By Richard K. Morgan

Takeshi Kovacs Novels

Altered Carbon

Broken Angels

Woken Furies

Market Forces

Thirteen

The Steel Remains

The Cold Commands

THE COLD
COMMANDS

THE COLD
COMMANDS

Richard K. Morgan

BALLANTINE BOOKS NEW YORK

Published in the United States by Del Rey, an imprint of The Random House Publishing Group, a division of Random House, Inc., New York.

DEL REY is a registered trademark and the Del Rey colophon is a trademark of Random House, Inc.

Published in hardcover in Great Britain by Gollancz, a division of The Orion Publishing Group.

ISBN 978-0-345-49306-4
eBook ISBN 978-0-345-52303-7

www.delreybooks.com

9 8 7 6 5 4 3 2 1

First U.S. Edition

Book design by Karin Batten

The Cold Commands is for V.
who has given me something to hold

I tell you, it's no game serving down in the city.

—J.R.R. Tolkien,
The Two Towers

THE COLD
COMMANDS

CHAPTER 1

When they got down into the fringes of the forest beyond Hinerion, Gerin saw the heat shimmering off the scrublands ahead of them, and knew the crunch had come.

Live or die, this was the shape of their last chance.

"We're going to broil out there," he told the others that evening as they sat in their chains and waited to be fed. "You hear the march-masters talking? It's another six weeks to Yhelteth at least, all southward, hotter every step of the way. You think these motherfuckers are going to give us any more water or food than we're getting already?"

"Of course they will, idiot." Tigeth, city-pallid and ponderous, and apparently too bone-fucking idle to want his freedom at any real cost, snorted, sniffed, and blew his nose on his fingers. Like half the men on the coffle, he was coming down with a cold. He wiped the snot away on the ground and glowered at Gerin. "Don't you get it? They have to *sell* us when we get to Yhelteth. How they going to do that if we don't make it, or if we're starved to the sinew by the time we arrive? Maybe you're too young or stupid to grasp the fact, marsh-foot, but this is *commerce*. We're worth nothing to them dead."

Marsh-foot.

In some quarters of Trelayne, it was insult enough to bring down an instant formal challenge and a duel at Brillin Hill Fields with the dawn. Elsewhere, it would simply get you stabbed and dumped in the river. As with everything else in the city, assumptions were general but wealth and station defined your specifics for you. And upriver or down, the Glades or the harbor-end slums, the common truth held—no one in the city of Trelayne would easily let word stand that they might have marsh dweller blood.

Gerin had grown up in the marshes and he wouldn't have lived in the city if you'd paid him. He let the epithet pass, the way he'd watched his kin put up with it for as long as he could remember.

Too much else at stake right now.

"You ever see the trawlers come in at harbor end, Tigeth?" he asked evenly. "You think every fish in that net makes it to market?"

Chain links rattled impatiently at Gerin's shoulder. A tight, angry voice in the gathering dark.

"What are you talking about—fish?"

It was another city dweller, Gerin didn't recall the name, this one more gaunt and work-worn than Tigeth. He'd barely spoken a word in the week they'd been marching; at rest stops, he spent the bulk of his time staring off into space, jaw set and working as if he had the last shreds of a tobacco twist between his teeth.

Like most of his kind, he still didn't seem able to get his head around the enormity of what had been done to him.

"Shit is what he's talking," Tigeth sneered. "Doesn't know any better. I mean, look at him; he's a stunted little marsh brat just like any other you'd see down at Strov market, reading fortunes or twitching for the crowd. Can't read, can't write, chances are he can't even count above five. He's got no idea how commercial concerns work."

Gerin smiled bleakly.

"Well, since you and everyone else on this coffle was sold for debt, I guess that makes us about even."

Tigeth swore and lunged at him. Brief, impotent rattle of chains and a chorus of protests as the move dragged at the other men where they sat. The gaunt man grappled Tigeth back, held the fat man's twitching hands a few inches off Gerin's face until Tigeth gave it up and slumped down again.

"Sit quiet, you fucking twat," the gaunt man hissed. "You want a march-master on us? Want to end up like Barat?"

Gerin's gaze switched involuntarily to the set of wrenched and empty manacles they still carried with them on the coffle. Big, tough Barat, a harbor-end pimp by trade, had come to the auction block the same way as Gerin—through the criminal courts. In the pimp's case, it was some business about cutting up the wrong slumming noble when he got rough with one of the girls. Said noble turns out to have Glades connections, the Watch get off their lazy, drink-sodden arses for a change and ask some questions, break some uncooperative heads. Someone talks, Barat lands in jail long enough to spit in his accuser's upriver face rather than cringe, ends up on the coffle as a result. Standard stuff, that same old city song.

Barat the pimp brought with him an arrogant dislike for the debt-slaves he found himself chained to, and he spent the first three days of the march taunting them to explosions of ill-judged violence, which he then slapped down with practiced thug ease and a sneer. For some reason, he'd left Gerin mostly alone, but the coffle chains were generous enough that he got to lay hands on at least four or five other men before the march-masters grew tired of the spectacle as sport, and started instead to resent the chaos it caused.

On the third day, the fifth or sixth outbreak of brawling, two or three of the caravan's mounted overseers and owners rode back down the line to see what all the fuss was about. One of them was a woman, and when the march-masters had kicked and cursed the coffle back into order, she beckoned their chief over, leaned down in her saddle to talk to him, and sent him back to his colleagues flushed dark with chagrin. Gerin never heard what was said, but he knew what was coming the same way he'd know a change in the wind off the marsh.

He chose not to share the knowledge with Barat, and the pimp was apparently too slum-stupid or iron-headed to work it out for himself. He started another fight later that same afternoon.

The march-masters took him at midday latrine stop the following noon, just across the river from Parashal. Four of them at once, grim, leather-faced men with long wooden clubs in hand and eyes that glinted like mica. They held him down and opened the manacles with the bolt cutters they all carried at their belts like weapons. It was an act whose irrevocability turned the pimp to snorting and kicking like a terrified horse when he saw it.

But by then, of course, it was far too late.

They dragged Barat thrashing and roaring into a nearby copse, and there they took their time beating him to death. It was close enough for the sounds to carry—solid, meaty thwacks, like a butcher chopping joints apart; high, awful shrieks that very shortly broke down into pleading and gurgling moans; finally a silence that was worse than either, as the sounds of the beating went on. Gerin had seen more than his fair share of brutality, out on the marsh and in the streets of Trelayne both; but even for him, the killing seemed to take forever.

Elsewhere on the coffle, less hardened men—and these included earlier victims of Barat's thuggish bullying—bowed their heads and stared at the ground they sat upon. One or two crammed fingers to their mouths like women, and choked back vomit. Gerin made it halfway to a sneering disdain before he realized he, too, was trembling with reaction.

Or, he told himself a little giddily, *just coming down with Tigeth's Hoiran-cursed fucking cold.*

Presently, the noises stopped and the march-masters emerged from the trees, trading guffaws, grinning like well-fed wolves. They carried their clubs at rakish shoulder arms. One of them swung his manacle cutters idly to and fro in the other hand, slashing at the knee-high grass. The implement's pincer end was dipped with blood, bright where the midday sun caught it as it swung.

And later, the unspoken knowledge settled among the silent captives, also grinning, like some new, skull-headed companion on the coffle—the understanding that it could have been any one of them in Barat's place.

"Yeah, and speaking of that," Gerin told them grimly, when Tigeth had quieted under the gaunt man's admonition. "You think that's the only empty set of cuffs you're going to see on this chain? Every day we don't make the market in Yhelteth is coins dripping through these fucks' fingers. You think they'll stop or slow down for anyone who can't hack the heat once we start across the scrub?"

"They have to *sell* us," Tigeth insisted petulantly. "It isn't in their interests to—"

"They have to sell *some* of us, Mister Commerce. Enough of us to make it pay. Like I said before, you think a trawl skipper cares if he spills a few fish on the dock when he unloads?"

"How old are you, son?" someone asked curiously.

Gerin skinned an urchin grin in the gloom. "Fifteen. And contrary to what Mister Commerce there tells you, I *can* count above five. I count thirty-five coffles on this caravan, thirty-two head on each. That's eleven hundred and twenty, less Barat, and you saw what happened to him. You think any one of us is worth the extra water or the wait while they coddle us along? This is march or die, people, and Hoiran gather in the hindmost. You're not citizens anymore, you're slaves. You fall down out there, they'll maybe kick you a couple of times to see if you can get up again. But if you don't . . ." He spread his hands in the manacles, shrugged. "They're going to cut you loose and leave you to die right where you fell."

"Maybe that's true," said the gaunt man slowly. "But maybe we just like to think it'll happen to someone else. Hell, maybe it *will* happen to someone else. We've all made it this far."

There was a murmur of agreement through the huddled figures on the chain. But as it died down, the gaunt man was gazing blankly southward, and he seemed unconvinced by his own argument.

"Never been in a desert," he said to no one in particular. "Never seen that before."

Someone else sneezed violently.

"I've seen march or die," said another man seated farther away. Half his face was nightmarishly scarred, poorly healed burns so severe that even in the failing light you could see the puckered contours of the scar tissue as he moved his head. "In the war, on the retreat from Rajal. Kid's right, that's how it works. They left the wounded where they fell. Made us march right past them, you could hear them calling after us, pleading. Begging us not to leave them for the lizards. And we weren't even slaves back then, we were still citizens, we were *soldiers*."

Tigeth made an exasperated noise. "It's not the same, that was a *war*. It's not the same thing at—"

"What's the matter, big man?" The gaunt captive stared at Tigeth with open dislike. "You reckon some rich Yhelteth widow's going to buy you for a scribe and butler just cuz you can read and write? Think you'll be too good for minework or carrying a hod till you drop?"

"Nah, just too fucking fat for it," someone jeered.

"Too fucking fat for a widow 'n' all," said someone else. " 'Less she buys him for a cushion."

General laughter, low and mean. Tigeth bristled.

"He isn't going to be fat by the time we get there," said the Rajal veteran quietly. "March like we got ahead of us, he's going to be just as burned down and blistered and broken as everybody else. If he makes it at all."

Quiet welled up in the wake of the words. The captives looked at one another as the message sank in. Most of them had doubtless seen some casual brutality since they were arrested and sold; maybe a few of the younger and prettier among them had suffered—like Gerin—the same inevitable dungeon rapes as the women who now marched on separate coffles. But by and large these men had not yet had to face the idea they might die.

Faint, feverish chills moved along Gerin's spine as he realized that up until now, neither had he. In all his twisting and scheming to get out of this, he'd envisaged a lot of bad outcomes, but none involved his own extinction. He'd foreseen various brutalities, improvising off those he'd witnessed himself in the past or had heard in campfire tales. He'd relived the memories of his rape in the debt cells, imagined that it might well happen to him again who knew how many times. He'd even brooded briefly, and unable to repress his shudders, on the chances of castration, which they said wasn't uncommon for male slaves in the Yhelteth trade.

But he'd never once imagined his life might end. Never really believed *he* might be the one cut loose and abandoned, begging and babbling as the coffles trooped on into the desert glare. Never thought it could be *him*, Gerin Trickfinger, fifteen years old, life barely begun, lying there too weak to move, too weak for anything but husked prayers to the Dark Court, Hoiran or Dakovash, Kwelgrish or Horchalat, Firfirdar or fucking *anyone* who might be listening out there, entreaties bargaining down like a roped and filled bucket let slip through weary fingers and back down the well, hope failing; prayers to be rescued, then prayers simply to be found, albeit by more slavers or bandits; finally the simple plea that thirst and heat might kill him before he felt the first darting, tentative tugs at his flesh, as the scavengers circled his twitching body and the vultures spiraled down to take his eyes . . .

He shivered—this *fucking* cold—and stared miserably around at his fellow captives. The gaunt man looked across at the Rajal veteran.

"You, scar-face. You think you'll make it?"

The veteran grimaced. Against the scarring, it wasn't a pretty sight. Gerin thought of tusked and fanged statues he'd seen in the candlelit shadows of the temple to Hoiran at Trelayne's southern gate. And they said that dark spirits were drawn to malformed and mutilated flesh. His father had once told him . . .

The scarred man shrugged.

"Probably would, yeah. But you got to think like that. It's all over if you don't."

"Right."

"Look," said Gerin, desperate to shrug off the shiver of his own sudden fear. "I'm not saying most of us won't survive. That's not the point."

The veteran's ravaged features turned, fixed on him. With the onset of night, the long gleaming scimitar edge of the band could now be seen clearly, slicing out of the clouds overhead, spilling a soft, uneven light on whatever the Dark Court deemed it appropriate to touch. Some of that light seemed to catch and gleam in the man's eye as he looked at Gerin.

"What is the point, then?" he asked softly.

It felt oddly like staging, like one of the tricked-up little pieces of street drama he helped set off down at Strov to pull in an audience or milk passersby for sympathy. As if there was a correct, fixed answer to this. Gerin, having no idea what that might be, looked around at his fellow captives and their stares.

He cleared his throat.

"We're none of us used to desert heat," he said. "And half of us are already coming down with the fucking snots and sneezes. We're going to be sick and stumbling tired. We get a few days into the scrublands on the rations they're feeding us, doesn't matter who survives, who doesn't, *none* of us is going to be in any fit state to make any kind of escape. This is our last chance for that."

"Escape?" Tigeth snorted phlegmily. "You stupid fucking—"

And the Rajal survivor cuffed him savagely across the head. Tigeth yelped and fell over sideways with the force of the blow. He opened his mouth to say something more but the veteran stared him down and Tigeth thought better of it. Then the scarred man's gaze swung back to Gerin again. He opened one chained hand in invitation.

"If you have an idea, lad, I think now might be the time to spit it out."

CHAPTER 2

The blade came up, caught blinding sunlight along its leading edge for a moment, and then snicked inward.

Egar the Dragonbane grunted. Tipped his head a fraction of an inch sideways and felt the steel scrape skin. With a major effort of will, he kept his neck where it was and stared up at the barbershop ceiling.

It was harder than he remembered.

"Do not disconcert yourself, my lord," the barber purred. He thumbed the gathered soap foam off his razor and flicked it into the basin. Angled in close for another draw up the Dragonbane's lathered neck, voice turning a little tighter with concentration. "You are in Yhelteth now, crowned queen of civilized cities. In this chair have sat visiting dignitaries from every corner of the known world. All left with throat intact."

Egar fixed him with one baleful eye—no easy thing to do with his head at the angle it was.

"I have done this before, you know."

"Well, my lord, you'll be pleased to hear that makes two of us." The barber wiped his blade clean again and tilted his customer's head back the other way. "Just so, and hold there. Thank you. Though I don't recall having had the pleasure of serving your worthiness previously. Was it one of your steppe brethren who recommended me?"

"My steppe brethren wouldn't pay your prices."

True enough—in fact, most Majak went bearded in Yhelteth pretty much as they would have back home on the northern plains. Why pay good money to scrape hair off your face that was just going to grow back the following week? Why, for that matter, scrape it off at all? Kept the sun off, didn't it? Tickled the wenches, let them know they'd been with a man, not a boy. Trim it back if you had to, if the grooming standards of whichever imperial mercenary brigade you'd signed up with required it, but otherwise . . .

The barber frowned a little as he bent and peered at his handiwork. "I beg to differ, my lord. In *fact,* I had a brace of your brethren in here only last week. Young lads, not long in the city by the way they talked."

Egar grunted. "Then they're getting better pay than I did at their age."

"Perhaps so. They wore the livery of the Citadel Guard, as near as I recall."

"Fucking *Citadel?*"

A flickered glance at the barber to see if this would cause offense—the imperials were funny about religious matters, had this clerk-arsed unforgiving book of rules to their observances, and very little sense of humor where it was infringed upon. Ordinarily, Egar could give a shit if he offended them or not, but it doesn't pay to upset a man who has a razor at your throat.

"Yes, well . . ." Immersed in his task, the barber was apparently unmoved by any stirrings of religious fervor. He took the blade up under Egar's eye, back to the ear, strokes as smooth and practiced as the voice and the bland platitudes it uttered. "The ranks of the Sacred Guard were much depleted in the war, my lord. Martyrdom called multitudes of the righteous away."

"Yeah, didn't it just."

Egar had seen some martyrdom operations during the southern campaign, and they sickened even his well-worn mercenary soul. Waves of men and boys, some of them barely twelve or thirteen years old, hurling their bodies forward against the lizard lines with the name of the Revelation on their lips. Most struck at best a single blow before the reptile peons clawed or chewed them down. They died in their screaming thousands out on the field while the commanding invigilators looked on and offered prayers for victory.

At Egar's side on an overlooking promontory, one of the other Majak mercenary commanders spat in the dirt and shook his head.

And they call us *berserkers?*

But Yhelteth was like that. It lulled you along with its shaves and its baths, its book learning and its law; and then, abruptly, when you least expected it, you saw the vaunted trappings of imperial civilization cast aside, like the cloth and baked clay of some wealthy leper's mask, and you were abruptly face-to-face with the leering horror beneath—a violent, tribal people, smug in their own assumed superiority and a faith that licensed their dominance wherever they could make it stick.

It doesn't pay to have too many illusions about us, Imrana once told him soberly. *Take the Black Folk out of the equation and we'd probably still be a bunch of bloodthirsty horse tribes squabbling over turf.*

The barber finished up his bladework, wiped Egar's face and neck down with a moist towel, and brought a burning taper to scorch away the hairs growing from his ears. It was a painful process—set the hair on fire for a scant second, slap it out again with a cupped palm, repeat—but Egar submitted with a stoic lack of protest. He was hitting close to forty now, and had no desire to be reminded of the fact every time he looked in a mirror. Ears sprouting hair, gray in the beard and pelt, creases in brow and jowls that eased but never fully faded as his expression changed; it was all starting to pile up in ways he didn't much like.

Nor did he like the space it was starting to rent in his head.

Back out on the steppe the last few years, he hadn't really noticed the changes, because outside of shamanry, reflective surfaces weren't something the Majak had a great deal of use for. But now, returned once more to the imperial city, Egar was forcibly reminded that Yhelteth prized fine mirrors as a sign of wealth and sophistication. Both homes and public buildings boasted a wide and ornate selection, lurking at unexpected locations in halls and reception rooms wherever he went. Imrana's house was particularly well supplied, as befit, he supposed, her position at court, and her need to maintain a polished outward beauty. *In the end,* she said, a little bitterly, facing him in warm perfumed bathwater one evening, *despite wealth, despite wisdom, despite contacts and court alliances, I am still a woman. And I will be judged on all counts for that single fact, via the cursed fucking geometry of how pleasing I am to the eye. Cheekbones and arse cheeks are my destiny.*

I think you're undervaluing a couple of other assets there. Lazy rumble of lechery in his voice, reaching forward to cup one slumped breast and thumb the nipple. Refusing to meet her tone with any seriousness of his own. *Tip to tail, it's all pretty pleasing to my eye. And a couple of other organs, too, in case you didn't notice.*

It got him a faint smile. And—what he'd been angling for, really—she put a hand on his already swelling prick, where it floated fatly between his legs in the bathwater.

Yes, an effect I'm quite sure any unlaced tavern wench half my age would produce in that selfsame organ just by brushing up against it. You can't crawl back inside what you once had, Eg. You have to live with now. And now I am old. Practically a crone.

He snorted. *You're not yet forty, woman.*

Though privately he suspected that she probably was, and a couple of years besides. Truth be told, it wasn't something he'd ever given a lot of thought to. Years ago when they'd first met, with the war still raging and nothing certain to grab on to but the day you were given—well, then things were different. The fact Imrana was a handful of years older than him had given her a darkly exotic allure, a frisson he was unused to in his more usual brothel tumbles. Age and court sophistication were the heady perfumes she was steeped in, a rising, maddening scent that hit him like patchouli or rose oil, and filled him with a restless, indefinable hunger.

Now, with thoughts of age creeping up on him as well, her vanguard battles against the same enemy troubled him more than he liked to admit.

Yeah, Dragonbane. Troubles you almost as much as that escutcheoned

*fuck she's got herself for a husband. And you don't much like to admit that,
either, do you.*

Ah. That.

*Yes, that—Knight Commander Saril Ashant, back from assignment in
Demlarashan, where he steadfastly and selfishly didn't manage to get himself killed by the rebels he was putting down. Came home instead, covered
in glory and claiming as rightful reward a couple of weeks' furlough complete with nightly conjugal . . .*

Leave it alone, Eg.

"Will there be anything else, my lord?" The barber was down to a
strictly unnecessary brushing off of collar and shoulders. "A massage
perhaps?"

Egar reckoned the brutal handling his ears had just had was probably about his limit today. And the confines of the barbershop felt suddenly tight. He shook his head, made an effort to dump his brooding.
He got up out of the chair and fumbled for his purse. Saw the big, freshly
shaven man in the mirror do the same. It caught him out as ever—*shit,
that's a lot of gray hair!* For something to say while he dug out coins, he
asked:

"And you say these compatriots of mine come in here a lot?"

"Regularly, yes, my lord." The barber took the proffered payment.
"Any message for them?"

The Dragonbane stared the mirror down, trying not to let a sudden
weariness show through. What would he say? What message could he
possibly pass on to young men possessed of all the idiotic, indestructible
confidence he'd owned himself when he rolled into town a couple of
decades back?

Enjoy it while it lasts, it sure don't last long, maybe?

Get paid well for the years you give?

If they were getting Palace Quarter shaves on a regular basis, they'd
already learned that lesson better than he could teach it.

The man in the mirror frowned at him. The barber hovered. Behind
the traitorous weariness, another sensation coiled, restless, like smoke;
like something summoned but not yet called to tangible form. He tried
to name it—could not.

He shook it off instead.

"No message," he said, and stepped back out into the sun-blasted brightness of the street.

HE WALKED AT RANDOM FOR A WHILE, LET THE FLOW OF HUMANITY through the Palace Quarter carry and soothe him. Women in brightly colored wrapping, like toffees too numerous to choose from, and the heady slap of perfume across the eyes as they passed. Slaves and retainers in the livery of this or that courtier's service, bent beneath upholstered saddles piled five feet high with burden, or—the lucky ones—bearing some lettered and sealed communication from one lordly house to another. A noble trailing an entourage in his wake like noisy gulls at the stern of a fishing skiff. Here and there the odd brace of City Guard, sun smashed too bright to look at across their cuirasses. Beggars and street poets not dirty, deformed, or disruptive enough to be worth the effort of moving on.

Faint, twining scents of fruit and flowers from a market somewhere close. The broken rhythms of the sellers, crying their wares.

Heat like a blanket. Street dust stirring beneath the tramp of feet.

Egar drifted on it all like a swimmer with the current—nursing for a while the still-sharp, piercing pleasure of just *being* here, of having come back to this place he never thought he'd see again. But in the end, it was no good. His eyes tracked inevitably up and west, to the stately, tree-shaded white mansions along Harbor Hill Rise. To one particular mansion, in fact, with the mosaic dome cupola at its southern end, where *right now probably* . . .

Come on, Dragonbane. Really. Leave it alone.

Too late. His gaze stuck on the cupola's polished wink and gleam like a blade in a frost-chilled scabbard. He felt his mood sour. Felt the unreasoning anger flare, the way it always did.

. . . right now probably, sucking him off in that big bed . . .

Grow up, Eg. You knew you'd have to live with this. Besides—a sly, steppe nomad wit intruding, relic of a man he sometimes wondered if he still was—*it's way too close to prayer time for that sort of thing. He's a pious little fucker, remember. She told you as much.*

As if in confirmation, the prayer call floated out from a tower somewhere behind him. Egar put up half a twisted grin for a shield, and hung on to it. Memory of Imrana was inextricably bound up with the plaintive skyline ache of that sound.

In the early days, when passion flared between them at every touch, at every loaded look, transgression against the appointed hour of prayer would light her up like a taper soaked in oil. Her eyes wide, her lips flexed apart, the arched tension of appalled delight on her face at what he was doing to her, at *when* he was doing it to her. Occasionally, he'd catch the waft of memory from those days, and go hard to the root just thinking about it.

And then later, settling more comfortably into the harness of their mutual attraction, they still spent postcoital evenings out on her apartment balconies, wrapped up in each other's tangled, sweat-slick limbs, listening to the evening call and watching the sun melt into layers of heat and dust over the western city.

His smile waned, turned ugly with the weight of current events. *Knight fucking commander or not, Dragonbane, one day you should just . . .*

He grabbed the thought by the scruff of its neck. *Enough.*

Time to be elsewhere. Definitely.

HABIT TOOK HIS FEET SOUTH, PUT HIM ON THE BOULEVARD OF THE Ineffable Divine. He didn't think Archeth would be back from An-Monal yet, but there was always Kefanin to talk to in the meantime. Ishgrim to leer at, if she chose to put in an appearance. And anyway, he reminded himself, a little sourly, it was his job to keep an eye on them all; it was the genteel pretense he and Archeth maintained—that his place as long-term houseguest was paid out by informal security duties on her behalf.

That this amounted to not much more than being visible—and visibly Majak—about the place was not discussed. Nor were the small purses of silver coin that showed up regularly in the pockets of his attire when it came back from cleaning and was laid out in his rooms.

He tried not to feel too much like a kept hound.

Truth was, the Citadel raid on Archeth's household was the best part of three full seasons in the past now, and the way it had worked out, it seemed unlikely the same powers would try again. Menkarak and his kind had backed off. There was a ticklish equilibrium in place across Yhelteth these days, like some massive set of scales hanging in the sky above the city, one cupped, brass weighing bowl dipped over the imperial palace, the other riding the air above the raised crag and keep of the Citadel.

No one wanted to disturb that balance if they could help it.

He felt it again—that same coiling restlessness, familiar but just out of reach.

Could always look for a real job, of course. Dragonbane.

He could, and with that name attached, there'd be no shortage of offers; you mostly had to look in graveyards for men called Dragonbane—the ones still walking around were few and far between. Any regiment in the city would kill to have one as a commander, or even a color officer. But a command, even a sinecure command, would mean responsibility—requirements to attend reviews and a hundred other tedious regimental affairs of one beribboned sort or another, when he'd really rather be out on a sun-soaked balcony somewhere, fucking Imrana or drinking and shooting the shit with Archeth. And a *real* command would be worse still—the way things were right now, he'd more than likely find himself deployed south to Demlarashan to supervise the slaughter of yet more deluded, poorly armed young men who had evidently somehow not managed to get their fill of war last time around.

The war; the years as clanmaster back on the steppe afterward—it still clogged him. It sat in his stomach and throat whenever he thought about it, the morning-after feel of too much undigested food and wine from some overblown feast the night before. He didn't care if he never held another command in his life.

He was done giving other men orders.

Let the dumb fucks work it out themselves, for a change.

He pitched up at Archeth's place in no better mood than that. Got in off the crowded street and paused in the cool shadows of the gate arch to wipe sweat from neck and brow. The two young guardsmen stationed there nodded warily at him. More warily than you'd expect, given that he'd played dice with them a couple of times at shift change.

He forced a grin.

"All right, lads? Seen the Lady Archeth at all?"

The man on the left shook his head. "No word yet, my lord."

Shrug. Kefanin, then.

He crossed the sunstruck cobbles of the courtyard, went inside, and rattled about the house a bit until he finally discovered the eunuch talking to Ishgrim in one of the enclosed garden patios out back. Egar didn't catch what they were discussing, but they seemed to his jaundiced eye to be getting on altogether too well for a young woman shaped the way Ishgrim was and a man with no balls. The slave girl was laughing, tipping her long candlewax-colored hair back from her eyes. Body curves shoving gratuitously at the yellow linen shift she wore, straining the material at hip and breast. Kefanin made some convoluted gesture with both hands, shook out a red silk handkerchief, and spread his fingers wide so it hung between them. A small cascade of white rose petals drifted down onto the stone bench between them. Ishgrim gasped, clapped her hands like a small child. Her breasts gathered up and inward with the action, not like a small child at all. Egar felt a throb go through his groin at the sight.

Not what he needed right now.

He coughed and made himself known.

" 'Lo, Kef."

The eunuch got hurriedly to his feet. "My lord."

"No sign of Archeth, then?"

"No. Ordinarily, I would have expected her back by now, but . . ."

"But once she gets up there to that house full of phantoms, who the fuck can tell." Egar's voice came out gruffer than he'd intended. "Right?"

Kefanin's lips pursed diplomatically.

"Would you care for some refreshment, my lord?"

"No, I'm good." Egar glanced down at Ishgrim, wondering, not for the first time, where Archeth found her restraint. If the girl had been *his* slave—a gift of the Emperor, no less, it doesn't get much more legitimate than that—he would have plundered those curves fucking *months* ago. Would have lit her up like a steppe-storm sky, put a fucking *smile* on her face for once, instead of that perpetually downcast look she dragged around the house all the time like a bucket of used bathwater.

Ishgrim flushed and shifted on the stone bench.

"Are you going to tell him?" she asked in a small voice.

Silence. Egar switched a glance between the two of them. "Tell me what?"

"It's nothing, really." Kefanin waved a dismissive hand. "Not worth—"

"Tell me *what*, Kef?"

The majordomo sighed. "Well, then. It seems we are being subjected to a little more clerical brinkmanship. The Citadel wish once more to remind us of their existence."

"They're out there *again*?" Egar hadn't noticed coming in, and an odd sense of shame crept through him at the realization. *Some fucking hound, Eg.* "Guys on the gate didn't say a thing about it when I came in."

Kefanin shrugged. "They are on loan from the palace. They don't want unnecessary trouble."

That ticklish fucking balance again. Egar remembered the wary looks the guardsmen had given him. Felt a fierce grin stitch itself onto his face.

"They think *I'd* cause unnecessary trouble?"

"My lord, I do not know if—"

"Leave it with me, Kef."

Voice trailing out behind him as he walked away. Riding an upsurge of varying emotion now, at whose heart was that same vaguely familiar restlessness he couldn't pin down. He strode back through the chambers and halls of the house. Across the blaze of the courtyard. Under the brief, cool caress of the arch, past the startled guardsmen—*assholes*—without a word. Out once more into the bustle and tramp of the street.

Paying attention now, he spotted them easily enough—there, under one of the acacia trees planted in twinned rows down the center of the boulevard. The lean, drab-robed figure of the invigilator and, flanking him in the cooling puddle of shade, the inevitable brace of men-at-arms; cheap bulk and professional scowls, lightweight mail shirts under surplices with the Citadel crest, short-swords sheathed at the hip.

There was a twinned flicker of motion as both men clapped hand to sword hilt when they saw the big Majak come striding through the traffic toward them. Egar nodded grim approval, let them know he'd seen it, and then he was planted firmly in front of the invigilator.

"You've got the wrong house," he said conversationally.

The invigilator's face mottled with anger. "How do you dare to—"

"No, you're not listening to me." Egar kept his voice patient and gentle. "There's obviously been some mistake back at the Citadel. Pashla Menkarak isn't keeping you up to date. When he sent you down here, didn't he tell you how dangerous it is to stand under this tree?"

The invigilator flashed an inadvertent glance up at the branches over his head. Egar dropped an amiable right arm onto his shoulder, just above the collarbone. He dug in with his thumb. The invigilator uttered a strangled yelp. The men-at-arms came belatedly to life. One of them raised a meaty hand and grabbed Egar's free arm.

"That's en—"

Egar clubbed down with the blade of his right hand, felt the invigilator's collarbone snap beneath the blow like a twig for kindling. The invigilator shrieked, collapsed in a sprawl of robes and choking pain. By then Egar had already turned on the man-at-arms who'd grabbed him. He locked up the grasping hand with a Majak wrestling trick, put the man into the trunk of the tree face-first. The other man-at-arms was a heartbeat too slow in reacting, and did entirely the wrong thing—he went for his sword. Egar swung a shoulder in with his full body weight behind it, trapped the man's sword arm across his chest, and smacked him in the temple with the heel of one palm. At the last moment, something made him pull the full force of the blow, and the man went down merely stunned.

Meanwhile, the one he'd put face-first into the tree was still on his feet, blood streaming from a broken nose, and he'd also decided it was time to bring out the steel. He got the sword a handbreadth out of its scabbard and then the Dragonbane kicked his legs out from under him. He went down in a sudden heap. Egar stepped in and kicked him again in the head. That seemed to take care of things.

Behind him, the invigilator was still screeching and thrashing about on the ground in his robes like some kind of beached manta ray. An interested crowd was starting to form. Egar looked up and down the street for reinforcements, saw none, positioned himself carefully, and kicked the robed form hard in the guts. The screaming stopped, was replaced by a ruptured puking sound. Egar planted another solid kick, higher this time, and felt a couple of ribs snap against his boot. Then he crouched beside the invigilator, grabbed him by the throat, and dragged him in close.

"Look up there," he said bleakly, and jerked the man's head upward for emphasis. "Pay attention, because I'm only going to go through this once. See that window? Second floor, third across from the arch? That's *my* room. It looks directly out onto the street, right here. Now I know that you people and the lady of this house have some prior history, but here's the thing: I don't fucking care. And more important, I don't want to have to look out of that window and see your scowling face fucking up my view. Got it?"

Gritted teeth snarl. "I have an ordained right—"

Egar slapped the rest of the sentence out of the man's mouth.

"We're not discussing *rights,* my friend. Do I look like a lawyer to you? We're talking here about a polite and reasonable personal request I'm making, to you and all your bearded chums. Stay the fuck away from this house. Take that back to Menkarak, make sure he spreads it around. Because anyone who doesn't get the message, I will be forced to hurt, probably very badly. And if *you* ever come back here again." The Dragonbane dug his index fingernail in under the invigilator's chin and lifted his face closer. Looked into his eyes to make it stick. "Well, then I'll kill you. Okay?"

From the man's face, he judged the message conveyed.

He got up, looked around at the tumbled, twitching bodies, and the goggling crowd that had gathered.

"Show's over," he said brusquely. "Nothing to see here."

And there it was, something in the words as he spoke them, some echo of the elusive feeling he'd been carrying around all day—which now slid out from the shadows and took on recognizable form.

Bored, he realized with a slight shock. *Dragonbane—you are bored.*

CHAPTER 3

Later, with the band muffled up in thickening cloud and the last of the daylight gone to a fading orange glow over the trees to the west, the march-masters set about building campfires. Tinder sparked and flared at intervals across the low open ground where the thirty-five coffles of slaves were huddled against the growing chill of night. Gerin watched the flames spring up, and counted—four, no, five of them among the slaves and another smaller one farther out where the overseer's tents were pitched. None was close enough to cast more than the faintest radiance on the men in his coffle—a gleam here and there on a few pale, city-bred faces like Tigeth's, the odd glint of an eye catching the light as someone turned their head. But mostly, the slaves made a rumpled and undistinguished mass of shadow in the gloom.

There was a faint, watery itching in Gerin's eyes and throat. He felt suddenly, ineptly weak.

He forced it down. *No time for that now.*

Those march-masters not tasked with the fires began the lengthy business of feeding and watering their charges. They moved outward among the slaves in ones and twos, dealing out the odd casual kick or blow to open passage. The men overseeing Gerin's coffle at least seemed in rough good humor as they went around, slopping cold stew into the shallow wooden bowls with reasonable attempts at accuracy, taking the trouble to hand out the chunks of stale bread rather than just throw them, here and there grunting the kind of gruffly soothing words you'd offer a well-behaved dog. Gerin put it down to Barat's absence—with the troublemaker off the chain and left to rot, there'd be no more unwelcome attention from the overseers, and that had to be good. Now they could all, slaves and march-masters together, get on with the practical business of reaching journey's end in peace.

Gerin forced down mouthfuls of the gelatinous stew, gnawed at a corner of his bread. He swallowed hard, breathed, swallowed again, and—

Abruptly, he was *choking.*

Choking—thrashing—flailing hard in his chains, so the manacles gouged at his wrists and ankles, and the men around him panicked back as far as their own restraints would let them. Clamor went back and forth.

"What the—"

"Look out, look *out,* he's having a fi—"

"Fever! It's the coughing fever!"

"Get him the fuck away from m—"

"Poison, *poison!*"

"Don't touch the fucking food!"

"Spit it up, man. Spit it the fuck *up!*"

And then the new cry, the new terror. "*Possessed, possessed!* The Dark Court has him. *Hoiran comes!* Don't let him touch you, he'll break the chains like a—"

"Hoiran! Hoiran! *Abase* yourselves, it is—"

"Hoiran walks!"

"Back, get *back*—"

The march-masters arrived. Gerin was barely aware of them, vision torn back and forth in splinters as his neck spasmed front and *side*, front and *side*, front and *side*. The spittle was gathering in his throat—he coughed and spat desperately, felt it start to foam and blow on his lips. A dimly seen form stooped across him, a fist clobbered inaccurately down. The blow glanced off the side of his head. His spine arched, and he made deep snarling noises at the base of his throat. A second march-master joined the first.

"Not like that, you fucking twat. Get a grip on his—"

"Yeah, *you* fucking try to—"

"Just hold him *still*, will you!"

Someone got fully astride Gerin, tried to pin him down by the arms. He thought he recognized the march-master's face from days earlier—hair grizzled and receding beneath a knitted wool cap, brow creased, and eyes worried. Another younger, angrier face loomed behind him and to the side. Deep in the fit and foaming, Gerin glimpsed the second man raising a fist wrapped in metallic knuckle-duster gleam. Saw the way he angled carefully for the punch. This one would break his face for sure.

Something thin and glinting whipped loosely upward in the night air, dropped down again over the younger man's head—Gerin knew it for a length of chain. He dropped his Strov-practiced spasming like a peeled cloak, hinged furiously up against the grip on his arms, nuzzled into the older march-master's neck like a lover.

He bit deep and hung on.

The march-master yelped and tried to smack him away. The younger man's steel-loaded punch misfired, hit his struggling companion in the shoulder. Then the chain pulled taut, ripped him backward and tumbling away. Gerin locked his jaws on the older man's neck, got his hands up to help the clinch. The other slaves on the coffle crowded about, prevented retreat. The march-master was bleating now, stumbling, trying to elbow a path clear. Flailing to get Gerin off him. The woolen cap got knocked askew on his balding head, then away, into the confusion. Gerin rode the struggles, felt his nose bloodied from a random blow, ignored it, ground and sliced and scissored with his teeth, worked at tearing a ragged hole in the man's neck. Skin, sinew, tiny gobbets of shredded flesh and there, *there*, the tiny, wet-pulsing pipe of the artery. He spat loose, let go. The march-master staggered back, eyes wide on Gerin's in the poor light, mouth gaping like a plea. He slapped a hand to the wound in his neck, felt the damage there, the swift pulse of his life running out over his fingers. Made a kind of moaning sound and fell over gibbering.

"Get his fucking bolt cutters! *Now!*"

It was the Rajal veteran, through gritted teeth as he sawed the length of chain link back and forth across the younger march-master's throat. His fist were up and doubled about the chain in an attempt to keep the worst of the strain off his manacles—still Gerin saw how the veteran bled at the wrists from the pressure. The march-master thrashed and kicked, booted legs lashing out, trying to find purchase. But the dull metal links had sunk deep in the flesh at his throat, and his eyes bulged inhumanly large as he choked, filled with the desperate knowledge of his own death. Gerin darted in, grabbed the cutters from his belt. He wrestled with the unfamiliar angles of the tool, trying to make it bite on the edge of his ankle cuffs.

"You motherfuckers!" Heavy blow across his shoulder. "Get on the fucking ground, you piece of sh—"

Gerin staggered, did not quite go down. The third, newly arrived march-master snarled and slammed the club into him again, from the side. It put him in the dirt this time. The march-master stood over him a single hard-breathing second with club raised again—and was clawed down by the other men on the coffle before he could strike. An awful, wailing yell came up from the ground where he hit. Chained forms piled onto him.

"Cut me loose, son. Do it quick."

It was the gaunt man, arms out-thrust. Gerin hesitated an instant, then fastened the bolt cutters on the man's manacles. He heaved and twisted, forearms aching from the effort. For one sickening moment, he thought the cutters would not work. Then the manacle bent, and split, and tore.

"That's it, that's it," the gaunt man almost crooning. "Guild-level iron, my arse. Look at that shit. Fucking skimp-shift Etterkal smiths."

The second manacle went almost as easily, and then the gaunt man had snatched the bolt cutters from Gerin's sweat-slick grip. He hefted them like a weapon. Gerin felt his mouth dry up.

"Come on," the man snapped. "Hold 'em out."

It was like his father speaking—Gerin obeyed in a daze. The gaunt man set the bolt cutters to his manacles, snapped each one open in turn with a powerful doubled crimping action. He did Gerin's feet almost as fast, then his own. He tore off the broken cuffs, straightened up and laughed—a sudden, fierce burst of joy that had something animal about it. He clapped Gerin on the shoulder, almost flooring him again with the force of the blow.

"Fucking amazing, son. Never seen anything like that."

Elsewhere, other men had laid hands on the other two march-masters' bolt cutters and were now about the squabbling uncertain task of trying to free themselves or one another in the dark. The scar-faced Rajal veteran rose up, like something summoned, from the corpse of the man he'd killed. He tugged his chains loose from the red-raw gape of the march-master's burst throat and offered them up. Gerin felt a shudder run up his spine at the sight. The veteran shook the chain impatiently.

"You two going to stand there congratulating each other all fucking night?" he growled, and nodded out across the gathered slave caravan to where the commotion was now general. "We've got a couple of minutes tops before someone with a sword gets here. Come *on*."

Gerin followed the gesture, saw the truth of it. Dark figures waded about through the disarrayed coffles, trying to trace the source of the uproar. Most held up torches or brands pulled hurriedly from the campfires. Dim glint of blades unsheathed in their free hands.

The gaunt man set the cutters to the veteran's manacles, broke them apart with no more effort than he'd needed before. The veteran jerked his hands impatiently free of the ruined metal, then bent and pulled each foot free of its snapped ankle cuff in turn.

Behind them, a shout split the night.

"There! Monkgrave's coffle!"

"They're . . . *Get them! They're loose!* Fucking get in there and . . . "

Still bent over his ankle cuffs, the veteran twisted his head toward the voices. Gerin saw him grimace and nod to himself. Then he got carefully back to his feet, curled a hand around each freed wrist in turn and breathed in deeply, grunted as if surprised by something.

"You'd better get out of here," he told the gaunt man.

"I, you, but . . . "

The veteran took the bolt cutters gently from him. "Go on. Take the kid, get up into that tree line quick, while you still can."

"And you?"

The veteran gestured at the confusion around them, the other men struggling to free themselves in the dark. "Friend, if someone doesn't buy us some more time, this is all going to be over quicker than a priest's fuck."

"Then I'll stay, too."

"You fight in the war?" the veteran asked, as gently as he'd taken the cutters.

The gaunt man hesitated. Lowered his head, shook it slowly.

"Reserved trades," he said. "I was . . . I'm a blacksmith."

The veteran nodded. "Thought it had to be something like that. Way you cut that iron. Look, there's no shame in it. Can't all be swinging the steel, you know, someone's got to actually make the fucking stuff. But you got to know your specialty."

He swung the cutters absently, feeling the weight in them. It made a sound through the air like a scythe. The blacksmith stared at him, and the veteran's scarred features creased in something vaguely resembling a smile. He gestured with his newly acquired weapon, up to where the trees thickened toward forest.

"Go on, get moving, both of you. Head for the trees." The smile became an awful grin. "Be right behind you."

They turned from the lie, the impossible promise in his ruined face, and fled.

The scarred man watched them go. Yelled curses and stumbling behind him as the first of the sword-wielding march-masters kicked their way through to the scene of the revolt. His grin faded slowly out. Amid the chaos of men scrambling to be free, tugging at their chains, and screaming for cutters, he turned to face the newcomers. Two men, both wielding swords, one with a torch upraised. The veteran felt a muscle twitch, deep under the scar tissue in his face.

"You!" The first march-master saw him, lifted his torch, and peered. He pointed with his sword. "Get down on your fucking knees. Do it now."

The veteran closed the gap with three swift paces, ignored the sword, got inside its useful reach before the march-master could grasp what was happening. He loomed over the man.

"We left them behind," he said, as if explaining something to a child.

Moth-wing blur of motion—the bolt cutters, slashing in at head height.

The march-master staggered sideways, face torn open from the blow, one eye gone, socket caved in. The torch flew away in a splatter of sparks. The march-master made a broken howling sound, dropped his sword, and sagged to his knees. The veteran was already turning on his companion. The second man got the reverse swing of the cutters across his face as well. He fell back in fright, blood oozing from the gouges, sword clutched upright like some kind of magical ward against demons. In the fitful glow from the dropped torch, the veteran came on, snarling.

"Orders," he said to the uncomprehending march-master, and hacked him in the head with the cutters, once, twice, until he went down. "They *made* us leave them."

For a moment, he stood like a statue between his two felled adversaries. He looked around in the fitful torchlight as if just waking up.

The second of the armed march-masters was on his back, head twisted to one side, skull a ruined cup. The first was propped on his knees and one trembling arm, trying to hold his shattered face together with the other hand. Weeping, gibbering. The veteran spotted the man's fallen sword, grunted, and let the bolt cutters fall. He took up the sword, hefted it a couple of times, then settled into a two-handed grip, whipped around and heaved it down on the injured march-master's neck. Passable executioner's stroke—the blade sliced spine and most of the neck, dropped the man flat to the ground. The veteran flexed, cleared the blade with drilled precision, looked down for a moment at the damage he'd done.

"We heard them screaming after us for fucking miles," he told the man's corpse.

More cries, the rush of something through the night air, a savage, incoherent yell. The veteran pitched about, saw the next march-master in mid-heave behind the downward slice of a morning-star mace and chain. The veteran seemed to just drift out of the way of the flail blow as if in a trance, let it come down and snag in the grassy ground. He stepped in close, like a newlywed to his bride, and swung the sword at belly height as the march-master struggled to get the morning star's spikes back out of the ground.

"Some of them *cursed* us," he grunted on the stroke.

The march-master screamed as the steel bit through leather jerkin and into the unprotected flesh beneath. The veteran hauled and sliced through, cleared the blade out under the man's ribs at the back.

"Some," he said conversationally, "just wept."

Beyond the collapsing ruins of the man he'd just gutted, he faced three more torch-and-steel-equipped figures. They were holding back now, aware of the corpses of their comrades littering the ground, aware that something serious was happening here. They huddled shoulder-to-shoulder and stared.

But behind them, others were coming.

The veteran settled his grip on the sword, angled it toward the gathering march-masters, and jerked his head for them to come ahead. Torchlight painted him massive and flicker-shadowed behind the blade.

He made them a grin from his scarred and ravaged features.

"Do I look like a fucking slave to you?" he asked them.

And though, finally, they would bring him down with sheer weight of numbers, none who heard him ask that question lived to see the dawn.

CHAPTER 4

There was an iron alloy tree in one corner of the courtyard, gleaming where the late-afternoon sunlight played off features in the gnarled metal bark. Sharp black shadow ran out from the trunk like spilled ink, then split into branching rivulets that spread out across the stone paving, as if in search of something. Archeth sat well out of reach on the courtyard floor opposite—booted legs propped up in front of her, warmth of the sun-drenched courtyard wall at her back—and watched the rivulet shadows creep toward her. She bit into an apple she'd plucked from another tree in another courtyard, one that humans might have been a little more comfortable with.

Nothing grows at An-Monal, the superstitions whispered across Yhelteth like the wind. *Nothing lives there.*

Like most things humans believed, it was missing the point. The iron alloy tree was not alive in any conventional sense, true, but every year the blue-black leaves it lifted against the sky would rust through as winter approached, speckling and staining first to a purplish red, then to pale orange, and then finally to a stark silvery white that crumbled and turned to glinting ash in the breeze. And then, every spring, the leaves slid back out of the alloy bark like tiny blades unsheathing, like a winning hand of cards spread out on the table before your eyes.

The quiet metallic process had been going on for as long as Archeth could remember, which was coming up on a couple of centuries now; and—despite a slew of idiot prophecies about such things ceasing when the Kiriath abandoned the world—when the last of her people's fireships did finally submerge in the An-Monal crater and something seemed to tear for good in Archeth's heart, the tree never missed a beat.

She wasn't really surprised, could have told the prophesying priests it was a stupid idea from the start. Her father's people prided themselves on creating processes and artifacts that did not need them to officiate over.

We are what we build, Grashgal once told her cryptically, in the brief months between the end of the war and the Departure. *Forces older and darker than knowing forced knowing upon us and long ago locked us out of paradise. There is no way back. The only victory against those forces is to build. To build well enough that, when we look back along the path of exile we have engineered, the view is bearable.*

If there's no way back, she begged him, *then why are you leaving?*

But by then it was a rancid argument. Grashgal could no more sway the Council of Captains than she could herself. The aftermath of the war had broken something in the Kiriath, had horrified them in some way that was still mostly obscure to her. They wanted out. After thousands of years of settled inertia, they were making plans again, drawing charts and asking their machines for counsel their own delicately damaged minds could not provide. Down in the workshops at An-Monal, the welding torches raged blue-white again, and sparks cascaded vermilion and gold down the curved iron flanks of the fireships in dry dock. The Helmsmen stirred in their brooding, mothballed darkness, and pondered the questions put to them, and said it could be done.

Involuntarily, she glanced left across the courtyard, toward the arched entrance and the paths that wound down to the workshops beyond. Ghost memories of the clangor faded out as she came back to the present; sharp acid taste of apple on her tongue and the warmth of the sun on her skin. She'd been down to the workshops that morning, had wandered the deserted iron gantries and crane platforms, leaned there and stared at the few fireships left behind in the cobweb gloom, until the familiar tears, the ones she'd been biting back for months now, came welling up and spilled burning down her face like some Kiriath etching chemical she'd been careless with.

And left her emptied out, but feeling no cleaner inside.

It's the krinzanz, Archidi. She'd quite consciously not packed any when she left the city this time. Two days away, three at worst—how bad could it be? Now she had her answer. *If you will go on these wildly optimistic cold quit jags.*

She cleared her throat. Took another bite at the apple and shaded her eyes against the lowering sun. The tree branched low, not much over head height for a human, and spread intricately tangled limbs upward and out—a dispersal derived not, Archeth knew, from any sculptor's observation or skill, but from certain mathematical musings her father's people had incubated in the hearts of their machines like song. She remembered swinging from those branches as a child, plucking at the emerging leaf blades one spring and being shocked to discover that they were burning hot to the touch.

She ran wailing to her mother at the time, got her burned fingers salved and bandaged, and when she asked questions, got the usual human explanation for these things.

It's magic, her mother said tranquilly. *The tree is magic.*

Her father let her get well into her teens before he disabused her of that notion. Maybe because he didn't want to hurt his wife's feelings, maybe just because he found it easier to discipline Archeth—who was growing up tough and scrappy—as long as she believed he really was a necromancer burned black by his passage through the veins of the Earth. Though, truth be told, it hadn't taken Archeth long to see through that one—if, for example, Flaradnam's journey through the twisted places really had burned him black, then how did you explain *her* ebony skin when she'd never been allowed closer than a hundred feet to a lava flow or the crater's edge at An-Monal? It made no sense, and sense was something that she clung to from an early age.

Then again, from that same early age, Archeth could also see there was something going on beneath the surface of her parents' relationship, something that reminded her of the stealthy bubble and churn of the magma in the eye of An-Monal. The sporadic eruptions it occasioned scared her, and she knew that magic was one of the subjects that would invariably cause the tension to bubble over.

I have explained *it to you,* she heard him shouting one evening when she should have been in bed, but had crept out to read by the radiant globe on the staircase wall. *No magic, no miracles, no angels or demons lying in wait for unwary human sinners. You* will not *fill her head with this ignorant dross. You* will not *chain her this way.*

But the invigilators say—

The invigilators say, the invigilators say! Crash of something crystal flung at a wall. *The invigilators* lie, *Nantara, they lie to you all. Just look around you at this piece-of-shit torture chamber of a world. Does it look to you like something ruled by a benign lord of all creation? Does it* look *as if someone's up there watching out for you all?*

The Revelation teaches us to live so that the world will become a better place.

Yeah? Tell that to the Ninth Tribe.

Oh. Will you blame me for that now, too? Her mother's own not inconsiderable temper rising to the fight. *You, who helped Sabal the Conqueror fall on them, who planned the campaign and rode at the head of our armies with him to see it done? Who came home splattered head-to-foot with the blood of* infants?

I killed no fucking children! We did not want—

You knew. The black acid tones of mirthless laughter in her voice now—Archeth, eight or nine and used to various degrees of being told off, knew the small, frightening smile that would be playing about her mother's lips, the kindled fury it signaled. *Oh, you knew. You talk of lies, you knew what he would do. You dream about it still.*

You weren't there, Nantara. We had no choice. You can't build an empire without—

Murdered children—

Civilization doesn't just grow, *Nantara. You have to—*

You lecture me about ignorance and lies. Take one clean fucking look at yourself, 'Nam, and tell me who's lying.

And so forth.

So, tough common sense notwithstanding, Archeth learned early to stay away from the topic of *magic,* to just let it slide, and subsequently that habit proved tough to unlearn. When she started receiving her—characteristically patchy and distracted—tutoring in Kiriath matters from Flaradnam and Grashgal, the mark of those first fifteen or so years was on her. Magic still looked pretty much like magic to her, even when it apparently wasn't. And there was something deeply buried in her, something human maybe, inherited from her mother's side, that wanted to just accept the magic, just leave it at that rather than go through all the awkward detail of *understanding.* Many decades on, long after her mother had lived out her human life span and died, Archeth could sometimes still feel herself looking at Kiriath technology through Nantara's eyes. In nearly two centuries, she had never quite managed to shake the eerie sense of unnatural power it radiated.

"Are you brooding, child? Or simply coping badly without your drugs?"

Dark, sardonic voice without origin, snaking through the sun-split air to her ears. As if the deep-rooted stones of the An-Monal keep itself were talking to her.

She closed her eyes. "Manathan."

"A safe bet, wouldn't you say?" As ever, the Helmsman's tones rang almost human—avuncular and reassuring but for the tiny slide at the end of each syllable, the caught-breath slippage that seemed like the rising edge of a suppressed scream. As if the voice might at any given moment suddenly shift mid-sentence from intelligible sound into the shriek of steel being driven against the grindstone. "Or have you started believing in *angelic presence* and *divine revelatory grace*? Are the locals getting to you, daughter of Flaradnam?"

"I have a name of my own," she snapped. "You want to try using it occasionally?"

"Archeth," said the Helmsman smoothly. "Would you be so good as to join me in your father's study?"

The door was set in the wall at her back, almost beside the place she had chosen to sit. She rolled her head sideways to look at its black, rivet-studded bulk. Faced front and studied the declining sun for a while instead. She bit into the apple again.

"If that's intended as defiance, daughter of Flaradnam, it's a pretty poor fist you're making of it. Perhaps you should abandon abstinence as a strategy for the time being. It doesn't seem to do much for you. And you are still young enough to take the damage."

She chewed down the mouthful of apple. "What do you want, Manathan? It's getting late."

"And your entourage at the river will not wait? That seems unlikely, my lady *kir*-Archeth."

Irony dripped off the title, or at least seemed to—with the Helmsmen you could never quite tell. But the rest of Manathan's sentence was unquestionably the understatement of the day. Unlikely wasn't in it—the imperial river frigate *Sword of Justice Divine* would hold station until Lady *kir*-Archeth of the clan Indamaninarmal chose to come back down from communing with her past at An-Monal, no matter what hour of the day or night that might be. The captain of the vessel and the commander in charge of the marine detachment aboard had both been charged by the Emperor himself to protect her life as if it were his own, and while the Holy Invigilator attached might not in theory be bound by such secular authority, this one was young and fresh to his post and quite evidently overawed by her presence. Which wasn't an uncommon stance. The Kiriath might be long gone, but their status and mystique clung to Archeth like a courtier's perfume. She'd wear the rank it bought her for human generations to come.

Occasionally, she wondered how it would be when those generations had finally passed, when all those who actually remembered the Kiriath and the Departure were in their graves, and only the tomes in the imperial library spoke of her people anymore.

She wondered if she'd still be sane by then.

The shadow of the iron tree reached out, touched her finally at the toe of one boot.

"Daughter of Flaradnam," said Manathan sharply.

"Yeah, yeah." She levered herself up off the wall and to her feet. Tossed the core of her apple away across the courtyard. "I hear you."

THE RIVER FRIGATE HAD BEEN BUILT FOR THE OCCASIONAL USE OF none other than his majesty Akal Khimran the Great—whose original

idea for the ship's name, before politics intruded, had been *Crocfucker*—
and its master's suite staterooms were better appointed than some local
lordlings' mansions Archeth had guested in on her travels. And while
Akal's son Jhiral, now Jhiral Khimran II, probably hadn't set foot aboard
the vessel more than twice since his father died, neither had he ordered
it decommissioned or struck from its original purpose. The fixtures and
fittings endured, then, in all their regal splendor. There was a full-wall
library in the lounge, a dedicated map room alcove off to one side, and
a table fit to feast a dozen men set beside the broad stern window. Ornate astrolabes and telescopes stood sentinel at the corners of the room,
and the walls were hung with portraits of venerable historical figures
from the Khimran imperial line.

That the earliest of these were little more than sheep rustlers and
mountain bandits had been tacitly ignored by the court artist, and all
wore some kind of anachronistic circlet or crown to confer retrospective
gravitas. With the cabin lamps lit, they formed a solemn, shadowy backdrop to the meeting Archeth called.

Similarly serious, the faces that looked back at her from around the
table. Maybe it was the portraiture exerting its intended influence,
maybe just the proximity to An-Monal and all that the volcano's haunted
bulk implied. Senger Hald, the marine commander, sat grim and watchful where he could see the door, seat set back a little from the table as if,
even here, he couldn't be wholly sure that they would not be burst in
upon and attacked. Lal Nyanar, the frigate's captain, was a little less obviously tense. But holding his vessel at the eerie iron quays of An-Monal's
abandoned harbor was clearly making him uncomfortable, and it was a
demeanor that soaked into the other ship's officers present. And Hanesh
Galat, appointed Holy Invigilator to the ship, knowing approximately
how well liked he wasn't by the secular officers of the crew, just looked
jumpy and upset. It didn't help that the Citadel was fast coming around
to the doctrinal position that the Kiriath Helmsmen were demonic pres-
ences imprisoned in iron to prevent them tempting or otherwise mis-
leading the sons of the Revelation.

Not that I uh, actually accept that tenet, Galat had hastened to assure
Archeth one afternoon at the rail, as the frigate forged its way upriver
toward An-Monal. *The Revelation is subject to such revision of course,*

through the wisdom of learned debate and prayer. But I see no reason to adopt every position proposed in the Mastery, simply because it is proposed. And I uhm, you know, actually I cherish the part your people have played in Yhelteth's rise to its holy destiny.

How very enlightened of you. Archeth had promised the Emperor she would be polite. *I'll be sure to keep that quiet when we get back. Wouldn't want you getting in trouble with your superiors.*

He flushed, and left her largely alone after that.

Which was what she wanted, but now she wondered if antagonizing him had been wise. She doubted he could derail the intentions of Nyanar and Hald if they chose to back her—an invigilator's so-called supreme moral authority was actually a pretty tenuous thing when it butted up against the blunt pragmatism of the Empire's career military officers—but he could certainly pour some cold ecclesiastical water on any enthusiasm she managed to generate in men who, to be honest, were already looking decidedly dubious about the turn events had taken.

"We are a small force," Hald pointed out. "And we don't really know what it is we're dealing with. Would it not make more sense to carry this news back to Yhelteth and organize a fully equipped expedition?"

It would—except for the fact that, under current circumstances, Jhiral wasn't about to spare such a fully equipped force for anything that didn't involve securing the northern borders or holding the line against rioting religious idiots in Demlarashan. And while the young Emperor had no time for the warmed-over superstitions muttering out of the Citadel these days as dogma, he didn't have much time for the Helmsmen, either. Certainly, he wouldn't trust one any farther than you would a steppe nomad with your wife. And in this he was, for once, representative of the people he governed. An-Monal stood empty and decaying for a reason.

So no, she fucking *couldn't* go back to Jhiral with this one, and Hald probably knew it. She paced her words for conciliatory aplomb.

"I do not believe, Commander, that this is an operation requiring much military force. Certainly nothing that your men could not handle. Manathan was vague, but—"

"Vague indeed," rumbled Nyanar. "A messenger in need of escort. Quote, unquote. That's not much to go on."

"And not much out there." The frigate's second officer nodded soberly at the map they'd spread across the table. Pinned out between a pair of heavy silver paperweights carved like slain dragons, the thick yellow parchment showed the full extent of the Y'hela River as it reached back from Yhelteth and the coast, past the huge bulk of the volcano where An-Monal was built, and then on into the interior. The land around it was largely arid and featureless. No cities marked. "If this is a messenger, then where's he come from?"

"Shaktur, perhaps?" Someone trying to be helpful.

"They are already represented at court," Hald said. "And anyway, if this messenger's come all the way from the Great Lake, why does he suddenly need an escort now? We're deep inside imperial territory here. No barbarian incursions, no banditry to speak of. Compared with the eastern marches, this is a pleasure park."

"From the south, then?"

Nyanar shrugged. "Same applies. Anyone coming up from the desert has to pass through rougher terrain than this. They made it this far, they don't need our help with the last leg."

"Unless they're in trouble," Hanesh Galat offered unexpectedly.

Everyone looked at him. He blushed, seemingly as surprised as anyone else that he'd spoken up.

"That is," he pressed on, voice gaining a little force as he spoke. "Perhaps in coming this far, the messenger and his party have suffered privations that mean they can go no farther without our help. In which case, it would actually be our bound duty under the Revelation to bring aid to them."

Archeth shut her mouth. Cleared her throat.

"Well, quite," she said.

An uncomfortable silence settled around the table. It was an instinctive reaction where matters of doctrine were concerned. No one who valued their position in Yhelteth society would ever willingly be seen to call the tenets of the Revelation into question, least of all where those tenets had just been subject to interpretation by an accredited invigilator. However . . .

"My concern," said Hald carefully, "is that this may be a trick. Maybe even an ambush of some kind. The Helmsman has said that this messenger is *waiting* for us. Is that not so, my lady?"

"*Will* be waiting for us, yes."

The marine commander gestured. "Yes. Will be waiting for us, or is already. In either case, my lady, and outside of sorcery, how is that possible?"

"I don't know," Archeth had to admit. "High Kiriath is a complicated tongue at the best of times, and the Helmsmen frequently speak it in arcane inflections. Maybe I'm just not translating very well."

Yeah, Archidi, and maybe that's lizardshit. Maybe you've told these humans exactly as much as you want them to know, because anything else is going to make their support even harder to enlist. Maybe there are details and questions you'd really rather they left alone, not least so you can do the same and just concentrate on this bright new thing the Helmsman has brought you.

This bright new thing . . .

"DAUGHTER OF FLARADNAM." MANATHAN'S TIGHT-EDGED TONES FELL somber in the cold air of her father's study. Shadows across the walls, broad fading angles of light from the high windows as the afternoon closed down outside. "There is a message for you."

"What message?" Not yet paying much attention, working with her tongue at a shred of apple peel caught in her teeth, looking absently around at the room instead, wondering as always where exactly in all this architecture the Helmsman was actually located. It was something she'd never managed to persuade Flaradnam to tell her.

"Well, a message of some importance, I imagine." Impossible to read if the Helmsman's voice was edged with exasperation or not. "Since the messenger is coming all this way to deliver it to you in person. Speaking of which, he will be *here*, more or less. And"—she thought she caught some subtle amusement in the voice—"he will *wait* for you."

A twist of reddish light kindled at one corner of the room, unwrapped into a floating map of the local region. She wandered over, made out An-Monal, the volcano's cone, and the city itself on the western slope. The road down to the harbor, the flex of the river as it skirted the volcano and backed off into the eastern hinterlands. Symbols she could not understand flared yellow across that portion, some kind of path laid out in an arc across the desert, and finally a pulsing marker, some fifty or sixty miles upriver.

"Here?" She shook her head. "But there's nothing out there."

"Well, then you'd better hurry up and collect him, hadn't you? Wouldn't want him to go hungry."

Archeth passed her hand through the phantom fire, not quite able to suppress the shiver of wonder it always engendered when the contact did not burn. She'd grown up with these things, but where some aspects of her father's heritage had worn smooth with use over the years, others were still a jagged shock every time they manifested. She rubbed at her hand anyway, instinctively.

"And you say this messenger has come for me?"

"You might say that, yes. Of course you might also say he's come for the whole human race—plus a few offshoots that don't really fit the description anymore. In these times of transition, it's hard to know how to phrase these things. Let us just say that your heritage fits you best for the role of message recipient."

Archeth stood back from the bright glare of the map. Unease stirred through her.

"And you cannot simply give me this message yourself?"

"No, I simply cannot."

Unease stoking now, sitting in the base of her belly like some coiled thing. It wasn't often you heard the Helmsmen admit to limitations—most of the time they were sulkily self-assured in their superiority, and even when Archeth thought she might have detected some boundary of word or deed they weren't prepared to cross, the block was usually shrouded in evasive gibberish of one sort or other.

"Cannot or will not?"

"Where you are concerned, daughter of Flaradnam, I don't see that there is any practical difference between the two."

"No? What about the difference of me not going to meet this messenger because I don't think you're being honest with me."

"Well, it's your message." As if the great stone shoulders of An-Monal itself shrugged at her. "Suit yourself."

Quiet gathered, like the cobwebbed shadows in the corners of the room. The map burned in the gloom.

"Look," she said finally. "That's a lot of arid wasteland out there. We could spend days searching an area that size."

"There will be a sign," said the Helmsman succinctly. "Look to the east for guidance."

Which, for all it sounded like some faintly mocking parody of reve-latory text, was also Manathan's last word on the matter. Attempts to get clarification were rebutted with the mild admonition not to *waste time, daughter of Flaradnam.* Archeth, who'd seen the Helmsman behave like this before, gave up and slammed her way back out to the courtyard to saddle her horse. It was a fair few hours' ride down to the harbor, and she wanted to get there before it was fully dark.

But on the road down, jolting tiredly in the saddle, she noticed the feeling in her belly that she'd mistaken for unease, and realized that it was nothing of the sort. Noticed in fact that it had warmed and spread, had become a faint pitter-patter of excitement throughout the web of her veins, and a slowly building, suffocating eagerness in her chest.

She clucked her horse into a trot.

"ERROR OF TRANSLATION OR NOT," SAID LAL NYANAR. "WE ARE STILL waiting for this signal the Helmsman promised us, and it has not come. That alone ought to give us pause."

"We *are* paused." Archeth gestured through the window at the iron quay and the glimmer of campfires built there on the dock. Impatience bubbling up in her now—time to wrap this up. "No one is suggesting we break camp and head upriver right now. Tomorrow morning will be quite soon enough, and that gives us time to lay sensible plans."

"If—"

"Charts for instance." Breaking smoothly into Nyanar's continued objection before it could build any more steam. "I understand perfectly, Captain, if you're concerned about our ability to navigate safely in the upper river at this time of year. But presumably we have summer charts aboard for just such an eventuality?"

The captain bristled visibly.

"I have no fears about navigation, my lady, but—"

"Excellent. Then we need to focus on available landing points along the southern bank in the area Manathan has indicated. Can I leave that in your capable hands?"

She let silence do the rest. Nyanar glanced around the table for support he had no hope of enlisting, then subsided. Even Hald wasn't going to directly gainsay an officer of the court with her mind so obviously made up.

"I am"—head slowly inclined—"yours to command, my lady."

"Good. Commander Hald, then. I believe we shou—"

Lightning raged.

Out of the east, flickering, harsh and brilliant, so furious it seemed the broad stern window must shatter inward with its force. It drenched the room, drove out every shadow with silent, blue-white glare. It washed their faces clean of the hesitant, yellowish, document-poring lamplight within. It lit them frozen in place.

And faded.

From outside, she heard the yells of Hald's men and the crew. Saw figures leap to their feet around the campfires, saw the detail of everything on the quay laid out dim in the wake of the glare. Feet thundered on planking overhead. Babbling confusion as the sudden brilliance inked out and left them all blinking at each other in the gloom.

"The *fuck*?" Hald, courtly manners forgotten for a moment, blown back to more soldierly roots by the shock.

"What *was that*?" asked someone else in a shaking voice.

Archeth didn't answer. She already knew; she didn't need to hear it said. So it was left to young Hanesh Galat, displaying an ironic composure and humor she would not previously have credited him with, to lean forward and state the obvious.

"That," he said, looking across the table at her, "was what I believe you'd call *a sign*. It would appear that Manathan's messenger has arrived."

Thunder rolled in behind his words.

CHAPTER 5

The hunt went on into the night.

At first, it was raw panic and confusion, yelling and the excited bark of hounds still chained up back at the camp. Crash of fleeing bodies through the underbrush around them as those who'd gotten free trampled and flogged their way up the wooded slope. Fading glint of firelight behind them amid the thickening picket of the trees. Gerin seared his throat with panting, felt himself stung bloody across the face with the backswing of unseen lowered branches as he came through them in the blacksmith's wake. He blundered on, terror of the hounds driving him like a lash.

He'd seen them on the march: great gray shaggy-coated wolf-killers with long heads and mouths that seemed to grin sideways at the slaves as they paced restlessly about on their leashes. The fear they aroused was primal. Once, out on the marsh as a child, he'd seen a man brought down by dogs like these, a convict of marsh dweller family escaped from one of the prison hulks in the estuary and floundering desperately homeward in some blind hope of sanctuary. Gerin had been little more than four or five years old at the time, and the noises the man made as the hounds pulled him down stuck in his head at a depth reserved for horrors more basic than he had language for.

But the memory brought with it conscious thought.

He snatched at the blacksmith's shirt, dragged on his staggering bulk, caught another branch in the face for his trouble. He spat out pine needles, wiped his running nose, and groped after words.

"Wait—stop, *stop!*"

Panting to a halt, the two of them, in some dry ravine declivity fenced around with saplings and thick-foliaged undergrowth. They stood and propped each other up, grabbing after breath. Off to the right, someone crashed on through the trees, too separated from them to make out in the dense brush and moving away, galloping, tramping sounds receding. The cool, resin-smelling quiet of the pines came and wrapped them. Abruptly, the knotted mess of stew in Gerin's stomach kicked, crammed hotly up into his throat. He doubled over and vomited. The blacksmith just stared.

"Fuck you stop me for?" Though he didn't move.

"No good." Gerin still bent over, hands on knees, coughing and retching. Threads of snot and drool, silver in the faint light, voice a thin thread itself. "Running, like this. No good. Got hounds."

"I fucking *hear* the hounds, kid. What you think we're running for?"

Gerin shook his lowered head, still breathing harshly. "No, *listen*. We've got to find—" He spat, gestured. "—water, a stream or something. Got to lose the scent."

The blacksmith shook his head. "What is this? Now you're an expert on being chased by dogs as well?"

"Yeah." Gerin got shakily back upright. "I am. Been losing the Trelayne Watch and their mutts out on the marsh most of my life. I'm telling you. We have got to find some water."

The blacksmith snorted, muttered something inaudible. But when Gerin cast about, picked a direction, and started forcing his way through the tangled foliage again, the man followed him, wordless. Perhaps it was credit given for the way the foam-and-fit trick had worked, perhaps just a more general faith. There was a wealth of lore talked about marsh dwellers in the city: That they could scent water on the breeze and lead you to it was a common enough conceit. Gerin took a fresh grip on his fear and tried to believe the myth as much as his city-bred companion seemed to.

Surreptitiously, he squeezed blood from a small cut on his face, mingled it with spit on the ball of his thumb, and blew softly on the resulting mix. Under his breath, he muttered the swift prayer to Dakovash he had learned at his mother's knee:

. . . salt lord, master of shadow and shifting winds, out of the wind's cold quarter and the west, hear me now and put forth your crooked hand for me . . .

And maybe it was simply the custom of childhood, the simpler sense of self it brought around, or the fleeting memory of a mother's warmth, but now the undergrowth seemed to give a little more easily before him, the branches and brambles to scrape his abraded skin a little less, and the ground underfoot to firm up and guide his steps.

The forest opened and breathed them in.

THEY STUMBLED ON THE STREAM ABOUT AN HOUR LATER, FAINT CHOR-tle of running water and a ribbon of broken, bandlit gleam in the base of a shallow valley. The sounds of pursuit seemed to have ebbed away to the north, and they paused on the saddle of land overlooking the little river. Time to peer and grin at each other before they went loping down between the trees, breathing more easily now for the more considered paths they'd taken. It was a little like waking from a nightmare. Heads less stuffed with fear, room for thoughts other than just staying ahead of the hounds, room enough that Gerin was starting to feel the raw weals the march in manacles had left on his ankles and wrists. The feverish tremor in his limbs, the parched rasp in his throat as he breathed.

They hit the water's edge, dropped to their knees, and drank in sucking gulps.

"You knew this was going to be here?" the blacksmith asked him when he finally came up for air. "You could really smell it like you said?"

Gerin shook his head, because in all honesty he wasn't sure anymore. *Something* had been driving him, that was all he knew. He dragged muddied hands through his sopping hair and over his face. Winced as the water stung his manacle sores.

"We need to get off the bank," he said. "Stay in the center and head downstream or up. Dogs can't follow that."

"How long for? This water's fucking freezing."

"A while." Gerin already wading in, up to his calves. "They'll run the dogs along both banks looking for scent, but it takes time to do that. And they have to pick a direction. That gives us a coin-spin chance either way. And I know some other tricks when we get farther along. Now come on."

The blacksmith grumbled to his feet. He joined Gerin in the middle of the stream, picking his way awkwardly over the stones on the bottom.

"All right, marsh boy," he said. "You've done pretty well by us so far, I guess. Can't hurt to see what else you—"

He choked to a halt. His expression splintered in shards of disbelief and pain. He made a helpless noise, lifted one hand toward Gerin, then back to his own chest where the iron head of a crossbow bolt stood an impossible six inches clear of his suddenly bloodied jerkin.

"Stand where you are!"

The cry came from the downstream bend of the river. Gerin's head jerked to the sound. Bandlight showed him three march-masters floundering upstream in thigh-deep water near the far bank, a pair of dogs held slavering at the short end of chain leashes. Black and silver, the bulk of the men and the dogs, the splash of water around them. The man with the crossbow stood apart, had his discharged weapon down, braced on a flattish boulder at the bank, cranking up awkwardly for another shot.

Blood bubbled out of the blacksmith's mouth. His eyes locked on Gerin's.

"Better run," he said throatily, and fell facedown in the water.

"Stand, slave, or we shoot you down!"

Gerin saw the blood smoke muddily out from under the blacksmith's floating body, the soaked folds of the man's jerkin and the crossbow bolt sprouting stiffly from his back. He saw, down at the river bend, the crossbowman still struggling with his weapon. He felt the moment tilt under him like a skiff's deck in choppy water.

He whirled and fled.

Upstream, six frantic, plunging steps and out, onto boulders at the bank, wet print slap across stone on hands and slipping feet, scrabbling up to the yielding earthen forest slope above and into the trees. Behind and below, he heard the dogs let slip, the sound of the men cursing and splashing. He tore off time for one final panic-eyed look over his shoulder, saw the blacksmith's spread-eagled floating form cradled in the river's arms, the dogs surfing about in the water near the boulders, barking furiously up at him, but seemingly unable to climb out.

He fell back into the grip of the nightmare.

The slope was steep; he kept having to drop to hands and knees to stop himself from tumbling back down. The resin scent of the pines clogged in his throat as he scrambled upward. The march-masters were big, burly men for the most part; it came with the territory of what they did for a living. Amid the trees, he could probably stay ahead of them. But the dogs . . .

Only a matter of minutes before they found a way up.

The climb began to shallow out, the trees thinned. The slope became a broad, saddle-backed ridge, edged with eroded stone bluffs on the river side. A cool wind hooted off over the rocks, cut through his soaked clothing, chilled him to the bone. Gerin got properly to his feet, sagged into a staggering run along the top.

Something dark stood waiting in his path.

Gerin's heart was already thundering in his chest, but it seemed to ice over as he saw the gathered black form ahead. For a single second it seemed he was looking at something blown together out of twisted remnants of bark and trees limbs charred to death. The figure was a sharp aberration in the smooth, bandlit open ground on the ridgetop. He slammed to an involuntary halt at the sight, and it was only then he understood he was looking at a man, a tall, cloak-wrapped warrior with the jagged rise of a broadsword pommel over his left shoulder, the stab of the scabbard out from his right-hand flank, the arms folded.

Overseer!

But it was not, and somehow, somewhere in his panicking brain, he knew that much already. He stared up into a gaunt face that might have been handsome once but was now clamp-mouthed and hollow-eyed and scrawled along one side of the jaw with a thin, snaking scar like the ones they gave to disobedient whores in the city. He met a gaze that offered no more passion than a fisherman watching his motionless line.

"Dakovash?" he husked. "Is it you?"

The figure stirred, gave him a curious, sidelong look.

"No," it said, in a surprisingly gentle voice. "And I haven't seen him up here, either. Were you expecting the Dark Court?"

"I . . ." Gerin shivered. A sneeze came and racked him, loud and sudden as surf bursting on the rocks at Melchiar Point. "I prayed for the Salt Lord's intercession."

The figure wiped fastidiously at its doublet with one hand. "Are you from the marshes, then?"

"Y-yes. I was—"

Behind him, the scrabbling of claws over rock and the full-throated whoop of the dogs as they saw their quarry. Gerin thrashed soggily around, saw the first of the pack hammering toward him, all teeth and grayish bunch-muscled sprint, felt a scream clog up in his throat—

At his shoulder, he heard the swordsman say something in a language he didn't know. Saw, out of the corner of his eye, an arm lifted, a brief sign sketched on the air.

The hound yelped.

Skidded to a snarling halt a dozen yards off. It snapped and snarled again, but would not come closer. The swordsman with the scarred face took a step forward, made another sign, and spoke again. A finger wagged, gestured at the edge of the nearest bluff. The dog got up and limped hurriedly to the edge, looked down, looked back once at the cloaked figure, and then threw itself off into space. A long howl floated up, a crash of tree boughs breaking, and then silence.

The rest of the pack howled in unison with their fallen leader, but would not come ahead. They slunk back and forth on their bellies at the fringe of the trees until the swordsman took two more impatient steps toward them, spoke and signed again, and then they crawled whimpering away into the sanctuary of the forest, and fled.

"Now," the newcomer said in his gentle voice. "Perhaps you'd like to tell me your name, lad?"

"Gerin," Gerin managed, still shivering. "They call me Trickfinger, it's because when I was still a boy I could—"

The figure twisted about, gestured impatiently. "Yes, I'm sure it's a fascinating tale. You can tell me all about it later. You're from the slave caravan?"

"Yes. We escaped. But they're right behind m—"

"Don't concern yourself with that. Your luck has just changed, Gerin Trickfinger. I am—"

The pain came and hit him a colossal blow in the side. Gerin blinked. For a moment, he thought the swordsman had stabbed him. He stumbled and sat down clumsily on the blufftop, legs out like a child's. He looked down dully, and saw the quarrel sticking out under his ribs, the blood leaking out around it. He looked up at his new companion, met his eyes in wondering fear and something that felt ridiculously like embarrassment. He felt treacle-slow and stupid. He made a hesitant smile.

"Shit, they—"

And now, in the eyes that had been as dead as stones, he saw something flare up. The figure made a tight, harsh, sobbing sound and swung around, one pale hand already up and tugging at the broadsword pommel. The blade came up and around and out—some trick scabbard, Gerin thought muzzily, must be open all along one side—and it glimmered in the bandlight.

Two of the march-masters had made it to the top. The crossbowman was already cranking for his next shot; the other held his sword two-handed, covering his comrade, breathing heavily but ready to scrap.

"Escaped slave," he panted. "No need for you to involve yourself, good sir."

"But I am involved," said Gerin's new companion in an awful, shaking voice. "I'm a son of the free cities, and so is this boy. And this doesn't look very much like freedom to me."

The man with the crossbow finished his crank, crammed a new bolt into the channel, and got his weapon lifted with obvious relief.

"I won't babble politics with you, sir," the other march-master said, more steadily now. "I don't make the laws, I'm just doing my job. Now if you don't want the same breakfast as this *slave* just got, you'll let us collect the scalp and be on our way. Just be a good citizen and stand back."

"But you have no weapons to make me."

It was like a thunderbolt cracking across the space between them. Gerin, watching it all unravel, saw the crossbowman drop his charged bow as if it were hot, gawp down at his empty, open hands in disbelief. The other march-master held up his sword in a loose-fingered grip and the weight of the weapon tugged it away, let it tumble to the stony ground.

The cloaked figure reached them in less time than it took Gerin to draw his next agonized breath. It was as if the space around the newcomer had folded up like a picture on a page, had let him step across the crumpled edges between. The blued-steel blade cut about, chopped the crossbowman's belly open from the side, licked back up to take the other man through the throat. Blood splashed black in the bandlight, and the two men went down in choking, screaming ruin.

Movement in the shadows beneath the trees. The third march-master came flogging to the top of the slope, short-sword in hand. His voice was hoarse with effort, and furious.

"Guys, what the *fuck* did you do to my hounds? They've gone completely—"

He jarred to a halt, words as well as steps, as he saw the bodies of his comrades and what stood over them. His voice went up a full octave, came out shrill.

"Who the fuck are—"

"You're just in time," the figure rasped, and the blue blade flashed. The third march-master had time to blink at the glimmer of metallic light in his face, then he saw his view tip and tumble and spin, pine trees and cloud and patches of bandlit sky rushing by—he had that single moment to think he'd been pushed over the edge of the bluff—and then a painful thud, vision unaccountably dimming out now, taste of dirt in his gaping mouth, and his eyes came to rest on a final, closing glimpse of something he might or might not have had time to recognize as his own collapsing, blood-gouting headless corpse . . .

The swordsman watched the body fall, then turned back to Gerin, who still sat splay-legged on the ground, head drooping forward now.

The cloaked figure crouched in front of the boy, touched the wound gently around the quarrel, and grimaced. He put down his blade and lifted the boy's sagging chin. Gerin looked back at him blankly for a moment; then a child-like smile touched the corners of his bloodied mouth.

"Doesn't hurt anymore," he mumbled. "Did we get away?"

The figure cleared its throat. "After a fashion, yes. Yes, you did."

"That's good then."

They looked at each other for a little longer. Blood ran out of one smiling corner of Gerin's mouth. The figure saw it and let go of his chin, put one hand cupped against the boy's lacerated, muddy cheek instead.

"Is there anything I can do for you, lad?"

"Out on the marsh," the boy said indistinctly. "Salt in the wind . . ."

"Yeah?"

"Mother says . . ."

"Yes . . . Gerin, right? What does she say, Gerin?"

" . . . says don't . . . get too close to . . ."

The swordsman put a single knee to the ground. Waited. After a moment, tears ran out of the boy's eyes and blotched on his lap.

"Fuck them," he wept. "Fuck them all."

He did not lift his head again.

Ringil Eskiath kept his hand cupped at Gerin's cheek until he was quite sure the boy was dead. Then he picked up his sword, and got quietly to his feet. He looked down at the small body for a while, and then away across the top of the rock bluffs, toward the distant, dotted fires of the slave caravan's camp.

"*That* I think I can do for you," he said meditatively.

CHAPTER 6

He had Kefanin wake him before dawn. He stumbled downstairs for a breakfast his stomach didn't really want, and stepped out into the courtyard under a sky fading dark blue from black. The sun was still a good hour under the horizon, and a crisp desert chill held the air. He filled his lungs with it, and was surprised to find, as he crossed the yard, a cheerful energy in his stride that hadn't been there the day before.

Purpose.

It was the first time in weeks he could remember having any.

He made good time on the boulevard; traffic was minimal compared with the brawling chaos that would claim the streets later. A handful of tradesmen with their barrows, some slaves carrying bundled wood for kitchen fires, the odd merchant setting out on horseback for somewhere requiring an early start. Once, a short column of soldiers passed him, marching to a muster somewhere. Egar heard the cadence as they overhauled him, made them for Upland Free Marauders, and grinned in recognition. He'd fought alongside the Upland Free a couple of times, had liked them for their hill-tribe manners and disdain for all things urban. More than any other imperial soldiers, they'd reminded him of his own people, back when that wasn't such a bad thing.

They tramped on, double-timing it behind a mounted captain, and left him behind in the graying light. The chant faded out on the morning air.

Egar split from the boulevard a few hundred yards farther on, crossed the river at the Gray Mane bridge and then took the long, winding incline of Immortal Glory Rise. He reached the top just as the sun poked its new-forged glowing edge above the eastern skyline. A pause to get his breath back—really must start some kind of serious training again soon, the most exercise he'd had for months now was Imrana—then he turned and surveyed the long blank walls of the building behind him.

The Combined Irregulars barracks—rows of slit windows along the upper levels, sliced view of the parade ground quadrangle beyond the tall iron gates. Figures already moved there in the shielded gloom, pairs of them in stylized, repetitive combat motions while a drill instructor's voice bellowed exasperated abuse.

Egar grinned at the sound, and went to announce himself.

The five halberdiers on the gate were Imperial Sons of the Desert, scarified southerners to a man, slim and almost desert-dark enough that you might have mistaken them for Kiriath until you looked in their eyes. Egar met their young, ordinary stares one by one as he rolled up, identified the squad sergeant by his sash, and gave the man a friendly nod.

"Here to see Commander Darhan," he said breezily. "Tell him it's the Dragonbane."

It got him startled glances, and exactly the response he wanted. The sergeant made an almost involuntary bow and gestured at one of his men to carry the word. Watching, Egar wondered idly what these particular desert sons made of the whole Demlarashan mess. The ritual scars on their cheeks were a good sign—it was a practice frowned upon by the Citadel—and they all seemed comfortable enough in their brand-new rig, which was certainly not what he'd been led to expect. The court gossip Imrana had fed him recently was laced with references to the renamed regiment—the previous *Holy* Sons of the Desert was now deemed a little too ambiguous in its implications for loyalty—and tales were rife of devout officers refusing to wear or subtly defacing the newly ordered colors.

Yeah, well. Court gossip. Like fucking old women around a campfire.

"Eg?" A delighted bellow from the gate. "Eg the fucking dragon spanker? Get in here, man! Where you been? Thought you were off working bouncer for some cut-rate whorehouse or something, found your level at last."

Darhan the Hammer, corpulent but still imposing in his padded black instructor's gear, beard trimmed down to something approaching a groomed appearance, graying hair bound back in a ponytail. He propped the gate open with one hand, held a wooden staff casually in the other. Egar moved through the loose cordon of the halberdiers and raised a fist in greeting. Darhan bumped it with his own, and Egar saw his knuckles on that hand were torn up and bleeding. He nodded at the damage as he went in.

"Nice job. What's the matter, old man? Recruits getting too fast for you?"

Darhan snorted. "Yeah, little fuck thought he was. He's lying down now, reconsidering. Little lesson in pain management."

"Majak?"

"Yeah, and worse yet, he's a runty little Skaranak just like you were." Behind the calculated tribal slur, the fierce old grin. "What do they do to you Eastland herdboys up there, Eg? Barely dropped out between their mother's legs, they all think they got a map to the whole fucking world and everything in it."

"Called pride, Darh. Course, I wouldn't expect a soft, city-dwelling Ishlinak twat like you to understand that."

"Oh, city dwelling, is it?" The Majak instructor dropped his staff with a clatter, put up fists in a mock-guard. "Old twat is it?"

"Well you *call* that pile of hovels down by the river a city, but . . ."

"Mouthy fucking whelp!" Darhan threw a joke-slow punch at Egar's head. Egar blocked and grabbed, and the two of them clinched and wrestled about in the gateway like a couple of young buffalo bulls in mating season. The southern guardsmen looked on with a uniformly sober lack of expression—they didn't get it at all. Why would they? You had to be Majak to understand. Back on the steppes, Ishlinak-to-Skaranak, you couldn't talk like this without blades coming out. But the first thing Darhan the Hammer bashed into your thick steppe nomad skull when you got to training with him was that *down here there is no Skaranak, Voronak, Ishlinak, you're all just ignorant mothers' sons from the same featureless shit-hole stretch of buffalo pasture, and your gracious, imperial employers have exactly the same amount of contempt for you all. And you know what, they're right, so leave your tribal horseshit at the door and let's get on with turning you into soldiers, shall we? Stop fucking nodding, you, that's what we around here call a rhetorical question.*

Darhan broke the clinch—Egar let him—and clapped a violent arm around the Dragonbane's shoulders.

"It's fucking great to see you, Eg. Just come and have a look at these idiots we're working on, see if it brings back memories."

IT DID.

Across the training yard in the strengthening morning light, the paired young men went back and forth with yells and the volleyed knock of staff on staff. Darhan stood by the south wall with a mug of hot stock cupped in his injured hand and gestured at his charges.

" 'Bout a month," he said reflectively. "I reckon that's the most I've got before the palace comes calling and packs them all off to Demlarashan. They're emptying the barracks as fast as I can train them up. You think these ones'll be ready?"

Egar squatted with his back to the wall, his own mug drained and set aside. He watched the exercise with narrowed eyes. In among the lines, someone fumbled and dropped his staff. His opponent stumbled into him as he bent to pick it up. Another pair of trainees stopped what they were doing to laugh at the mess. A trainer rushed in, bawling.

Egar rubbed at his newly shaven chin.

"Is that what we around here call a rhetorical question?"

Darhan sipped from his mug and grimaced. "I know. Thing is, regional command's saying it's not going to take crack troops to break this thing—not that Jhiral's got any to spare with all that swamp demon shit going on up north—so they'll take whatever we're turning out here, whatever they can get at short notice. They're saying it's just the usual desert moron suicide brigade, but—"

"But a lot of them."

"Right." Darhan stared at the trainee lines as they formed up again. "Remember the reptile peons?"

Egar chuckled, but the sound was rusty in his throat. "Trying to forget."

"Yeah, well."

"Ah, come on, they had fangs and claws and a tail lash they could break your fucking leg with. Not going to be the same thing at all, is it?"

"Let's hope not." Darhan downed his stock, threw out the dregs on the training yard dirt. "So anyway, what you doing up here, Eg? You looking for a job or something?"

"No, mate. Just some information."

"About?"

Egar squinted into the brightening light across the yard. Now, with the sun up and another human being around to broach the subject to, his newfound sense of purpose suddenly seemed a bit foolish.

"You heard anything about any of the brothers down here taking the Citadel's coin? Hiring on officially, I mean. Livery, the whole works."

"*Citadel?*" Darhan blinked. "Don't think so. Reckon I'd remember pretty well, too. Not like the holy robe mob were ever very keen on our kind. Where'd you hear this anyway?"

Egar gestured vaguely. "Around. You know how it is. Just thought I'd chase it up, see if . . . " He gestured vaguely.

"If what?" Darhan was, he knew, looking down at him quizzically. "What's your end of this, Eg? Why should you give a shit?"

Why indeed?

Come on, Dragonbane. Make some sense a fellow steppe thug can follow.

"Thing is, Darh . . . " Slow and measured. Laying it out in words for the first time since he'd had the idea, and pleased it didn't sound quite as half-arsed as he'd expected. "I've got this bodyguard gig right now. High ranker at court, and she's had some scrap with the robes. Happened last year, but it doesn't look like it's going to go away. I'm just looking for a back door in. Try to get some intelligence, maybe some advance warning set up from inside. Figure another Majak might see it my way, and help me out."

"Or not." Darhan, dubious. "There's still a code of sorts going around, Eg, even these days. Take their coin, you owe them the fight. That's still what I'm teaching up here, anyway."

"Yeah, but the fucking *Citadel*?" Egar glanced up at his old trainer. "Come on."

Quiet close in, the yells and messy rattle of staff play across the yard. Darhan stared out at his men.

"You ever run into Marnak?" he asked distantly.

"Sure. Last year, back up on the steppe." Egar chuckled to cover a sudden stab of regret. "Old bastard never seems to age."

"He didn't think about coming back south with you?"

"No chance. He's happy up there, Darh." Egar didn't add that the circumstances of his own departure hadn't allowed for Marnak to express a preference one way or the other. "Found his place in the world, I reckon."

Darhan grunted. "He ever tell you we fought opposite sides of a couple of battles, back when he was taking League coin? Back when we were young?"

Egar couldn't remember.

"Never mentioned it," he said breezily. "You making a point or something?"

"My point is, Eg, there was a time, Marnak might have killed me if we'd ever come face-to-face on those battlefields, and he would have done it without blinking. Same goes for me—the Empire paid my wages, I killed their enemies for them. Still do when there's call. If those enemies turn out to be Majak, turn out to be Ishlinak-Majak even—well, that's a damn shame, but there it is." Darhan turned to look at him intently. "You don't want to lean too much on that tribal thing, is what I'm saying."

Egar levered himself unhurriedly to his feet.

"That sounds like a warning, Darh. There something you're trying to tell me?"

For a moment, their gazes locked. Then Darhan snorted, shook his head, grinned at the ground. Looked up, still smiling.

"You're a fucking idiot, Dragonbane, that's what I'm trying to tell you. You, and your loyalties. Going to get you killed one of these days. Look, a couple of decades back, it was the League and the Empire, right? Then the lizards came and stirred everything up so we were all friends in the grand human alliance. And afterward we went right back to killing each other, League and Empire, same as it ever was."

"You don't need to remind me, Dar. It's why I went home."

"Yeah, but now you're back. So I guess things didn't work out the way you hoped up there. Life on the steppe not how you remembered it?"

Egar found a grimace of his own. "Don't ask."

"Yeah. What I thought. So like I said, you're back and now it looks like the palace and the Citadel might end up going at it for a while. So what, Eg, so fucking what? Politics. It'll pass, just like the lizards, just like the war. Let it go, stand aside if you can. At a minimum, make sure you don't get caught in the middle unpaid."

"Been paid, Darh." Egar made a formal bow, Yhelteth horse-clan style, hinged fingers of each hand locked together to form a flat double fist at chest height. It was the first thing they'd learned as recruits into the imperial war machine. The first physical thing Darhan the Hammer taught them. "You made me that smart, at least. Look, I've got to go. Clients to shake down, whorehouses to frequent, you know how it is. Do me a favor, though. If you do hear anything about the robes hiring Majak enforcers, could you send me a runner? They'll get me on the Boulevard of the Ineffable Divine, number ninety-one."

"Yeah, right. The Boulevard."

"Yeah, it's just a temporary thing. Till I get my own place, you know."

"Fuck, right, off."

"Seriously." Egar winked. "Make it worth your while. I'll come up and buy you a beer."

"Yeah, you'll buy me a fucking barrel if that really is your address. Fucking court puppy. Get out of here, before I come with you, see if they don't need someone to feed their fucking dogs or something."

They bumped fists once more.

"Good to see you again, Darh. Thanks for the soup."

"Hey, any trainee of mine, fallen on hard times. The least I can do, y'know. A cup of gruel."

"Hospitality worthy of the ancestors, truly."

"Yeah, your ancestors, maybe."

Egar grinned, forked an obscene shaman's gesture at the other man for farewell, and walked. He was halfway across the yard, still chuckling in the sunlight, when Darhan yelled after him. Egar stopped, turned about to field what was likely going to be some parting obscenity about his tribe.

"Yeah?"

"Just occurred to me." The old instructor's voice pitched effortlessly to carry over the shouts and blows of the ongoing staff drill. "Probably came to the wrong place. You really want to chase this Citadel hire thing, why don't you try the Pony Stringer's. Same crowd as ever down there."

Egar frowned. "That place? Under the Black Folk Span? I thought it burned down years ago."

"Yeah, it did. They rebuilt it. Been open a couple of years now. They're calling it the Lizard's Head."

"Oh, that's fucking original."

Darhan shrugged. "What you going to do? They've got the head."

CHAPTER 7

The imperial trade legate was less than impressed.

"When slaves are shackled in Yhelteth," he sniffed, peering out at the slow gray creep of dawn across the scrub, "they *stay* shackled."

Poppy Snarl held down an urge to stab the man right under that neatly kept little fucking goatee he wore. Wouldn't have been hard to do it, either; two steps across the tent, he barely topped her by an inch and a half anyway, and like most imperials she'd met he was mannered and perfumed like some harbor-end ladyboy with delusions of courtly station. Useless piece of shit. He'd done nothing but bitch about the conditions on the march since they set out, and the endless comparisons with how much better things were done in Yhelteth were beginning to wear her down. She didn't like the imperials and their oh-so-fucking-superior airs, even at the best of times. And this—well short of cock-crow, the night without sleep, nearly an entire coffle of male merchandise somehow escaped, or killed or crippled beyond salable worth in the attempt, close to a dozen of her march-masters dead or dying, and another dozen still out unaccounted for in the hills—this was definitively *not* the best of times.

Still—fingers forced, through a major effort of will, to remain loose on the hilt of the fruit knife she was using to peel a breakfast apple, a bland diplomatic smile put on like makeup—she needed this man's good graces. They all did. Preferred supplier status was not something the Empire granted lightly, and Trelayne was not the only city in the League jostling for position now that Liberalization had opened up the trade again. *Play nice,* Slab Findrich had advised her over a celebratory pipe before they left. *Let him feel superior, if that's what gets his ink on the parchment. It's just business, you've got to suck it up.*

Yeah, easy for you to say, she'd snapped. *You're not the one going to be on the road with him for a solid two months.*

Findrich just fixed her with his leaden eyes. He wasn't much for histrionics.

We're legitimate now, Poppy. An equally leaden patience in the rasping, pipe-cooked voice. *This is how it's done.*

Yeah, this was how it was done. Like the war all over again. The perfumed fucking imperials standing around like priests at an orgy, while she and her League muscle scrambled to get a tourniquet on the escape. Findrich's legate pal and his high-tone bodyguards hadn't lifted a finger all night except to examine their fucking nails in the firelight.

They were just *so* fucking above it all.

Her palm itched where the knife lay across it. She settled for imagination, chopped deep into the apple with her blade, and sliced off a glistening chunk. Chewed it and swallowed.

"Of course," she said smoothly, "I'd be most grateful for anything I can learn from our more advanced colleagues in the Yhelteth slave market. It's part of the reason for this trip. But right *now*, I'm afraid we—"

Scuff of boots outside the tent flap.

"Milady?"

"Irgesh. Good morning. Are we accounted for, finally?"

The lead march-master ducked his head into the tent. Red-eyed and weary from the night's hunt. "Uhm, in fact no, milady. Still missing eight. It's just—there's someone here to see you."

"To see me?" She raised one groomed brow. "At this time of the morning? Is he from Hinerion?"

"Not sure, milady." Hastily, spotting the smolder of exasperation in her face. "He . . . he's not a commoner, that's for sure. Noble-born, no question."

Snarl sighed. "Oh, very well. Tell him I'll be out. But if it's the Hinerion border patrol commander, he's a bit bloody late."

"Yes, milady."

Irgesh ducked out with visible relief. Snarl set down apple and knife and wiped her hands on a cloth.

"Sent out to Hinerion when all this kicked off," she muttered. "He's had the whole fucking night to get his men out the gate, and now he shows up when we've done all the work ourselves. Sometimes I wonder why we pay taxes."

The imperial legate stroked his chin.

"As I have said numerous times, worthy merchants such as your-selves could not fail to benefit from an allocation of imperial levies along the major trade routes. A hand in trading friendship that my Emperor would be only too happy to extend if you might persuade the League Assembly in that direction."

Snarl looked at him bleakly. "Yeah, you're right. You have said that numerous times."

She found her cloak and snugged it around her shoulders. Looked briefly into the tent's tiny dressing mirror at the caked makeup, the sleepless eyes, the creeping signs of age. She hesitated a moment, then made an exasperated gesture, a spitting sound, and left everything the way it was. She stalked out into the dawn, let the legate follow or not, as he wished.

It seemed he did wish. She heard the tent flap again behind her as she swept past the burned-down campfire and the standing march-master guard. The huddled mass of slaves stretched away into the gray-ing gloom around her, thankfully quiescent now after the chaos of the night before. They'd had to beat down at least three or four other coffles aside from the one that had so mysteriously come apart, as understanding of the escape spread through the caravan. She thought, glancing back through what had happened, that it might have been touch-and-go there for a while. Could easily have ended up with a full-blown chain revolt like the one at Parashal last year.

"Eight remaining," the legate said at her shoulder. "That's little enough wastage. My advice would be to call off the search, strike camp, and not waste more valuable journey time."

"No." Tight-lipped on the monosyllable. Snarl spotted the newly arrived nobleman down the rise from the tents at one of the other fires, in conversation with Irgesh and a handful of the imperials. She headed downward, trailing explanation in tones just this side of polite. "I don't work that way, I'm afraid. I don't know how you handle these things in the Empire, but we're staying put until the runaways are all accounted for."

"But eight slaves, Mistress Snarl. So small a loss is—"

"*My* loss, my lord legate, is the major part of that coffle, counting these eight or not. And there's not one damn thing I can do about that. What I can do is make sure nothing like this *ever happens again.*" She felt her temper slipping. Bit down on her words for a clamp. "We are going to make examples here, soon as the sun comes up. And the word is going out for future fucking reference: Nobody, no-*body* gets off the chain on one of my caravans and lives."

The legate muttered something in Tethanne. She didn't know the language well enough to follow what he'd said, but guessed it for an insult. She was past caring. If Hinerion had sent help, they stood some chance of getting out of here today. If not, she'd have this watch commander's balls. She reached the dying embers of the campfire, felt the faint wash of warmth it still radiated into the dawn chill. She drew breath to speak.

The new arrival showed no sign he'd noticed her approach—he stood with face and spread hands turned away, toward the ashen fire, evidently feeling the cold as well and trying to soak up some of the remnant heat. Rich black brocade cloak over broad swordsman's shoulders and what looked like a Kiriath blade and scabbard across his back. Snarl blinked, impressed despite herself. If the weapon was real and not one of the cheap replicas knocked out by forges across the League since the war, then her guest was a noble indeed. No one else outside the Empire could afford Kiriath steel, and across the free cities it was something of an ultimate in terms of status. Even in Trelayne itself, there were only a handful of men who—

"Hello, Poppy."

She went very still. That voice alone, but then he turned slowly to face her.

That face.

They'd told her he was changed, back in Trelayne. Those who'd seen him, those who claimed they had. The stories were all much the same. Scar-faced, empty-eyed, eldritch—all trace of the young warrior who'd thrown back the Scaled Folk from the battlements of the city now eaten away from within by some consumption beyond human naming. At the time, she'd scoffed—it was the same basic rap they ran for every street thug, marsh creep, or coastal pirate the Watch had yet to bring to justice. Stood to reason—you had to have some rationale for why you'd let him face you down and get away. Why, against all the odds, he kept slipping through your fumbling law enforcement fingers. Why the men you commanded were not enough, why your bounty hunter's blade hadn't been up to the task of taking this one down.

Eldritch. Sure. *Glamorous, shadowy, and unhuman. Walks through walls.*

A crock of shit.

Perhaps, Findrich admitted, as they talked it through one early-spring evening. *But for all that, we* have *lost our dwenda patron, our very own walker-through-walls, and the rumors say it was Ringil that took him down. They say—*

Oh, they say! They say? Slab, give me a fucking break! When does the mob not rock itself to sleep with folklore and wish fulfillment? Do you really think we could rule these idiots the way we do if they didn't have their myths to cuddle up to around the fire at night?

She knew Ringil Eskiath, perhaps as intimately as anyone alive, and she didn't think it likely he was much different from the arrogant aristo prick he'd always been. A little older and colder with the war years, maybe, but who wasn't.

Now, suddenly, as she met his gaze, she was no longer sure.

"Ringil," she managed urbanely. "Do I have *you* to thank for this impromptu insurrection?"

"No. They thought of that themselves."

The voice was a soft rasp, not much over a whisper, and the hollow eyes might have been looking right through her. He wore his long black hair gathered back in a loose queue, and that scar they all talked about was a bone-white scrawl along his jaw, seemingly tilted at her for inspection. Something defensive about the way he did that. And he'd lost some weight since she saw him last.

"Well." She forced a laugh, covering, looking for the angle. He'd walked into camp alone, was not even wearing armor beneath the cloak. "I confess I'm a little surprised to see you here, Gil."

"Yes, I imagine you are."

"You do know there's a price on your head now?"

He nodded. "Fifteen thousand florins. The Sileta brothers came looking to collect last month."

Somewhere low across Poppy Snarl's shoulders, a faint shiver came alive. Back in Trelayne, there were the usual tall-growing weed-garden rumors about the whereabouts of the Sileta family. The street said they were somewhere out on the marsh, hiding from the Watch. Or they'd run off to Parashal behind some brothel connection a cousin had there.

Or they'd been eaten by demons.

The street said a lot of things, most of which you had to sieve repeatedly for superstition, wishful thinking, and flat-out lies. But on this occasion the gleaming residue of truth remained: The Sileta brothers, toughest and most feared of the harbor-end ganglords, were currently nowhere to be found.

She shrugged it off, barely missed a beat. "I don't imagine they'll be the last."

"Probably not. It *is* a lot of money."

The imperial legate waded in. "Am I to understand that we are here bandying words with an *outlaw*?"

Ringil shot the man a disinterested glance. "And you are?"

"I do not answer to—"

"He's the Empire's vested interest," Snarl said succinctly. "And these are his sworn personal guard you're bandying with. Now really—perhaps you'd better tell me what you're doing here."

The hollow-eyed stare again. "Can't you guess?"

"No, I can't." She fought down the faint shiver again. Found the threads of her anger once more. "To be completely honest with you, Gil, my best guess up to now was that you'd crawled back to that shit-hole little mountain town you saved in the war. You know, back to where they still think you're some kind of hero and don't mind you buggering their sons."

"Oh, they mind, Poppy." A thin smile. "Even there, even where they owe me their lives, they *mind*. But what are they going to do about it? You can't control a son the way you control a daughter. Can't just lock him in the house or beat him to a pulp like you can with your wife. Not once he gets older than about fifteen, anyway. Too much chance he'll hit you right back."

"They don't have the cage in this . . . Gallows Gap, wasn't it?"

"Gallows Water. The gap is above the town. And yes, they used to have the cage. Hung up right there in the town square." Ringil's expression hardened. "Except the first summer I was there, I had it cut down."

Small silence. Irgesh and the imperial bodyguards exchanged glances. Everyone seemed to be waiting for something.

"How very . . . flamboyant of you," Snarl said finally. "I suppose I shouldn't be surprised. But you still haven't answered my que—"

"I'm here to kill you, Poppy."

Now the silence came back in like roaring surf. The moment pivoted around Ringil, dizzying, high-fever intensity, like the world rushing away. The legate's neatly barbered mouth shocked open, the stealthy settling of hands on sword hilts among the—*count them off, two, three, four*—imperial soldiers. Irgesh, already ahead, less of a fighting threat by his stance, but mistrustful since the stiffening of his mistress when she saw who her guest was. It all fell into place like pieces of a puzzle solved, the geometry of the moment and the fight to come—the heat of the dying fire at Ringil's back, just the way he'd maneuvered to have it, the men and what they would assuredly do in the next few seconds, and, somewhere out beyond it all, Seethlaw's voice across salt black emptiness, echoing off sea cliff stone.

I see what the akyia saw, Gil. I see what you could become if you'd only let yourself.

He saw the legate's signal, finger-twitch-small, but screaming loud to his senses as a battlefield death. Heard the minuscule grating of imperial blades coming loose all around him. Felt the fight sheet upward like oil-fed flames.

He let go.

The dragon-tooth dagger, dropped from his left sleeve into that hand—he gripped it blade-down, was already spinning, right hand up and reaching past his ear for the jutting pommel of the Ravensfriend at his shoulder. The sword's rough-woven grip seemed to weld itself into his curling palm, seemed to kick eagerly as he tugged on it. The engineered Kiriath scabbard split along its outer edge, spat the Ravensfriend free as he drew.

The imperials had cleared their weapons, too.

He went to one knee. No thought to the motion; it was as if a revolving storm of forces put him there. Vaguely, he knew a cavalry scimitar went scything over his head. He seemed to unfold from the bisecting line of his own rib cage—dragon tooth curving left and into the nearest imperial's thigh, Ravensfriend right and under the scimitar's cut. He supposed it chopped the man somewhere between throat and belly—was moving too fast now to find out or care.

Screams.

And somewhere, Seethlaw, laughing . . .

He left the dagger where it was, came up out of his dropped stance. Got a two-handed grip on the Ravensfriend and reversed his guard. Backed off a pair of blades on the rising edge of his sword and gained himself a couple of steps of fighting ground. The Kiriath steel licked out again, impatiently, took Irgesh across the forehead, and the overseer staggered back howling as blood flooded down his face. It was a sword-tip slash, not fatal, not even very damaging, but in the screaming, red-tinged chaos of the moment, Irgesh could not know that, and would not be given the chance to find out. Ringil blocked another imperial blade, got in close on the turn and snagged a leg in behind his opponent's feet. Hook hard, and the man went over, sprawling backward into the smoking ashes of the firebed. He yelped and rolled, his cloak catching fire in a dozen places. Ringil closed on Irgesh, beat aside a clumsy cutlass block, and skewered the man in the guts. Twisted the blade and withdrew. The overseer made another noise, low and grinding, and the Ravensfriend came loose in a burst of blood and whatever Irgesh had had for breakfast.

Ringil whirled about snarling. It was like some noise a Yhelteth war cat might make as it sprang. Blood droplets sprayed the air, off the swinging arc of Kiriath steel, fine as summer rain.

The imperials reeled apart, away from the thing in their midst.

One was down, dead or dying or just in shock from that first upward chop into his chest—the Ravensfriend liked bone pretty much as well as flesh these days, and Ringil himself couldn't say how deep the cut had gone. The others were not in much better shape, one rolling and yelling in the firebed trying to put himself out, a second fighting to stay upright with Ringil's dagger in his leg, only one unharmed, and now Ringil moved to meet him.

But they were imperial soldiers, they were a high-ranking imperial's honor guard. Drawn from altogether finer cloth than Snarl's marchmasters, and not quite what Ringil had been expecting. The man in the firebed shucked his cloak and rolled clear, would be back on his feet in seconds. The stabbed soldier was reaching awkwardly down, eyes fixed on Ringil like he was hungry. The uninjured soldier stepped forward to cover his comrade, locked up Ringil's attack. Sour scrape of steel as the blades met. The other man got hold of the dragon-tooth dagger and yanked it out of his own flesh with a single gritted roar. He straightened up, teeth still bared in a savage grin—and dragged himself right back into the fight.

Fuck.

At the corner of his vision, Ringil saw Poppy Snarl look out across the huddled slave caravan for her men.

Saw her eyes widen in shock.

No time for that. He met the two standing imperials in a zigzag blur of steel, deflected both blades and took a slice across his ribs for his trouble; if the injured man's leg was bothering him, it didn't show. Ringil kicked out viciously, tried for a knee. He missed, could not afford the instability or time it would take to try again, dropped hastily back, caught a blurred glimpse of the burned man rushing him from the side, and swung about to meet the assault.

Barely in time.

The Ravensfriend blocked like something alive, took the brunt. The sword chimed and quivered, his attacker's steel glanced off it, turned the force of the rush a vital couple of inches. Ringil pivoted with it, flashed out a hand on instinct, grasped something, a buckle on a tunic, an edge of stiffened cloth, jerked the man forward off balance. The imperial plunged past him, stumbling. Ringil tripped him, put him down. No time to bring the Ravensfriend down for the kill—the others were on him—he settled for a glancing kick to the downed soldier's head—

Sensed, somehow, the hurtling edge of steel at head height behind him—

Ungainly sideways leap—over the sprawled body, and just ahead of the scything imperial blade. He felt it touch his queue, flip the bound ponytail of hair, felt the cool wind of its passing. He landed awkwardly, breath caught up, only half convinced his head was still on his shoulders.

And whipped about at guard. Tight grin on his face with how close he'd come.

The remaining two imperials came on. The body of their fallen comrade slowed them down. But behind them, the legate had finally managed to draw a sword of his own, was brandishing it not entirely unhandily. And Poppy Snarl was on her knees in the dirt beside Irgesh, scrabbling for his weapon. Ringil felt the balance tilt, felt what he'd planned sliding out of reach, felt—

Straight-line crow-flicker black.

Like a mother hushing unruly boys, but impossibly swift. A rippled fleeting past him through the air, and the two soldiers slammed to a halt, spiked about with sudden, black-fletched arrow shafts. Throat and eye, chest and belly.

Eril's men, taking no chances.

Yeah—took their fucking time about it, though.

The imperials spasmed, gurgled, and went down, dead or near enough to make no difference. Puff and drift of dust up around their bodies. The man at Ringil's feet moaned and twitched, but showed no sign of getting up.

Ringil let his breath out. Surveyed his victory.

The legate, clutching his sword at an uncertain guard. Poppy Snarl, crouched beside her slaughtered march-master, blinking at what had just happened. And out among the sea of huddled slaves, Eril's men moving forward. They wore the assumed garb of the march-masters they'd murdered in the night or the captured slaves they'd imitated coming into camp. They held an irregular assortment of weapons, stolen or already owned, among them at least half a dozen recurved bows drawn to a cautious half-taut readiness. Eril himself led the gathering circle, a bloodied knife in each hand and the matching daubs of close-quarters slaughter still on his face.

Ringil stepped nimbly over the man he'd kicked in the head, booted Snarl sprawling into the dirt as he passed her, and put the tip of the Ravensfriend at the legate's throat.

"Drop it," he suggested.

The legate's sword fell out of his fingers. Ringil lowered the Ravensfriend and waited for Eril's men to reach him. He met Poppy Snarl's gaze where she lay watching him from the ground. Surprised at the quick pulse of hate it still generated in him.

Flushed with relief, the imperial legate decided on bluster.

"This—this is an *outrage*. Do you have any idea *who I am*?"

Ringil turned to look at Eril.

"Do we have any idea who he is?"

The Marsh Brotherhood enforcer shrugged. "Some Empire merchant fuck, right?"

"*I am the Yhelteth Emperor's direct, empowered legate to your countrymen!*"

Ringil nodded. "He is, unfortunately. See that brooch on his shoulder? Yhelteth diplomatic seal. And I'm willing to bet he's got—"

He grabbed up the legate's left hand.

"Yep, the ring, too." He let the legate's arm drop in disgust. "This is the last fucking time I trust Brotherhood spies to get my intelligence for me."

Eril looked embarrassed. In the months they'd been harrying Trelayne's slavers, he'd pulled Marsh Brotherhood favors for Ringil where he could, but the Brotherhood itself hadn't been particularly cooperative about it. In the end, sworn-sons-of-the-free-city bullshit aside, they were criminals trying to buy their way into upriver respectability, and Ringil's terrorism wasn't any more comfortable for them than it was for the slavers. And Eril, blood debt notwithstanding, was a mid-ranking enforcer, acting alone and out on a limb, with very limited pull.

Surprised it's lasted even this long, really.

Well—you did save his life.

Ringil sighed and cast a brooding glance around. Daylight already strengthening in the east, washing the first faint color into the tree line and the sandy terrain below. The night gone to bleaching shreds of darkness in the west, and all around the thousand eyes of the slaves and their new saviors, all seemingly resting on him.

An imperial legate. Great.

"Perhaps now," the legate stormed. "You realize the gravity of your error."

"There's no error here," Ringil told him.

They hauled Poppy Snarl to her feet and held her pinioned for Ringil's inspection. There was some jeering and groping along the way—Snarl had aged well on the proceeds of Liberalization and the new trade. She still had a bright sheen to hair and eyes, a harsh-boned beauty in the face and curves in all the right places. Hands pawed and squeezed at the more obvious options. She flailed and spat, her clothing tore. Someone—it was hard to keep track of the men Eril hired, Banthir, was it? Or Hengis?—retrieved Ringil's dragon-tooth dagger from the dirt and brought it to him, wiped carefully clean. The man bowed for respect and handed the weapon over. Ringil nodded absent thanks, tucked it away.

Snarl head-butted one of her captors, sent him stumbling. Raucous laughter from the others.

"Got a temper on her, this one."

"Soon sort that out. Just needs a good splitting is all."

"Get in the fucking queue, man. You don't—"

They quieted as Ringil approached. He still held the Ravensfriend unsheathed in his hand. Snarl bared her teeth at him.

"What the fuck do you think you're doing, Gil?"

He considered her for a moment. "I'm just the messenger. Does the name Sherin mean anything to you?"

"Oh, for Hoiran's *sake*! Slab said you were . . . " Snarl bucked again between the men who held her pinioned. "This is really about some whining idiot second cousin of yours? You know, when Findrich told me that, I didn't believe him. I said you were too fucking smart for that shit. *Had* to be something else. What the fuck happened to you, Gil? You used to be a *player*."

Ringil backhanded her across the face. Someone among his men voiced a low, hooting cheer. He started to feel vaguely sick.

"I asked you a question, Poppy."

By then she could see it coming, knew her hand was played out. A blank, street-tempered defiance hardened her features. She spat at him, spittle threaded with blood from where the blow must have cut the inside of her mouth. She put on a dreadful, death's-head smile.

"What do *you* think, hero? You think I keep count of every piece-of-shit slave I buy, every bad-debt auction knockdown that falls in the net?"

"This particular piece-of-shit slave was my cousin."

"So fucking what? You want to believe I was there personally when they broke her? Grow the fuck up, Gil. This is a business. You think I *care*?"

Ringil remembered where and how he'd finally found Sherin. Remembered what had been done to her.

He looked into Poppy Snarl's eyes. Saw nothing there he could defeat.

"Take her away," he said woodenly. "Do what you will. But leave her alive."

Mob roar of approval from the men. Ringil held himself immobile and watched as they started to drag her back, started tearing at her clothing again where it was already ripped. She growled deep in her throat and thrashed against them. A breast spilled free, was grabbed and bitten into like fruit. Snarl yelled in pure fury. Someone levered her legs open, grasped brutally between. Another yell, sobbing this time, another chorus of whooping as the men heard, and saw. Then they lifted her bodily away, and closed around her like rats on rotting meat.

He stood. He stood and watched.

"Hengis." Sudden shudder—he came to life and grabbed Hengis by the arm as the man drifted to join the rape. *"Hengis."*

"Jengthir, my lord."

"Jengthir." He nodded jerkily. "I mean it. If she dies, so does the man who caused it."

"Course, my lord, no worries. I'll see to it. Got a tender touch, I have."

Jengthir grinned at him, tugged free, and was gone.

Ringil turned away from the boiling thrash of men, now collapsing to the ground, and the woman he'd given to them. He wanted to wipe a hand across his face, but dare not risk the gesture. He caught the legate staring bulge-eyed.

"Fuck are you looking at?" he snarled.

"You cannot do this." The imperial was whispering it in Tethanne, maybe unaware he was speaking at all. "The Emperor will—"

"Will *what?*" Ringil followed the language shift, strode up to the legate, and smashed him in the mouth with the pommel of the Ravensfriend. The imperial went over backward with the force of it, and Ringil stood over him. Voice shouting to drown out the noises behind him. "The Emperor will *what? Tell me what your fucking Emperor will do!*"

The legate put a hand to his broken mouth, brought it away bloody, stared disbelieving at the wet red dripping off his fingers. Ringil dropped to a crouch beside him, forced his voice down to a corrosive, conversational rasp.

"If I know that fuck Jhiral Khimran, the only thing he'll do when he hears about this is have it turned into some piece of harem fantasy theater, and then sit back and watch until he gets it up enough to join in. But I wouldn't worry about it, your excellency, it isn't going to be your problem."

Behind them, Poppy Snarl shrieked and sobbed, and the men raping her roared with ribald delight. The legate heard, gaped at Ringil as if he were something summoned out of a crack in the Earth's crust. He was trying to crawl backward, away from the gaunt, scarred face and what he saw in it, but his cloak was under him and he got no purchase. His boot heels slipped and slid on silk.

"What do you . . . " He was mumbling, numb with terror. "What do you think you're—you're doing?"

Ringil set aside the Ravensfriend, shook the dragon-tooth dagger from his sleeve. He grasped the legate firmly by the hair with his free hand, pulled his head back hard. He leaned in close, near enough to smell the man's terror-soured breath, near enough to bestow a kiss.

"I'm abolishing slavery," he said.

And opened the imperial's throat.

CHAPTER 8

They cast off mooring from the iron quays an hour after dawn—
a leisurely enough start by military standards, but Archeth wanted
plenty of light in the sky to reassure the men. She stood at the starboard
rail and watched as the *Sword of Justice Divine* drifted out on the swirl of
the river, started to turn in the current, and then stiffened and quivered
as the oars dug in along her flanks. The stroke drum boomed belowdecks,
the pulse of it throbbing up through the planking under Archeth's feet,
and she heard the caller start the cadence:

> Bring me the Head of the Whoreson Pimp
> *—Severed at Dawn! Severed at Dawn!*
> Bring me his Best Whore all 'tired in Silk
> *—I've Whoresons to Spawn! Whoresons to Spawn!*

Bring me the Purse that the Pimp stole from me
—*All Emptied Out! All Emptied Out!*
Bring me . . .

And so on.

She let it wash over her, faint smile of recognition and then the words rinsing out in their own familiarity. Not a bad choice of chantey—the brutal shore-leave bravado in the lyrics might serve to bolster some nerve in men who'd gone to their bedrolls the night before amid mutterings of sorcery and demonic visitation.

And hadn't woken up much better.

The frigate slugged its way upriver to the beat of the drum, the sky to the southeast now flushed deeper with the glare of a sunrise still hidden behind the long shoulder of An-Monal. Archeth leaned on the rail, eyes screwed up against the light, staring at the distant smoke.

It hadn't changed since daybreak—a single, thin column in rising charcoal, like some craftsman's sketch line drawn on the brightening blue tile of the sky. She'd woken at dawn to the sounds of the men as they spotted it. Graying light from the east outside her cabin window, and excited calls back and forth, building to a small storm of debate and disconcerted oaths, until Senger Hald came down the gangplank and bellowed them into quiet.

If he had misgivings of his own, he hid them well. Tasks were reaffirmed, the camp along the quays was struck, the frigate loaded for the off. The marines went about their work efficiently enough, but she heard their voices as they passed muttering back and forth below her cabin on the quay. They were mostly devout men, in their own rough fashion, and this was just too close a match for some of the more lurid prophesying rants in the chapters of the Revelation dealing with the Last Battle for the Divine. Demonic fire by night, and now something was burning in the east. Draw your own conclusions.

The sun slid up over the slope of the volcano like an incandescent coin, unstuck itself from the skyline, and started to rise. Archeth yawned and thought she might need more coffee. She hadn't slept well in her stateroom. Had, in fact, rolled back and forth the whole night, tugged in and out of dreams, as if the frigate were plowing through heavy seas.

Chalk up another delight to quitting the krinzanz. She didn't remember the detail of the dreams, except that her father walked in them, and was not well, and warned her constantly of something whose impending form and nature she had not yet learned enough to grasp.

You must try, she thought she recalled him pleading. *You must keep trying.*

Big, blunt hands braced forward and wide apart on the table of scattered charts, eyes that glittered in the gloom, and a thin moaning outside the window that might have been someone in pain, or some Kiriath machine she did not understand, or possibly both.

If you do not try now, who will? Who is left, Archidi?

And then she knew, with the abrupt certainty of dreams, that he was dead, and she was next, and the thin moaning could only come closer, pressing up to the glass, peering in and she was—

Awake. Like the snap of a twig underfoot.

Staring across the cabin into empty gloom.

And so on, again and again, as the night wore slowly down on the hard-edged grind of her thoughts. Until dawn seeped in at the window like some pallid, halfhearted salvation, and gifted her with temporary purpose.

A second yawn swamped her. She blinked in the sunlight, took the hint, and went down to the galley. On her way back up, hands cradled around the warm ceramic mug, she ran into Hanesh Galat.

"Good morning, my lady."

"Yeah." She was already past him on the companionway, heading up. Trying not to hear as he called after her.

"Might I, uhm, join you?"

She made an indistinct noise, which he apparently took for assent. He trailed her to the rail, leaned there a diplomatic distance off her right elbow.

"A beautiful morning," he said, awkwardly.

She stared down at the wash of orange-gold on the rippling water, the glistening churn of the oars. *Krinzanz, krinzanz—my soul for a quarter ounce.* She held herself down to a stark civility. "I guess."

"Well, uh . . ." Galat hesitated. It made him seem oddly boyish. "You see, I'm from the north, originally. Vanbyr, near enough. We aren't so lucky with the sun up there."

Or anything else, lately, she just stopped herself from saying.

But scenes from the rout of the Vanbyr uprising marched by in her head like a column of leering trolls. Shrieks and smoke, the hovels burning in the countryside, the choking, pleading figures thrust back inside at pike-point when they tried to stumble out. Severed heads kicked like footballs in the cobbled city streets, infants thrown from upper windows and spitted on swords for sport while their mothers wept and howled and were raped to provide more conventional recreation for the imperial soldiery.

It was the Emperor's command, and it was carried out to the letter. Akal the Great wanted an example made, a lesson given in what happens when an imperial border province gets ideas about independence. And all who were at Vanbyr agreed that the lesson had been given with magisterial force—though detail was of course decorously reworked to suit the court's finer sensibilities. As for the man himself—aging and increasingly infirm from the toll of the injuries he'd sustained during the war, Akal was unable to ride with his army to Vanbyr, and so did not see the various ways in which his forces covered themselves in glory.

Archeth, as attached court observer for the action, had been only too viciously glad to bridge the gap, to bear accurate tidings home to her ailing Emperor, and recount them to him in careful, repeated detail, while he lay on his sickbed and muttered about necessity and would not meet her eyes.

After the succession, when the court murmurs against Jhiral started, she surprised herself with the withering tide of contempt she felt for those who murmured and the selective memories of the father they apparently retained.

And she was almost glad when Jhiral's reprisals began.

Almost.

"You came to the capital while you were young?" she asked Galat, for want of something to chase out the memories.

"Before the uprising, yes." Maybe he'd seen the shadow pass across her face. He cleared his throat. "I was selected for the Mastery at nine. It was a great honor for my family."

"I suppose so."

"Yes. *Service to one's fellow man may take many forms, but those who serve the Revelation are privileged beyond measure.*"

Archeth deadpanned it. "They certainly are."

"But for all that, I think my father would have liked, maybe even preferred me to hold a commission. We are traditionally a military family."

"Then your father must be delighted with the recent direction of the Mastery's teachings. *Every faithful adherent shall then consider himself a warrior for the cause of the righteous, bearing not only the word of the Revelation, but also its holy sword.*"

Hanesh Galat cleared his throat again. "There is actually some textual debate about the intrinsic meaning in that last image."

"Not according to Pashla Menkarak there isn't."

Another awkward pause, long enough this time that Archeth glanced around to see if Galat was still there. He looked sheepishly away.

"Arch-Invigilator Menkarak is, uhm, a very learned man. A fine scholar of the Revelation and an incisive interpreter of doctrine. A fine writer, one of the Mastery's finest. But as I am sure he would accept, his opinion is mortal and therefore potentially flawed."

"You've met him?"

"Uh, not personally, no."

"Didn't think so."

A silence opened up between them, and she thought maybe now he'd piss off. But no such luck. His hands mated and twisted on the rail, he shifted about as if tethered there. She could feel him marshaling the words in his throat, dismissing them, selecting again. In a better mood, she might have helped him out.

But she wasn't in a better mood.

"This, uhm, disenchantment with the Revelation's temporal representatives," he tried finally. "It's not unexpected for me."

"No?"

"No. I am quite aware that your recent interactions with the Citadel have not been, shall we say, amicable. I have been . . . made aware of that."

Archeth's last direct interaction with a representative of the Citadel had involved slitting his throat in broad daylight on a public thoroughfare. She kept her eyes on the passing riverbank and her tone even.

"You have a diplomatic way with words, Invigilator Galat."

"Yes, uhm, thank you." He would not look directly at her. But he seemed to seize some kind of courage as he blushed. "We are not all in accord with Arch-Invigilator Menkarak, my lady. We are not all filled with hate. You should perhaps keep that in mind."

And then, to her surprise, he actually did leave her to herself.

SHORTLY BEFORE NOON, THE *SWORD OF JUSTICE DIVINE* PLOWED INTO A mudbank not listed on the charts, and stuck fast.

There was no warning—just the sudden jolt and then a shuddering, groaning sound under the hull, like some monstrous donkey they'd just hit. The deck jumped violently, and tipped. Archeth staggered with the impact, would have gone over on her arse but for Senger Hald's steadying hand on her shoulder. A couple of the younger marines standing about nearby did go over, to jeers and general hilarity from their peers. Somewhere below, the boxed horses voiced protest. And on the galley deck, yells and groans from the rowers. They were seasoned rivermen, they knew what the noise meant.

The caller cut across it. "Back oars! *Back oars!* One! Two! Put some fucking muscle into it, you pussies!"

Archeth and Hald made their way across the tilted deck to the rail and peered over. Nothing to be seen in the muddy brown churn of the water, but it was clear that despite the exhortations of the caller, the oarsmen were shoveling in vain.

"Come *on*! My baby sister rows harder than you cunts! *Back oars*— like you fucking mean it! One! Two!"

The oars dug in. The water boiled. The caller's abuse intensified. It went on that way for a couple of minutes, then they heard Lal Nyanar in the captain's nest at the prow, bellowing for them to stop. A moment later he came up on deck, glowering.

"We're stuck," he reported superfluously. "Going to have to put teams ashore and drag us off with ropes. The only good news is, we're not far down from our landing point. This is a meander—you've got decent beaching shingle right across from us on the other bank."

Hald shrugged. "Then I guess we do it from here."

He and Nyanar divided up the men, leaving the bulk with the ship to help on the ropes. The remaining detachment lowered three landing boats, got equipment and Hald's and Archeth's horses aboard through the hull hatch, and then rowed across to the beaching point. There were a couple of tense moments as a giant desert croc hit water farther upstream and came nosing log-like and curious across the wake of the boats. Senger Hald detailed men with cranked and loaded arbalests at the stern of each boat, set others to calm the horses, and then quietly doubled the cadence of the rowers. At first the croc seemed undecided whether to follow them in to shore or not, but finally it showed them a yellow-black armor-plated tail and rippled off downstream, seeking easier prey.

You could hear the tautly held breath let go from throats in each boat as the creature swam away.

"Fucking things," muttered one of the younger marines.

His companion on the opposite oar was older, temples and stubble showing gray. He grunted and showed his teeth on the stroke.

"Think yourself lucky, son. That's a *dumb* lizard you're looking at. Some of us were around when the smart ones came calling."

And he met Archeth's eyes as he leaned into the next pull.

She could not recall his face from the war. Maybe she'd stood near him in the battle lines, maybe not. There'd been thousands of faces, most of them gone now. More likely, she was simply emblematic—the jet Kiriath features, the stature, the eyes; mementos for a time now gone, when, at the hour of humanity's greatest need, men and women like her had stood at the head of every army Yhelteth put into the field.

"Ganch," someone said, farther back in the boat, "why don't you give it a fucking rest with the war stories, huh?"

General laughter. Ganch himself joined in with it.

They beached without further incident, the men still giving one another queasy grins as they splashed overboard into knee-depth water, to drag the boats ashore. There was some overloud hilarity, some horseplay, evaporating as Senger Hald called muster and pulled out the men selected for the reconnaissance party, twenty in all. He gave them a brief sketch of intentions, ordered the remaining men to set up camp by the boats, then mounted up alongside Archeth and shot her a dubious glance.

"Well then, my lady—let's get this done."

They rode up through the silent desert air, tracking the smoke. Ancient, broken lava flows in a desolate, tilting landscape around them, no respite from the sun as far as the eye could see. There was some low-growing scrub initially, but as they left the river behind and climbed An-Monal's skirts even that started to thin out. The volcano loomed in the sky at their backs like a living, watching presence. No more conversation out of Hald, in fact no sound at all but the horses' hooves, the clink of harness iron, and the crunching tramp of the men's feet behind them.

They found the tree about an hour in. It was a caldera oak, native to the flanks of An-Monal, and usually a majestic, welcoming sight in territory as arid and unshaded as this.

Something had burned this one to a crisp.

Senger Hald reined in and raised his hand. The sound of marching feet died off. They came to a halt beside the blackened skeleton of the oak. There wasn't much to see—the tree's foliage was gone completely, but the charred branches were still smoldering into the blue crystal air. Archeth prodded and wheeled her horse about, leaned out and wiped one hand across the charred trunk of the tree. Her fingers came back greasy and thickly smeared with ash.

Muttering from the men ranked behind her. She studied the ash on her fingers, listening without appearing to.

"Those trees don't fucking burn, man."

"Yeah, what do you know? Wood burns. Any wood, sooner or later."

"No, he's right, Trath. My old man grew up on the lava fields north of Oronak. He always said you could pour two gallons of lamp oil all over one of those trees and you'd not do more than scorch the twigs."

"Yeah? So how did this happen? I mean, you got eyes to see it, don't you?"

"I see it, yeah. I don't like it."

"Oh, and what did you expect? Got Monal glowering down on us from back there, got a burned-black for a guide. You think we—"

"Shut the fuck up, man! Sergeant's coming up, he's going to hear you."

She stopped listening, let the words slip away like leaves on the river's skin. But she knew they were looking at her—she felt the swift, stolen glances like pinpricks across her neck and shoulders. And though the sergeant did come up the line from the rear and bellow for quiet in the ranks, she knew that back at camp tonight the stories, the restless tales, would flicker back and forth in the firelight, myths about the Volcano and the Volcano Folk, and an uncle they had who'd once, no, just listen to this, back when he was a young man and the Kiriath used to . . .

So forth.

"Were you expecting this?" Hald asked her quietly.

She shook her head. "Nothing like this, no."

The unspoken word hung in the air between them.

Dragon.

IT WAS NOT A DRAGON.

It was not, in fact, very much of anything at all.

Beyond the first tree were others, similarly cremated, leading on toward the central column of smoke and then, abruptly, a broad, shallow bowl scooped in the canted ground of An-Monal's colossal flank. Here, the only remaining trees were charred down to tall, jagged stumps, reminiscent of stakes and leaning at odd angles. Along the upper edges of the bowl, the reddish desert itself had blackened from the heat, and farther down toward the center the blackening gave way to a glassy pale substance that shone rainbow-iridescent in the sun.

The smoke column rose serenely from a crumpled pile of something at the bottom of the bowl. It was the finishing touch that made the place look eerily like a small copy of a volcanic crater.

Archeth dismounted and stood staring down.

We came all this way for . . . that?

Heat shimmer rendered the central object's shape trembling and indistinct at this distance, but she thought it resembled nothing so much as the slag excrescences sometimes generated by the black iron machinery of the Kiriath brewing stacks south of Monal.

Manathan, if this is meant to be some kind of Helmsman joke, I'm going to take an engineer's hammer to your fucking innards.

If I can find them.

"Leave your horse," she said tiredly. "She won't be able to walk on that stuff anyway. And tell the men they'll need to be careful—it's going to be slick as a waterfall rock face down there."

Senger Hald swung off his mount and joined her. He shaded his eyes, peered down into the crater space. "The same as the Kiriath ramparts at Khangset and Hanliahg, is it not?"

"At a guess, yeah. Kiriath moldings are formed using a lot of heat, and I'd say there was a lot of heat here last night, too."

She waited while Hald gave orders to the sergeant, squinting into the heat haze and the rainbow glare from the glass. At Khangset, she'd seen the reptile peons try to climb the defenses her father's engineers had put in place; she'd watched them make two or three yards at most before they lost any kind of grip and went lashing and snarling back down into the sea below, claws raking impotently on the glassy slope.

She wondered, staring down into the bowl, if this, too, was a kind of defense.

"Do you intend to spend the whole day up there spectating, daughter of Flaradnam?"

For one stretched moment of shock, she thought the voice spoke solely to her. It had the same intimate word-in-your-ear feel as Manathan when he addressed her around the keep at An-Monal. But then she saw the way Senger Hald had stiffened, the way the marines stared about them with hands on sword hilts, and she understood that the air around her was filled with the rich, ironic, and slightly off-kilter tones.

"Yes—you I'm talking to." Its tone was higher pitched than Manathan's, almost feminine, and the jagged edge-of-unreason element was jumpier, more in evidence. "You and that gaggle of natives you've brought along. Could you perhaps cultivate a modest sense of urgency? Manathan insisted you were good in a crisis, but I'd have to say he appears to have overstated his case."

Hald was at her side, bearded features taut and watchful. "My lady?"

"It's all right." Archeth raised a hand to indicate the calm she didn't feel.

"It knows your name, my lady."

"Oh, indeed," said the voice acidly. "It also knows *your* name, Senger Hald. And the names of all your men, except for the tall one with the dueling scars who, for some reason, is using an alias and cannot actually remember what he was once called. I'd look into that if I were you—it seems inappropriate for a crack imperial unit."

Archeth looked back at the men. They were all clutching at charms or making signs. A number of them wore dueling scars, it was impossible to be sure which man the voice had singled out, but mistrustful glances went back and forth. Someone needed to lock this down, fast. She cleared her throat, lifted her chin a little for want of a more specific direction to address herself in.

"You are the messenger Manathan promised?"

"No, I'm a random demonic voice in the wilderness." From down in the crater, there was a loud *crack*. "Of *course* I'm the messenger, daughter of Flaradnam. Don't you see the smoke? Now would you be kind enough to get down here and arrange some transport back to Yhelteth for me? It really is a matter of some urgency."

And, in the heat haze at the center of the crater, sudden movement.

CHAPTER 9

They were still raping Poppy Snarl when the red edge of the sun cleared the scrubland horizon to the east.

Ringil sat on a rise near the overseers' tents and listened, staring into the early sunlight as if it were the wind. He was out of meaningful distractions; he'd cleaned the Ravensfriend with lengthy care, put it to rest in the scabbard on his back; he'd watched Eril's ragtag mercenary crew check on the bodies of the march-masters and the imperials, slitting the odd throat where necessary but mostly just looting pockets; he'd searched Snarl's tents for anything remotely useful, upending boxes and ripping the seals off parchment rolls, perusing ornately written documents that were either numbingly banal or in impenetrable cipher.

Pointless, all of it—the sounds of the rape stalked him whatever he did, Snarl's screams winding down to sobbing and finally a low, infrequent moaning; the men's grunting hilarity chasing an oddly similar decline, as if the less resistance there was, the less they were comfortable with what they were doing.

It was the sound of the war, all over again.

Eril came and joined him, squatted at his side. Ringil nodded his acknowledgment, didn't really look at him.

"How'd we do?"

"Pretty good all around. We lost seven men in the fight here, plus another four still unaccounted for, might have gotten lost in the forest. Couple of wounded. Pargil, the big fat guy? He got his arm hacked up pretty bad, probably going to lose it when we get him to a surgeon. But he can walk for now. The other's gutted, we'll have to carry him. No one else got worse than gashes."

Ringil ran the count in his head.

"That leaves eighteen."

"Nineteen. There's that old guy we took on at Hreshim's Landing last week."

"Right. Forgot all about him."

Quiet—and seeping into it the small, muffled noises that Poppy Snarl still made. The grunting of the men. Eril seemed to read something in Ringil's face as they listened. He cleared his throat.

"You want me to stop that?"

Ringil switched a glance at him, saw how the Marsh Brotherhood man flinched from it. He looked away again, into the sun.

"I mean." Eril hesitated. "You said, you didn't want her to . . ."

"Die?" The word ghosted out of him. He made an effort, pulled himself back in from the gray margins of his own thoughts. "Poppy Snarl came up in harbor end. She was running with the Brides of Silt before she was ten years old. Bossing them by the time she hit fifteen. It takes more than a gang rape to kill someone like that."

Eril thought he heard a reluctant admiration behind the words. He shifted on his haunches, cleared his throat again.

"Okay, but . . . these men, you know, they're not exactly . . . well, with the purse we had, how fast we had to do the hiring, they're not going to be the most—"

"Soldiers rape," Ringil said harshly. "Regardless of what they're paid. It's what they do. You think this is the first time I've had to listen to . . ."

His jaw tightened. He came to his feet abruptly, as if levered there by some mechanism Eril couldn't see.

"Fuck this shit," he whispered.

He stalked down the rise to where the latest in a short, scruffy queue of men was heaving himself up and down on Snarl's spread-eagled naked form. The man had his breeches down to his boots, his unbuckled sword belt, sword, and sheath cast aside in a hasty tangle. He made a throaty gasping sound each time he thrust into the woman under him.

Ringil grabbed him by the unkempt hair and pulled him off. Got a strangled yelp from the man, dumped him sideways across his discarded belt and sword.

"That's enough."

The interrupted man scrabbled halfway to his feet, one hand cupping down to cover his still-erect and throbbing prick, the other fumbling for the hilt of his sword. His face was a mask of slit-eyed fury. His voice came out choking.

"You. Fucking . . . "

Fingers found and fastened on the sword hilt.

"Do it," Ringil told him. "Give me a reason."

He held the stare. Hoped for the two heartbeats it took that the man wouldn't back down. Because this one—he could feel it trembling through him now—this one, he'd do with his bare hands.

The man's prick shrank and shriveled, hung like the neck on a plucked and slaughtered hen. His fingers slipped free of the sword hilt. He looked away, dribbled out a feeble, halfway laugh.

"Yeah, all right. Whatever." He got awkwardly to his feet, tugged his breeches up his legs as he rose. "No fucking loss anyway. Had better up against a wharf post in Baldaran."

Ringil thinned his lips, found the serrated edges of his front teeth with the tip of his tongue. He still wanted to kill this man.

"Get your gear back on," he said tightly. He jerked a thumb over his shoulder, brushing the hilt of the Ravensfriend with his loosely curled knuckles. "Go do what you've been paid for. Get down there and start cutting the shackles off these people."

The man hesitated, licked his lips. Something cheering seemed to occur to him, and the frown cleared off his face. He buckled his breeches closed, bent, and picked up his sword. As he straightened up, Ringil stepped in close and grabbed him by the shoulder. Got in his face and nailed him with another stare.

"And you leave the women alone. You've had all the fun you're going to today. I catch you trying this with anybody else, I'll hamstring you and leave you out here for the hyenas. Got that?"

Stiff silence, and the death-house reek of the man's breath in his face. Ringil's free hand curled into a fist at his side.

"I *said:* Have you got that?"

The man swallowed, then dropped his gaze. He tugged sullenly free of Ringil's grasp, stepped back.

"Yeah, man, I got it, I fucking got it—all right? Just leave me the fuck alone. What did I do, huh? What did I fucking do?"

He slouched away down the slope, jerking angrily at his sword belt where it had settled too high on his waist. Ringil turned to watch, and his gaze swept across the line of men still waiting there.

"You too. Fun's over. We set these people free, we see that they're fed. Jengthir, you make sure that's what happens."

The men looked at one another doubtfully. Jengthir cleared his throat.

"My lord, it's uh . . . that's going to take a long time. We're not—"

"*Do I look like I want your fucking advice?*"

Jengthir flinched. He turned and muttered something to the men, gestured down the slope. They went, but not particularly fast, and with resentful glances cast back across their shoulders every second step. Ringil caught each glance and stared it back down. He could feel the command begin to unravel around him. Could not make himself much care.

At his feet, weak, coughing laughter.

He looked down. Poppy Snarl had propped herself up on one shaky elbow, was working to fold her legs back under her. Her mouth was broken and bruising fast across one corner; blood had run and crusted there. One eye was swollen almost closed, and there were bites everywhere on her exposed flesh.

"Lost the taste for your vengeance, have you, Eskiath?" She folded her arms across herself. She was starting to tremble, but still she stared up at him defiantly. "Fucking rich kids, you're all the same. No guts when it comes to the crunch. Spoiled stupid little Glades-blood queer. Findrich and the rest are so fucking wrong about you. You're soft as pox pus."

"It isn't my vengeance," he told her distantly.

"Oh, yes." She bared her teeth, spat at his feet. "Poor little Sherin. Is this what she wanted done, then?"

"No. She just asked me to kill you." Ringil took the dragon-tooth blade from his sleeve. He crouched to Snarl's height. "She didn't say anything about protecting your honor until I did it, though."

"Honor." An awful bubbling laugh came up out of Poppy Snarl's throat. "Oh, but how the other half live. *Honor?* You think, you *really think* this is the first time I've been raped? You think it's the *tenth* time, maybe? The twentieth?"

"I don't care, Poppy."

"Fuck you, Eskiath. You think I would have lived past *fourteen fucking years old* in harbor end if I'd broken as easily as your little bitch cousin? You tell them back at House Eskiath I was a dozen times the woman Sherin ever was, and before I was half her fucking age. You tell them I said that."

"No, I won't," Ringil said quietly. "I'll tell them you died screaming and begging for mercy."

"Well, you always were a fucking liar." She jerked her chin up at him, bared her throat, and sneered. "So what are you waiting for, you mincing aristo cunt? Get it done, why don't you."

AFTERWARD, HE LEFT HER BODY WHERE IT LAY AND WENT DOWN TO stand among the coffles she had owned. Around him, the mercenaries went about with manacle cutters and much bad grace, setting free the slaves and throwing stale bread at their feet. None who passed him would meet his eye.

The men under your command may well hate you, he'd once written, in a treatise on modern warfare that never saw publication. *And who can blame them? They see you dine on fine wine and meat while they subsist on gruel. They sleep under canvas and you under silk. They make do with rusting hand-me-down mail while you gleam in personally tailored plate.*

*And where battle is joined against known and human foes, they know that
if captured, you will likely as not be feted by noble commanders on the
opposing side and ransomed safely home, while they will likely be tortured,
mutilated, or killed.*

*Who, without the careful massaging of illusory tribal pride or the
promise of rape and pillage, would* not *hate their commander under such
circumstances?*

Of course, the Scaled Folk had come along and changed a lot of that.
They didn't differentiate—grunt-level soldiery or noble flesh, apparently it all tasted pretty much the same to them. Stumbling on the bar-
becue pits and cracked and blackened human bones the lizards habitually
left behind at their camps, the League's soldiers acquired a sudden, icy
understanding of their common humanity and what it stood against.
They were no longer fighting to plant a flag somewhere pointless, to
avenge this or that slight to honor in the endless squabbling negotia-
tions of the various noble families and city fathers who owned every
fucking thing the eye could see.

They were fighting not to be eaten.

The clean, cold clarity of it washed over the young Ringil Eskiath—at
the time a sinecure-posted junior liaison officer with Trelayne's Majak
mercenary units—like bathing at the Falls of Treligal. Where other men,
other commanders from the noble families of the League, recoiled in
horror before the change, Ringil embraced it like the tight-muscled
torso of an unexpected back-alley lover.

It carried him through the war. It sent him up against the lizards at
Gallows Gap fully expecting to die, and it made a hero of him instead.

And then, in the sick-to-the-stomach, hungover morning light of
their victory over the Scaled Folk, like so many of those tight muscled
back-alley lovers over the years, the promise of change melted from his
side, and was gone.

At the time, it took him a while to understand what had happened.
He was still young back then; he really had believed in the change. But as
the norms shifted again, back to what had been before or near as fuck,
his enduring belief started to get in the way. Later, it came close to killing
him. Came closer in fact than the Scaled Folk had ever managed—toward
the end, it had taken Archeth's intervention to save him, to wake him to

the fact that they'd saved humanity from the lizards so that said humanity could go right back to wallowing in the same pit of ignorance and
oppression it had seemed so comfortable with before.

He walked away.

Away from the honors and the offers, away from the collapsing unity
between League and Empire, away from the thousand petty squabbles
and land grabs the war had degenerated into. He spat out what he could
of the taste the war had left in his throat, and among many other pointless exercises sat down to write his treatise.

Hate, then. Since it's so fucking popular again.

But hate, he reminded his putative audience of young, up-and-coming
noble commanders, *is a curious emotion, often akin to love, in fact resembling love much as your image in the distorting mirror of a penny shriek-
house resembles you. And even more curious—in the white heat of combat,
the shriek-house of men killing and dying for causes undefined, passage
across that mirror surface is sometimes possible. Make that transition, step
through somehow, and their hate for you may transform, as well, into a
pure, consuming love for which they may well follow you and give their
lives.*

It was, he'd readily admit, weird beyond belief, but he'd seen it happen that way, more than once, in the raging chaos of the war, like quick-
silver magic, like so much else that happened to him in those years.
Twisted, and wonderful, and strange.

But that was the war and that was then.

Here and now, on the scrub-plain borderlands outside Hinerion,
with a ragged band of the cheapest mercenary castoffs his depleted
purse could buy, there would be no transformations. There would be no
wonder.

He was trapped behind the mirror, and he knew it.

So he watched the freeing of the slaves, and tried not to feel, as his
men evidently already did, that it was all a colossal waste of time.

Tried not to feel at all.

The slaves themselves seemed for the most part to have reached a
similar state of numbness. Some few scrambled to their feet as soon as
the chains came off, grabbed the bread they were thrown, and hurried
away toward the fringes of the forest in ones and twos, glancing back

over their shoulders all the way; others, mostly the women, grabbed at the hands of their liberators and tried to kiss them or wept. And got startled curses and shruggings-off for their efforts. But these were the minority. Most just took the food and gnawed at it where they sat, staring into some hollow distance they'd excavated for themselves during their captivity. Perhaps they didn't believe what was happening; perhaps they thought it was a trick. Or perhaps they no longer cared one way or the other. Certainly, if they grasped the fact they were free, it didn't seem worth very much to them.

Ringil—who'd seen a lot of what freedom this world had to offer, and still somehow found himself standing here empty with a raped woman's blood on his hands—had to wonder how far wrong they actually were.

The sun climbed in the east, chased out the last of the night's cool. The events of the dawn seemed to recede with the change, as if the butchered corpses of Snarl and the legate and their men were detritus left by some battle in a ghost realm just parallel to the real world. Ringil shook off a shiver at the thought, at memories attached to it, and tried to soak up some of the new sun's warmth. There was a tiny personal drumming in his ears, more felt than heard, and his vision seemed abruptly darker. Another shiver. He wondered glumly if he might be coming down with a cold.

Swift running footfalls, crunching across the ground behind him.

He whipped about, one hand reaching up for the pommel of the Ravensfriend. Saw Eril sprinting down from the top of the rise to meet him, one hand flung out, chopping the air westward.

"Riders to the west!"

Jagged awareness, like waking in terror from a flandrijn pipe dream. The distant drumming fell out of his head and into the morning quiet, resolved into what it was: a sound he knew from half a hundred battlefields past—the tremor through the ground of an armored cavalry detachment at the gallop.

Eril was bellowing now.

" 'Ware riders!"

Around Ringil, the mercenaries heard, too, and took up the cry—

" 'Ware riders!"

"Riders!"

"Fucking heavy horse!"

Bawled warnings, chaining together like lightning before the storm, and then, suddenly, the random crisscross of sprinting men, leaping and kicking their way through the huddled slaves, heading for the tree line, for horses maybe, ultimately for anything the horizon might offer. Ringil tried to grab one of them as he pelted past, was spun around by the man's momentum and left grabbing after a fistful of empty air. The man ran on, still bawling.

Heavy horse!

Ringil had seen it put more seasoned men than these to flight. Armored cavalry—for anyone who'd ever had to face some, it held an ingrained terror worse than any sorcery. Back before the rise of the Yhelteth imperium and the foundation of the League to stand against it, heavy horse was the deciding factor time and again in the endless squabbling wars between the Naom city-states. It smashed through defensive formations; it shattered morale. Even the Majak had been known to break under armored cavalry assault. Expecting this bunch of castoffs to hold together, well . . . he gave it up as pointless, hurried up the slope to meet Eril instead. Turned about to stare westward as Eril pointed again.

"There. Left of the bluff, where the tree line breaks."

No detail yet, but Ringil saw the pale boiling of the dust cloud. No doubt about it.

"Hinerion," he said grimly. "Word got through, then."

"Yeah, looks that way." Eril eyed the dust, and the wooded terrain that separated them from where it was rising. "Heavy horse won't cut through those trees, they're too dense. They'll have to keep to the road."

Ringil nodded. "Gives us about time to saddle a horse."

"Already saddled. Up behind the tents. Come on, I've got the old man watching them."

They went up the slope at a run. Found the old man from Hreshim's Landing stood between the heads of two shaggy-maned mares, face tilted down under a grubby skirmish ranger's cap. He wasn't holding the reins, but he had one hand pressed lightly to the side of each animal's head and he was crooning to them, some garbled gibberish that put

Ringil's teeth on edge. He looked up as his commander approached, and the sunlight gleamed red off one eye.

"So it's not to be a stand, sire?"

"No it's not," Ringil told him shortly.

"A pity. An old man might imagine himself dying well, fighting at the right hand of the hero of Gallows Gap."

Ringil stopped, peered suspiciously into the old man's weather-tanned features. As far as he remembered, neither he nor Eril had mentioned his true identity to any of the mercenaries they'd recruited over the previous weeks. But the old man just looked innocently back at him, face devoid of apparent mockery or deceit.

Got no time for this shit, Gil.

"This isn't Gallows Gap, old man." Voice tight with memory. "And the war is over. We've done what we came here to do. We're leaving."

The old man's head lowered in deference. "Very good, my lord. And your mounts are ready for you, as you see. The best two I could secure."

Past the old man and the two animals, Ringil caught sight of something on the ground. He stepped sideways around the right-hand horse for a better look. Saw three tumbled corpses—by their mismatched weapons and ragged apparel, members of his own mercenary troop. The other horses had moved back against their tether lines to give the dead men as wide a berth as possible, and now they blew and whinnied and shifted nervously about, in marked contrast with the two the old man had selected. Ringil stared at the corpses, then at the old man's sword, still sheathed across his back in echo of the way Ringil wore the Ravensfriend. He frowned.

"And your own mount?" he asked.

The old man offered him a crooked grin. "Oh, I shall not require a horse to evade capture, my lord. I have other and better means."

"Yeah? Such as?"

—no fucking time for this, Gil—

But the old man only grinned again, and touched the brim of his skirmish ranger's cap in silence, as if that were answer enough. Ringil shrugged and took the reins of the horse on the left, ushered her about for space, and swung up into the saddle. He doubted the old man would easily evade capture, ranger training or no—not if Hinerion's border watch had been roused as it seemed. But he was in no mood to argue the point. He had his own escape to think about.

"Well, I'm obliged to you then." Ringil raised a hand to his brow in salute. "Good luck."

"And to you, my lord."

The old man put a sweeping bow behind his words, and once again Ringil could not be sure if he was being mocked or not. He looked across at Eril, now also in the saddle, but the Marsh Brotherhood man gave no sign he saw anything amiss. Ringil shook it off—whatever it was—and urged his horse forward.

"Look to your own safety, old man," he said gruffly. "While you still can."

He passed the corpses, glanced down at one of them and then wished he hadn't. He jerked his gaze back to the tree line, scanning for the broken pine tree and the hidden defile it marked out, the path that had brought them to the encampment from the river. It was a goatherd's track, not made for riding, but with a little care and good horsemanship they should pass.

Yeah, we'd better. Ringil's mouth twisted sourly. *Don't like the alternatives much.*

The distant drum of the approaching cavalry was distant no longer, and as he looked north to where the road emerged from the thinning woodland, Ringil thought he spotted the flash of desert sunlight on armor through the foliage. He kicked his horse into a canter.

The old man stood and watched them go. Smiling faintly.

Down on the flat ground, the slaves who had not run earlier were milling about in a listless simulacrum of the panic among those who had freed them. Ringil and Eril cantered through the mess, heading for the marker pine. Mostly, those on the ground got out of their way, but one young mercenary—Ringil recognized him from the queue for Snarl—stood his ground, brandishing a battle-ax without much sense that he really knew how to use it. There was a cheap helm askew on his head, and his face was white with fear. He stepped in, yelling.

"Don't you fucking leave us, you fatherless piece of—"

Ringil nudged his horse left, booted the mercenary full in the chest as he passed him, and rode on.

At the tree line, Eril reined about and stared back. He shook his head.

"Armored cavalry's going to make mincemeat out of those guys."

"Yeah, well they've been paid," Ringil growled, and ducked his head as his horse picked up the start of the path.

But as the trees closed around them, he thought back to the corpses around the old man, and he shivered. One of the mercenaries had fallen faceup, neck lolling to the side, throat tugged stickily open on the long, neat slash that had bled him out. No different from a hundred other sneak killings Ringil had seen over the years. But the man's eyes were frozen wide open in the grime of his face, and his expression . . .

In over a decade of soldiering, Ringil had never seen horror so clearly printed onto a set of human features.

A low-hanging tree bough brushed his shoulder. Sunlight speared between the branches, dappled the ground. Somewhere in the quiet of the forest, a bird called to its mate.

Ringil shivered again.

Shook it off. Sneezed.

Coming down with something. Definitely.

CHAPTER 10

One of the Nine Eternal Gifts from the Kiriath to the Khimran dynasty, the Black Folk Span did exactly what its name implied—it bridged Yhelteth estuary with a leaping arrogance of architecture that dropped Egar's jaw like a gangplank the first time he saw it. Gleaming black iron, hung up in the air from shore to shore like some dark lord's rainbow, like a bow chopped out of pure night and then planed and polished and bent to purpose by forces beyond dreaming. Glassy cables, each as thick around as an archer's arm, fell from the structure in twinned rows a thousand strong, flashing translucent in the sun, holding aloft a carriageway broad enough for two dozen armored men to ride abreast and not jostle one another.

In time, he got used to it, the way he did to the Kiriath themselves. All part of life in the big city. But the Span went on casting its shadow over him in a more practical sense for quite a while after. The carriageway it lifted across the water came ashore on the north side a full thirty feet overhead and didn't hit the ground proper for seven city blocks beyond. And down at the water's edge, in the shadow it cast, stood the Pony Stringer's Good Fortune, a raddled old tavern dedicated to the memory of some young horse trader from the city's earliest history who'd apparently been lucky enough to rescue some of his livestock from drowning on a beach at this very spot. Or something. Horse-related tales and legends were ten a penny in Yhelteth; after a time they all blurred into one another. Anyway, the so-named tavern was a known haunt of mercenaries and freelance street muscle from way back, and a clearinghouse for all manner of professional opportunity. Recruiting officers drank there regularly, ganglords and minor merchants dropped in from time to time to assess the available talent, and for a couple of coins hard-up men of violence seeking employment could always leave a name and current doss address behind the bar.

Much of his young mercenary life in Yhelteth, Egar had thought of the Pony Stringer's as more of a home away from home than any of the billets or lover's lodgings he'd happened to be crashing in between deployments. Even later, with rank and officer's lodgings to call his own, he'd habitually find his way down there to drink away the slack summer afternoons in the shade of the Span. Or he'd close out the place at dawn and stumble groggily outside between a brace of supporting barmaids, head tipped back to stare up and up and up at the soaring alien architecture, and often as not go teetering backward onto his arse with the dizzy, wine-soaked wonder the sight could still inspire.

And when he went home for real after the war, and a fellow Skaranak came riding through years later with news that, among other things, the old Pony Stringer's had burned to the ground, Egar surprised himself with the pang of nostalgia it pricked in his belly.

If he'd known the place was standing again, it would have been his first port of call. For far more reasons than simple information.

Come on, Dragonbane. The past is dead and cairned. Let's stick to the present, shall we.

The present turned out to be a basic but not unappealing two-story in stone and white stucco. Supporting beams for the upper story protruded an unfinished couple of feet out of each wall, and the woodwork hadn't yet taken much weather. Egar spotted a couple of beam ends still showing the red drip stain of a carpenters' guild stamp. On the dusty ground between the tavern and the water's edge, equally rough-sawn trestle tables stood about, and the place's new name was lettered across the shore-facing wall in cheap gilt characters a foot high. The rising sun glanced off the gilt and gave it an illusory early-morning shine.

And just as Darhan had promised, there was a small iron cage hung by a short length of chain from one of the beam ends at the tavern's corner. The severed head sat inside for all to see, mummified black and listing sadly to one side, like some overlarge turnip left way too long at the back of the larder. At some point, someone had sheared off the creature's lips to better reveal the fangs beneath, but even so it was a pretty pitiful sight. Egar felt a grimace take his face as he stared up at the trophy.

"That's a Scaled Folk," a small voice at his side said solemnly.

He glanced down and saw a boy of about five with a grimy face and stuck-up, filthy hair. One chapped and reddened hand held a wet cloth streaked with soap curds. Egar nodded.

"It certainly is."

"It's dead now, though."

"Yeah, looks that way. Did you kill it, then?"

The boy looked at him as if he were mad. "I'm seven."

"Right. Stupid question." Egar stifled a yawn and looked around. "Is your father about?"

Flicker of confusion across the young face. "My father's dead. Laid to rest with honors, his sins cleansed."

It was recitation—learned cant. The boy must have thought he was asking if his father was *abroad*, condemned to wander the Earth in spirit for want of a properly officiated burial.

Abroad, about—his Tethanne had never been great in the finer points.

"Ah. With honors, eh? He was a soldier, then?"

The confusion smoothed out, gave way to a waxing pride that had clearly been taught as carefully as the clerical cant. "My father died fighting dragons in the war. He died defending the Emperor and his people."

"That's good. Something to be proud of, then. So look, who around here is—"

"Gadral? *Gadral?*" It wasn't quite a full bellow, but the boy jumped as if the head in the cage had suddenly opened its eyes at him. "If you're out there jawing with your little cunt mates again, I'm going to give you such a fucking hi—"

The voice dried up as its owner loomed in the doorway and saw Egar standing there. The man narrowed his eyes against the early-morning sun.

"Help you, pal?" It wasn't a helpful tone.

Egar let the moment stretch, took the time it gave him to read the other man. Big by Yhelteth standards, a heavy, once-muscular frame now beginning to blur at the edges with age and easier living. Sun-darkened face seamed and pouched, but still some trace of military bearing, something a little deeper etched than levy standard. A butcher's chopper held casually in one meaty, blood-sprinkled hand.

Egar nodded at the clumsy blade. "Making soup?"

Brief clash of gazes while the other man took the trouble to read him, too. The chopper lowered, hung slack at arm's length.

"Yeah. Week's End stew. You want some?"

"I'll start with a beer. Work up to it."

"Sure." The other man nodded him inside. As Egar stepped past and found a stool at the bar, he heard the publican cursing the boy out again. But he thought there was a little less heat in it this time, and the man came inside pretty quick.

"Your boy?" Egar asked, as his pint was drawn.

"Is he, fuck. My boy died under arms at Shenshenath, when the lizards came. That's just my whore's son. Came with the territory, y'know. Someone's got to feed the little shit."

"Right."

The other man set the filled pint glass down on the bar between them. "Stew is going to take a while. I got bread and oil, you want it while you wait."

"Sounds good."

The publican disappeared behind a grubby curtain hung across the kitchen entrance, leaving Egar to his pint. Low voices, clatter of plates, and then the dull, repeated thud of the chopper into a wooden board. The Dragonbane sat in the stale, beer-scented gloom and the dusty, filtering light from shutters still not opened. He sipped his beer. It wasn't bad.

Presently, a tall, haggard-looking woman came out carrying a platter with his bread and oil. She stopped in her tracks when she saw Egar but then gathered herself quickly enough and set the food down on the bar. She charged him one elemental for the platter and the beer, looked relieved when he paid up without a fuss, and then went outside. Egar heard her murmuring to the boy.

When she came back in, he said, breezily: "Guess you don't see that many like me in here?"

"What?" Voice faint.

"Steppe dwellers. Don't get a lot of them? I was wondering because—"

"Not so early," she said and fled back into the kitchen.

Egar raised his eyebrows and went back to his pint. More lowered voices in the kitchen. The chopper chunked once, definitively, into wood. The publican came out through the curtain, glowering.

"What's your fucking problem, then? I said she was *my* whore, I didn't say she was up for grabs."

Egar set his drink aside with care, and looked at the man.

"Just making conversation," he said softly. "Where I'm from, reasonable men can talk to a woman without it meaning anything. You seemed like a reasonable man when I came in, but maybe I was wrong about that."

The publican hesitated. Sunlight filtered into the low-beamed space and the quiet. Somewhere, a beer tap dripped into its tray. The moment stretched.

Went away.

"Yeah, all right then." An ungracious shrug. "Let it go. Got a brother served up at the Dhashara pass, he always did say you lot let your women run riot. Mouthing off like they were men, riding horses, carrying weapons, shit like that."

"Been known to happen," Egar agreed.

"Yeah, well, that shit won't wash down here. This is Yhelteth, this is the Empire. We're civilized. Women know their place. And truth is, I'm about fucking sick of the trouble we get from your kind coming in here." Grudging, bitten off. "No offense."

"Oh—none taken. What kind of trouble would that be, then?"

"Only a big fucking fight a couple of weeks back. They put out two windows, and one of my serving girls lost a finger. Had to call the City Guard. Like I said, I'm sick of it. You going to live in a civilized city, you've got to act civilized, too. You know?"

Egar pulled a face. Brawling at the Pony Stringer's Good Fortune hadn't ever been out of fashion as far as he could recall.

In fact, some of his best brawls . . .

"What was this fight about, then?"

"Fuck would I know?" The publican swabbed irritably at his bar with a fetid-looking cloth. "Some tribal shit? Not like I *speak* northern, is it? All I know is, one minute everybody's drinking and yelling back and forth like normal, next thing it's fists and blades. Half of them in Citadel threads, too—I mean, that's just . . . "

He gestured helplessly, a man losing his grip on the changing world.

"Citadel rig, huh?" Egar, voice elaborately casual, sipping his beer. "That's unusual."

"Yeah, tell me about it. When I was a kid, they wouldn't have let an outlander set foot inside a temple, let alone fucking pay them wages to do it."

True enough. It was a time Egar caught the tail end of, arriving in Yhelteth a decade and a half ago. A time when a lot of taverns were still calling themselves the Majak's Head, still sporting iron cages very like the one outside this place to prove the point. He remembered burning one to the ground in the Spice Quarter one riotous summer night. A mixed-bag company of other steppe nomads, out staggering drunk on furlough. Summer heat, booze-tightened tempers, just waiting for the right tinder. Some heavyset Ishlinak, ax in hand, bawling that that was his fucking *uncle* up there in the cage, rot-eyed and blackened . . .

They burst in, boots and brutal-indignant rage. Broke faces and furniture, tore women's clothing, grabbed torches from brackets on the wall. Roaring encouragement to one another. Whirl and toss—up behind the bar, in amongst the crowded tables. The straw across the floor went up, flames thigh-high in seconds.

And then it was all discordant screams and chaos, and a stampede for the doors.

He remembered making it outside, standing there grinning into the blaze as it built. Remembered the fire leaping out of windows, chewing at the low eaves. The head in its cage, flame-wrapped and roasting until the bracket charred too much to take the weight and the cage tumbled to the street, still on fire. The roof timbers took—cheap wood, poorly seasoned—burned rapidly through, and crashed in with a roar. The watching Majak roared with it.

Whirling, red-orange sparks on a cinnamon wind.

Akal the Great, always shrewd in his lawmaking, brought in an ordinance the following year. War against the League had brought the Majak south in their mercenary thousands—you could no longer afford to offend them. The tavern names changed.

No one recalled what happened to the various heads. Most, in truth, had probably never belonged to genuine Majak in the first place.

" . . . and he should fucking know better. That's all I'm saying."

Egar blinked back to the present. Scent of stale beer and the sifting, low-angle sunlight. He'd evidently missed a chunk of the publican's rant.

"Yeah?"

"Yeah. Look, don't get me wrong. I got nothing against you people, right. Really. And I still serve Harath in here just the same as anyone else, same as I always did before. I just think you got to know who you are, is all. Can't make a decision like that just because you're cunt-struck. He really wants to convert, hey, fine with me. Revelation says it's for all men to make that choice—even outlanders. But you can't turn around later and say you want out just cuz your little whore fucks off and dumps you. That's apostasy, it's serious shit up at the temples. He can't blame the ones who still carry steel for the Citadel when they give him the cold shoulder."

"So." Egar made a quick estimate on the shape of what he'd missed. "You're saying this Harath started the fight?"

"I'm saying he was here, is all. And I've seen the way he gets when the others are around. Starts yelling about the old gods, how the Citadel is full of shit. You can't expect to talk like that and not get a kicking."

"True enough." Egar turned his tankard back and forth a little on the bar, frowning. "You know where he flops these days?"

It got him a funny look. "Yeah, and what's it to you?"

Shrug it off. "Sounds like this guy I'm looking for, is all. Mother's cousin's son, it's the same name. Bit of a fuckup by all accounts, but I'm supposed to check on him. No big deal. Family. You know how it is."

"Tell me about it."

"Does he still come in here? Since the fight, I mean."

The publican glowered into the middle distance for a moment or two. Maybe he was remembering the broken fixtures.

"Try up on the An-Monal road, other side of the Span," he said. "Someplace above a pawnshop, I heard."

CHAPTER 11

They reached the river without event, followed the sounds it made and the flash glimpses through sun-metaled foliage that the path afforded them. They tracked along the eastern bank for a while until finally, a hundred yards downstream from the last set of rapids and craggy falls, the trail broke cover and went to the water's edge. It was the same fording point they'd used coming in, and they already knew the water never went worse than waist-deep. Still, Ringil dismounted there into the long grass and stood for a while, watching. He wanted, he told himself, to check the far bank for any sign of an ambush before they crossed.

Getting a bit jumpy in our advancing years, aren't we, Gil? What's the matter, you planning to die old and in bed all of a sudden?

Not planning to die at all just yet.

It was a beautiful day, drowsy with heat and insect hum. Late-morning sunlight lay on the water in splashes too bright to look at directly. Ringil shaded his face and screwed up his eyes, peered across to the trees on the other side. It was about thirty yards, an easy crossing for the horses, no swimming required.

If there was anyone in the trees, they were keeping very still.

There's no one in the fucking trees, Gil, and you know it. This is local militia and the border patrol we're dealing with here, not a skirmish ranger advance party. They're all back at Snarl's encampment, butchering your men and probably the slaves as well for good measure. Just face it—you got away from this one without a scratch.

Nonetheless, he took the reins and led his horse into the water on foot, moving slowly, ready to scoot back and use its bulk for cover if the far bank suddenly sprouted militiamen with crossbows. He tested each boot-hold on the river bottom, and he never took his eyes from the greenery.

Behind him, Eril dismounted and followed suit.

They crossed without a word, wading through the soft swirl of water at their waists and a curious sun-touched silence that seemed to exist separated from the muted roar of the rapids upstream. A pair of birds bickered brightly and chased each other in dipping flight a scant couple of feet above the surface of the river. Pine needles and bright yellow specks of forest detritus slid by on the flow. It was—

The corpse was on him before he knew it. Bumping at his side in the water, carried on the current. One trailing arm wrapped around his hip like the final effort of an exhausted swimmer.

"Fuck!"

The curse jolted loose, as if punched out of him. Nerves still raw from the morning's slaughter, cranked newly taut again from watching the bank ahead; he flinched like some upriver maiden touching her first erect cock. Floundered back, hands up and warding, almost off his feet with the shock.

Just about had the presence of mind to let go the reins and not drown his fucking horse.

Hoiran's sake, Gil. Get a grip.

He found his footing, reached back to the horse, and clucked at it. The dead man caught at his waist, seemed inclined to cling there. A little embarrassed at being so girlish, Ringil cleared his throat and looked the body over. He saw drenched clothing bubbled full of air at the back, facedown under a floating mop of lank, dark hair. Crossbow fletches standing stiffly clear of the water where the quarrel protruded from the man's back.

Some dark and weary war-stained impulse made him reach down and touch the corpse at the shoulder. He rolled the man in the water, pulled the clinging arm gently loose, and turned the body faceup. It told him nothing. Nondescript Naom face, about forty, worn with hard-scrabble living, and a couple of small scars that didn't look like the result of combat. The sharp end of the quarrel jutted a handbreadth out from the chest. The floating hand that had until a moment ago been wrapped around Ringil's waist was blunt-fingered and scarred from a lifetime of labor, but it had raw manacle sores around the wrist, leached pale and whitish pink by the water.

The corpse opened dead black eyes and stared up at him.

"Better run," it hissed.

This time the shock held him rigid, came shuddering in along his veins like icy water and put cold clamps at his temples. His grip on the corpse clenched as if to drown it, he heard his throat make a locked-up sound.

A hand fell on his shoulder.

"You all right, mate?"

Eril's voice, concerned. He'd led his horse up level with Ringil's, was peering at his companion curiously. Ringil blinked back at him, and something shifted in the sun-bladed air. He stared down at the heavy, black-barked tree branch in the water and the death grip he had it in. The crooked twist and reach of one arm off the main body, the way it tried to roll in the swirl of the river's flow.

It was just a chunk of tree.

"Must have washed down from near the bluffs," Eril said. "Seen a lot of fallen trunks choked up in rapids and falls back there. Something that size, the whole tree's probably gone in, got jammed, and now it's rotting off a piece at a time."

Ringil cleared his throat. "Yeah."

He let go of the branch and stepped back to let the current take it. Watched it drift downstream to the next bend in the river, the lifted arm still wagging slightly from the motion, as if waving good-bye.

He watched it out of sight. Cleared his throat again.

"There's nothing in those trees," he said brusquely, and led his horse forward again, wading hard for the bank.

"YOU RECKON WE CAN RISK THE CARAVAN ROAD?"

This high up, they could see it from where they sat—a thin, pale line snaking through the wooded uplands east of Hinerion, lost repeatedly to forest and valley shadow on its way north. Ringil narrowed his eyes against the sun, as if at that distance he'd somehow be able to pick out the glint of plate armor and lance-points on the carriageway. He shook his head.

"By now they've got the City Guard out in force. Checkpoints strung every five miles or less, looking slant at anybody with a sword and no good reason for travel. I don't want to have to fight my way through that."

Eril nodded glumly. For him, it was the road home. "But south is going to be the same, right?"

"South is going to be worse. When the Yhelteth authorities hear what happened to their legate, we'll be lucky if this doesn't turn into a full-scale diplomatic incident. The border patrol are probably down there right now trying to look like a crowd—just in case the garrison commander at Tlanmar loses his temper and decides it's time for a punitive frontier raid or six." Ringil pressed thumb and forefinger to his eyes, which had started to ache in their sockets. Sank his chin on his hugged-up knees and sighed. "Truth is, it's a fucking mess. And we're stuck right in the middle of it."

"Right." Eril shrugged and shuddered like a dog shaking off water. Lay back on the flat, angled rock where they were seated. He was a phlegmatic man, not much given to worrying about things he couldn't change. He put his arms behind his head and looked up at the brilliant blue sky. Yawned and closed his eyes. "So I guess we wait it out."

Ringil shot him an envious look. Patience had never been one of his strong points—he'd learned some in the war, because it was either that or die in a hurry, but beyond that basic cornerstone of self-preservation the habit never really took, and age hadn't helped the way it was sup-

posed to. Thirty-one years old and he'd still walk into pretty much anything as long as he thought he could walk out again.

Sometimes when he wasn't even very sure of that much.

He stared down the pale granite slab to where their boots stood upright, knee flaps folded down inside out, drying in the sun. Socks draped
out to the same purpose. Under the soles of his naked feet, the rock
where he sat was warm to the touch and smooth. It was a soothing feeling, like the soft breeze out of the west that kept the full heat of the sun
at bay, and the knowledge that their vantage point was well chosen—
clear views back down the valley to the river they'd crossed and over
pine-covered slopes on all sides. You'd see trouble coming before it got
within a hard hour's upward slog of the top.

Their bellies were filled, black bread and cured meat from the sad-
dlebags, cool water from wineskin canteens refilled at the river.

There was birdsong among the trees, and the soft sounds of the
horses as they grazed in the clearing a little farther down.

A hawk, hanging motionless a hundred yards out in the crystal air.

Snarl was dead, as planned.

So what the fuck's eating you, Gil?

He looked again at Eril, felt the same stab of envy, and saw abruptly
what lay at its root. The Brotherhood occupied an odd niche in Trelayne,
trading on their much-vaunted historical lineage to avoid being classed
as the bunch of organized criminals they basically were. That meant
giving ground from time to time if some overly brutal piece of extortion
or murder upset the Chancellery and the Glades classes enough to stir
up a law enforcement response. As a Brotherhood soldier, Eril would be
well used to sitting out the heat from his work, out on the marsh with
trusted retainers or in some backwater harbor town down the coast
until his lodge master could smooth things over back in the city. Strictly
a matter of patience—in the end, you always went home.

All well and good, for those who have homes to go to.

Trelayne.

He glanced instinctively northward at the thought, though from
here it was probably more like northwest. Trel-a-lahayn, Blessed Refuge
on the Trell, fabled merchant metropolis, rising in walled and towered
splendor from the mists and mazed safety of the great river's estuary

marshes. Trelayne—League Queen of the northern city-states, and the closest thing to an imperial capital anybody outside Yhelteth could lay claim to. Trelayne, the unquestioned cultural and political heart of the civilized north.

Write it off, Gil. Let it go.

Gingren had disowned him in front of the Chancellery. *My son, war hero or not, has in his recent activities gone far beyond the pale. Debt-slavery is an established pillar of our society, without which the good economic function of the city cannot be guaranteed. It has been voted on and signed into law with all due solemnity, and it is not for any citizen, however privileged their position, to gainsay that decision. It is not for any man, Glades-born or not, to terrorize merchants in good standing in a legal trade.*

Break their legs, burn their homes down, murder their agents. Stuff like that.

I thus declare my son Ringil now and forever exile from the Glades House Eskiath, and proscribed outlaw within the territory of Trelayne.

They'd posted copies of the declaration alongside his wanted poster in market squares and at crossroads all about the city, the seal of clan Eskiath stamped into the parchment beside that of the Chancellery, assurance if any was needed that Gingren would not seek blood vengeance in private against the bounty hunter who managed to bring Ringil down. Though truth be told—even now, it brought a small, bleak smile to Ringil's lips—you'd be hard put to find a Trelayne bounty hunter who could read much more than the large lettered price at the top of the poster.

There'd been a sketched likeness to complement the written description, unflattering but to the point. Long black hair, worn pulled back; long white scar scrawled across otherwise finely drawn features. Mouth thinned, drawn down at the corners, and more lines in the face than Ringil liked to think he owned. The eyes were dead. *Known to carry Kiriath steel and a Majak dragon-tooth dagger.*

Knight graduate of the Trelayne Military Academy, they did not mention. No point in putting off the punters. The accent was on the five-thousand-florin reward, and a noisy rumor that certain parties within the slave trade cabal of Etterkal would triple that money for a rapid result. Word-of-mouth and greed, leavened through with the poverty and desperation the war had left in its wake, would take care of the rest.

There was no going home.

Ringil stared at his stranded boots some more. Behind him, Eril had started to snore slightly. He sighed and rolled his head back to loosen the tension in his neck. Screwed up his eyes against the glare of the sun.

Shadow fell chilling across his face.

"So, the illustrious Ringil of House Eskiath."

He flinched, violently. Eyes jammed abruptly open, lunge headlong, half blind in the sudden blast of sunlight, sideways across the smooth rock to where the Ravensfriend lay discarded in its sheath.

Knowing at some instinctive level that he was wasting his time.

Up in the ready crouch anyway, one hand on the hilt of the sword, the other wrapped low on the scabbard as Grashgal had taught, so the blade would clear through the engineered split down the side without taking off his fingers on its way.

He blinked about in the bright air, looking for the voice.

"Or would Ringil of Gallows Gap be fairer nomenclature?"

Something seemed to happen to the light. It was like coming in out of the sun on a summer afternoon in the Glades, the sudden gloom before your eyes got used to the change. As if the day were pale blue fabric of some kind, and something could come and abruptly drench it through.

A cloaked figure stood watching him, less than half a dozen yards away.

Slouch hat shading a face that was oddly hard to draw detail from— later, all Ringil recalled was the smile that clamped the thin lips shut, and a cold, speculative light in the eyes. The cloak, now he looked closer, was a stained and worn patchwork of leather mendings, one upon the other until it was hard to tell where, if anywhere, the original material remained. Blunt, sailor's hand stitching, and here and there amid it all the embroidered runework of a charm against mutiny or storms. He remembered Egar's muttered, half-disbelieving words in the stolen ferryboat as they fled downriver—*just like they say in the fucking legends, man; sea captain's cloak and hat, the whole thing. Just standing there.*

Just standing there.

No weapon.

No way—no *fucking* way—anything human could have crept up on him like that.

Ringil eased up out of his crouch. He did not relinquish the Ravensfriend. There was a deep pulsing in his chest and something in his hands that should have been trembling but was not, was tighter and sweeter and scared him more because he didn't know where it might go. The world was changed about him, even the birdsong muffled away by the Presence. His eyes flickered briefly to Eril's prone form, saw the man's sleep-softened features and he knew that whatever happened now, his companion would not wake until the stranger was gone.

So.

Like bending an iron poker, he forced his stare back to the newcomer. Met the cold and curious eyes, the waiting in them.

"You're late," he said harshly.

The clamped smile loosened a little, showed teeth. "You were expecting me?"

Ringil shook his head, and the tiny motion seemed to give him back a small measure of control. From limestone depths and the memories of Seethlaw, he summoned an awful, precipice calm.

"Not me. Talking about someone I met last night, some marsh dweller kid name of Gerin—he was asking for your help, back by the river. Right before he died, he told me he prayed to the Salt Lord for intercession. Begged for it, I'd guess, the state he was in. So what's the story, Salt Lord—you don't hear so good these days? Got to scream our prayers a little louder, do we?"

The eyes held him, attentive and mildly amused, as if he were a Strov street performer with a less than averagely tiresome act.

"Is it really this boy's unanswered prayers that so upset you, Ringil Eskiath? Or another boy's, long ago?"

Ringil's knuckles whitened on the hilt of the Ravensfriend. "You think I'm upset? When I'm upset, Salt Lord, you'll know all about it."

"Should I take that as a threat?"

"Take it any fucking way you want."

Because while one component to that thrumming in his hands and chest and blood was certainly fear, a swooping shadowy terror of what stood before him, the fear was really nothing he had not felt before, and thrumming along with it his blood sang with other things, just as dark, that he had long since learned to welcome in. And while he had never been face-to-face with a denizen of the Dark Court before—had in fact not believed until very recently that they even existed—he *had* been eye-to-eye with other things that most would count just as soul wither-ing, and the truth was, his soul had not withered very much.

He took a pine-perfumed breath from the forest around him, held it, plumed it out again like fumes from a well-rolled krinzanz smoke. He widened his eyes at Dakovash, and he held the Salt Lord's gaze.

A quiet like the world waiting to be born.

But Ringil thought that, for just a moment, the mouth below the slouch hat might have bent at one corner. There and gone, the sour trace of amusement, and something else he could not quite name. The sigh that followed sounded, to his Glades-bred ears, a little manufactured.

"Do you really consider that a fit way to talk to your clan deities?"

Ringil shrugged. "If you wanted veneration, you should have shown up while your supplicant was still alive."

"Has it occurred to you that maybe I heard Gerin Trickfinger's prayers, heard the forward echoes of them long before they were even said, before he was even *born*, and that help *was* sent?"

"I was there. If you sent help, it didn't show up in time."

"Well, as you say: *You* were there."

Ringil's eyes narrowed. "And what the fuck is that supposed to mean?"

The figure matched his earlier shrug. "Take it any way you want."

Which sat in the washed granite-and-gloom space between them for what seemed like a long time. Finally, Ringil bent and lowered the Ravensfriend carefully to the rock under his feet. He straightened up, felt a long shiver run through him as he did. He folded his arms tight across his chest.

"What do you want, Salt Lord?"

"Ah. So your insolence is calculated after all. No risk in disrespecting the Dark Court if it needs something from you, eh?"

Ringil stared back through the creeping chill in his bones. "No gain in respecting a demon lord who cannot be summoned when he's needed."

He thought he saw something spark in Dakovash's eyes.

"Oh very droll," the voice whispered, suddenly uncomfortably close and intimate, though the figure did not appear to have moved. "But what if you're wrong, little Gil Eskiath? What if you're wrong and we don't need you as much as you think? What then? What if I just cut my losses and take offense and *melt your fucking bones down, right now, in your still-living flesh?*"

And like a nightmare made real on waking, Ringil felt it start, a crawling, searing sensation along the edges of his shins and forearms, down his spine and into his guts like a bucket hitting well water, the beginnings of true pain buried deep under his skin, the fleeting premonition of how it would be, how he would dance and flail, and scream without surcease as the fire ate him from the inside out . . .

"Feel better now, do we?"

He goes to his knees with the sudden force of it. Catches a breath already turning scorched and acrid in his throat—

Is catapulted away, elsewhere.

Smooth, cooling breeze, and a low, silvery gloom that instinct and fumbling recognition tell him are not the Salt Lord's to command. Breath sobbing in his throat—the pain is gone. He kneels at the heart of a place he knows: an Aldrain stone circle, mist shrouded, the looming impassive half-hewn monoliths scabbed with dark moss patches and lines, and overgrown around the base.

For a moment, something leaps alive in him at the sight.

Seethlaw.

But the circle is empty. Anything that happened here is long over, and if the stones witnessed it, the way he thinks he remembers, then they have nothing to say on the matter now. Ringil gets to his feet out of silence and long grass soaked with dew. The knees of his breeches are damp and cold with moisture. He stands there, aching in the throat once more, and this time it's nothing anyone has done to him but himself.

He tips back his head to see if that'll relieve the pain, but it doesn't.

Overhead, Seethlaw's dying, pockmarked little sun—the thing he called *muhn* instead—sits high in a murky sky and scatters its second-rate light. Tatters of ragged cloud whip in from a direction that might be the west, sweep briefly across its feebly glowing face, almost blotting it out as they pass. It's the wind, he supposes, pushing the cloud that way, that fast, but he feels abruptly as if it's the *muhn* scudding past overhead at dizzying speed while the rest of the sky stands rock-solid still.

For one disorienting moment, he tilts with it, and almost falls.

—*Seethlaw*

He's been back to the Gray Places more times since Ennishmin than he likes to count, back to the Aldrain realm he first walked in at Seethlaw's side. He knows you can find the dead there, along with other, less reliable ghosts, the ghosts of what could or should or might have once been, *if only.* So—like grinding a loose tooth down into the soft bleeding gum of his fear—he goes looking. Sometimes cooked on krinzanz fumes and mad with a generalized grief he no longer knows how to contain, sometimes wakeful straight and possessed of a mind so cold and clear it scares him more than the madness. He goes looking for the dead, and they come to him in droves, just as they did before. They make their cases, present their alternatives to him, the way that, no, look, they certainly have *not* died, that's rubbish, he misremembers, they're as alive as he is, can't he *see* that . . .

You don't argue with the dead. He learned that early on. Argue and they grow angry, build vortices of rage and denial in the webbing of whatever holds the Gray Places together; if you aren't careful, they drag you in there with them, and damage whatever delicate mechanisms of sanity keep you centered in your own version and understanding of what's real. Better by far to let them have their way, and you go yours. There's a state of mind you need for it, something like the slightly fogged and thoughtless competence you find underlying your hangover the morning after a night lit up with krinzanz and cheap tavern wine. You cope, you move on.

You keep looking.

He never found Seethlaw. He doesn't know why, doesn't for that matter know what he would do or say if he ever did find him. It's not as if they parted on good terms at the end.

But the search is a compulsion, a deep insistent tug with no more governed sense to it than the deep salt pull of the currents that flow past the point at Lanatray where his mother keeps her summer residence. More than once, as a boy, he swam out too far and got caught up in the implacable grip of that flow. More than once, he saw the shore swept away to a flat charcoal line on the horizon, and wondered if he'd ever make it back to land alive.

Once, after Jelim's death, he let the tow take him and didn't care much one way or the other what happened next.

What happened next, as near as he recalls, was that the water bore him up despite his best efforts to drown, as if wet muscular hands were gathered under his neck and chest and thighs, and somehow, as the sun declined and the light above the swell thickened toward dark, he found the shore creeping in closer once more. It seemed the ocean didn't want him. The current spat him out miles down the coastal sweep of the beaches, he came in staggering and exhausted in the surf, and the waves cuffed him brutally ashore like blows from his father's sword-grip-callused hand.

Yes, and I don't suppose it ever occurred to you to wonder about those helpful hands, now, did it? Sardonic voice at his ear—he whirls violently about to face it, sees a shadowy form slip between two of the standing stones, trailing edge of a cloak and gone before he can fix on it. The voice drifts behind in its stead. *Never occurred to you to wonder what exactly it was that was holding you up in the water all that time?*

A chill wraps the back of his neck, stealthy, prehensile. The damp division of webbed fingers, pressing firmly up.

He shudders at the touch. Shakes it off. Cannot now recall if the memory is real or if Dakovash has reached back and placed it there.

Oh yes, that's right. I'm just making all this up. The merroigai were never there, you swam in to shore all by yourself, of course you did. Beyond the stones, the Salt Lord's voice prowls, not quite in step with the flitting shadow of his form. There's an angry agitation to both, like the flicker and spit of an oil lamp flame dying down. *Fucking mortals. You know, it's— I am so sick of this shit. Where's the respect? Where's the supplicant awe? I thought you, Ringil Eskiath, you of all people . . .*

A long pause, the figure stops between two monoliths and faces Ringil with one pale hand pressed claw-like to its chest. The face beneath the hat is all shadow and gleaming teeth and eyes like a wolf. The voice rasps out again.

Look at me, Eskiath, fucking look at me. If you can't manage respect, then at least grow a sense of self-preservation, why don't you? I am a lord of the Dark Court. *I'm a* fucking demon god. *Do you have any idea what I've done to the flesh and souls of men a thousand times as powerful as you'll ever be, for no other reason than they spoke back to me the way you do, as if you had the fucking* right? *Look at me.* I am Dakovash. *I stole— when I was still young—when this whole fucking* world *was still young— I stole fire from the High Gods, and forged it into a new weapon against them. I commanded angels in battle, brought bat-winged demons out of the dark to overthrow the old order, I crossed the void as a fucking* song *so that the old order would fall. I broke those fuckers in battle over the arch of this world when none could or would do it but me. And you think you're going to judge me? Judge me on some fifteen-year-old marsh brat that couldn't lift a fucking broadsword to save his life? What am I supposed to do* with *that?* Train *him?* The Salt Lord throws out one arm, rakes crooked fingers through the darkened air in some paroxysm of exasperated disbelief. Somewhere behind him, thunder rumbles through the Gray Places. *What—find some fucking monastery on a mountain someplace and pay his board and lodging for a decade among* kindly warrior monks, *all so he can grow into his ascendant power, fulfill his destiny, and become The One? Give me a fucking break, Eskiath. You really think that's how it works?*

I wouldn't know how it works, Ringil says flatly. *You're the demon lord here, not me.*

The Salt Lord's hand drops to his side. *Well, then try giving it some thought, why don't you? Apply that finely tutored mind of yours to all those bullshit hero-with-a-high-destiny legends you people are so fucking fond of telling one another. You really think, in a mudball slaughterhouse of a world like this, where war and privation harden whole populations to inhuman brutality and ignorance, where the ruling classes dedicate their sons to learning the science of killing men the way they consign their daughters to breeding till they crack—you* really think *the gods of a world like that have got no better thing to do with their time than take some random piece of lowborn trash and spend long years carving him into shape for a cat's-paw?*

*I had—*Ringil swallows on an abrupt gut-swooping gust of insolence that licks up in the pit of his belly like flames—*no idea that time was so precious a commodity among the denizens of the Immortal Watch.*

Beat of silence among the shrouded stones. Then Dakovash grunts, as if from some old pain returning.

Not many call us by that name any longer.

Ringil shrugs. *Not many can read. Or care about any past beyond their own fucked-up selective remembrance.*

He thinks the shadowed figure smiles at that.

You sound bitter, hero.

Do I? Ringil gestures impatiently against the returning chill in his bones. *I'm not the one complaining about a lack of supplicant awe, though, am I? I'm not the one short of time for my immortal designs.*

More quiet. Framed on either side by the silent monoliths, the Salt Lord seems to be studying him as if through the bars of a cage.

Finally, he says this:

The march of time is broken, Ringil Eskiath. Something in that softly rasping voice that might be admission, concession, or maybe just a bone-deep weariness. *The bounds of possibility come adrift around us, the old certainties are all in their graves. Cats can no longer be considered alive or dead.*

Cats . . . ?

The skeins are tangled. Some butterfly shaman up in the north beats his puny fucking wings and the storm gathers before you know it. Chaos gathers, like a bad poet's verse. We run damage control, but the rules of engagement have changed. You think we're any happier about it than you? We've got our balls to the wall here, hero. We're fighting half blind, nothing works, not the way it should, not anymore. Which being the case, well . . . A shrug. *Let us just say that in a situation like that, you work with the tools at hand. And speaking of which—*

Like a scything shard of darkness, the Ravensfriend, still in its scabbard, pitches through the gloom from the Salt Lord's pale grasp, through the gap between the standing stones, and onto the long, wind-matted grass at Ringil's feet.

Try not to drop that again. You're going to need it.

I—teeth now clenched for a swirl of reasons, fear, anger, the growing cold, that he cannot unpick—*am not your fucking cat's-paw.*

But the space between the two stones, when he looks up from his sword, is empty. Only a faint breeze, wandering through as if following the sword, touching his face with cold.

It leaves traceries in the mist like the motions of a languid hand in water.

The Salt Lord is gone.

EYES OPEN, ON BLINDING BLUE SKY.

He blinked, vision tearing up from all the sudden brightness. He propped himself up a little and rubbed hard at his eyes. He was back on the flat rock under a declining afternoon sun. The Ravensfriend lay at his side. He rolled over, reached convulsively for the sword. Discovered he was shivering despite the warmth still in the day. More than shivering, actually—a feverish chill rode his bones and racked him with a desire to curl into a ball. He coughed, and found a razor's edge in his throat.

Great. And now he remembered the boy sneezing on him the night before. *Marsh flu, that's all I fucking need.*

He levered himself to his feet and stared around. Treetops nodding in the breeze, the thickly wooded slopes and the unattainable road north threading between. Over everything a blue haze of distance that seemed to be thickening.

Shadows a little longer than they'd been.

Farther up the rock, Eril snored throatily, one arm cast up to shield his eyes from the sun, but otherwise unmoved since Ringil had last looked at him.

The hovering hawk was gone. And no sign of Dakovash. It could all have been—*yeah, right*—a dream.

Chaos gathers, like a bad poet's verse.

He looked westward, frowning.

Hey now, come on. That's just stupid . . .

Is it? He turned the sudden glimmer of it carefully, panning for some truthful assessment of its value. *Got a better plan, do you, Gil? State you're in?*

He held down a fresh bout of shivering, wrapped his cloak tighter about himself, and crouched beside Eril's sleeping form. Made a tight *hssst* he knew would waken the Marsh Brotherhood enforcer without fuss.

Sure enough, Eril's eyes slid open at the sound, as wakeful as if he'd only closed them a moment before. His hand was already on his knife hilt.

"Yeah?"

"Time to get moving," Ringil told him.

Eril got to his feet, staying low, and didn't argue. He looked about at their unchanged surroundings, then back at Ringil, curiously.

"Did I miss something?" he asked.

"No," said Ringil briskly. "You didn't miss a thing. But I've got an idea how to get us out of here."

CHAPTER 12

It called itself Anasharal.

Archeth had never seen anything like it. The Helmsmen of her youth came large and semi-visible at best—mostly they were in the walls, or the hulls and bulkheads of the fireships, like helpful rats out of some fairy tale or shelved talking library books. They engaged you in solemn conversation, sometimes they solved your problems for you—or at least told you why they couldn't—and they could manipulate numerous aspects of the Kiriath domain in ways she'd never been able to think of as anything but magical. As a child, she'd gotten the impression some of them were taking a slightly scary avuncular delight in guiding her, and not always along paths her parents approved.

But one thing they weren't was mobile.

Later, when the engineers started stripping some of the old fireships preparatory to leaving, she saw why: The component parts came out into the light like giant iron organs and loops of intestine surgically re-moved. Angfal, once Helmsman for the wrecked flagship—rough translation—*Sung Through Lava Like the Petal of an Autumn Rose on the Scorching Late-Summer Breeze,* now hung on the walls of her study in Yhelteth, looking discomfortingly like a huge, gross-bodied spider ooz-ing through from the next room. But the impression was fleeting at best—Angfal could no more move unaided than the next fat keg of ale waiting in a tavern cellar.

Anasharal had limbs.

It wasn't a feature that was immediately apparent. Archeth and the eight men Hald detailed to go down with her came awkwardly across the glassy surface in the bottom half of the crater, aping the motions of wading through cold water on a stony shore, and found themselves star-ing at something rather like a moldy, half-eaten pie that someone had mistakenly put back in the oven. The heat shimmer rose off a roughly hemispherical knobbed gray carapace cracked neatly apart across the middle. It was the gray crust itself that was smoking, but where the crack ran through, there was a faint white mist that spilled steadily out onto the glassy ground and crawled about there in wisps that gave out a faint, sorcerous chill. Peering into the space the mist was vacating, they saw a nested hollow about four feet across, something like an opened rose with its heart punched out. In the middle, something like a huge egg was rocking back and forth.

The men drew back, doing their best not to step in the puddles of chilly mist. They looked to Archeth for guidance. She shrugged.

"We do not understand how to help you," she said flatly, to the air in general.

"Yes, just a moment."

Another loud cracking sound. A couple of the marines jumped vis-ibly. One whole quarter of the broken gray crust fell abruptly aside and lay there like a chunk of abandoned wasps' nest. From the gap it left, the thing that had rocked back and forth within came scrabbling out like some gigantic crab looking for food.

Oaths laced the air. The soldiers backed up even farther. Archeth tried not to; it wouldn't have looked good.

The crab-like thing finished extricating itself and dropped to the floor, where it lay for a moment, feebly twitching one or two of its limbs as if exhausted. A pair of halberds swung down off marine shoulders and prodded inward.

"That really won't be necessary," said the voice. "Nagarn, Khiran, thank you. You can put those away."

The named halberdiers gaped at each other. Their weapons drooped in shock. The crab-like thing propped itself up and waddled sideways in the gap, then collapsed again. Archeth crouched to look closer. The new arrival was fully three feet across at the widest point, smooth and featureless gray on top, apart from a scattering of thumb-sized optics glowing softly blue or white. At a glance you could be forgiven for thinking you were looking at some Kiriath-grown metallic giant mushroom— until it moved. But even then, she saw, there was something awkward about the motion. The legs folded out from sculpted recesses in the lower half of the creature, but they seemed to work poorly, as if unused to supporting the thing's weight.

"It will take three or four of you to pick me up." Briskly, as if it had heard her thoughts. "I suggest we improvise some kind of sling."

SHE LEARNED ITS NAME AS THEY CARRIED IT, GRUNTING AND SCUFFLING with the weight, up the slope of the crater. Later, once they'd together the suggested sling out of horse blankets and two halberd shafts and were on their way back to the river, she also got a vague, lengthy, and rather improbable sketch of its life story told in archaic High Kir, which she soon grew weary of trying to stay focused on. Like most Helmsmen of her acquaintance, Anasharal liked the sound of its own voice and seemed largely immune to modesty.

" . . . and in return for which services, I was flung up into the heavens by the grateful king, set among the stars to gleam there in guidance for all travelers of good heart forever after."

"Yeah?" Archeth, riding alongside the sling and its carriers, slouched back in her saddle. "So what are you doing back down here, then?"

There was more snap in her voice than she'd intended. Relentless desert heat and the constant darting glances from the men that wrapped her in with this burbling chunk of sorcery and iron—it all added to her mounting irritability. But more than any of that was the dawning real-ization that when Manathan had spoken of messengers, she had assumed—rushed to assume—that he meant the Kiriath themselves, returning somehow, in some fairy-tale improbable fashion, from the veins of the Earth into which they had disappeared.

Instead, she had this.

"I really don't think, daughter of Flaradnam, that you or any of your, uhm, friends here could remotely comprehend the complexity of deci-sion making involved in letting me fall to Earth at this precise moment. Command decisions, I'm talking about, taken in an arena so cold and empty that it would render your body a block of ice in a heartbeat and boil your blood in your veins."

"I think you mean freeze."

Anasharal was silent for a moment, motionless in the sag and jog of the horse-blanket sling. Dry, metronome crunch of marching feet on either side—but even the men carrying the sling looked down, surprised at the sudden quiet from their cargo.

"You did say cold." Archeth, twisting the knife.

"Think what you will." Like clockwork wound back up—she couldn't be sure if the voice had turned sulky or was sneering. "It won't affect anything that matters. Your perspective is as Earthbound as any mortal. I, on the other hand, have seen the rise and fall of king-doms across the continents and through the ages, witnessed the passing of the Aldrain and the bloody, midwifed renaissance of Men, watched the brief, multitudinous lives of humans spinning by like dandelion seed on the wind, wrestled with the almost—but actually not quite—incalculable mathematics of it all, and I'm telling you not to bother trying to comprehend any of it or me. Just follow my instructions and try to keep up."

"We are carrying you," Archeth pointed out.

"Yes, as your horse carries you—but I doubt you've tried to teach the beast basic algebra."

Seemingly satisfied with this retort, Anasharal lapsed again into si-lence and stayed that way until they reached the boats. There, it seemed to derive a childish satisfaction from startling the marines who crowded around the sling to see what their comrades had brought back. It called various of them by name, asked after their individual circumstances in perfect Tethanne—Ganch, if the reptile peon bite wound in his shoulder still gave him trouble in winter, Hrandan whether he preferred assignment on the river frigate to his previous duties at Khangset, Shalag how he'd found his time in Demlarashan and if things down there were as bad, in his opinion, as they were all saying. It was the most blatant piece of showing off Archeth could ever recall, even from a Helmsman—and like all such tricks, it was spellbinding.

In the end, Senger Hald had to bellow for order over a drawn blade to get his men back about their tasks and everybody onto the small boats.

The good news, though, was that Lal Nyanar had succeeded in refloating the *Sword of Justice Divine*. He met them at the hull door as they embarked the horses, rubbing his hands briskly, clearly pleased with himself. Hard sunlight slanted down through the open hatch, caught dust motes dancing in the damp gloom of the belowdeck. Painted a bright stripe across the satisfaction on Nyanar's face.

"So then. What did you find?"

"They found me," said Anasharal. "And it took them long enough."

Nyanar jumped. He stared at the inert chunk of metal the men were carrying onto his ship in its horse-blanket sling. You could see him struggling to make the connection with the irritable voice that had just spoken into his ear.

"It's like a Helmsman," Senger Hald told him, stepping off the bobbing small boat and aboard the frigate. "A Helmsman fallen from the heavens, it says."

"But—so small?"

Hald spread his arms eloquently. Both men looked at Archeth.

Great—like I know any more about this than you do.

She faked a command confidence. "We have no reason to doubt its word. We'll find out more when we get it back to Yhelteth."

"Yeah—just—wait a minute." Nyanar gestured at the men carrying the sling, and they set it down on the planking with evident relief. "We have no reason to trust it, either, whatever it is. This could be a, a trickster demon. An evil spirit enchained in iron."

"Oh, *charming*."

"It needed us to carry it here," Archeth said shortly. "I really don't think we're in any danger."

"No physical danger, perhaps. But what of our souls?"

"Lal Nyanar—if Mahmal Shanta could only hear you now. What would he think of the man he once named his most promising student. His most promising . . . collaborator?"

Nyanar's gaze flickered back to the Helmsman. Now the fear was plain to see—the mention of Shanta had only made matters worse. He faced Archeth with features set.

"This is my vessel, my lady. My command. If I invite something demonic aboard, who knows what power I accord it over us all. I will not allow this."

The dust motes danced. The frigate's hull creaked softly around them in the sun-barred gloom. Men waited, stood there in the cool or crouched out on the bobbing small boats in the heat. They were all watching her.

As usual.

Archeth sighed. "All right. Where's Galat? Let's get an invigilator's opinion on this, and then maybe we can all go home."

SHE'D EXPECTED HIM TO INSIST ON A CLOSETED INQUISITION, A CABIN alone with Anasharal, or maybe even—to cleanse the frigate of any potentially demonic taint—a tented retreat somewhere along the arid shoreline.

But Galat was almost careless of the details. He suggested they bring Anasharal up to the rear command deck, where the spread canvas shades would keep the sun off but let the breeze blow through. More comfortable for everyone, really. And this would allow those men not about their duties elsewhere to hear the deliberations and be assured that their leaders, spiritual and military, acted in their interests as well.

Fuck me, Archeth thought behind an impassive mask of acquiescence. *A true believer.*

The end result was that the *Sword of Justice Divine* sat at anchor while Anasharal was placed on a small ceremonial carpet in the shade of the canvas on the command deck, facing Hanesh Galat who knelt formally on a similar carpet with a Citadel scribe cross-legged at his side. Some murmured recitation, call-and-answer style, between the two men, and then the scribe took up his pen and scroll. Nyanar, Hald, Archeth, and a couple of the frigate's senior officers sat on cushions in a semicircle around. And a small gaggle of sailors and marines with nothing better to do loitered on the main deck below, listening for whatever scraps of the proceedings the breeze would carry down.

Galat began his inquisition with formal introductions of all concerned, and then went straight into a series of labyrinthine clerical pronouncements. Archeth, unable to make herself sit for more than a couple of minutes, prowled about at the shoreside rail, trying to kid herself that the scratching impatience she felt to get home was not krinzanz withdrawal. Images of her bedroom at home kept spilling into her mind—a wooden box of rolled twigs beside the bed, fragrant smoke through the cool night air, the icy rising tide in her head, and Ishgrim, perched prettily on the bench by the window casement as she sometimes did, *or sprawled naked and voluptuous and pouting on the disordered divan the way she never had, but some day, some fucking day* . . .

She shrugged it off. Her body had never been subtle in the messages it sent.

But perhaps Manathan was right. There'd be plenty of time in the centuries to come to wean herself off the krin. Right now . . .

" . . . so in any real sense you would have to accept that it's impossible for me to prove to you what I am. *Demon* is an arbitrary term, not so much a definition as an admission of a gap in a definitional framework, which . . ."

Right now, this was doing her head in.

Hanesh Galat seemed to be enjoying himself, though.

"But the Revelation clearly states—"

"Yes, your Revelation has textual criteria for defining a demonic entity, of course it does. But only by dint of a so-called deformation of nature, in other words via the acts said demonic entities indulge in and more important via human perception of the *unnatural and negative impact* of those acts on the human sphere and the physical world. So a demon that did not act in either the human sphere or the physical world, or at least did not give cause to perceive unnatural and negative impacts in those spheres, could not be defined as a demon as such. For that matter, though the textual authority is thinner, one could say the same of a similarly inclined angel."

Galat blinked. "You mean to say that demons and angels could be mistaken for each other?"

"No, what I'm saying is that, just as with men, demons and angels cannot be effectively defined, in the temporal sphere at least, *except by the actions they take in that sphere.* That a lack of temporal agency on the part of either one leads to an impossibility of definition until some concrete action is taken and humanly perceived. And then, since this is the origin of definition, it is the act that must be judged, not the enactor."

"But then, you're also arguing—implying, anyway—that angels and demons *are not immutable spirits!*"

Senger Hald rolled his eyes. Lal Nyanar glanced surreptitiously up at the position of the declining sun.

"Well, if you follow that implication to its textual corollary in the Revelation at Hanliahg, yes," Anasharal said smoothly. "But I ask you, is that such a bold step? I'm not suggesting anything that has not already been given considered debate in the Ashnal verses. The limitations on temporal knowledge are readily acknowledged, as is the imperfection of human senses in perceiving or even imagining a spiritual realm. Spirit is inherently unknowable from the context of the Earthbound soul, and so the Revelation, on its own admission, can only be partial."

"There is the behavior of nonhuman spectators to consider, though." Galat enumerated on his fingers. "Indirect intelligence that we achieve by observing the reactions of natural denizens in the animal kingdom. Dogs skulk and howl, spiders and other vermin may be attracted to—"

"Well, I think you'll find that the horses did not react to me at all."

"The horses *were* uncomfortable," said Hald, patently seizing on something that might move the proceedings along.

"That was the trees." Archeth, dismissive, moving to lean on the rear rail. Down on the main deck, the gathered men had evidently found other, more engrossing things to do and long ago dispersed to do them. "The burning spooked them. You'd get the same thing if the ship caught fire."

"Well, burning the trees might be seen as a deformation of nature," Galat allowed, but you could see that his heart wasn't really in it.

"Do men not also burn wood for their own, natural purposes?"

"Yes, but the purpose is an intrinsic . . . "

So it went on until the sun fell below the trailing edge of the canvas shade and started getting in their eyes. Perhaps noticing this, Galat hurried through some concluding formal remarks, cited a verse or two from the Revelation at Shaktur, and then solemnly pronounced the Helmsman welcome among them as a Permitted Being.

The scribe signed off and dabbed the scroll dry.

For the others, it was like a spell breaking. Hald, Nyanar, and the ship's officers piled to their feet, grimacing as they stretched cramped limbs, and headed down to the main deck. They left Hanesh Galat still seated, staring at Anasharal entranced.

"Fascinating," he mused. "The implications. *Fascinating.*"

"I take it we're in the clear then," Anasharal asked Archeth in High Kir. "We'll have no more interference from these idiots?"

Galat glanced up at Archeth when he heard the Black Folk tongue, but any suspicion in his expression was softened by the blatant wonder that still held his face. Archeth made a small, reassuring gesture, then turned her attention to the Helmsman where it sat on the carpet, carapace gleaming dully now in the long rays of the late-afternoon sun. She drew closer. Followed the language shift.

"If you're talking about the Citadel, then yes, we're done. This one's rank permits him to write opinion directly into the Quotidian canon. That's not the same thing as the Revealed canon, so it's not set in stone. It can be disputed at Mastery level. But that's unlikely to arise. They've got a few other clerical fish to fry right now."

"Just as well. Immutable spirits, indeed. Morons."

It was the first time since the war that she'd seen a Helmsman treat the Citadel with anything other than complete disinterest. Curiosity prickled at her.

"I wouldn't have thought it would matter that much to you. It's not as if they can harm you in any way."

"No, but a certain amount of cooperation will be important."

"Cooperation in what?"

Long pause. "That's not important right now, daughter of Flarad-nam. The important thing is to get back to Yhelteth with all speed."

She stood over the iron thing and suffered an overwhelming urge to kick it.

"Yes, you keep saying that. But you don't explain why."

"Why?" Abruptly, there was a snap in the Helmsman's voice. "Be-cause, daughter of Flaradnam, something dark is on its way. That's why. And it's nearly here."

CHAPTER 13

*H*inerion, the Trelayne poet laureate Skimil Shend once wrote, *is less a city in itself than some weak, far-flung echo of the capital it strives at every turn to imitate. It is a cultural and architectural cry that lacks conviction, the coarse cant of some mongrel urchin in the street who has perhaps heard Great Oratory somewhere and knows somewhat how to copy its more obvious features, but has neither the breeding nor the education to truly understand what it is he echoes. Worse yet, this is an urchin rubbing shoulders in the common mob with fellows whose blood origins, worse than uncertain, are most assuredly alien. For Hinerion belongs almost as much to the Southern Scourge as it does to the League. It is nominally in League territory, yes, but tell that to the dusky-faced multitude who throng its streets, jabbering in a variegated confusion of tongues where Naomic is no more honored in dominion than Tethanne; tell that to the imperial merchants whose vessels mob the harbor with their foreign flags* *and the mercenaries who with the thinnest of documentary justification come and go on the streets of what is called a League city as if they trod the tiled thoroughfares of Yhelteth itself. They tell me Hinerion is a frontier town, and it must be lived in as such, but from what I see about me at every turn, that frontier is as thin and seeping as the soiled bandage on a war wound that may never heal.*

Ringil knew Shend—had in fact fucked him a couple of times in his youth, in curtained alcoves at fashionably seedy parties in the warehouse district—and he was inclined not to judge the poet's vitriol too harshly. Like a lot of wordsmiths, Skimil was a delicate soul, exiled to Hinerion at the time of writing, and evidently not handling it very well. That old Trelayne story, the sudden trapdoor fall from grace. Jostled from your upriver residence on charges of *seditious composition* or some such shit, summoned to explain yourself before the Committee for Public Morals, and rapidly deserted by your up-until-then generous patrons—it must have been a rude awakening, and Ringil, who'd fallen foul of the Committee himself as a younger man, could well imagine the hole it would have punched in Shend's brittle sense of superiority. The sudden, chilly desperation that might come whistling in through that hole. You'd write—allowing that that was your given talent—pretty much *anything* if you thought it might curry enough favor to banish that chill. And anti-Yhelteth rhetoric was a safe enough drum to beat if you wanted to ingratiate yourself with the great and the good in Trelayne. Add a judicious seasoning of sycophantic praise for the city and its pontificating elders, and who knew what might be achieved if your friends could only get what you'd written to the attention of the right people.

In Shend's case, it took the best part of three years, but the steady stream of letters to friends and family, loudly professing love of Trelayne and horror at the mongrel mixing of its culture with others, finally did the trick. The poet went home behind a full pardon and a deal with the University to publish his letters as a collected whole titled *The Distant Beloved.* Ringil had read it, took it with him on the northern expeditionary campaign and subsequently used its pages to wipe his arse.

About one thing, though, Shend had been accurate. Hinerion was indeed a mongrel city, a seething mishmash of influences from north and south, belonging wholly to neither and thronged with men passing through in both directions.

It was one of the things Ringil, on previous visits, had most liked about the place.

Now it made it the perfect place to hide.

So they rode in through the Black Sail Gate toward dusk, subsumed in a gaggle of arrivals off ships whose masters had no certification to enter the main harbor and must dock a mile and a half down the coast from the city walls. The secondary harbor was a shabby affair, little more than a collection of jetties off a mud beach into deeper water and an array of flimsy wooden shacks strung out along the dirt road into town. Tavern, brothel, and chandler's store, there was really little else to see, and the City Watch pointedly did not extend its protective remit to any of it. With that in mind, most shipmasters hired cheap mercenary cover to protect their vessels at anchor and to escort their passengers and cargo to and from the city. Hard-bitten thugs on horseback and the well-used steel they carried were commonplace on the Black Sail Road, and there was no reason Eril and Ringil should not pass as such. Both of them were grubby and travel-stained enough, and Ringil had bagged his black brocade cloak in favor of a cheap woolen wrap from the chandler's store. And he'd bound the Ravensfriend's scabbard tightly with strips of shredded saddle blanket back in the forest, daubed firegrime and ashes all over pommel, hilt, and guard until you could no longer tell the weapon for what it really was. His face was similarly grimed to soften the impact of the scar and mask his feverish pallor, which latter he was concerned might be taken by some sharp-eyed sentry for the possible onset of plague.

Might as well have *fucking plague, the way I feel right now.*

Quit whining, hero.

He gritted his teeth to hold down the shivering, and hoped his blank and fevered stare would pass for standard fuck-off profession-of-violence detachment.

He needn't have worried. The guard detail at the gate, bored and yawning to a man, spared the two of them no more than a cursory glance while the captain took and pocketed the levy. They were not even asked to dismount. The crossed pikes lifted out of their path, the captain waved them through.

THE TOUTS SURGED INTO THE ROAD AS SOON AS THEY PASSED INSIDE the gate, most of them boys not over the age of ten.

"Rooms, good sirs, rooms. Fine ocean view."

"Stabling of imperial quality, imperial-trained grooms . . . "

"Fine wines, my lords, and fine females to serve them. Girls *practiced* with the neck of a bottle, know what I mean, my lord?"

Ringil urged his horse level with Eril's.

"Get someplace close to the harbor," he muttered. "But not so close we have to smell it. Views down to the docks, I want to be able to see what's moored."

Eril nodded. "On it."

"Then meet me down in the main square. Bounty office, under the south colonnade."

"Right." Eril gave him a narrow look. "You okay?"

"No," said Ringil shakily. "But there's fuck-all I can do about it right now. See you down there."

He wheeled his horse aside, out of the flow of the main thoroughfare and onto one of the steeper, less used alleys that led more directly down into Hinerion's center. The horse didn't like it much, but he stroked her neck repeatedly as they worked their way downward, talked down her worry as soothingly as he could with the continual jagged shivering coming up through his sternum and along his limbs.

"You and me both, girl," he murmured. "You and me both."

Down at the south colonnade, he put away the trembling with a grunt, like a book he hadn't much enjoyed, and dismounted by the bounty office rail. He tied the horse, found an urchin to watch it for a coin, and stepped in under the colonnaded roof. The doors to the bounty office were propped wide; yellowish lamplight spilled out onto the paving and the ragged huddle of men stood or seated around about. They were a dozen strong, and their profession announced itself with the here-and-there gleam of cheap, notched steel; an ax slung across a broad back and peeking over the shoulder, a sword whose owner made do with a loop of rope at his belt in place of a scabbard; a couple of nasty-looking Parashal knives, a Majak-style staff lance that you could tell at ten paces was a fake.

In general, the men were a match for their weapons, grubby and scarred and worn down by use.

Well—don't suppose you look too shiny yourself at the moment, Gil.

The gathered company appeared to have drawn the same conclusion. They looked up incuriously as he stepped into the light, made him for one of their own, and went right back to the muttered conversations and dice games that had occupied them before. One grizzled older warrior jerked a long-bearded chin at him in a fashion that might have been meant amiably.

Ringil returned the nod, put on a stock Yhelteth accent but stayed in Naomic. "Busy tonight. Something going down?"

"You haven't *heard*?" A pale, eye-patched swordsman, turning from some minor dispute he was having with the owner of the fake Majak lance. "Road scum took down a big fucking slave caravan this morning. Less than ten miles outside the city walls. Broad fucking daylight. Set about five hundred slaves free and killed the fuck out of everybody else. Where've you *been*, man? The whole fucking city's buzzing with this one."

Ringil gestured. "Came in the Black Sail Gate half an hour ago. Laraninthal of Shenshenath. First time back in League territory for a year. How many heads we talking about?"

"Lot of enough for the everybody," someone grunted, crude mimicry of Gil's southern accent, laced with the archetypal imperial's stumblings in Naomic grammar. There like a blade, like the teeth in a sneer, and then just as suddenly shed for a bored, sour-edged disdain. "Just get in the fucking queue, southman."

Some snickering in the wake of the comment, and it seemed to center among the dice crew. The bone cubes rattled down and the man who'd thrown them glanced up at Ringil, to see if offense had been taken. The studied blankness in his eyes said he didn't much care one way or the other.

"Twenty, thirty heads at least," the bearded warrior said hurriedly. "Got to be, those caravans are well protected. Seems like the border patrol got about a score of them, fighting a rearguard, but the rest escaped."

Ringil broke gaze with the dice man, looked in instead through the doors of the office, where a clerk sat yawning at a desk, poring over an open tome with a quill. Behind him, a couple of others bustled about with more ledgers and capped scrolls. A handful of other bounty hunters had chosen to stay inside, seated at the edges of the room and watching the paperwork.

"So." The urge to shiver made it easier to fake the Yhelteth accent, kept his jaw tight and guttural on the Naomic syllables. "Fifty outlaws, hiding in the forest. Sounds pretty vague to me. That all they've got?"

Eye-patch shook his head excitedly, flung thin, hanging threads of greasy hair about his pallid features. Behind the vertical scar that sat above and below the patch as if skewering it, he was younger than Ringil had noticed at first.

"No, man, that's not all. They're saying these guys had, like, this *sorcerer* for a leader, some magicked-up fuck down from Trelayne, carrying a Black Folk blade. They say he's already wanted up north for treason, already got a *twenty-five-thousand*-florin price on his head."

"Twenty-five thousand . . ." Ringil let his voice die off in carefully textured disbelief. "That does not seem likely."

"I'm serious, man. They took some prisoners, got them up at the Keep and they're putting them to the question. Some of the slaves, too. That's the word coming down. Fucking sorcerer, man." The young bounty hunter nodded in at the clerks. "Go ask for yourself, you don't believe me."

Ringil tipped him a skeptical look, then shrugged and stepped past, over the threshold of the opened doors and into the lamplit confines of the office.

The clerk looked up as he came in. "Yes?"

"Man outside says you're hunting a sorcerer."

"That's unconfirmed." The clerk put his quill aside and knuckled tiredly at one eye. "We had a raid on a caravan coming down the Trelayne road last night, attackers still at large. Probably a lot of them. We're waiting on names."

"How much you paying for heads?"

"Fifty per. Hundred if you bring them in alive. Maybe get you more later if the caravan owners put up a reward."

"Alive?" Ringil pulled a face. "In Tlanmar, they pay me seventy per, dead or alive. That's Empire elementals, too, comes out at a hundred and twenty florins' worth, near enough."

The clerk shrugged. "So go back to working for Tlanmar. Here, you'll get fifty florins per head, a hundred per captured prisoner. You want on the list or not?"

Ringil made a show of grumpy indecision, caught the bounty hunters in the corner of the room nudging one another and grinning at the
display. He judged the performance a success, cleared his throat, and
made an ungracious gesture.

"Well, then. I will go on your list, yes. Laraninthal of Shenshenath.
Captain, retired, Sixty-second Imperial Levy. Put me down."

"Some fucking retirement," said one of the bounty hunters quietly.
"Eh, pal?"

Low, noncommittal laughter among the others. Ringil turned to face
the speaker. Saw a League military-issue cloak and tunic that had both
seen better days, a sword sheathed in leather at the man's belt and another slung naked across his back. The man's features and close-shaven
skull were scarred in a couple of places with blade damage, and part of
one ear was chopped away. But there was no challenge in his face, and
the comment seemed to have been meant without harm.

"I served a cause," Ringil said stiffly, sticking to the role. "I served my
Emperor and defended my people. That was payment enough for me."

The shaven-headed man nodded. "Yeah. And now you're hunting
bandits in a foreign land for fifty florins a pop."

"There's no brawling in here," the clerk warned. "Start anything and
your name comes off the list. That goes for you too, Klithren."

The bounty hunter waved it off. "No one's brawling, inkspurt. Just
working men here, trading air and waiting on the names so we can get
to work. Right, Shenshenath?"

Ringil nodded curtly, turned back to the desk. "About this sorcerer.
Outside they're saying he's worth twenty-five thousand florins up in
Trelayne."

"I already told you," said the clerk, writing laboriously, not looking
up. "That's not confirmed. All we know for the moment is that the leader
of the attack was a northerner and he may have used a Kiriath blade."

"Got a description?"

"Yeah. Tall, scary, and a scarred face."

More dry chuckling among the bounty hunters. It was a sketch that
would have fit at least three of the men in the room, and probably half
of those who stood outside as well. It was a caricature for a campfire tale.

Well, so are you these days, Gil. So are you.

The clerk scratched to a halt on the ledger page and reached to dip his quill. He glanced up at Ringil, as if surprised to see him still standing there.

"That's it, we're done. You're on the list. Come back at first light or take a seat and wait, your choice."

"Do you expect names before dawn?"

"The Keep does a pretty good line in questioning," Ringil's shaven-headed new friend offered. "I doubt any of the road scum they took are going to stand up for long. Some'll be injured, some just cowards. They'll break right down."

No doubt.

Ringil had seen prisoners put to the question before, and some of them most assuredly not cowards. In the end, it made no difference. Everybody broke.

Yeah. Broke and said just exactly whatever the fuck they thought their torturers wanted to hear. I did it, yes, I'm guilty, oh yes. With poison, yes, that's right. With a blade, yes, just as you say, a blade I threw in the sea. With black magic I did it, yes, yes, you're right, magic and the help of miniature fucking pixies.

He had the measure of the men he'd hired—*and then abandoned, Gil, let's not forget that bit*—and he knew most would give up everything they knew at the first searing application of heated iron to their flesh. Fortunate, then, that they knew so little. Scarcity of detail would anger the interrogators, who in a case like this would be under a lot of pressure to deliver results, and the awful logic of that situation would roll right along, would push them way past the norms to make sure there really was no more to be gleaned. So their captives would have to go on suffering despite their initial confessions, would go on screaming out whatever names or facts still floated intact in the stew of their terror and pain—along with any of a hundred crazed embellishments based on the hit-and-miss exhortations of their tormentors. Truth or lie, sane or not, the captives would offer up *anything*, any shrieking, sobbing, shuddering stream of contradictory gibberish they believed might take away the agony, might *just please stop* this dungeon-dim nightmare of crushed and split and fire-scorched flesh.

So yeah—they'd say it was a northern sorcerer with a magical blade and scars on his face; they'd say it was an imperial renegade in full Kiriath mail at the head of a squad of border skirmishers; they'd say it was fucking *steppe nomads* if you halfway suggested it to them. Any grains of truth in it all would be stamped and mangled beyond useful recognition.

"Rumors and lies and campfire smoke," he summarized later for Eril, over spiced wine and cleared platters in the tavern. "Right now, that's all they've got."

The Marsh Brotherhood enforcer nodded. "Think it'll stay that way?"

"For a while, yeah. They think they've got a couple of dozen demoralized bad guys hiding out in the forest somewhere. Lot of tough, impatient bounty hunters are going to think that's too good a chance to miss. Come morning, they'll be riding out to see if they can't get an early piece of the action."

Eril snapped a long shard of bone out of the fowl carcass on the table between them, lounged back, and commenced picking his teeth. Watching, Ringil surprised himself with a sudden, forceful recollection of Egar doing much the same thing, and—equally surprising, equally abrupt—he felt his eyes moisten.

. . . the fuck? He hadn't thought about the Dragonbane in months.

He blinked down the moisture in his eyes. *This fucking flu.*

Eril took the bone shard out of his mouth, pointed pensively at his companion with it. "And if they send to Trelayne? Confirm the price on your head and get sketches posted around town?"

Ringil shook his head, tried wearily to keep his thoughts together. "Going to take a while, even if they do. Use a bonded courier there and back, it's still the best part of a week. A lot more if they let it run through normal channels. Meantime, they've got a few other, more pressing concerns."

His companion frowned. "Such as?"

"Such as trying to keep the murder of an imperial legate quiet. Right now, I guarantee you, they're shitting milk and sugared biscuits up at the Keep. They need all the time and quiet they can buy just to work out how they handle the Tlanmar garrison commander when he finally comes calling. This is a frontier town. They've got a lot to lose if that boils down badly."

"No one mentioned the legate down there in the square, huh?"

"No one. Like it never happened."

Eril grunted. He was a career criminal; he understood the dynamic. Ringil poured them both more wine.

"Yeah, like that. And there's something else." He set down the flagon, picked up his goblet, and studied its contents without much enthusiasm. Hinerion, as Shend had been fond of whinging, wasn't exactly famed for its viticulture. "These guys have got the best part of a thousand captured slaves milling around now with no apparent owner. That's a lot of quick cash for the city if they can parcel it out before anyone gets down here from Trelayne to claim ownership."

"Oho."

"Yeah. My best guess? Sometime in the next couple of days, you're going to see an open auction for city coffers. And I doubt very much they'll be sending any bonded couriers to Trelayne until that's done."

"Gives us some time, huh?"

"Yeah." Ringil sipped his wine. Grimaced and put it down again. "Gives us some time. So—you see anything good in the harbor?"

The Marsh Brotherhood enforcer gestured with his bone shard at the cheap glass panes of the window they sat beside. The snug was on the ground floor of the inn, and it was full dark outside by now; but even through the grubby, distorted glass and the lanternlit gloom beyond, you could make out gathered thickets of mast-tops over the roofs of the intervening houses.

"There's a caravel flying marsh daisy pennants tied up at the south dock. Couldn't make out the name from here, even with the spyglass, but she doesn't look familiar." A shrug. "No reason she should. Half the merchantmen out of Trelayne fly those pennants now, just to scare off pirates."

"But they've got to be paying dues, right?"

"Dues, yeah." Eril pulled a sour face. "But that doesn't have to mean much of anything anymore. When I was coming up in the city, you knew the name and rig of every keel flying the daisy, and you knew the crew on those ships would be solid Brotherhood to a man. These days . . ." Another shrug. He stabbed at the fowl carcass with his bone shard, left it sticking there. "These days, it's like every other fucking thing. Comes down to haggling."

Ringil tried to muster some enthusiasm. Eating seemed to have pushed back his fever a little, and the marsh daisy vessel had the gossamer feel of luck come calling. Dark Lady Firfirdar, seated on her iron throne, blowing the ghost seed off her fingers and into their path, so it danced and lit their way.

"Well, look," he said reasonably, holding off a deep, rolling urge to shiver. "At a minimum she's out of Trelayne, and going back there at some point. Now with that, and maybe some haggling like you say, or just a judicious bit of leaning on the captain—I'd say we're nearly home dry."

Eril nodded. "Lean on him's right. I'll fucking—"

Quick rapping at the snug door. Both men stiffened and swung to face the sound. Eril's hand slipped under his coat without fuss. Ringil loosened his sleeve where the dragon-tooth dagger was stowed.

"Yes?"

The door opened a crack. The boy who'd served them earlier stuck his head and one scrawny shoulder around the jamb.

"My lord Laraninthal?" Stumbling over the Tethanne syllables, nervousness taut in the hurried tones. His face was pale and sweaty in the lamplight. A cool combat tension soaked into Ringil's limbs, settled there.

"Yes?"

"Uh . . . Somebody here to see you, sir. It's uh . . ." The boy swallowed, licked his lips. "They're soldiers, my lord."

CHAPTER 14

He found the pawnshop easily enough—there were several on that stretch of the An-Monal road, but only a couple offered rooms above. Counting the time spent to climb one of the staircases in the dizzying Kiriath architecture and then walk the Black Folk Span across, the whole search took him not much more than an hour.

The pawnbroker, a wiry old man with a patched eye, bought the line about family the same way the Lizard's Head publican had. He waved Egar through musty gloom and out again to the shop's backyard. Rickety outside stairs went up the wall above them to a row of doors under the eaves.

"Second room," he said wheezily. "Tell him I'll need him tonight."

Egar went up the stairs. Laid knuckles on sun-bleached wood a couple of times.

"Fuck do you want?" someone bellowed, in bad Tethanne.

Sounds like a hangover in there. Egar grinned and called back through the door in Majak.

"Is that any way to talk to a brother?"

Sudden quiet. He thought he heard the creak of someone moving off a cot. Sensed the weapon lifted stealthily from its resting place against the wall.

"Harath? Let's not get off on the wrong foot here, son."

The voice behind the door came back, matching Egar's change of tongue.

"What do you want, *brother*?"

Youthful sneer and an Ishlinak twang on it, blunted somewhat by time away from the steppes. And the thick, unmistakable smolder of mistrust. Egar chose his words carefully.

"Could take a while to explain that. How 'bout I buy you some belly lining and a pint?"

"That fuck Alnarh send you? He wants me dead, he should have the balls to come down here and do the work himself."

"No one sent me. I got some questions I'd like to ask you, is all. About the fight down at the Lizard's Head."

Footfalls across the boards inside. Egar judged the other man was still a good three feet back from the door, and probably off to one side. It was the same basic precaution he would have taken himself. If the door got smashed suddenly inward, you'd want the space.

"I'm not a big fan of the Citadel myself, see. Thought maybe you could help me out."

Silence. A floorboard creaked. Harath cleared his throat.

"I didn't get your name, brother."

"Egar. Of the Skaranak. They call me the Dragonbane."

Coughed laughter. "Yeah, *right.*"

"Look." A spurt of genuine anger licked through him. "You going to open this fucking door or what?"

A final quiet, but the tone of it had changed, and Egar knew he was getting in. He waited. A bolt slatted back. The bleached wood paneling swung inward a grudging handbreadth and a young Majak face glowered out from around the jamb. Wispy beard, long unkempt hair across the bloodshot eyes. Harath of the Ishlinak stared blearily at the Dragonbane for a couple of seconds, but seemed not to see a threat.

"Anyone tells you I started that fight, they're a fucking liar."

Egar nodded. "Why I came to ask your side. Want to let me in?"

The younger man shrugged gracelessly and shoved the door wide. Backed up a couple of paces and held out both arms like a seller displaying his wares—or a man as he submits to being frisked by the City Guard.

"Sure. Mind your head."

The room behind the door was hot and cramped, jammed under the eaves as it was. Stoop height only except in the very center. Harath filled the space simply by virtue of standing up in it—he was a big lad, still slim with youth but built in the shoulders and thighs from a lifetime of horsemanship and staff lance practice. Behind him, Egar saw a low cot under a tiny window, stained and tangled sheets, a threadbare cloth curtain that did little more than strain the sunlight blasting into the room. A chamber pot sat in one corner, but the bearish reek of the room was general.

"Share hearth and heart's truth, break bread and sup under a shared sky." The ritual disarming welcome phrases didn't really work once you got down off the steppe and into a city, but Harath mumbled through them nonetheless. "The warmth of my fire is yours."

"As grateful kin, I take my place."

"Yeah, well . . ." Harath showed the skinning knife he'd been holding at his back. Made an apologetic gesture with it. He stuffed the blade into the sheath on his belt and stood there yawning—slept-in shirt and breeches, hair a tangled mess even by Majak standards. Night-before breath that Egar could smell on the yawn from a yard away. "Can't be too careful, you know. Can't even trust the brothers in this fucking place. And I don't mean Majak across the board, guys like you—cuz that's always been a bit iffy, right? I'm talking my own fucking Ishlinak blood-bond kin here."

Egar pulled a face he hoped was sympathetic. Mostly, he was trying not to breathe too much of Harath's secondhand air.

"Hard to believe, something like that. Yeah."

"Believe it, old-timer." Harath wandered back to the cot and sat down hard enough to make the timbers crack. "This fucking city. Gets its teeth into you, you know. Sometimes wish I'd never set eyes on the place. Fucking Alnarh, I knew him back in Ishlin-ichan. Knew his kin out on the steppe. Sure, he was a bit of a mouthy prick, even then, but you could always trust him in a scrap. Trust him to get a brother's back."

"I hear he's a convert now," Egar hazarded. "What's that about?"

"Yeah, it's fucked up." Harath scratched at his belly through the shirt. "I mean, we all did it, the cash was too good to turn down. No conversion, no commission, so we figure what the fuck, it's only like marrying some Voronak tart or something; you got to make libations to all their pointy-faced little ice gods, else you're never going to hear the end of it from her family, right? Same thing here. There's this number you do, offering up your blade to that book they've got. Bunch of reciting, some incense, and you're in."

"So what went wrong?"

"Fuck knows. We had this squabble a few months back over a slave girl. Waggle-arsed little package from up in the League, you know what they're like, right?"

Egar nodded absently—lurid images of Ishgrim dancing behind his eyes.

The Ishlinak mustered a weary grin. "Had udders on her like you wouldn't believe, brother. And when I jumped her, well, Alnarh took that hard. He's a jealous fuck at the best of times. But, nah . . ." Harath sank fists in his own hair, dragged the heels of his hands down his face. Shook his head. "He was acting weird way before that. It's like he was buying into the Revelation for real. When he talked about it, he got this look in his eye. Starts telling us to stop using Dweller names around him when we curse. Some shit about offending the angels. I mean, come on. I expected the others to call him on it, couple of them are way closer kin than I can lay claim to, I think Larg's a full cousin or something. But they just let it go. And then when Menkarak comes calling, it's a whole—"

"Menkarak?" A moment too late, the words already out of his mouth, Egar realized the way he'd jumped. "Pashla Menkarak, you talking about?"

"That's right." Harath looked up. "Listen, Skaranak, don't take this the wrong way, but what the fuck's your interest here?"

"Ahh, the usual." Trying belatedly for mercenary nonchalance. "Took blade pay from a court noble and now she's into it with the Citadel. Fine as far as that goes, but then I hear they've been hiring brothers, and that's new. Never figured I might end up fighting my own kind when I took the purse."

Harath shrugged morosely. "Coin is coin."

"Yeah—speaking of which, the old guy downstairs told me to tell you he needs you tonight. If that makes sense."

A grimace. "Sense enough."

"He got you strong-arming for him?"

"Debt collection." Harath yawned and gestured. "This fucking city. Got to cover the rent somehow, you know how it is."

"Been there once or twice when I was your age, yeah."

"Not going to pretend I like it much." The young Ishlinak picked up the chamber pot and peered into it, grimaced again and put it down. "Thumping some poor kid about to get money back he borrowed to buy a ring or impress his friends. Or—like last week—some war widow trying to feed her kids when they just doubled the rice tax. Lot of the time, I'll just stand there behind the old fuck with my arms folded. With the widows, that's usually enough. They don't have the money, they'll take him behind the curtain, or get the daughter to do it. He's good like that, most times he'll let it slide, you know. But fuck, man, if I'd known back in Ishlin-ichan I was going to be making my bread like this . . . "

"Coin is coin," Egar reminded him.

"Yeah, well it's a pretty small fistful. By the time he writes off the rent, lucky if I'm eating two squares a day." Harath's face changed, seemed abruptly younger. "You really a Dragonbane like you said?"

"Yeah. I am."

"Takes some balls, huh?"

"And some luck." Egar chopped down the subject. "You didn't think about going up the hill, then? Sign up for Demlarashan, get some coin that way?"

Harath stared at him. "I did two tours down there last year. That was enough for me. Fucking shit-hole. You ever been?"

"In the war, yeah." Egar shrugged. "Different then."

"Well, I wouldn't know about that. But I'll tell you something for nothing, Dragonbane—they're all fucking nuts down there now. I reckon it's the heat."

Egar remembered the heat, like some solid bronze idol of a fat man he had to carry around everywhere, seated weightily on his shoulders, fat burnished thighs wrapping around his neck, pressing down on his chest. The steppes in summer could be sweltering—but it was nothing compared with Demlarashan heat. And Harath was right, the locals were mostly barking mad. He didn't blame the Ishlinak. He wouldn't go back himself if he could possibly avoid it.

Not even to look at the bones of that fucking dragon.

"Tell you," the young Ishlinak muttered. "Demlarashan, it's a waste of fucking time. The Empire's never going to rein them in, doesn't matter how many men they spend. Those guys got nothing better to do down there than string each other up over spelling mistakes in the fucking Revelation. Might as well give it up now and go home. I mean, it's not like there's anything down there worth having anyway. It really is a shit-hole. Nothing grows, you're lucky if you can keep goats. So let them keep their goats and their fucking rock temples and gibberish texts and acres of fucking sand. Who gives a shit?"

Egar looked around for somewhere to sit down, but there was only the cot. The room was growing oppressive.

"Well, next time I'm up at court, I'll be sure and pass on your strategic advice."

Harath shot him a hungry look. "You really gigging for a noble, huh?"

"Yep. Like I said."

"Good purse, yeah?"

Egar nodded. "Very good. You want to get some lunch?"

THEY FOUND A TAVERN IN A STEEP BACKSTREET WITH VIEWS OUT ACROSS the Span and the estuary. Harath apparently knew it from his high-rolling days before Menkarak fired him. They took a table out on the balcony. Ordered some hair-of-dog to blunt the edge of the Ishlinak's hangover.

"Wasn't him personally, mind you." Harath, surfacing from the suds of his ale. "They got Alnarh to tell me. Which he did with a big fucking grin on his face, the cunt. Said if I couldn't *comport myself like a man of faith,* I had no business standing guard over Citadel property. Like *he* wouldn't have jumped that bitch if she'd given him half a look."

"So it was about this girl then?"

Harath stared off across the water. "Oh, I guess. Like I said, Alnarh was acting twitchy well before that, but yeah, that seemed to send him over the edge. Fucking nuts, it's not like he couldn't have had his pick from the others."

"The others?"

"Sure, they're keeping a whole gaggle of them up there. Some boys, too, if that's your thing."

Egar frowned. "Up there? At the Citadel?"

"No, man—Afa'marag." Harath jerked a thumb over his shoulder, upriver. "The old horse stringer's temple, up by the locks. Menkarak had it opened up again in the spring. Creepy fucking place. You didn't know that?"

"No. And what are they doing up at Afa'marag? Aside from corralling slaves?"

"Fuck knows. I never bothered getting that close, they were paying me well enough just to keep an eye on the gate and take food into the slave pen. Alnarh and Larg volunteered for sanctum duty, arse-licking around Menkarak as usual." The young Ishlinak shook his head. "Way too much purifying prayer and memorizing bollocks in it for me. Who needs that shit?"

The food came. Harath plunged in. Egar watched him eat, picked at his own plate for appearances. Mostly, he was thinking it through. Shuffling Harath's grumblings together with what he already knew from Archeth's briefing the previous year, and Imrana's court gossip since. Trying to assemble it all into a hand you could bet something on.

Invigilator Pashla Menkarak—son of Grand Invigilator Envar Menkarak, and a big noise now in his own right, it seemed. A loud voice among the new crop of humorless asshole invigilators they were apparently cultivating up at the Citadel these days. *Renowned writer of clerical opinions and interpreter of holy text*—Imrana read that one out to him from a court communiqué she had secondhand a couple of months back. She reckoned he'd once been a pretty canny political animal, but now he was openly critical of the Empire's failure to properly consolidate conquests of infidel territory in the north after the war. The King's Reach suspected direct links with the Demlarashan tendency, but it seemed they couldn't prove it yet, and with the way things were between palace and Citadel right now, that kept Menkarak safe.

Archeth had gone head-to-head with the fucker last year at court, and the Emperor backed her play. Teetering moments when it looked like the tensions between palace and Citadel might crack wide open. But cooler heads from the Citadel forced an apology, and Menkarak skulked off into the tall grass. There'd been no further direct clashes, but behind every shot the Citadel had taken at intimidation since, Archeth reckoned you could count Menkarak's hand, or the hand of invigilators who shared his dickhead views.

Whatever the little turd was doing upriver would bear a look.

"You reckon you could get me in?" he asked.

Harath looked up over a laden fork. "In where? Afa'marag? Doubt it. Alnarh told the others not to have anything to do with me after I got thrown out."

"Yeah, I wasn't really thinking about going in the front door."

"Ohh." A slow nod. The Ishlinak shoveled the forkful of food in and grinned through it as he chewed. "All right, I got you. Yeah, that's doable. Place is ancient, it's falling apart. Got a whole stack of places you could break in with not much more than a bent pin. Show you that if you like, sure."

"What about coming in with me?"

Harath hesitated. Swallowed his food and sat back. "What is this, Skaranak? What you want to get in there for? Come on, really. Man, if you're looking for some cheap League pussy, I can take you to a couple of—"

"It's not about the girls." Hurriedly. "The boys, either. Like I said, this Menkarak's on the other side of a blade gig from me, and I'm just looking for an edge. All I want to do is get in there, poke around for a bit, see what I find. Get out again without making any noise."

"I don't want to get in a fight with any of these guys. Not with steel."

"We won't."

" 'Cause they used to be my friends, right? Wasn't for Alnarh, they probably still would be. All that shit down at the Lizard's Head? That only kicked off because I bought Elkret a drink and Alnarh told him to pour it away. Fucking prick."

Egar sat forward. "Son, look at me. We won't get in a fight with your friends. We won't get in a fight with anyone. We get in, we have a look around, maybe ask a couple of questions to some of these slaves, then we get out. Do it right, no one has to even know we were there. But I need you to show me the way in, and I need you to watch my back for me while I'm inside. You do that, I'll see your rent covered for the rest of the month, and top you up fifty elementals in cash into the bargain. Save you having to go out on widow-battering duty for a while."

Harath settled back to his meal again. Shrugged. Chuckled as he broke bread. "Okay, man, what am I going to say to that? You got me. Coin is coin."

"Coin is coin," Egar agreed. "And I'm going to throw in another twenty when we're done. You want to know what that's for?"

"Sure." Throwaway gesture—the younger man's attention didn't come up off his plate. "Hit me with it."

"That's to keep your mouth shut. No drinking down the Lizard's Head, yarning about how you broke into a Citadel temple with a Dragonbane for company."

A noncommittal grunt. "Does sound like a good yarn, that. Worth a few beers."

"Hey." Egar snapped his fingers under Harath's nose. Got him eye-to-eye. "You listen to what I'm telling you, Ishlinak. Twenty. On top. Mouth shut. I'll want your blood oath on that."

"Okay, Dragonbane, *okay*. Relax. I'm just fucking with you. Blood oath, you got it."

"Good."

Egar sat back, looked out at the Black Folk Span and the river while the other man ate. Across the city, the day was tipping over, noon heat spilling down toward afternoon. He watched the traffic threading across the Span's ebony thoroughfares, wagons, riders, the plodding majority on foot. Some troops, sun glinting off their helmets and mail. A slave coffle, dust plastered, stumbling into town and journey's end.

He caught the loose thread of the thought. Looked across the table at Harath.

"This slave girl. You reckon she knows anything?"

The Ishlinak grinned down at his food, still chewing. "Knew plenty, brother. Couple of tricks she had, telling you, man . . . "

He shook his head in bemused delight.

"Like that, huh?"

"Like that." Harath swallowed and reached for bread. Leaned across the table and gestured with the chunk he'd torn off. "Look, I got to reckon the last couple of years, I've had more pussy than a clanmaster's eldest sees in a lifetime. I must have seen the inside of nearly every brothel the Empire has, from Dhashara to Demlarashan. But that's still got to be one of the best fucks I ever had."

It was common enough talk—Urann knew he'd done enough like it when he was Harath's age. But just on the off chance . . .

"She ask you for anything in return?"

The other Majak laughed. "Sure, man—what do you think? Get her out of there. What else is a slave going to ask you for?"

"So what happened to her?"

Harath, slopping up gravy with the torn chunk of bread, shrugged and didn't look up. Shook his head as he chewed.

"Dunno, never saw her again. Why?"

CHAPTER 15

Ringil met Eril's eyes across the table. Their swords were up in their rooms with the cloaks and baggage. He kept his voice soft and nonchalant.

"Soldiers, eh."

Eril made a show of lounging back in his chair. "So what do they want, lad? Is it the Watch?"

The boy shook his head, licked his lips again.

"No, my lords. They are irregulars."

There was a pleading quality to his expression as he looked at his two customers. Not so long since the war swept through here. Hinerion's walls had held well enough against the Scaled Folk, but the border skirmishing that followed between imperial and League forces was brutal on the inhabitants. Standard tavernkeeper's wisdom for the whole region: Forget uniforms or nominal allegiances—if it wears a weapon and scars, it's no safer than the next starving wild dog. Feed and water with care, walk like you're carrying dragon eggs, and never, *never* get between rival packs.

"All right," said Ringil, rising. "We'll come out and talk to them. Nothing to worry about."

But he had a moment—allowed himself the self-pitying luxury of it as he got up from the table—to wonder if Dakovash hadn't taken demonic offense at his earlier insolence and set him up, whispered the plan to come to Hinerion into his head and let him believe it his own, all so that he could be caught like a rat and dragged down to the dungeons and a death by screaming inches.

He shivered.

This fucking flu.

Outside, through the candle gloom and smoky air in the main bar, he made out half a dozen bulky figures ranged about the place. The unmistakable, rigid jut of weaponry from their silhouettes, at hip and over shoulder, the instinctive space the tavern's other clientele accorded them. One or two were idly bullying the customers and serving girls. Smacked lips and slurping sounds as the crockery-laden women tried to squeeze past, the inevitable pawing hands, stoically endured. At one table, a thickset axman leaned low over the board, getting in the diners' faces with a mock-friendly grin and the kind of intrusive commentary that demanded either weakly smiling capitulation or offense taken and a fight.

Ringil went by and jolted him heavily with one hip, jarred the man's leaning arms so he slipped mid-sentence on the table edge and nearly fell.

"Oi!"

It was more yelp than bellow, outrage beaten upward in pitch by surprise. But the axman came back from his stumble with a scary fighter's grace, pivoted and grabbed Ringil by the arm, dragged him back around.

"Fuck do you thi—"

And his voice died out from under him as Ringil met his eyes.

They were close enough for the reek of the man's breath to plaster Gil's face like something solid, to feel that it was congealing and smearing there. Ringil said nothing, just looked at him.

It felt, for one flickering moment, as if there were black wings at his back.

The axman broke. Dropped his eyes, dropped his hand from Ringil's arm. Turned away.

"Wanna look where you're fucking going, man," he muttered.

"Same might be said for you, Venj." The voice was a good-natured rumble that Ringil recognized. "Thought you said you were a skirmish ranger in the war. Don't they teach all-around awareness at all times, or some such shit?"

It was the shaven-headed bounty hunter from the office. He loomed up at the axman's side, one cautionary arm out loosely across his comrade's chest, a gesture that looked restraining and protective in about equal measures. He was taller than Ringil had realized when they talked before. He grinned with the assurance of a man used to dominating whatever room he was in.

"How you doing, Shenshenath?"

"I am. Well."

"Klithren. From the bounty offices."

Ringil got a firmer grip on his fake Yhelteth accent. "Yes, I remember. You have come looking for me?"

"Yeah, how about that?" The bounty hunter tugged at his mutilated ear. "See, some of us got sick of waiting for the Keep to put up its list. Going to ride out at dawn, see if we can't flush this bandit scum out of the forest and worry about the names later. Wondered if you wanted in."

Ringil grappled with his fever-blurred wits. "Me?"

"Yeah, well, I pride myself on being a judge of men with steel. And you're like me, you've held a command. Got the rank, the experience. Man like that, be glad to have you ride with us."

"Uh." Ringil glanced across at Eril. The Marsh Brotherhood enforcer shrugged.

"Your pal here's welcome along of course," Klithren said quickly. "I didn't know you were mobbed up. Thought you'd come in alone. Seemed like a man alone, you know. But this fella looks like he can handle himself. You'd be welcome to ride with us too, pal."

Eril inclined his head. Ringil said nothing. Klithren looked from one to the other.

The silence stretched.

"So, uhm, look." Briskly. "I figure an even split with the boys here, your man included, plus you and me take a captain's tithe on whatever total we bring in. Sound about right?"

Ringil made an effort, brought a hand to his chin, rubbed at his stubble as if giving the offer weighty consideration. He held it for as long as he dared, head tilting dizzily with the thought of riding out at dawn in hard pursuit of himself.

"Yes," he managed. "Yes, that. That would be acceptable. The rates. Good. And you say at dawn?"

"Yeah. Going out the Dappled Gate. You know how to get there?"

"Yes, I . . . the Dappled Gate. Of course." *Stop fucking* mumbling, *Gil. Get a grip.* "On the eastern wall. Yes."

"So you're in?"

Ringil pulled himself somewhat together. "I will be there, yes."

"Good." The bounty hunter looked triumphantly around at his men. "Told you, didn't I? The imperial knows a paying opportunity when he sees one. Here, give me your hand on it, Shenshenath."

Ringil took the clasp, gripped the leathery swordsman's palm in his own, forced pressure into his fingers and a smile. Klithren squeezed back, only about half as hard as a war hound's bite.

"See, now *that's* what I'm talking about." Once more, he seemed to be addressing his companions rather than Ringil. "That old Alliance magic, just like back in the war. No stopping us now, eh?"

Some halfhearted assent from the other men. The axman glowered and didn't join in. Klithren evidently didn't care. He turned Ringil's pulped hand loose and waved a dismissive arm.

"Ah, ignore them, they're a bunch of fucking pussies. I've been at them over two hours not to just sit on their arses down there waiting for the city to loosen its purse strings like it's some virgin taking off her shift. If we'd acted this way when the Scaled Folk came, there wouldn't be a city still standing on this coast."

"Hoy." The axman's glare shifted focus to Klithren. "I fucking stood with *my* city. I was on the walls of Trelayne when the lizards came, and I threw them back into the ocean. And I was part of the levy sent down to clean up the mess here before that, when you border rats couldn't hold the line. So don't come the superior fucking warrior with me."

Klithren cocked his head. A slow, comfortable grin lit his features.

The axman saw it, but it took a couple of moments for him to catch up. He was in a Hinerion tavern, after all; his comrades were—it appeared from their scowls—mostly from Hinerion. The border rats comment had not gone down well.

"Venj," Klithren said fondly. "You are a grumpy old fuck. And if you weren't such a dab hand with that ax of yours, I would probably have to kill you. We all know you married a *border rat's* daughter, so why don't you just get over the fact you don't live in *the capital* anymore, and let's leave Shenshenath here to get some sleep. Dawn'll be 'round soon enough for all of us."

It was masterfully done. The tension leaked out of the room, grins leaked in. A guffaw came from way back in the tavern gloom.

"Oh, the pain of exile," jeered someone, none too quietly.

Muzzy from his fever, Ringil jerked a hot-eyed glance toward the voice before he realized it was not meant for him. He caught a flurry of motion at one table; much looking away or hiding of faces in goblets. Ringil detached his gaze carefully again, found himself looking instead into Venj's mutinous face. The axman stared at him for a couple of moments, then snorted and turned to Klithren.

"Are we done here? Can we *please* get out of this shit-hole now?"

Klithren shrugged. "Sure. Got what we came for, didn't we? See you in the morning, Shenshenath. Dappled Gate, right?"

Ringil nodded. "Look for me there at dawn."

The bounty hunters left. They went in grimly assured quiet, watched fearfully and equally silently by the tavern's clientele. They shouldered their way out through the standing customers, knocked back the main door so it clunked hard into the wall, and ducked out under the lintel, here and there a man pulling his back-slung weaponry down to stop it snagging.

Ringil and Eril watched them go.

"Got this knack for making friends, don't you?" the Marsh Brotherhood enforcer said, deadpan.

Ringil peeled him a sour look. The door swung shut on the final broad-shouldered back, and chatter sprouted across the quiet like weeds.

"So," said Eril. "The harbor?"

"The harbor."

THE SKIPPER OF THE *MARSH QUEEN'S FAVOR* POURED THEM RUM FROM A scuffed leather flask and did his best to seem pleased. But he was not a gifted actor.

"Of course, for any Brother of the Bloom in need . . . "

He gestured vaguely, as if he hoped something in the cabin around them would sufficiently underline his loyalty to the marsh daisy pennants he flew. Following the gesture around, Ringil saw no likely candidate for the task. It was a pretty squalid space they sat in, cramped and rot-smelling, and fairly indicative of what they'd seen of the vessel as a whole so far.

"Good," said Eril bluntly. He drained his shot glass and put it back on the table. "I'm glad to hear that. So what we'll need from you is cabin space for the duration, somewhere as far away from prying eyes as possible. And a dawn departure."

The skipper blinked. "Dawn?"

"Yes. You told us your cargo's already stowed."

"Well, yes, the *cargo.*" The skipper made a visible effort to regain his shipboard authority. "But I do have other passengers to consider as well."

Eril leaned forward. "Are you trying to tell me there's no cabin for us?"

"No, no, far from it, brother. We have four cabins disposable aboard the *Queen;* it would be my honor to guest you in, uh . . . "

"Two of them," prompted Ringil.

The skipper swallowed. "Yes. Two. But one other cabin is nonetheless occupied by a, uh, a lady of the realm, and she does not expect to join us until late tomorrow morning."

Eril sat back. "A lady of the realm, eh?"

He swapped a glance with Ringil. Ringil shrugged, sniffed at his shot of rum and put it carefully aside untouched.

"I'll go," he said.

A little later, trudging up from the harbor with a brace of the *Marsh Queen*'s huskier crewmen at his back for porters, he thought maybe he should have drained his cup after all, the same way Eril had. Rough as the liquor was, the shock of it in his throat and belly might have gone some way to anchoring him a little more firmly to the cobbled street underfoot and its attendant reality. Might have stopped this queasy sense of *seepage*. As it was, he was now dealing with the uneasy sensation that the whole nighttime substance of Hinerion could at any moment shrivel away around him, like so much poorly painted morality-play backdrop canvas tossed onto an end-of-season bonfire; and when that happened, it would leave him drifting alone in a muggy, gray-tinged void with no way back.

It's the fever, he told himself patiently. *Not like you haven't had one before. Few more days, some sea air to clean your head out, you'll be sharp-edged and smoking as a harbor-end whore on krin.*

Krinzanz. His hand crept automatically to the pocket it was stowed in. *Now, there's an idea.*

But it wasn't really. He'd debated long and hard with himself whether or not to use some of his dwindling supply to beat out the symptoms of whatever he'd caught from the sneezing slave boy. In the end, an iron campaign frugality won out. He was down to his last thumb-sized twist of the krin, and there was no telling when he'd next be able to buy some more. Hugging the coast and allowing for favorable winds, *Marsh Queen's Favor* might make harbor at Baldaran in a couple of days, but then Baldaran was an odd town, full of neatly maintained temples and pious little fucks in the magistrature. There'd been a public order ban in force on *noxious substances* the last time Ringil was there.

After Baldaran, it was Rajal, almost twice the distance again, and a searing, sand-and-spat-blood combat memory for every yard of shore-line once they got there. He wasn't sure he'd be going ashore at Rajal if he could avoid it.

And after that, well . . .

After that . . .

Decision time, Gil.

The street took a bend to the right, and above cheerily lit windows the hanging sign outside the Hero's Respite Inn came into view—some suspiciously clean-looking knight at restful ease on a carpet of lizard corpses. Lettering above his head in gilt-edged red. So it seemed the skipper was competent to chart a course, on land at least. *Seven streets up, the crooked lane to the left and follow the torches until the bend with the temple on the right. The inn stands at the corner opposite. Room Eleven. Ask for the Lady Quilien of Gris.*

So far, right on the money.

Ringil checked to see his husky escort were still with him—in fact they'd been dawdling so as not to get ahead of the man who'd given them coin—and realized abruptly just how slow he'd been, climbing the shallow incline of the streets up from the harbor. He nodded curtly at the men, and stood still in the street to catch his breath. The moment tilted alarmingly beneath him. His vision webbed across in gray at the edges; he felt sick and empty.

He covered for it with a measured stare across to the ornate statue-work on the temple's façade—Hoiran's customary tusked and fanged ferocity pared down here to something a little more urbane and close-mouthed, perhaps influenced by traffic with the south and its penchant for studiously human religious figures. But for the massively muscled shoulders and an alarming, overly well-toothed grin, the Hoiran depicted here could almost have been a Yhelteth holy man, hands raised in benediction. At his flanks, the other members of the Dark Court ranged out in bas-relief like some hard-bitten mercenary command whose services the Dark King was trying to offer you. They were equally toned-down of aspect but still possessed most of the weapons and items of iconic power accorded them in more northerly tradition. Oddly, there seemed to be a gap in their ranks on Hoiran's left. Ringil was too jangled to focus and work out who wasn't there.

In the dim guttering of the street torches, he thought the figure of Dakovash tipped its head a fraction and winked at him.

Did not.

He leveled his breathing, snapped a glance over his shoulder, and caught his escort watching him curiously. They averted their gazes as soon as he looked around, found something apparently fascinating instead about the brightly lit windows of the Hero's Respite. From the interior of the inn, a suddenly audible wash of laughter. It sounded harmless enough. Ringil looked from one man to the other, cleared his throat, and turned his back on the darkened temple.

"Let's get on with this," he muttered sourly. "Shall we?"

He stalked up to the door of the inn and thumped it open. Stood on the threshold. A startling waft of chatter and the tangled aromas of roasting meat and coffee washed out to meet him. Warm yellow light escaped through his legs like a cat, spilled out onto the cobbled street behind. Ringil stood and peered inside like some visitor from another, chillier world.

Under bright lamps and hanging candelabras, a crowd of rosy-cheeked, well-dressed diners sat at cloth-covered tables, eating with the leisurely self-assurance of men and women who had never gone hungry. Staff in cheery scarlet livery waited on the tables, and more somberly uniformed hired muscle stood around near the bar, riot batons looped casually on their belts. The floor was freshened with sawdust, not straw, and *stringed music,* for Hoiran's sake, lilted from a screened dais at the far end of the room.

Ringil saw faces glance up unhurriedly from their platters as he came in, register his arrival, and then go back to dining with as little concern. Small smiles and shrugs, a disinterested comment back and forth. If the sword on his back was noticed, it excited none of the anxiety Ringil had seen in the other tavern when Klithren and his men came calling. In fact, at one table a satin-clad young woman turned and eyed him with open and rather predatory interest, before her friends' chorus of shocked mirth and expostulation brought her back around to face her food.

Ringil let a thin smile flicker across his face in response. He crossed to the bar.

"I'm looking for the Lady Quilien of Gris? I understand she's lodged here."

The bartender wiped a cloth across the bar-top. He surveyed Ringil and his companions, shot a sidelong glance at the closest of the hired muscle. He sucked at his teeth. "Is she expecting you?"

"No. But if she still plans to take passage on the *Marsh Queen's Favor* tomorrow morning, she'll need to see me." Ringil nodded upward to the stairs and landing over the bar. "Room Eleven, isn't it?"

The bartender put down his cloth.

"Wait here," he said. He moved down the bar and leaned over to mutter in the ear of one of the uniformed men. The man looked at Ringil, clearly wasn't much impressed by what he saw, but shrugged and pushed off the bar, then made his way to the stairs and up. His footfalls clomped overhead on the landing gallery, then faded. Ringil waited and watched the diners. The bold woman in satin sent him a couple more arch glances and whispered to her friends. He looked about idly for some male attention in the same vein, but could not find it.

"Get you something while you're waiting?"

Ringil was about to say no, then recalled his abandoned glass aboard the *Marsh Queen's Favor* and the ensuing regret through the climbing streets, the tilting gray vagueness that would not leave him alone. The sense that he was not anchored enough in things outside his own feverish head.

Yeah, like getting drunk is going to help that.

Fuck it. Battlefield tonic, right? He remembered Flaradnam after the battle at Rajal Beach. Iron hip flask raised, seamed black face grim and gashed with something you couldn't really call a smile. *Kill or cure, Gil.*

"Rum," he said, and indicated his porters. "For them, too."

The bartender raised an eyebrow at that, but he set up the glasses and poured accordingly. Ringil tossed a couple of coins onto the bar-top, glanced up at the sound of clomping footfalls on the landing overhead. The uniformed muscle, coming back downstairs with a bemused expression on his beefy face.

"You can go right up." He apparently couldn't believe it.

Ringil grunted as if he expected no less. He knocked back his rum—this one wasn't bad—and upended the empty glass on the bar.

"Stay here," he told his escort.

Upstairs, the landing gallery cornered right, into a narrow passageway with doors on either side and small candelabras in the ceiling every ten feet or so. The receding dimensions of the passage seemed to sway very slightly in the guttering light the candles gave, as if the inn were a ship that had already put to sea. Ringil resisted the temptation to put bracing hands against the walls as he walked.

The door to Room Eleven was ajar.

He stopped dead when he saw it. Something black and whisper-edged ghosting up through the layers of flu and alcohol, right hand flexing at his side, left reaching across to loosen the sleeve he kept the dragon knife in. The corridor was far too narrow for the Ravensfriend to be useful—any fighting done here would be close and sweat-palm desperate.

Just what you need right now.

Ringil eased closer to the far wall to get an angle of vision on the cracked door. Silence battened down in the corridor, stuffed itself into his ears like black water. He watched with fatalistic calm as the gap between door and jamb thickened, as the door hinged slowly and soundlessly back on itself and opened the room beyond to view.

A dog stood in the gap, looking steadily up at him. Pricked ears and slanted amber eyes in the gloom. Long gray muzzle, and a ruff at its throat as thick and glossy as one of his mother's winter mufflers.

Dog? That's a fucking wolf, *Gil.*

Ringil stared back into the amber eyes. Had he been less fuddled with fever, he might have reached for the *ikinri 'ska,* the words and gestures he'd used against the dogs at the river, the marsh dweller lore learned from—

—*Hjel,* leapt into his head, *tight-limbed, hot-eyed young scavenger prince in rags, who seems, despite evasive conversational maneuvers to the contrary, to somehow already know you as he tilts wine from a leather skin, catches your eye in that way you recognize, invites you to stay and admits yes, he's heard of Trel-a-lahayne all right, his forebears were its rulers, but it's a dead legend now, man, fallen to an unknown evil out of the south a thousand years ago—and then he leads you to tumbled white ruins on the marsh to prove his point—*

The Gray Places were full of that shit, full of the wreckage of what you thought you knew about the world, full of people and places that could or should not be, and aching absences where what you expected was suddenly *not.* But with time you learned, you handled the ache, you let the current carry you, and you took what it offered you along the way; you lay down, for example, beneath damp marsh dweller canvas like some childhood fantasy of escape, lay down with hot-eyed scavenger princes who smelled faintly of wet earth and wood smoke, and owned all manner of useful tricks of sorcery with plants and animals.

And when you woke, some uncounted series of days and nights later, and your companion was gone with his tent and wagon and the rest of his grubby clan, and the Gray Places as often had faded with them, burned back to the hard-varnished texture of whatever portion of the real world you'd washed up in with your dreams—then, still, the scents of your fucking lingered on your flesh, and the *ikinri 'ska,* in your own reality no more than myth and marsh dweller superstition, was harsh in your head, and real as a blade . . .

The wolf, or dog, perhaps bored with all this, twitched an ear at him and turned its long gray head away. It yawned, exposing slick white fangs as if for inspection, closed up its muzzle again with a hollow snap, and walked away from him, back into the room. Ringil, beginning to suspect that the rum had been a bad idea after all, went after the animal, one wary step at a time.

At the back of the room was a section for washing and dressing, screened off by an opened iron concertina frame hung with thick muslin curtains. The dog crossed to the leading edge of the screen, peered in, and then seemed to leap up onto some high platform behind the drapes. A poorly defined shadow moved across the muslin, and a woman's voice drifted languidly out to him.

"You wished to see me?"

Ringil cleared his throat. "I've come from the *Marsh Queen's Favor*. Our departure has been brought forward."

"Really?" A sudden edge on the urbane tones now. "And there I was, given to understand we need not depart until I chose to present myself aboard tomorrow morning. Your captain is a fickle man when his purse is filled."

"He is not my captain."

"But fickle nonetheless."

"Possibly so, my lady. I really wouldn't know." Some ghost of court-bred manners past struggling to assert itself as he spoke. It was a part of himself he took out from time to time, like some age-worn keepsake of youth, and was always surprised to find how much he missed it. "But though it grieve me to carry the message, I am very much afraid that your ladyship will need to present herself aboard before dawn, or the ship will sail without you. I have brought men to ease the transport of your effects."

A slight pause.

"Well. They send me a knight errant. And I have, I suppose, been less than courtly with you."

Motion across the muslin again. The Lady Quilien of Gris stepped out from behind the screen and paced toward him, toweling riotous dark hair dry with one hand as she came. Apart from the scarlet flannel towel she was using, she was completely naked. She offered her free hand in a—

Naked?

She'd done it with such aplomb, such utter lack of care or self-consciousness, that it took him those first few paces and the outstretched hand before he realized the fact. He supposed that a man with more conventional appetites might have spotted it faster—youthful breasts, belly, thighs, all on open display—but even there, he wondered how many such men would be prepared for the complete lack of acknowledgment this creature offered for her state of undress. Ringil had known his share of successful sluts, numerous of them among the nobility, and there were quite a few he remembered who'd have no problem pulling a trick like this if it were for the right visitor to their rooms. But in all of those women, at the heart of all their artifice and display, there was always the arch stare, the tilted head, the intimate signal that this was a game of stakes. They deployed their bodies and their availability exactly the way you'd deploy a regiment across a battlefield, with every bit as much ceremony and command.

This woman was not deploying herself.

The Lady Quilien of Gris wore her pale and shapely body as if it were some cheap garment she'd borrowed from a friend and just that moment thrown on.

"You wished to see me," she said simply. "Now you do."

"I, uh . . . " Ringil took the offered hand and pressed it to his lips, something mechanical to do while he got his head together. The Lady Quilien of Gris was clearly insane. "Thank you, my lady. But might I suggest that you are not as, uhm, open, when my porters come to collect your luggage."

"Oh, I won't need *them*." Quilien took back her hand, brought it to her face. It seemed, for a moment, she was about to sniff or lick at her knuckles, but then she suddenly remembered herself and dropped her arm to her side instead. "I travel very light, you see."

She was still holding the red flannel towel to her head in her other hand, as if to stanch the flow of blood from some recently acquired scalp wound. She smiled brilliantly at him from under the cloth and the damp mass of her hair, but there was something vacant in the way she did it, as if smiling were something she'd only recently learned to do. She tipped her head, but it was a jerky, inelegant motion, and he heard her neck click as she did it. In the uncertain light, he had the sudden sensation that the color of towel might indeed be blood-soak, and the off-key gestures the sign of a brain damaged by some brutal blow to the skull. The wide, empty smile stayed and stayed. Saliva gleamed on the points of the teeth. Her eyes seemed to stare through him at something else.

Ringil felt a brief quiver of something, made it for pity, and fell back on his original verdict—here was some touched-in-the-head scion of a rural House too embarrassed to keep her at home or consign her to one of the newfangled asylums pioneered in Parashal since the war. A House wealthy enough to pay instead for an endless round of pilgrimages to shrines of reputed healing somewhere far from Gris.

Wherever that was.

"Are you quite sure that—"

"You are very kind, nameless knight. But I assure you that anything I need for travel will be in my cabin when I arrive."

So perhaps she had porters of her own. Or imagined she had. Or—

Whatever. Feeling increasingly like a man in the wrong place, Ringil contented himself with a courteous nod.

"At dawn," he reminded her.

"Yes. At dawn." Almost absently—her interest in him seemed to have abruptly waned. She was looking past his shoulder and slightly downward. "And now, since I see there are men waiting for you, perhaps you should go to them. It was nice meeting you."

Her arm was out again, hand held up, but oddly, as if it were something she thought might belong to him rather than her. When he took the hand and raised it to his lips, she looked at him with blank surprise, as if she'd had no idea her limb had moved from her side.

Ringil fixed on a courtier's smile, let go of the arm, and made a bow. Got himself hurriedly back out of the room and into the passageway. Surprised to find the breath tight in his throat.

It wasn't that madness bothered him much anymore—Hoiran knew he'd seen enough of it during the war to become accustomed.

And in the Gray Places, it was practically the key to survival.

But somewhere, elsewhere, in whichever rural backwater shit-hole it counted itself lord over, Quilien of Gris's family ate and drank and slept without her under their roof, knowing she was tipped out into the world and groping about with her scrambled sense of self to make whatever poor tapestry of day-to-day living she could. They knew that, and they had let it happen, and they lived with it daily in complicit, well-heeled tranquility. Perhaps they spoke of her sometimes, in strained and distracted tones, their oceanic complacency driven back every so often by storms to reveal the reefs of memory and care. Or perhaps, on some patriarch's orders, they did not name her at all except in whispers.

In any case, they had abandoned her; had counted it their best strategy.

At least she's got the dog.

Funny, he'd forgotten all about the dog.

CHAPTER 16

His Imperial Radiance Jhiral Khimran II was executing traitors in the Chamber of Confidences when they got back.

Archeth had Anasharal brought up to the palace anyway. She'd known the Emperor since he was a child, had watched his ascension to the throne—apparently with a few less illusions than the rest of the court, because she seemed to be the only one not shocked when the purges started—and she knew he was going to demand to see the Helmsman as soon as he heard about it.

He might even put the executions on hold.

So she went, unenthusiastically, along the sculpted marble corridors in the Salak wing of the palace. Went deeper and deeper, toward the screaming, while krinzanz need scraped at her nerves like knives. The smooth-walled architecture gleamed and curved and swept, palely voluptuous around her, mostly tones of muted jade and amber, but veined through in places with stark copper or black, and studded at intervals with conquest pieces—artwork and sculpture dragged here from every corner of the Empire and jammed into alcoves or nailed onto walls that didn't really suit the purpose.

And the shrieks and pleas for mercy echoed off the polished stone, chased one another down the corridors, ambushed her around corners, like the ghosts of the conquered dead, somehow trapped in the marble heart of the imperium that had vanquished them.

THE SALAK STONEMASONS AND ARCHITECTS WHO BUILT THE CHAMBER of Confidences—so the story went—committed quiet suicide when they learned what had been done with their work. Archeth was a child at the time, and would never know for sure. As she grew up she suspected a more pragmatic truth behind the tale: that his Imperial Radiance Sabal Khimran I had had the craftsmen murdered to ensure they never spilled what they knew about the various architectural tricks and secrets they'd so lovingly created.

Certainly had it in him, the evil-eyed old fuck.

Sabal the Conqueror, first of the Khimrans to really deserve the term *Emperor.* He'd died before she hit her teens, putting down some rebellion or other out on the fringes of the eastern desert. But she still remembered how he'd lifted her up as a small child, the secret look on his hawkish face, as if she were some incredibly precious vase he entertained notions of smashing apart on the floor, one swift and brutal stroke, while no one was looking.

She'd asked her father about that, many years later, when grief at her mother's death trawled the memory to the surface. But Flaradnam was deep in grieving of his own and disinclined to discuss Sabal, or indeed anything much else, beyond bitter monosyllables. *He would not have dared,* was about all she could extract. *He needed us—they all did back then—as they still do now. Whole fucking dynasty leans on us like a crutch. And Sabal knew I would have ripped his motherfucking mortal heart out if he'd harmed a hair on your head.*

Flaradnam lived through his grief and eventually put it aside—or at least learned to ignore it for extended periods—but they never really discussed Sabal again. The early excesses of Empire seemed to be bound inextricably in his mind with Nantara's death, and he skirted them in conversation as soon as they arose. And then, there was that *whole fucking dynasty* angle to worry about—Archeth was old enough now to be admitted to the Council of Captains, to take on her own role in the subtle steering of Yhelteth affairs that served the Kiriath for a mission, or a means to other ends, or maybe just a hobby. There was, her father told her repeatedly, important work to be done.

So forget Sabal the Conqueror, because his son was on the throne now—Jhiral I, a diffident, gentle boy Archeth had grown up playing tag with through the gardens and corridors of An-Monal and the palace in Yhelteth—and the succession was far from assured. Flaradnam and Grashgal spent quite a lot of the next few decades quashing usurpers, safeguarding borders and laws, hammering and tempering the newly minted Empire into something resembling a permanent tool of policy for the region.

And after Jhiral, there was Sabal II, seemingly a solid reincarnation of his grandfather's brutality and cunning and military prowess. At An-Monal, they all breathed a collective sigh of relief, and stood back to give him sword-room.

And then Akal the Great, perhaps the best of them so far.

And now Jhiral II. Hers to handle alone, for her sins. She sometimes wondered—she was wondering now—why she fucking bothered.

But old habits die hard.

She cleared a final twist in the milky, veined stone corridor—the shrieking hit her full in the face, she did her best not to flinch—and went under the heavy marble cowl of the entry arch, out onto the Honor promontory.

The execution party didn't pick up on her arrival at once—all attention was focused inward on the business of the day, and anyway with the noise the condemned were making, she could probably have ridden in on a warhorse in full armor and still not have been noticed. She counted about twenty men in all—executioners and apprentices in the somber gray and plum of their guild, a couple of robed judges, there to see sentence carried out, and then a scattering of whichever strong-stomached nobles felt they needed to curry a bit of imperial favor right now.

The Chamber of Confidences.

Under other circumstances, it was a radiant, beautifully rendered space. The Honor promontory was one of three blunt marble tongues—Honor, Sacrifice, Courage, the old Yhelteth horse-tribe trinity—extending at regularly spaced intervals from the otherwise circular walled circumference of a closed ornamental pool fifty yards across. Sunlight fell in through cunningly angled vents in the high dome of the ceiling—the marble blazed and shone where it took the rays directly. Elsewhere, reflection off the water put cool, rippling patterns of light and shade on the walls. A tented raft of rare woods and silks was ordinarily anchored in the center of the pool, a private retreat for the Emperor you could reach only by poled coracle, because you certainly wouldn't survive the swim.

But the raft was currently moored tight to the Sacrifice promontory, well out of the way. *Well, you wouldn't want to get blood on that silk. Take forever to get the stains out.* And four of the convicted traitors—three men and a woman—were already afloat, shoved out a safe distance from the promontory on their execution boards and drifting farther away.

Archeth tried not to look at what was happening to them.

She focused on Jhiral's back, the sumptuous imperial ocher and black of his cloak among the clustering matte palette of the executioners' garb. She held down a shudder—swore she'd never again try to quit the krin cold.

"My lord."

Hopeless—the shrieking drowned her out. The fifth man was thrashing and flailing as they dragged him to the manacles on the last remaining board. She thought, with a sudden freezing through her veins, that she might know him. Though beneath the marks of lash and heated irons, the distorting terror in the features, it was hard to tell for sure.

She cleared her throat—something seemed to be sticking in it—and tried again, louder.

"My lord!"

He turned. Heavy silken sweep of the cloak across the marble flooring, handsome features a little clouded, brow furrowed like a man struggling with accountancy he had no real taste for. His voice carried effortlessly. He was used to this.

"Ah, Archeth, there you are. They said you were on your way. But—as you'll see—I'm a little busy right now."

"Yes, sire. I see that."

The last execution board was an old one, gray wood swollen and split from repeated immersions, manacle screw plates spotted with lichen-orange rust. The board looked, she thought, not for the first time, like a generous wedge cut from some huge mold-coated cheese. Broad at the top end so the victim's head stayed a good couple of feet above the waterline, tapering to a narrow end at the bottom so tortured and manacled feet would lie submerged, leaking slow tendrils of blood into the water.

The pool dwellers were smart—Mahmal Shanta swore he'd once seen them using lure tactics to entice seal pups off beaches in the Hanliahg Scatter—and they knew well enough the sound of the underwater gongs lowered into the pool when there was to be an execution. They'd have squeezed in through the submarine vents in the base of the chamber that morning, would have been waiting below the surface ever since.

They'd be ravenous by the time the first board hit the water.

And then she could no longer beat the perverse urge, she could not keep her eyes away. Her gaze slid out to the water, to the four boards already floating there with their dreadful, shrieking, red-slippery writhing cargo.

In the wild, a Hanliahg black octopus would have wrapped tentacles around surface prey this large and dragged it deep, where it could be drowned and dealt with at leisure. Defeated by the bobbing wood and the manacles, the creatures settled for swarming the boards, tearing at the chained bodies with frenzied, suckered force, biting awkwardly with their beaks. So skin came off wholesale, gobbets and chunks of flesh came with it, finally down to the bone. Blood vessels tore—in the case of a lucky few, fatally. And occasionally, a victim might smother to death with tentacles or body mass across the face. But for most, it was a long, slow death by haphazard flaying and flensing. None of the creatures was bigger than a court-bred hound—they could not otherwise have squeezed in through the chamber's vents—and even their combined efforts were rarely enough to make a merciful end of things.

Jhiral was watching her.

She forced herself not to look away—the spray of blood, the

up-and-down flail of tentacles like thick black whips, the soft, mobbing purple-black shapes hanging off the wood and flesh, crawling across it. Her gaze snagged on a wild, wide-open human eye and a screaming mouth, briefly blocked by a thick crawling tentacle, then uncovered again to shriek to shriek, to *shriek* . . .

She turned to meet Jhiral's gaze. Locked herself to the casual poise it took to do it. *Slowly, Archidi, slowly.* Held his eyes, held the moment like a knife blade, loose for the throw. Warrior trick—funnel the noises away, to the edges of your attention, like the pain from minor wounds when the battle demands you gather yourself.

Jhiral gestured impatiently.

"So?"

"We have found a new Helmsman, my lord. It talks of threats to the city, to the Empire."

"A *new* Helmsman?" Jhiral's brows kicked up. "A *new* one?"

"Just so, my lord."

Jhiral glanced back at the last condemned man, the frantic scrab-blings he made against his captors as, finally, they managed to get him to the board. The Emperor seemed to be pondering something. Then he looked back at her again.

"Archeth—you would not by any chance be trying to avert punishment for your old pal Sanagh here, would you?"

So.

The bloodied, screaming features—the memory popped into place like a brutally relocated shoulder joint. Bentan Sanagh. They'd hacked his hair off in the dungeons, of course, and he was haggard with suffer-ing. And anyway, *pal* was not really accurate—she knew Sanagh only casually, through Mahmal Shanta and the shipwright's guild. A loud-mouthed idealist, quite brilliant in his way, which was probably what had kept him alive during Akal's reign, but he'd always lacked Shanta's instinct for self-preservation. Archeth had liked him well enough, shared some conversations, a banquet party or two. But she judged him doomed from way back, and kept her distance accordingly.

"Because Prophet knows," Jhiral went on with a long-suffering sigh, "his good lady wife's been writing to every worthy at court he ever shared a bribe with, trying to get his sentence commuted. We're all up to our ears in tearstained parchment. I imagine you're on the list as well, somewhere."

She was not. Perhaps her own habitual standoffishness had been noted. *Doesn't pay to get attached to humans,* her father told her bitterly, drunkenly, one night a few months after her mother died, *they only fucking die on you.* Or perhaps it was her black skin and her eyes and her volcanic origins.

Or maybe you missed the letter, Archidi. Maybe you were fucked up on krinzanz or brooding out at An-Monal or hiding in the desert.

"I was not aware of Bentan Sanagh's conviction, my lord," she said evenly.

"No?" Jhiral stared at her, she thought, almost resentfully. "No?"

"No, my lord."

Shrieking. *Shrieking.* Abruptly, the Emperor of All Lands rolled his eyes.

"Oh, just *cut his fucking throat,*" he snapped.

The executioners froze. Exchanged glances. One of Sanagh's arms flailed almost free.

"My lord . . . ?" ventured one of the braver men.

"You heard me. Stop wasting my time trying to get him pinned and floated. Just slit his throat, I'll witness it and we can all go and do something less . . . noisy."

More glances. Helpless shrugs. Sanagh had frozen as well, fallen silent against the backdrop of his fellow convicts' screams. It was hard to tell what expression his features held.

"Well? Get on with it!"

"Yes, my lord!" The sergeant executioner snapped to attention. He cleared his mercy blade, came forward and knelt at Sanagh's head while the others held arms and legs down to the board. Archeth caught one last glance of the blood-streaked face, the unreadable eyes, and then the sergeant's solid arm blocked her view. She never saw the blade slice through Sanagh's flesh. But a gout of blood leapt out across the gray wood, and it splattered on the copper-veined marble almost at her feet.

Jhiral looked around at the assembled company and nodded.

"Good. Well done." Out across the water, the shrieking went on, bouncing crazily off the sculpted marble walls, filling the air, seeking the ears like swarms of stinging insects. Jhiral still had to pitch his voice above it. "That's it, then—we can all get out of here. Thank you, everybody, you are dismissed. Khernshal, have somebody clean up this mess, would you."

The named courtier bowed gravely. Jhiral was already turning away. "Well, then, Archeth. Let's go and have a look at this Helmsman of yours, shall we?"

"Yes, my lord. Thank you."

"Oh, don't mention it," said the Emperor of All Lands sourly. "The pleasure is entirely mine."

The shrieking followed them out.

ON ARCHETH'S INSTRUCTIONS, THEY'D PUT ANASHARAL IN THE QUEEN Consort Gardens. It was an extension to the upper levels of the palace that hadn't seen much use since Akal's beloved third wife died in childbirth eleven years ago—a quiet, largely forgotten space, dusty colonnades and wind-rattled palms, here and there a haunting white-stone statue in the Salak style. The interior sections felt shadowed and secret, like long-abandoned ruins, scarcely part of any built architecture at all. The paths through the foliage were unswept, littered with fallen leaves, shaded into patchwork gloom by the spread of the largest trees overhead. A good place for meetings you didn't want noticed. No one came here if they could help it—some said the veiled ghost of the queen consort could still be seen on certain nights, prowling the gardens with her stillborn child gauze-wrapped and bloody in her arms.

But at the far side of all this, the gardens opened out onto an area of sunstruck white-stone paving, and balustrades festooned with pink-flowering creeper. There were broad granite benches, more statues, and a long balcony view. From here, you could look out westward across the city and the blaze of sun on broad waters at the estuary mouth.

The Helmsman had been placed on a central bench under the balustrade of the middle balcony. A squad of Throne Eternal stood uncertainly at guard beside it. They stiffened up as soon as they saw who was coming. Their commander came forward.

"My lord, I—"

"Relax, Rakan, it's only us. No need to stand on ceremony."

"Yes, my lord." Noyal Rakan, wound overly tight these days, it seemed to Archeth, wearing his recent promotion to his brother's rank like a helm and uniform cut a little too large. She felt sporadically sorry for the kid. He wasn't long out of his teens; his grief was still fresh and boyish. But he'd served in the Emperor's personal guard for the last seven years, and regimental custom for the Throne Eternal was clear, running a tight line back to horse-tribe family tradition.

"So this is our new metal friend, hmm?" Jhiral walked a circle around the Helmsman, looked it over with sidelong curiosity. "Doesn't *look* like much, I have to say."

"*Do not despise the beggar, grizzled and crippled at the corner,*" Anash-aral quoted tartly. "*For who can tell what households or kingdoms he may once have called his own. Life is a long dream whose end we cannot see, and he is perhaps but a premonition, a lucky warning you may yet take.*"

"Oh, it knows scripture, too." An imperial shrug. "But then they all seem to, don't they? Well, Helmsman—I'm told you have a warning for me?"

"It isn't for you personally, Jhiral Khimran. It is for your people."

A long silence. Rakan and the other Throne Eternal looked elaborately elsewhere. Archeth clamped down on a creeping grin.

"Then I'll be sure and pass it along," said Jhiral with an abrupt edge in his voice. "Now perhaps you'd care to give me the specifics?"

"And *warning's* really not quite the word either. You'd be better to see it as a tactical opportunity. The chance to get in ahead of your opposition."

"Are you talking about the League?"

"No, I am not. I'm talking about something that's going to make your border disputes with the League look like the pathetic schoolyard squabbles they always were. I'm talking about a darkness out of legend, a storm in the making, a long-buried nightmare brought to waking. I am talking about the end of your Empire, Jhiral Khimran.

"So you'd better sit down and listen to me."

CHAPTER 17

Downstairs in the bar, he bought the two crewmen another drink and then told them to head back to the ship. There would be no heavy lifting. Neither of them looked too unhappy about it. They drained their glasses, wiped their mouths, and slipped away with laconic sailor nods. Ringil let his own drink stand, leaned an elbow on the bar, and tried to get the room to stop its sporadic blurring in and out of focus around him. For a while, he watched the well-fed diners and tried to work up a modicum of dislike for them, but his heart was not in it. Mostly, he just wanted to lie down and sleep.

Yeah, well. Arse in the saddle then, Gil.

He propped himself up off the bar—it seemed harder to do than you'd expect for so simple a motion—paid for the drinks, and navigated his way to the door. Got himself out into the street, stood in the fitful torchlight for a while. Across the way on the temple façade, Hoiran grinned at him toothily. Ringil peeled him a sour return sneer, breathed in hard, and shook his head like a wet dog shedding water. The street tipped and teetered downward in response, inviting a fall. Ringil kept his balance with an effort, waited until everything settled again, and then started down the sloping cobbles, one jolting, jelly-legged pace at a time.

Get to the harbor. Get aboard the *Marsh Queen's Favor.*

By now, Eril would have been back to the tavern they were lodged at, would have seen to the selling of the horses, for whatever price could be had at such short notice and time of night. And by the time the sun came up and they were missed at the Dappled Gate, *Marsh Queen's Favor* would be standing well out to sea, beyond pursuit and the need for any more fugitive planning.

A cabin, a bunk, departure at dawn while he slept.

It was like a beacon, pulling at him.

"Ringil *Eskiath*!"

He lurched around. Realized too late the trap the name implied.

Stupid, stupid, stupid *fucking . . .*

"Well, well, well." Venj the axman, there on the corner of a cross-street alley, teeth bared in a savage grin. Bulky figures at his back, half a dozen or more. "Thought that was a dodgy fucking Yhelteth accent, if ever I heard one. Thought I knew the face from somewhere."

The war, the war, the fucking war. Was he ever going to run out of people who knew his face from some blood-soaked skirmish or other?

"Look," he fumbled.

"Look nothing." Venj spat on the ground. "I got family in Trelayne still, I hear the stories. Ringil Eskiath turned black mage, turned on his own family. Price on his head, for loosing slaves and killing merchants. And now there's some northern swordsman sorcerer down here raiding slave caravans. Doesn't take a lot of brain to put that together."

"Lucky for you then," Ringil said faintly.

He thought it got a couple of guffaws from the men at Venj's back. Didn't think it would help much, come the crunch. He held himself upright, tried to look like some kind of credible threat.

"You sure you want to do this, skirmish ranger?"

Sudden flinch in the axman's eyes. "That was a long time ago."

"Wasn't it just. I can let this go, Venj, and so can you. Just walk away."

"Walk away." The axman's tone was light, mock-reasonable, as if he were seriously considering the idea. Ringil felt something plummet in his guts at the sound. "Yeah, we could do that, couldn't we, boys? Just walk away—from a *twenty-five-thousand florin reward*. Yeah, why not?"

"It's fifteen."

Venj grinned. "Either fucking way, it'll do us."

Growl of approval at his back like surf. No way out, then. Ringil flexed his right hand at his side. Reckoned angles, but groggily—hopelessly numb. Recall of the fight at Snarl's encampment only that morning, now faded like some impossible dream of speed and power, some old soldier's tale of a youth and glory that never was. He'd have to get the Ravensfriend drawn; the dragon dagger wouldn't cut it against men like these. Not this many, not this type. But they were in so fucking *close* . . .

Venj watched it all going through his head and nodded.

"So, you going to come quietly, or do we have to hamstring and drag you?"

Fuck that. Make them kill you.

But he knew they wouldn't have to. Not in his current state, not with these numbers. And with the promise of a reward that high, Venj's men would take whatever risks and gashes they needed to bring him down alive. They'd bracket him, they'd crowd him, and sooner or later—

He went for the Ravensfriend.

Fevered flash grab—as fast as he could make his body do it.

Knew instantly he'd fucked it up.

It was there in the fumbled grip he got on the pommel, the jagged, grudging tug as he tried to clear the blade. Weary—inelegant—the motions of a man who did not *want* to fight. Venj must have seen it all, spotted the move even as it bloomed. He leapt in with a yell, grabbing for Ringil's sword-arm before it could swing down. Ringil twisted awkwardly aside, lashed out with a boot and felt it connect. The axman yelped and went over, sprawling and tangled. He lay in a cursing heap on the cobbles as his men rushed in. Their weapons glinted in the gloom.

Ringil got the Ravensfriend around in a soggy arc, managed to block the first opposing blade of the night. Chime of steel, but he staggered from the impact. Turned it into a backward lurch, tried for some fighting space. No fucking chance—they pressed in on him like excited dogs.

He swept his blade low, trying to scare them back, but they were a hard-bitten crew and they just grinned, and skipped the feint, and surged back in. Ringil parried as best he could. Behind the mob, Venj was back on his feet, ax drawn, bawling encouragement.

Something steel got through, he never saw what or how—the flat of it clouted him across the left knee with numbing force. His leg buckled, he could not brace it up. The Ravensfriend wavered. He saw a face full of scars, leering. Hands grappled and grasped, someone got to his wrist and bore it up; someone else ducked in and punched him hard and fast—once! twice!—under the chest. He might have ridden the first one out, but the second dropped him to his knees like a slingshot buck. He swayed there a moment, had time to notice he'd lost the Ravensfriend, and then he keeled over on his side, breath creaking in his starved lungs. Someone kicked him in the head for good measure; someone else laughed and spat on the cobbles near his face. He heard Venj's voice again, distantly, berating them about something or other.

Do I look like a fucking slave to you?

No, that wasn't Venj. It was hollow and toneless, and it seemed to come out of the air right beside Ringil's ear. He twisted his head up. Saw nothing. But he thought the others had heard it, too, because the excited surf of their voices rolled suddenly back into quiet.

"The fuck . . . ?" said someone.

Do I look like a fucking slave to you?

Something moved in the gloom of the nearest side alley. Ringil, still struggling to breathe, could not get enough of an angle to see clearly.

"Oi!" Venj trod forward. Ringil got a worm's-eye view of his boots. "This ain't your fucking business, chum, so put that blade up, and clear off while you still can."

Do I look like a fucking slave to y—

"Stop fucking saying that!"

Better run, said another voice, from the other side of the street. Ringil felt a chill smoking off him as he heard the words, though in his fuddled state he could not work out why. *Better run.*

"Right, that's it," said Venj grimly. "You were fucking warned."

Out on the marsh, said a third voice, as cold and empty as the other two. *Salt in the wind.*

Footfalls, impossible to tell from where. The swish of a sword blade making passes in the night air. One of Venj's men jerked out a string of curses, but there was a waking terror in his voice. Ringil twisted his head frantically, trying to see something, anything. Thought he made out a solid black figure standing in the shadows to his left.

Fuck them all, said the third voice, and Ringil remembered, with a sudden, gut-deep jolt, where he'd heard those words before.

Venj roared. "Come on then, you motherfucking—"

Dark rush of motion. Something like a whirlwind, closing from three corners.

Wrenched screams. Venj's bellow, turned suddenly castrated.

And a hot, wet pattering through the air, like a rainy-season downpour back home in Trelayne. As it fell on his face and the cobbles around him, he realized vaguely that it was blood.

RINGIL CAME ROUND WITH THE STENCH OF SOMEONE'S VOIDED BOWELS clogging his throat. He coughed and turned over on the cobblestones, rolled up against the familiar bulk of a still-warm corpse. His knee throbbed painfully and, somewhere not far off, he heard the sea. For a couple of moments he was confused, tangled in old memories, thought he was still lying hidden among the slain at Rajal Beach. Panic-stricken, he froze the cough in his throat. His pulse pounded. If the Scaled Folk were still prowling the breakwaters, looking for survivors . . .

The leaning bulk of a corner building, the cobblestones under him. Faint glow of street torches. He blinked. Memory swam up to him in all its ugly glory.

No Scaled Folk anymore, Gil. We slaughtered them all, remember?

He heaved himself into a sitting position. The cough jumped him, would not be held down any longer. He gave in and let it rack his chest, had to prop himself up on the corpse until the spasms passed. When it finally stopped, there was a sour, acid taste in his throat. He hawked and spat, wiped his mouth and stared around.

Well, it wasn't Rajal Beach, right enough, but whoever had been at work here could have given the Scaled Folk lessons in savagery. Venj's followers were scattered across the slant of the street in butchered pieces and broad pools of blood. The corpse Ringil was leaning on lacked both legs below the knee and one arm. Others were worse. He spotted a body ripped in two somewhere below the rib cage, another reduced to chunks of meat no larger or better defined than you'd see on a butcher's slab. Venj himself sprawled back against a wall, throat torn out, staring down with sightless eyes at his own opened guts. His ax was still gripped firmly in both hands. Other weapons lay about for the taking, one or two with their owner's disembodied hands still clinging.

A faint odor of scorched flesh and metal hung over everything. The slave market stink of branding.

"Interesting," Ringil mumbled, mostly to keep from thinking too hard about what he'd seen of his saviors. He patted the corpse on its intact shoulder, leaned hard on it, and used the leverage to get back on his feet. "And very handy. I think—"

"Hoy!"

Klithren hung there at a panting halt—he'd come up the rise at a jog. Naked disbelief slapped across his face like cheap paint as he stared at the slaughter in front of him. He grabbed at the sword in his belt. For one drop-stomached moment, Ringil thought it was all over, that Klithren would kill him now before he could even find his sword, let alone put up a guard with it. He met the bounty hunter's gaze, felt himself shaking his head numbly.

No more, no more.

"Hoiran's fucking balls, Shenshenath. Who did this?"

"I uh, I—" Then, abruptly, he was tumbling forward and Klithren let go of his sword hilt and darted in just in time to catch him and hold him up. His boot heels dug and scrubbed about on the cobbles; he tried to get purchase, but his legs were like marsh grass stalks. The bounty hunter made a hushing noise.

"Hey, hey. Easy, Shenshenath, easy. I got you."

He lowered Ringil gently to the ground. Put hands on him, checking for wounds. Ringil pushed him away.

"I'm fine—just gashes. Got hit in the head with something."

The bounty hunter nodded, took back his hands with an oddly propitiatory gesture. He crouched there in front of Ringil, still taking in the carnage.

"You see who did this?"

"They jumped us. No time." Ringil felt another cough coming on, rolled with it, played it up for all it was worth. He nodded weakly to one side. "Out of that alley. Like fucking demons."

"But . . . " Klithren's brow furrowed. "Must have been a lot of them, right?"

"Didn't see. No time." He kept his voice faint, tightened up the Yhelteth accent. "Couldn't tell."

The bounty hunter stared around. As his eyes fell on Venj, Ringil thought his mouth grew clamped. Thought his eyes suddenly gleamed.

"He found you, then? Venj. He tell you what he wanted?"

Ringil felt a chilly caution settle over him. He shook his head, feeling his way by inches. "Found me, yeah, in a tavern up there. Never told me what it was about. Something important, he said, but they hit us before he could say."

"Well, where the fuck were you all going?"

Another groggy headshake—work the act. "Dunno. Back to the square, I think. Bounty office. He seemed . . . excited."

Klithren sat back on his haunches. "Just doesn't make any fucking sense. He left me a note at the boardinghouse. Gone back to see you at the tavern, something important, he said. Supposed to meet him there. I get there, he's gone to the *harbor*, left word for me to follow. I get to the harbor, no one fucking there, either, and some wharf rat drunk tells me he saw men head up the street this way. *Heard* the fight, but by the time I got up here . . ."

Ringil nodded. At night, the sound of steel clash and dying would carry half a mile at least. He started to get up, found his legs a little stronger this time.

"Over quicker than you can piss," he said truthfully. And then, with mental apologies to Egar, "Thought I saw staff lances. And howling. You hear it?"

"Steppe thugs?" Klithren looked doubtful. "You think? Looks savage enough, yeah, but I haven't heard of a Majak company in these parts since the war wrapped up. Haven't seen any about town, either."

"So maybe I imagined it. Got hit in the head, like I said." Ringil cast about for the Ravensfriend, found it in a pool of blood. He wiped it down as best he could with rags from one of the slaughtered men, slotted it clumsily back in the scabbard on his back. Checked his sleeve for the dragon knife, settled it a little looser. Looked up and down the street for witnesses.

"Ah fuck, Venj. Look at you."

Klithren had wandered over to stare at the axman's corpse. Ringil came up on his shoulder, got a reflexive, flinching glance from the other man, the skirmish habit of years, and then the bounty hunter went back to brooding on his fallen comrade. Neck bent forward, the nape offered. Ringil felt himself hesitate.

"You know him long?"

A shrug. "Four, five years. That's a long time in this business, right? Came down here from Trelayne after the war, chasing some piece of pussy he'd fallen for when he was in uniform." Klithren crouched to eye level with the dead man. Sighed and pressed his chin to his folded knuckles. "He was an arrogant little fuck sometimes. But you couldn't ask for a better man at your back in a scrap. Saved my life a couple of times for sure."

"Guess this means we're not heading out the Dappled Gate after all."

"Nah, that was scuppered to fuck anyway. Didn't you hear?" Klithren looked up at Ringil. "Thought you might have. Thought *he* might have, maybe that's how come all this rushing around . . . "

Ringil felt his pulse pick up slightly. "Heard what?"

"Word just came down from the Keep." The bounty hunter said it almost absently, like he couldn't care less. His eyes were fixed on Venj's wounds. "No one goes outside the city walls until further notice. They're saying some of the slaves on that caravan got hit yesterday had the plague."

THE WORLD OPENS UP AND SWALLOWS YOU DOWN.

This is not new. You've spent the last decade of your life, at least, wondering how it'll burn down in the end. Before that, of course, you were too young and alive to really believe in your own death, but the war took all that away.

The war gave you death as a daily commonplace, an immediate possibility behind every badly timed sword stroke or stumbling misstep you made. Death was there at your side in the screaming chaos of battle, cutting down comrades and enemies alike, occasionally turning your way, ready for the least slip or sign that you'd *really had enough of this shit* and wanted the easy out. Death came to you, pensive quiet and sated in the aftermath, smirking up at you from the rictus grin of the men who'd died hard, hanging about at your back in the waning cries and weeping of the wounded beyond repair. Death was your friend, your confessor, your intimate companion, and though the seduction might be lengthy and sly, you always knew he'd get you in the end.

Just not like this.

Klithren went down behind the blow from the dragon-tooth dagger without a sound. Ringil, stirring from the dimmed moment of the act, saw he had used the weapon's pommel and that though there was blood in the bounty hunter's hair Klithren would live to fight another day. Make sense of that if you could.

Harbor. Get to the fucking *harbor.*

Where the night had by now settled down to seeping bandlight and an illusory, seaward-yearning calm—faint, irregular slap of waves against the pilings, soft stutter and creak of mooring ropes as they stretched with the shift of their tethered vessels on the swell. A trio of quiet drunks huddled like cormorants atop a pile of trawl nets at one end of the quay, mumbling sea chanteys and passing a wine flask back and forth. Ringil went past them at a limping trot, got a tipsy salutation from one, hurriedly shushed by his more circumspect—or just more sober—companions. Farther along, in the puddle of shadow cast by the customhouse wall, he caught the grunts and glottal clicking sounds of some sailor getting a cheap blow job. He thought he saw a queue of figures waiting there in the gloom.

Eril was draped at the rail of the *Marsh Queen's Favor,* smoking a krinzanz twig. He straightened when he saw Ringil approaching, pitched the twig into the gap between ship and wharf, and came down the gangplank with a grin. Ringil raised a hand to keep him back. Shook his head.

"Better stay where you are."

Eril's smile dropped off his face. He glanced about the darkened wharf, seeking enemies.

"Trouble?" he asked quietly.

"You could say that." Ringil was fascinated to discover that what he felt most was an obscure embarrassment. "You'd better tell the captain to get his crew together and slip ropes. Time for a smuggler's exit."

"And our other passenger?"

"They're calling a plague quarantine on the city, Eril. You don't get out of here right now, they'll lock the whole harbor up and your ride out of here as well."

"*Plague?*" For perhaps the second time ever in their acquaintance, Ringil saw genuine fear in Eril's eyes.

"Yeah. Seems some of the slaves had it."

The Brotherhood enforcer made the connection. The fear in his expression shifted into something else.

"You . . ."

"Yeah. Looks like it."

Silence stretched between them like distance, as if the gangplank were already up and the *Marsh Queen's Favor* drifting from the shore. Ringil made himself grin, guessed it must look pretty awful. Eril cleared his throat.

"I had a great-uncle in Parashal, got it back in twenty-eight. They say he lived."

Ringil nodded. Everybody had an uncle somewhere who'd survived the plague in some other place or time. It was a bedside platitude, cheap comfort you could hand out like some threadbare blanket you weren't going to miss.

"Sure," he said. "It can be done."

In Majak lands, Egar had once told him, you could cheat the plague of its victim if the tribe could find—read, in the constant tribal ruck of the steppes, capture alive in battle—a suitable substitute to sacrifice in place of the original sufferer. Given a man or woman of comparable rank and blood, the hovering plague spirit would take the offered life instead and depart with it. The original sufferer didn't just recover, they came back stronger than they had ever been before. Often they would rise to become tribal leaders or shamans in their own right. Such recoveries apparently took place overnight—sometimes, if the shaman had the Dwellers' favor, before the planned sacrifice had even been carried through.

Nice trick if you can pull it.

"My debt . . . ," Eril began.

"Is hereby canceled. I asked you to help me throw a burning brand into Etterkal, and we did that pretty effectively. I'm all done murdering slavers for now."

The Brotherhood enforcer could not quite keep the relief from soaking into his features. He made an uncharacteristically awkward gesture.

"I, uh, I sold the horses."

"Good. Get anything halfway decent for them?"

Eril shook his head, overvehemently. "Got fucked in the arse. Barely three hundred apiece and that's including the tackle. Fucking landlord's going to double his money just by sleeping on it. Here."

He dug a purse out of his coat, took a half step forward on his way to hand it over, and then remembered. He stopped dead on the gangplank. Ringil nodded, lifted one open hand toward him.

" 'Sokay. I'm not too far gone to catch stuff."

Eril hesitated, then tossed the purse across the intervening gap. A good, hard throw, to make sure it cleared the edge of the wharf. The weight and impact stung in the cup of Ringil's palm.

The two of them stood there looking at each other.

"What will you do?" the enforcer asked him finally.

Ringil weighed the purse in his hand. "I don't know. Get drunk, maybe. Don't you worry about me, Eril. You need to turn around and put your foot in that captain's arse. Get some sail hoist while you still can."

He turned away then, because the temptation of the gangplank's sea-rotted edge where it rested on the wharf was getting a little too much to resist. *Marsh Queen's Favor* sat there, four feet out from the quay, and the urge to cross that symbolic gap to safety was like krinzanz craving. Give himself any longer, and he'd do it, he'd start trying to talk his way into coming aboard regardless, rationalize his way past the obvious fucking shape of this particular truth, tell the tawdry fucking lies to himself that everybody did, *Look, this isn't plague, it's just a bad cold, be over it in a couple of days with some sea air to clear your head, you'll* . . .

Like that.

He grimaced. You could already hear the pleading tone of it all.

He walked away.

Got about three paces before Eril called after him.

"Sire?"

He stopped. Blinked at the honorific. In the best part of eight months, he'd never heard Eril use it to anyone. He turned back.

"Yeah?"

"I, uh, wanted to say. All that shit they say about you? The corruptor-of-youth stuff, the queer thing. Just wanted to say. I always knew they were a bunch of lying fucks. Knew it wasn't true. You're no faggot." He swallowed. "Sire."

Ringil remembered the times he'd caught himself staring with something worse than longing at Eril's exposed arse and shanks when they bathed in rivers on the way south. The hollow ache that stalked behind the lust.

He found the smile once more. Put it on.

"You neither, Eril. You neither. We're true men, the both of us. Now get out of here while you can. Go home. Fare well."

He put the gangplank and the *Marsh Queen's Favor* at his back again, and this time he kept walking.

CHAPTER 18

When they got up close to the black looming mass of the lock gates, the boatman shipped oars and threw out the anchor. It made a soft, swallowing *plop* as it went down. The boat tugged about silently on the dark flow of the river; the anchor cord went taut and held them.

"That's it, gents. 'S as far as I go."

"You could get us a bit closer to the shore," Egar suggested.

The boatman shook his head. "More than my hull's worth. The Citadel posted guards around the temple on that side months ago. See the torches? They catch me at this time of night with you two muffled up like that, well . . . Folk are liable to draw conclusions, aren't they?"

He gave them an amiable grin to show he'd already drawn his own conclusions but hey, no hard feelings, we all got to make a living somehow.

"So," Harath hissed at him. "You saying we gotta fucking *swim* across there?"

"Well, if you really want to, I suppose you could, yes." The boatman jerked a thumb back over his shoulder. "But there's a ladder, back there on the lock gate. It's a bit of a jump, but you should make it all right."

Egar waited to see if Harath could make the leap—turned out he could, and with wiry, youthful poise now he'd shrugged off his hangover—then paid the boatman out.

"Couple of hours," he said. "If we're not here, then wait. It'll be worth your while."

"Understood, my lord." The man stowed the coin beneath his jerkin and leaned aside to let Egar get up the sharp end of the boat. "Have a profitable evening."

"Yeah, you, too."

He took the leap—it was awkward, the unaccustomed weight of the knotted rope he was carrying slung tight across his body putting him off. He missed the ladder with one hand. But the other found a grip and he hung on, harsh grunt with the effort, beat the barn-door pivot of his body to the side, and got his feet on a rung. He grabbed a couple of breaths—dank, pitch-smelling air—then went stealthily up to where Harath crouched atop the lock gate in his black burglar's garb and charcoal smear. The Ishlinak nodded minimally toward the shore.

"Four guys," he murmured. "Same as before. They do paired perimeter in turns, the other two hold the gate. That puts all the blind spots exactly where they always were. I told Alnarh about that, but he didn't want to hear it. He's all *We are Majak, no one will dare.* Twat."

Egar stared at the crenellated bulk of the temple, the scrubby, cleared ground it stood on, the flicker and gust of a night guard brazier out front and the two figures gathered to its flames. Forty yards, fifty at most. He watched the bright yellow dapple of torches go along the darkened walls on the left and around the corner to the front, two vague forms beneath. He checked his knives and hoped he wouldn't have to use them. Killing other Majak wasn't something he'd ever really gotten used to—even if they were Ishlinak.

"Right then, you call it. Let's go."

They skulked along the top of the lock gate like rats, quick, purposeful spurts, cautious of balance on the foot-and-a-half width. Egar's pulse picked up with the nighttime slide of it all. He caught himself grinning. The torches paused partway along the riverward façade of the temple block, and Harath locked to a sudden halt in front of him. Ten feet to the ground, no time to do it and not be seen or heard. They crouched, waiting.

"Soon as the other two start moving," the Ishlinak warned him. "They'll be nattering back and forth, all four of them, like chucking-out time down at the Lizard's Head. No eyes to the left side at all. There—see that bush at the corner they've just passed? King's thorn—can't see a thing through it, even during the day. Sprint for it, hold there."

The torches reached the gate. The two new arrivals became clear silhouettes in the brazier's flare. Faint bass of voices, some laughter—indistinct echo off the temple walls and floating out over the water. The rhythm of it was Majak. Some jiggling with the torches, and then—

"Now!" snapped Harath. "Go!"

Off the lock, dark, sudden drop, soft crunch of impact on the ground below, spring up out of it running. Forty yards—*easy ground, Dragonbane, come on.* Behind him, he heard the swift brush of Harath's footfalls, following. The torches wavered away along the wall to the right of the gate. Darkness held the left side. Egar reached the king's thorn scraggle and crunched himself down into cover, trying not to breathe too hard. Harath piled in behind him.

The float of voices stopped.

Taut silence.

Harath put his lips to Egar's ear. "They spot us?"

Egar shook his head minimally, raised a warning finger. *No idea—shut the fuck up.* Eyes slitted against the gloom and glare for detail. Hand to knife hilt at his waist.

Soft mutter of another voice. The figures around the brazier shifted. A long laugh drifted out. Egar relaxed, eased his hand off his knife. Harath got back into a poised crouch.

"Along the left wall," he whispered. "Follow my lead, look for that crack."

And off again, like ghosts into the gloom. They hit the shadowed edge of the wall, scuttled along its darkened length. Ahead of him, Harath found the crack, reached up and swung effortlessly off the ground. Little fucker was good. Egar was only seconds behind him, but by the time he arrived the younger man was already eight feet up the wall above him.

That envy, Dragonbane?

He shook it off, checked the crack with his hands. Snaking jaggedly upward, a clean shear through the stonework, about four fingers wide, once-ragged edges worn smooth with time. It was pretty much what you'd expect from a building this old. There were fractures like it all over the city, anywhere a structure still stood that had been around back when the Drowned Daughters of Hanliahg vented their volcanic spleen and the Earth shook and the sky over Yhelteth turned black. *Not what you'd call comfy* was Harath's considered opinion. *Nowhere to rest, but you can hand-jam if you need to . . .*

Torch glow at the far end of the wall.

Egar hooked both hands into the crack, jammed his feet in below, made a braced sideways V with his body, and hauled himself up the crack. Sharp pinch of the stonework against his toes—the soft-sole boots he'd worn for the occasion were thin, and he had to angle his feet downward almost vertically to fit the confines of the crack. The torches rounded the corner and the two watchmen came ambling along the wall in companionable quiet. Apparently they'd run out of banter. And he was still less than ten feet off the ground. If either of them took the trouble to glance upward . . .

He worked his way higher, as close to silently as he could. Finger-width chunks of the fractured stone gave a little under his grip, made a tiny grating sound. *Shit, shit . . .* Sweating palms, powdering stone under the pads of his fingertips. He hurried his hold past the loose section—the haste undid him, one foot slipped out of the crack and he hinged around and out.

Fuck!

He forced one hand fully into the crack, closed it up into a fist, and twisted it sideways. The ragged stone bit into his flesh as the hand-jam took his weight. He hung there, teeth gritted, twelve feet off the ground, and tried to quiet his breathing as the guards walked by underneath.

Which they did. Right on by.

He let them get a decent distance beyond before he moved. Then, working as swiftly as he could without noise, he worked his loose foot back into the crack, loosened off the hand-jam into a more conventional hold, and climbed the rest of the wall without incident. He came over the crenellated top and found Harath seated with his back to the battlement, as relaxed as if he'd come up here to get some sun.

He sank down next to the younger man, breathing hard. Harath glanced sideways at him.

"All right?"

Egar held up his fist in the bandlight and spotted the tiny black trickle of blood. He licked it away, sucked the ragged edges of the torn flesh clean.

"Fine."

"They see you?"

"Yeah, they saw me. They said they'd give us an hour inside as long as we didn't break anything. You going to show me this fucking hole in the roof, or what?"

THE INSIDE OF THE TEMPLE HAD A MUSTY, STONE-DUST SMELL THAT reminded Egar of rock tombs he'd ransacked in Dhashara as a younger man. He kept expecting caskets, raised stone biers, or mummified remains racked in the walls. Instead, the spaces were broad and high and empty. Detritus crunched underfoot, but it was the leavings of decades without occupancy—stone and plaster powder fallen from the cracked ceilings, rat turds and grit and the tiny dried corpses of spiders. Somewhere, he could hear the sporadic drip of water falling in from the roof or some damaged cistern in the upper levels. There were a lot of holes up there like the one they roped in through; damage done by the same eruption that had cracked the walls. You could look up as you passed beneath and see the stars in the gaps.

Old, denied gods held up the ceilings.

"Remind you of anybody?" Harath whispered, nodding at one looming figure.

Egar glanced up at the muscled torso, the shoulder weighed down with horse tackle, the short, squared-off blade in the upraised hand, barely a knife at all. The tight-lipped, somber warrior face and beard.

"Yeah, Urann—without the teeth."

"Should think himself lucky he's got any face at all. They tore up some of the others in here so bad, you can hardly tell who they were meant to be."

Egar nodded, mostly to himself. It was pretty much the way of things, wherever the imperial writ ran. The Revelation didn't like competition.

They slipped past under the empty stone gaze of the statue. Harath gestured left—shallow stone steps, leading up. They took them two at a time, knives drawn for anyone they might happen to meet at the top.

Nothing. Shadows and dust. Tall, wood-paneled doors twice the height of a man, riddled with dry rot, wedged ajar on the gritty, detritus-strewn floor.

"This opens onto a gallery over the central hall," Harath told him when they got there. "Gallery runs right around. Get a good view from up there."

Egar nodded. He gripped one of the doors at its edge, decided moving it would make too much noise, and inserted himself sideways in the existing gap.

"Deep breath," said Harath judiciously.

It took rather more than that. The effort of holding his belly tight made Egar's eyes water, and he still scraped himself on the door edge, scraped the door open a farther grating inch, before he popped out the other side. He stood statue-still, teeth gritted, blade in hand, waiting to see if they'd been heard.

Harath came sveltely through after him.

The gallery was, as promised, a grand affair, sweeping round the hall fifteen feet up, broad and balustraded. Bandlight seeped in through tall windows long ago boarded up. Egar crept up to the balustrade in a crouch and peered through. Below him, he saw an expanse of the same derelict, debris-speckled stone flooring as in the previous chamber. Some remnant altar up at one end, looked like it hadn't seen use in a century, couple of squat statues standing around elsewhere, a few long wooden benches and . . .

He frowned. His gaze went back to one of the figures. He saw now there were five of them, four in a rough ring, the fifth more or less central . . .

Like something he'd once—

Height of a small woman or a child. Crude stonework, the facial features barely picked out. Stubby arms outspread as if for balance. Like mannequins for arrow practice, but dark and unyielding and dumped to floor height.

The memory cascaded—filtering soil of familiarity, and then the big rocks of recall, falling in his head.

Harsh gray light.

Some kind of beacon for the dwenda. Archeth, the morning following the skirmish, one boot on the tumbled figure lying facedown in the swamp. She was kicking at the thing with her heel, some monotonous residual anger working itself out. The wound across her temple was cleaned and livid in the thin morning light. *The marsh dwellers made them, way back when. Forms a link, somehow. Something to do with the kind of stone they used.*

He nudged Harath. "Where'd those come from?"

"Where'd what c—" The Ishlinak saw where he was pointing. "Oh. Beats me. They only had two last time I was in here. Pretty cheap shit by the look of it. Worse carving than the Voronak, and that's saying something."

"It's glirsht," Egar said absently. "Naom stone. They've got them set out like . . . that's got to be . . . compass points, right?"

The younger man shrugged, sniffed. "Could be. You want to see where they keep the slaves or not?"

"Yeah, yeah."

But he followed Harath along the gallery and through another decaying doorway with a lot of backward glances. And even after they left the hall, the squat black stone statues sat in his mind's eye like evil little dolls.

CHAPTER 19

After a while, the cormorants seem to tire of his company. They hop ungainly off the rock they've all been sharing, disappear one by one into the depths below. The last one cocks its head back at him before it dives. Utters a parched croak that might be farewell, and is gone. Ringil raises the flask after them in salute.

Puts it to his lips and finds it empty.

No wonder they left.

For a while, he resists the obvious implication in that. The rock is oddly pliant and comfortable beneath him, there seems no reason to—

Well, apart from that queasy, gray-white patch of radiance seeping through at the sky's eastern edge.

Something's on its way, Gil.

Best if you're not around for it to trip over when it arrives.

He makes the effort and gets to his feet. Swaying a little with the sudden height it gives him. He peers downward after the cormorants, gets nothing for his trouble but a vague gloom and the rising reek of fouled seawater. He shrugs. The fact that they were seabirds and he isn't doesn't seem to matter that much in the end. He takes the long step forward and plunges downward after them. Splashes into the—

Not water exactly, it's too sparse and fleeting for that. But for scant moments he thinks he sees bubbles rising through it, his breath ascending in a milky trail toward a surface stirred silver by his entry above. There's a brief, chilly prickling, like the splash of cold water thrown in his face, and then something lunges sharkish at him out of the murk.

Fuck!

He catches fragments of a glimpse—a circular mouth, dilated wide enough to swallow his head whole, the unbroken ring of a single taut lip rolled back and concentric rings of teeth erect in the throat beyond. It's the akyia, the thing that Seethlaw and Risgillen called the merroigai. Behind the nightmare head, the hint of a lithe, approximately human body bisecting into long, coiling limbs fronded with fins. A sleekly muscled arm, darting out, one clawed hand grasping for him, perhaps to save him from the fall—but he shrinks from it like a child from the clutch of the Marsh Wraith, and the fall takes him on.

Deeper yet.

If there was ever a surface above him, it's long gone now. The darkness presses around like some giant constricting serpent out of legend. Breathing is an effort, forcing him to shallow intake through trembling lips. His eyes ache from peering into the black, but something will not allow them to close. The sense that *something is coming* has not left him—he feels it plummeting down behind him, vast, shadowy, jaws agape. And he's *pinned*, less falling than hanging from some constructed torture table whose shape and extent he cannot yet see.

Pale and luminous, something else looms up out of the depths.

For a couple of shivery moments, he thinks it might be a jellyfish, one of the giant ones that wash up on the shores at Lanatray when the summers have been stormy. He remembers abruptly—himself at eight years old, alone, as he increasingly was, walking dazedly on rain-damp sand among humped and shivery-translucent mounds that rose almost as high as he was tall. For a few eerie moments in that early-morning light, before a fast-growing hardheaded pragmatism set in, he believed—wanted to believe—these might be the quivering, fled souls of whales taken by the harpoon off the Hironish isles.

They were not.

And this, now—he shakes himself back to the moment—is not a jellyfish.

It's a stone.

It seems to settle with this recognition, bobbing about at his feet with dog-like attachment. It wants to be friends. A softly gleaming chunk of masonry the size of a big man's chest, inscribed across the top of one facing with letters in old Myrlic script. Ringil tilts his head a little and deciphers the lettering:

. . . and the Keys of a City greater than . . .

Like something you'd see on the walls of some ruined temple in the older, marsh end of town, some eerie once-isolated shrine now drowned in a sea of modern housing as Trelayne's burgeoning outer districts spread—some of the stonework there is very old, it predates the Naomic ascendancy by centuries.

. . . the Keys of a City . . .

The stone startles upward, as if hauled on a ship's cable by weary men. Knee height, a hesitant bob or two, and then rising again, a hound called off by its *real* master after some case of mistaken identity. Perhaps, he thinks with blurry imprecision, the words are not intended for him to read at all, and this conjunction of man and building block is just some mis-stroke of destiny or demonic intent, a sword skating off a shield it's supposed to cleave, an axman's sure-footed brace slipping on mud, and down he goes on his arse before the cut can land. A life spared where no mercy should be looking down, a city sacked where it should stand against the besieging horde—an error in the Book of Days, some shit like that.

In his mind, he builds a suitably dismissive shrug, but finds he's shivering too much to give it physical form. His body is ceasing to feel like anything he owns or has much control over.

This time, it occurs to him, he might really be dying.

The chunk of masonry comes level with his head, and wobbles there a moment. Blind impulse—as realization catches up, he finds he's grabbed it. Is now hugging the worn-smooth contours of the lettered stone. He travels upward through the black, with a force that tugs and aches in his shoulder joints. The stonework is chilly against his face, the carved characters print their patterns into his flesh, he feels his body and legs rise devoid of weight until he hangs horizontally out from the stone like a windblown pennant at the mast.

The black around him is graying out.

A bruise-colored sky billows into being overhead, spreads itself to the horizon like a briskly snapped-out blanket.

He falls out of it.

Catches the sudden reek of salt water on the way down, the scent of fresh-cut kitchen herbs out of childhood memory . . .

He hits a surface that gives soggily under his weight. Water presses up from the ground and soaks through his clothes. He blows some of it, bitter and black-tasting, out of his mouth. Turns his head a little so he can breathe. Understanding catches up with the sense impressions of before.

He lies full length in a marsh, cold and clinging to a solitary chunk of stone.

Oh well . . .

Something stalks over his head like the fingers of a hand. He knows at once what it is, flails out with instinctive revulsion and flings the soft body away from him. Insistent squirming under his own body now, somewhere below his ribs, floundering panic—*fuck! fuck!*—and then the hot scissoring of jaws through his shirt and into his flesh as he rolls too late. A gossamer nuzzling at his neck, more soft, exploratory fingers. He swipes the touch away, comes frantically up on his knees. Cobwebs everywhere, plastering his arms, thick on the marsh grass around him like yards and yards of rotted gray muslin, he's in the burrow, he's landed *right on top of the fucking thing.*

He staggers to his feet, casts about, panting.

Rips loose sword, scabbard, cloak. Flings them away.

Brushes himself down with brutal strokes. Marsh spiders are communal, fiercely territorial, grow to a foot across if you're unlucky. A couple of bites from a big one is usually enough to finish a grown man. Ringil turns a taut full circle about, airheaded and struggling for balance as his feet shift and sink in the slippery springy turf and the ooze. The bite in his belly stings like scalding. He feels the slow, hot creep of the poison under the skin. He peers hard in the poor light, wishing he had a torch. Thinks he sees movement amid the coarse cobweb coatings and the marsh grass, but can't be sure.

He gets his breath back with an effort.

At his feet, the spider that bit him lies half crushed by his weight and flexing feebly. It's the size of a man's head. He stares numbly at it for a couple of seconds, then stamps down with convulsive anger until it dies.

It's all the energy he can summon. He stands swaying. The poison creeps some more in his belly, seems to be spreading. He rubs reflexively at the wound, then wishes he hadn't. Searing acid bites under the skin.

The marsh stretches featureless to the horizon. Thickly cobwebbed marsh grass in every direction, and an icy winter wind, knifing at his ears.

Great. Just fucking great.

He picks his way carefully over to his fallen sword and cloak, picks each item up in cautious turn and looks it over. He shakes three more fist-sized spiders out of the cloak's folds, finds another crawling on the scabbard and flicks it off. Stands a moment to make sure they all scuttle away. Then he fits the cloak across his shoulders—fighting the wind for possession—and fastens it there, hangs the Ravensfriend on his back once more, and stares defiantly around.

He reckons the cobwebs look somewhat thinner off to his left.

He starts walking.

Behind him, the abandoned chunk of masonry sits ringed in black water and offers its words to the empty sky.

. . . the Keys of a City greater than . . .

IT MIGHT BE THE POISON, MIGHT NOT. IN THE GRAY PLACES, WHO can tell?

He begins to hear a voice shouting down from the clouds, hoarse with anger but somehow soft as fine wool on his fingertips at the same time.

Just look at him down there . . .

Just look at him down there . . .

A female voice, or maybe something that knows how to imitate one, more or less. Faintly, eerily familiar. It comes and goes with the wind, seems to rush past him in sudden gusts, and then rush back. Ringil spins tiredly about, trying to face it.

. . . look at him . . .

The standing stones begin to flicker in and out of being around him, huge misshapen bars on some jail cell built for trolls, a circular prison that keeps pace with him as he walks. They chop the marsh horizon in segments for him, stand for a couple of soggy heartbeats, rising solidly out of the cobwebbed marsh grass, then vanish as he lurches toward them. After a while he learns to ignore the effect, much as you have to with so much else in the Gray Places.

He stumbles on, feeling steadily sicker with each pace.

. . . look at him . . .

Tilting vision of gray on gray, stone on emptiness, there and gone, there and gone . . .

Just look at—

He sags to a halt, feels the world go on a few steps without him as he stops. The voice goes abruptly silent, as if in interest at what he'll do next. He breathes in a couple of times. The wind jostles cold and blustering at his back. It's trying to shove him onward.

He lifts both arms. Calls out hoarsely.

Yeah, look *at me. Risgillen, is it? Go on and look: Ringil Eskiath, brought low. Is this what you wanted? You can't have wanted it any more than I did.*

No response. If Risgillen is out there, she isn't in the mood for a chat.

Can you blame her?

He can't really.

The ghost of the stone circle, painted like sunset shadows onto the backs of his eyes. The fleeting memories of Seethlaw—snarling, wrestling passion, cool flesh under his hands, the taste of the dwenda's come in his mouth like juice from some salt-sweet bursting berry on his tongue. The deep, clenching thrusts as he hauled and molded himself against Seethlaw's ivory-hard buttocks. The noises the dwenda made with each stroke.

And then the collapsing to the dew-soaked grass, the shuddering release, the laughter on the edge of weeping. The letting go, and all that came after.

He remembers suddenly how the stones kept Dakovash out, how the Salt Lord prowled beyond them but would not step through. How he threw the Ravensfriend in to Ringil like a man feeding meat to a beast whose cage he dares not enter.

Try not to drop that again. You're going to need it.

I am not your fucking cat's-paw.

Out of nowhere, a laugh coughs its way up into his mouth.

There's not much to it, certainly not much humor. But the smile it stamps onto Ringil's lips is down-curved and ugly with sudden strength.

He looks back the way he's come. The low-growing marsh vegetation is broken in a wavering line where he's passed. It seems he's walked out of the marsh spiders' territory without noticing. The cobwebs are gone. The smell of salt seems stronger now.

He rubs at his wound again, and this time when the pain sears, he breathes it in like a perfume from fond memory.

He casts about and thinks he sees the bright spark of a fire on the gray horizon.

He stares toward it for a long moment, waiting for it to vanish, the way every other fucking thing does around here.

When it doesn't, when it holds and beckons to him off the surface of the cold gray sky, he grunts and sets off in that direction. The cold wind at his back, hustling him on.

Well. What else you going to do now, Gil—stop?

From time to time, the stone circle flickers in and out around him as he walks. But it feels less like a prison now, and more like armor.

WHEN HIS GHOSTS START TO SHOW UP, HE'S ALMOST PLEASED TO SEE them. This, at least, is something he's used to.

Yeah, it's all right for you. Skimil Shend plods gloomily along beside him in cracked leather boots, poorly patched breeches and a white court blouse that has seen far better days. *You're not stuck in some stinking garret back in that miserable feces-reeking apology for a city. You're not an exile.*

Actually—Ringil pushes the pace as hard as the soggy ground and his shaky legs will let him—*I am.*

Oh, you call that exile? Chartered ambassador to the Majak plains, a sinecure purse and the writ of the city to cover your extravagances? That's not an exile, that's a license to plunder horny-handed horse-breeder arse. All those iron-thighed young things. Some punishment that's *going to be. I*—Shend thumps his chest with bombastic self-pity—*I suffered for my art.*

Oh, shut up.

But he has to wonder, just briefly and for all he's trained himself against such things, what shape his life must have taken in the world this alternative Shend belongs to. A Shend who never got to go home after all, and a Ringil who . . .

The aspect storm is a warp in the fabric of every possible outcome the universe will allow, Seethlaw once told him, camped out in the Gray Places with the aplomb of a Glades noble at a picnic. *It gathers in the alternatives like a bride gathering in her gown. For a mortal, those alternatives are mostly paths they'll never take, things they'll never do.*

He makes the aspect storm, he knows, every time he walks in the Gray Places. It blows around him in barely visible cobweb vortices, and the fragments of those alternatives swirl to him like storm waters pouring down into a drain.

You'd be living inside a million different possibilities at once. The—slightly drunken—opinion of a scholar in dwenda lore he knows back in Trelayne. *Imagine the will it would take to survive that. Your average peasant human is just going to go screaming insane.*

It certainly sounds like insanity: a Ringil not disowned, a Ringil cherished enough by family—*yeah, or maybe just soft enough to bend to family will*—that his transgressions meet with no worse sanction than an iffy diplomatic posting. He sees himself hurried urbanely out of that other Trelayne with face-saving rank, appointment, entourage. Sent in genteel disgrace a thousand miles northeast to the steppes, a place where his appetites can no longer bring the name of House Eskiath into disrepute because no one in Trelayne will know or care what he does there.

He wonders vaguely if he'd meet some alternative Egar out under those aching, open skies. An Egar who's perhaps not quite so resolutely and exclusively dedicated to pussy.

There's a feeling in his chest now, dangerously close to longing.

What if . . .

He stamps down on it.

You don't do that shit, Gil. There are no alternatives. You live with what is.

And you don't let your ghosts rent room in your head.

But he glances sideways at Shend anyway, can't quite repress the impulse, and it's not a pretty sight. The poet's once-fine features have sagged and bloated with his years away, and his hair is stringy with lack of care. His nails are bitten down to the quick, his belly hangs like a money changer's apron at his waist. That he woke up one morning in exile and just *gave up* is written into his flesh like branding.

Pouched eyes give Ringil back his stare. *What you looking at? See something you like?*

Look, Hinerion's not that bad, Ringil says uncomfortably.

Really? Then why are you leaving?

I'm not . . . leaving. Some unlooked for puzzlement in his voice at this. *I'm . . .*

Sudden, crushing image of a black sail on the horizon.

. . . dying . . . ?

Shend sniffs. *Looks like leaving to me. And in such exalted company.*

Ringil staves off a shiver.

I just don't see what the big thing is about life in Trelayne, he tells the poet. *You were broke more than half the time back home, always borrowing money off Grace of Heaven or the Silk House boys, then scrabbling to find the payback. How's that worse than pensioned exile in Hinerion?*

Shend stares morosely off across the marshland.

I don't expect you to understand. Why would you? You always did like to immerse yourself in the filth. I imagine you're quite as comfortable rubbing hips with our dusky southern neighbors as you are with any other riffraff.

Well, yeah. I fucked you, didn't I?

Oh! Oh! The Shend that Ringil remembers was more articulate. Not as shrill. *So it's come to that, has it? Well, I'm not the one with refugee blood running in my veins. I'm not the one with skin that tans in the sun like a marsh peasant's. I mean, how dare you! You're practically straight out of the fucking desert on your mother's side.*

Which, aside from shrill, is also inaccurate enough to be termed open slander and see steel drawn, at least in Ringil's version of the world. The southern refugee connections lie a good several generations back— Yhelteth merchants, driven out in some religious schism or other as the fledgling Empire convulsed yet again over clerkish points of doctrine— and by the time Ringil's mother was born, the lineage had been mingling pretty freely with the local blood for a while. In fact, rather too freely, some maintained, pointing to a number of unfortunate outlying branches on the family tree where marsh dweller ancestry was, let's say, hard to deny.

But Shend isn't likely to call that one out—like a lot of the petty nobility in Trelayne, the Shend clan itself has more than a few points of lineage with the whiff of the marsh about them. The trace physiognomy is there for all to see. Ringil chooses his riposte with cruel care.

You know, you shouldn't knock southern blood, Skim. Maybe if your mother'd come from the south, she could have arranged for you to have some cheekbones.

And you should just—just fuck off and die!

. . . die, die, die!

The last word seems to echo, inside Ringil's head or across the sky, he isn't entirely sure which. He grimaces.

Perhaps I will.

Raw silence, pressing in his ears, and the soft squelch of his steps in the marsh. Ringil looks around and sees that the poet, perhaps in some terminal paroxysm of offense, is gone, faded out with the echo of his parting words.

That scrap of fire-glow at the skyline doesn't seem to be getting any closer, either.

LATER, AS IF SHE'S SOMEHOW HEARD AND BEEN DRAWN BY SHEND'S slurs on her lineage, Ishil Eskiath puts in an appearance. Carefully skirting the fringes of another marsh spider infestation at the time, Ringil's surprised by how hard this is to take. He can't tell how far removed this woman is from the mother he knows back in the real world, but she seems genuinely happy, which to his mind suggests some considerable distance.

Lanatray, she insists brightly. *You always loved it there.*

I nearly drowned there, Mother.

He can't help it, the snap in his voice. Out of the corner of his eye, he sees her pull a face, but she says nothing. Another switch—the Ishil Eskiath he knows would never let him have the last word, least of all when he's just hurt her.

He sighs. *Look, I'm sorry. But you don't know me, Mother. You think you do, but you don't.*

Oh, Ringil, don't you suppose that's what every boy thinks about his mother?

She lays a hand on his. He flinches a little from the contact—there's something cool and not quite human about it. The ghosts in the Gray Places seem to lack the normal warmth of living things, and he supposes they must draw off some of his heat to keep going as they circle him. Perhaps that's what draws them, like moths to a lantern spark across the marshland gray. But—

I've known you longer than you've known yourself, she says.

He stares at the dull, thickly glistening swatches of cobweb across the marsh grass ahead of him. *Tell me what I'm thinking, then.*

Oh, the usual. Ishil's tone turns abruptly gemstone-hard and glinting. He feels a chill gust through him—suddenly, she's a perfect match for the mother he knows. *You wonder how I manage to live with the daily truth of marriage to your father and not just open my veins some sunlit afternoon in my bathwater.*

Well . . .

She laughs. Some of the hardness leaches back out of her voice. *You're such an old romantic, Gil. Just try to imagine for a moment you'd been born female. Breeding or brothel stock, these are your options. We just don't get to carry a blade and carve out our own uncompromising path through the world like the boys.*

He's known women who did, across the old warehouse district and down at harbor end. Admittedly not many of them made it out of their teens alive. He supposed not many had ever expected to.

Women know the price of things, Gil. We learn it hard and fast at our mother's knee, helping and caring and fetching and carrying, while our brothers are still playing at knights and foes without a care in the world. The world falls on us early.

You seem to be bearing up, he says sourly. *What's the secret?*

Children, she tells him with sudden warmth. *Bringing them into the world. Seeing them through it. You know that.*

He can't face the way she looks at him as she says it. He turns away, eyes pricked through, half blinded. He wonders, with an odd, quiet desperation, how many times the Ishil he knows might have looked at him like that without him ever seeing or knowing.

Is that why you're here? To see me through?

She laughs again, voice utterly unfettered this time. *I'm here to ask you about the wedding arrangements, Gil. The vow circlets for you and Selys, gold or silver? Red rose petals or white for her bridal path?*

What? he asks faintly.

And the invitations, the list? Will you really insist on snubbing the Kaads, or shall we let bygones be bygones? Come on, Gil, don't spoil your mother's proudest hour. I'm so happy for you both. Is that so strange?

It's so fucking strange he doesn't even want to think about it. He gestures at the cobwebs to buy time. *Listen, I'm not getting married to anyone unless we find a way through this first.*

Why don't you try over there?

To his annoyance, it proves a good call. There are patches where the webs are frayed and old, clogged with the sucked-dry corpses of insect life and small marsh animals. No sign of any stealthy, articulated motion within. He unsheathes the Ravensfriend just in case, prods about dubiously for a bit, then resigns himself to Ishil being right.

This way, then?

This way, she agrees. *Keep right on like that, it's your best path out of here. Now, what about the Kaads? Seriously. Your father thinks they should be there.*

I bet he does. Smashing grimly through the old web and the grass, the tiny, dried hanging corpses that swing and spindle about as he passes. *Chancellery politics never sleeps, does it?*

Oh, don't start, Gil.

So he doesn't. He lets her talk instead. And though he doesn't like to admit it, her voice, trailing at his shoulder, is oddly comforting.

What you don't appreciate, Gil, is that for all your father's cruelties and indiscretions, he has been a great shield through difficult times. You don't

*know what it was like back in the twenties. We didn't have the Scaled Folk
to unite us all back then. Yhelteth was a despised enemy—*

Yeah—*heading that way again these days.*

But she doesn't seem to hear him. *The raiding went back and forth at
the borders for* years, *Gil, news every other week of towns burned and
populations marched away in chains. And we were marked. No matter that
we were merchants in good faith, wealth in our coffers and a generation of
judicious marriage alliances. Still we had the red daub on our door, still we
were barred from the Chancellery. Stones thrown at us in the street, spat
upon with impunity by urchins. Southern scum, southern scum. In the
school we attended, the priests beat my brothers at every opportunity. One
of them struck Eldrin to the floor once, called him Yhelteth whelp, kicked
him from his desk to the door and out into the corridor. He was five. He
came home black and blue, and my father, shamed, could do nothing. My
mother went begging to the priests instead, and the beatings stopped for a
while, but she never spoke of that visit afterward as long as she lived. Do
you know how relieved my parents looked the day I married Gingren Eskiath? Do you know how happy I was for them?*

Were they happy for you?

No reply.

He looks back and sees that she, too, has left him.

CHAPTER 20

*I*n the time before this, the Earth was not the way you see it now.

In the time before this, the Earth was ravaged by endless conflict, fought over by races and beings you now remember only as myth and legend.

Weapons of hideous, unnatural power were unleashed, vast energies raged, horizon to horizon, the sky itself cracked open. The planet shuddered from the tread of the Visitors—enemies and allies too, the latter chosen in desperation from other worlds and places worse than other worlds, to hold the line against invaders who were probably in the end no more alien.

Whole nations and peoples disappeared inside storms that lasted decades.

Great jagged darknesses larger than mountains moved in the night sky, blocking out the stars and casting deathly shadow on those beneath.

Gates opened, in places no earthly passage should ever have been per-

mitted, and the Visitors poured forth, met in battle, coiled and recoiled, worked their alien technologies in causes it is doubtful those who enlisted them could ever truly comprehend. It was a conflict beyond human reckoning, and mere humans found themselves trapped, cornered, hemmed in on all sides by what had been unleashed.

So Humanity fought, hopelessly, generation after generation, endured unimaginable horrors, changed at levels once believed intrinsic, splintered apart and became a dozen disparate races in itself—as if only in dissolution could the race once called human hide sufficiently well from the carnivorous glare of alien eyes.

And then—finally, for reasons no longer well understood—the wars ended, the Earth spun on along its customary course in relative peace.

And those who were left squabbled over what remained.

"NO CHANGE THERE THEN," JHIRAL MUTTERED, AND ARCHETH GLANCED at him in mute surprise.

A brief and pointed silence, and then Anasharal's voice resumed, with biting schoolmasterly emphasis:

"Into, this, void . . . "

INTO THIS VOID, THEN, BURST THE DWENDA, THE ALDRAIN, THE WITCH *folk, glittering dark and beautiful, human at least in base form, and claiming a prior heritage, an ownership of Earth predating the conflict—though there were those who argued their memories were faulty, hopelessly distorted by their custom of dwelling for long periods in the realm of the Unrealized Possible; and others who believed that Time itself had been somehow collapsed, folded, or maybe just shredded in the wars, so that the past the dwenda claimed did not even belong, correctly speaking, to this version of the world.*

But such arguments were at best academic—the wars had weakened the walls that held such places apart from the unshadowed world, and the Aldrain were not disposed to debate with the existing populations in lands they considered their own by ancestral right.

They took the Earth by storm and built there, summarily, an Empire

*that lasted seven thousand years. Many, including the humans they domi-·
nated, called it glorious.*

*They brought magic as a way of life, they sprinkled it across the planet
like seed.*

*They stalked the night as absolute monarchs—and created a harsh
human oligarchy to serve them wherever and whenever the light of the
Realized sun struck too harshly for them to endure. A dynasty of kings,
endowed with dark powers, a bloodline of human sorcerers with whom
they mated and shared their heritage—to the extent that such heritage
could ever be shared with ordinary human stock.*

Most of the Dark Kings were insane.

*It took the enemies of the dwenda all of those seven thousand years to
learn the new rules—to master the new magic, to bend it to their will as the
dwenda so long ago already had.*

*Seven thousand years to bring the Kiriath through the hidden gates in
the bowels of the Earth, to summon a science and a people equal to the eldritch folk, to meet them in battle, to throw down their cities into marsh
and ruin, to scatter their armies and their human adherents. To bring back
a measure of sanity to the world.*

To defeat the Last of the Dark Kings.

THE HELMSMAN FELL SILENT.

"I thought—" Archeth began, then shook her head. "Doesn't matter."

But the pinched wick of suspicion still smoked in her head. There
were a lot of stories about how and why her people had arrived in the
world, most of them told by humans ignorant of anything resembling
actual facts. Come to that, even the legends the Kiriath themselves told
about the Advent were erratic and hard to credit. But Angfal, who hung
on her study wall like so much alien iron viscera and bulbous-limbed
swelling, had always been scornful.

*The Kiriath barely survived the voyage through the quick paths on their
way here,* he told her one fractious night as she tried to crowbar some
useful answers out of him. *They did not choose to come here, Archeth,
despite anything the Chronicles might claim to the contrary. They were*

shipwrecked here, and if they stayed it wasn't because they liked the scenery. It was because they were afraid that the return would break them.

Some of this she put down to bitterness—the resentment Angfal felt at being left behind. But still, she thought Anasharal's version rang slightly overwrought.

The Emperor had taken a seat on one of the granite benches near the balcony, back to the glare of the sun. His face was in shadow, richly oiled hair hanging forward to screen his features, but she read the impatience in how he was sprawled, the sideways tilt of his head. She wondered if she'd gotten in the way of a visit to the harem—if commanding the executions had left him with the itching need to fuck something.

He brushed invisible dust from his lap.

"You, uh, plan to actually *tell* us something about this Last Dark King? His name, for instance? Who he was, what he did? How any of this has anything to do with the here-and-now?"

"It is better not to name him," said the Helmsman somberly. "Better not to utter those syllables here."

Archeth rolled her eyes.

"Yes—we're not easily shocked around here," said Jhiral. "Feel free."

"Let us call him simply the Ilwrack Changeling, since it was that Aldrain clan who raised him in the Gray Places. Taken from a humble home on the marsh for the dark glimmer the dwenda prize so much in humans, brought up an Aldrain warrior, and ultimately given command of a dwenda legion, he rose to—"

"You know—" Jhiral was showing signs of real irritation now. "I've heard this humble-beginnings crap a few times before, Helmsman. Funny how no one can ever actually point to a living example, isn't it? Funny how in the end they're all legendary and dead."

Anasharal paused, delicately. "Oh, the Ilwrack Changeling is not dead, Your Imperial Radiance. Far from it."

Silence. Maybe it was the slow afternoon cooldown and the breeze blowing in from the river, but Archeth felt a tiny shiver creep across her shoulder blades. She glanced at Jhiral, who sighed heavily and examined his manicure. She read the little display as false. Emperor or not, Jhiral had grown up on this kind of tale like any other kid. His voice, when he spoke, could not quite shroud a tiny, chained tension.

"And . . . what is that supposed to mean, exactly?"

"Exactly what it says," the Helmsman said blandly. "When the Kiriath destroyed Hannais M'hen in the last stages of the Twilight war, the Ilwrack Changeling was at the head of the Aldrain forces and their human allies. But he was betrayed—some say by a lover, others claim it was a diplomatic deceit of the Kiriath. Perhaps, in the end, it was both. At any rate, when he discovered the betrayal, it's said he fell into a paroxysm of rage and grief, and was taken for dead. The dwenda forces fell back without his body, and vanished into the Gray Places."

"But he wasn't dead." Jhiral said, leaning forward a little despite himself.

"No. The dwenda were in disarray, they apparently misunderstood the situation. But a small group of his human supporters carried the body away and entombed him on an islet in the northern ocean."

"The Hironish isles?"

"Farther west and north than the Hironish. But in any case, the island does not appear on your maps."

Jhiral grunted. "Convenient."

"The story goes that the Changeling's Aldrain lover came later, in secret, to the tomb, but could not wake him. So he—"

"He?" The Emperor's lip curled. "*He?*"

"Or she," Anasharal amended. "The story is not clear on exact identity, only that it was a member of the Ilwrack clan. In any case, this lover cast an enchantment around the whole island, sweeping it up into the margin of the Aldrain marches. But the magic was hurried and incomplete, and it's said the island emerges from time to time and stands solid again in the ocean, though lit with witch-light and sometimes for only moments at a time."

"I've read about this," Archeth said slowly. "The Ghost Isle, the Chain's Last Link."

Jhiral looked at her. "You have?"

"Yes, it's a legend of the Hironish peoples, but there are some versions in Trelayne as well. Mariner tales—an uncharted island beyond the last in the Hironish Chain; ships sight it in the midst of storms, witch-lit in blue, there one moment, gone the next." She gestured helplessly. "It's a legend, you know. I always assumed . . ."

"Quite." The Emperor turned his gaze back to the Helmsman. "Are you trying to tell me we should be expecting a visit from this undead Changeling?"

"You've had some trouble with the Aldrain recently, have you not?"

Archeth and the Emperor swapped a look. The dwenda incursion at Ennishmin was a closely guarded secret. Outside of those who'd actually been there, only Jhiral and a tiny cabal of trusted court advisers and men-at-arms had been informed of the events. Two full legions of imperial levy now sat on the borders of the marshland between Pranderghast and Beksanara, ostensibly as a bar to raiding parties from the League territories to the north and west. The commander of the garrison at Khartaghnal had been apprised of what they were really watching for, but beyond that . . .

Of course, the creep of rumor was unavoidable. Faileh Rakan might have died in the skirmish at Beksanara, but a number of his men did not. The local population was decimated, but not wiped out. And among the survivors, some, even paid off and sworn to secrecy, even threatened with dire penalties—even Throne Eternal veterans—would drink and yarn and recall, and let loose dark hints and drunken fragments of truth.

"The dwenda were driven back," Archeth said carefully.

"Indeed. But, you see, the legend says that the Ilwrack Changeling will return when his adoptive people's need is greatest; more exactly, *when they have been thrown back in battle from their heart's ancestral desire, and are once more in disarray.* That's a more or less direct quote from the original Naom legend. See the corollary?"

Jhiral nodded. "Yes. What you think we should do about it is a little less clear, though. A preemptive assault on this sporadically manifesting island, perhaps?"

"That's clearly not possible." The Helmsman's tone was almost prim. "I am charged with offering *pragmatic* solutions to your difficulties."

"Not so far." Archeth found some of her Emperor's impatience seeping into her own mood. "If the Ghost Isle is inaccessible then—"

"You did not let me finish the tale, daughter of Flaradnam."

"Well, she's not stopping you now. Can we get on with this?"

"The Kiriath," said Anasharal smoothly, "had no way to counter the sorceries of the Ilwrack clan, or at least none that they could bring themselves to deploy. Instead, they built for safety. A city was constructed, standing above the waves south and east of the Ghost Isle. A watch was set."

"A city in the sea?"

There was a sudden, odd strain in Archeth's voice. Jhiral glanced at her in mild surprise.

"That is correct, daughter of Flaradnam. Commissioned and built by the clan Halkanirinakral, manned, initially at least, by its scions. The city was named An-Kirilnar—that's City of Phantom Hunters to you, your majesty—it was designed to shadow the Ghost Isle in and out of the Gray Places. But recently it seems to have returned to the world permanently—"

"*It's still there?*"

"Yes, it's still there, daughter of Flaradnam. Currently it stands in the ocean beyond the Hironish isles, as it has now stood for some weeks."

"Then we have to go there!"

"Archeth—"

"Yes, I would say that's an appropriate conclusion to draw."

"Archeth—"

"Can you . . . communicate with—"

"*Archeth!*" The Emperor's voice cracked like a whip. He got up from the bench and moved toward the balcony. His tone softened to a honeyed irony. "Would you be so good as to attend me within?"

"My lord." She hurried after him. "My lord, this is an opportunity to—"

"This is an opportunity to calm the fuck down, my lady *kir*-Archeth." Jhiral leaned in closer to her. In her tumbled state, she could not read it—menace or a plea for intimate confidence, the Emperor or the boy she'd watched grow up. The words came spaced. "Now walk with me if you will."

SO SHE WENT WITH HIM.

Out of earshot—though she wasn't convinced that was meaningful where the Helmsmen were concerned. Angfal never spoke to her outside of the study where he was hung across the walls like a nightmare in iron;

Manathan would speak to you anywhere within the An-Monal keep. She didn't know if ripping Angfal out of the fireship he had once commanded had in some way truncated a broader sense of awareness, or if the Helmsman was hiding its true reach. But she was tolerably sure that Anasharal, a being who could pluck personal details from the heads of the men it spoke to apparently at random, would not have a problem listening to a conversation maintained a few hundred paces away in the shade of the inner garden.

"If there really is a Kiriath city up there, my lord—"

"A city standing in the ocean?"

"An-Naranash in Lake Shaktan stands above the water in exactly the same way."

"Yes, so they tell me. And is abandoned."

Their voices were growing heated again. Archeth backed off, seated herself on a tall, arching tree root just off the path. Her pulse was up, her vision dizzied dim. Her thoughts skittered back and forth on the shiny jagged edges of krinzanz lack.

She forced calm.

"My lord, whether the city is abandoned or not is hardly the issue."

"Is it not, Archeth? Is it not?"

He had her—however hard she tried to crush the knowledge out. "My concern, my lord—"

"Is that you may yet find some of your father's race who have not abandoned the world." Jhiral sighed and sat down beside her on the root. His shoulder jolted her. He stared across the path into the foliage opposite. "I don't blame you, Archeth. Really, I don't. Who wouldn't like to call back their parents sometimes? But your need is transparent. Be honest. With me, even if you cannot with yourself. You are supposed to be my most trusted adviser. Can you—honestly—tell me this is about a threat to the Empire?"

She grimaced.

"I carried a warning to you last winter that we came close to ignoring, and look how that turned out."

"Yes, rub my face in that, why don't you."

"The facts remain, my lord."

"All right, don't milk it." Jhiral leaned back and peered upward into the canopy of the tree, as if he might discern a way out among the branches. He frowned. "You said after Ennishmin that the dwenda do not favor harsh light, that they can probably not abide the sun in these latitudes."

"That's not what I said, my lord. It's what the knight Ringil Eskiath said he *surmised* from his time among them. It's a supposition, nothing more."

The young Emperor nodded vigorously. "Yes, but still. Even in Ennishmin, where the sun barely breaks through the clouds, even in the pall of winter, the dwenda chose to fight at night."

"They could fight at night here, too."

"That was not what this . . . Eskiath *surmised*, though, was it?"

Most of the time I was in the Aldrain marches, it was dark or dim, like twilight. Ringil's hesitant theorizing rose in her memory. *One place we went, there was something like a sun in the sky, but it was almost burned out. Like a hollow shell of itself. If that's where the dwenda are from originally, it might explain why they can't tolerate bright light.*

"They still came to Khangset," she said stubbornly. "They ripped the town apart. And if the Helmsman is to be believed, the Ilwrack Changeling is not dwenda at all. He's an undead human sorcerer, wielding Aldrain powers. How, unaided, would you stop something like that?"

"You believe in this Ilwrack Changeling, then? Tell the truth, Archeth. Have you even heard of him?"

"No, my lord."

"Then—"

"But the timing is suggestive. Less than a year after our skirmish with the dwenda, and here we are, warned of an escalation in the conflict. Can we afford to ignore this as some kind of coincidence?"

"I'll tell you what we can't afford to do, Archeth. We can't afford to equip a full naval expedition to the middle of the northern ocean in the hope that it'll stumble on some figment of a mad machine's imagination. Quite apart from anything else, that's the other side of League waters. We sail there in force, it's a major diplomatic incident in the making."

"We are not at war with the League, my lord."

"No," said the Emperor glumly. "Not yet. But piracy is on the increase north of Hinerion. And I have it on good authority from the admiralty's spies in Trelayne that the League shipmasters' association is pressing for a renewal of privateer licensing. You know what that means. It always kicks off the same way."

Except when we kick it off ourselves by marching north in force.

She quelled the thought. She had no great love for the League, had always believed, as her father's people had—perhaps *because* her father's people had—that Yhelteth offered the better way forward.

But:

"Admiral Sang's . . . spies . . . are less than wholly reliable." She trod warily. "They've been known to exaggerate claims before."

"As has the old bastard himself. Yes, all right, Archeth, I know you don't like him." Abruptly, Jhiral was on his feet again, pacing. "But I've read the reports, and I don't think this is Sang beating the drum. We've seen this before, after all. Those mercantile little shits up north can't afford a war right now any more than we can, and they know it. But it won't stop them farming the unpleasantries out to private shipmasters and then taking a tithe on the booty it brings in. Their coffers fill up with plunder from imperial cargo, their diplomats shake their weasel heads in sorrow and deny all knowledge. And meantime, as if we didn't have enough to worry about down in Demlarashan and up at Ennishmin, we have to raid the treasury again to build navy pickets, or risk losing our own trade lanes to League competition."

"Maybe Admiral Sang is just looking for some new warships."

"I already told you I don't think it's that." Trace of a growl in his voice now.

"Besides which there must be a whole constellation of League trade interests on land who don't want any kind of war. The slavers to name but one. The League aren't necessarily bound to listen to what the shipmasters want. They—"

"Archeth, will you stop building castles in the air!"

"I"—before she could stop herself—"trust Sang about as far as I could throw his fat arse. He's not reliable."

"Oh, and the fucking Helmsmen are?"

Suddenly he was in her face. Hands clamping down on her shoulders, thumbs hooking in, cabled strength in the arms. She was forcibly reminded that if Prince Jhiral, heir apparent, had never seen anything of the war against the Scaled Folk or his father's earlier campaigns, had in fact never struck a sword blow in anger his whole life—well, neither then had he missed a day's combat schooling for anything other than sickness since he was twelve years old. There was a lot of muscle under the ocher-and-black draped shoulders, a lot of trained and channeled power.

But even with the krinzanz jitters, she could have put Bandgleam in his throat faster than he could blink.

Could have . . .

She met his eyes.

Perhaps he sensed it. He let her go. Straightened up.

"Archeth, you were at An-Naranash. You saw how it went down." His voice was back to regal, council-chamber calm. He gestured, throwaway, with one open palm. "All that Helmsman burbling, months to cross the desert, all the diplomatic wrangling with the nautocrats in Shaktur, the lake tolls and bribes, and what do we end up with? A mausoleum on stilts, centuries deserted, stripped of anything even remotely valuable."

She remembered. The slow-dying excitement in her guts as they swung in closer to An-Naranash's silent, towering bulk, and she saw the extent of the dilapidation. The clenched, sickening disappointment as she boarded at one massive, barnacle-crusted leg, climbed the endless damp-reeking stairwells, and prowled the echoing gloom of spaces as abandoned as anything she knew at An-Monal.

"It cost us half a million elementals to mount that expedition, Archeth. All because the Helmsmen said go. It's one of the biggest mistakes my father ever made. Do you really expect me to follow in his footsteps? Is that what you want?"

For that, she had no answer.

Because you forced the Shaktur expedition, Archidi, and you know it. It wasn't the Helmsmen, not really. You squeezed it out of Akal in his dying melancholy and regret, funds and men he could ill afford in the postwar mess, a paid penance, an old man's attempt to atone—the unspoken bargain that she would no longer torment him with the tales of what she saw at Vanbyr, if he underwrote the expedition and gave her the command. That she would, in some unclear fashion, absolve him.

Strange how you could become a man's god without noticing.

Akal died before she returned. It was probably just as well—she'd been in no fucking mood for absolution when she got back.

"Archeth, look." Akal's son, conciliatory now, leaning back toward the dissolute aristo loucheness he wore so well. "I'm not saying we don't take this seriously. Go do some reading, by all means. I know how much you love that clerkish shit. Chase up this changeling fairy tale in the Indirath M'nal. Talk to Angfal, if you can drag anything out of him. But for the Prophet's sake, cool off. Go get drunk, chew some krin—fuck it, get yourself laid, Archeth. Go play with that curvy little Trelayne trollop I gave you last year. Bet you still haven't touched that, have you?"

In a way, she was almost relieved. It was a side of Jhiral she found far easier to deal with, a role he'd been playing since his early teens, a thrust to which she knew all the smart parries and ripostes because she'd been making them for a decade or more. A decadence you could comfortably despise.

But she wondered, not for the first time, what he armored himself against with it.

Maybe it's not armor—maybe he just fucking likes it. Revels in it. Ever think of that?

Ishgrim sprang into her head, pale portions of flesh that begged for hands to cup and grasp. Long, smooth limbs to revel among. *Bet you still haven't touched that, have you? The smart bet, my lord.* Whatever mannered game Jhiral was playing with her over Ishgrim, he was winning it hands down.

She pushed herself upright off the arched root. Drew a long breath.

"I shall do some reading, my lord," she said.

"Good. Then we can leave it there, I think. The Helmsman should—"

"If," Anasharal said, out of the empty green-fragrant air, like any divine visitation. "I might interject."

Emperor of All Lands and Kiriath half-breed semi-immortal—their gazes snapped together like those of small children called in for dinner by an unfamiliar voice. Even Archeth, elder sister and halfway expecting this . . .

She built a shrug, elaborately casual.

"You've been listening to us?"

"You truly have a talent for stating the obvious, daughter of Flarad-nam. Manathan did mention it. He puts it down to your muddied half-breed blood. But oddly enough, you have still not spotted the very obvious solution to the impasse you face."

"There's no impasse here," said Jhiral, mustering some regal disdain.

"I was not talking to you, Jhiral Khimran."

It was an affront that would have earned any human speaker a swift and probably fatal trip to the palace dungeons. The Helmsmen—well, over the centuries the Khimran dynasty had learned to adjust. You didn't bite the hand that fed your power, for all it might be taloned and de-monic beneath that urbane, avuncular surface.

"Perhaps you'd better explain," Archeth said hastily. "What impasse?"

"The impasse you will face, daughter of Flaradnam, when you've done your reading, and you've satisfied yourself that an expedition to find An-Kirilnar is indeed necessary, and you still face the same stric-tures from this stuttering apology for an Empire's depleted treasury."

"Yeah, maybe you can just point us to a handy pot of gold," sneered Jhiral.

Again, the beat of silence Archeth was learning to interpret as re-proach. The icy schoolmaster tone.

"In point of fact, Jhiral Khimran, that is exactly what I am going to do. So once again, it would behoove you to quell your sense of throne room entitlement and listen carefully to what I'm about to say."

CHAPTER 21

Some unmeasured time later, still alone, but roughly on the bearing the ghost claiming to be his mother gave him, he stumbles across a paved track through the marsh.

It's not much to look at—scuffed and worn white stone, muddied black in the grain, a couple of feet wide at best, almost covered over by the marsh grass growing back in from margins long untrimmed and up between the cobbles. He shoves back a tuft with one boot, examines the paving curiously. It looks a lot like the paths through the Glades district in Trelayne, the paths leading among other places to the gates of his home—or at least the way they'll probably look a thousand years hence.

Without Ishil's guidance, it would have been easy to miss this.

He looks left and right, shrugs, and picks the direction that seems to lead closer to the scribble of firelight on the sky ahead. Almost unnoticed, some tiny increment of satisfaction thaws and drips inside him.

The going is easier now, no more soggy give with each step. The stone sounds firm under his heels, pushes back solidly as he walks, and though the cobwebs sweep in sometimes on either side, they never touch or cross the track.

Instead, eventually, he finds skulls.

Scores of them, maybe hundreds, dotted grinning out across the marsh on either side of the path. Each skull sits perfectly upright, atop a low tree stump whose wood has gone gray and cracked with age. A hundred and more leveled pairs of eye sockets, rinsed through with the cold wind, surveying the marsh horizon. But for that perfect sentinel rigor in every hollow gaze, these might be inventive cairns, built to the dead of some battlefield long forgotten, the fallen warriors of some race that preferred not to pile cold stones on the face of their loved ones in death.

But they are not cairns.

Ringil slows reluctantly to a halt where one of the skulls sits a couple of paces off to the left of the path. It still has hair, a fall of long dead gray strands plastered across the skull and over one eye, like magically straightened cobweb. He squats and brushes the hair aside, touches the bone behind, pushes gently against one yellowed temple. There is no give. The skull is cemented to the stump, just as its owner's still-living head once was. He's seen it before; it's Aldrain sorcery, a favorite terror tactic of the Vanishing Folk wherever humans tried to defy them. Seethlaw once told him that the heads would live indefinitely provided the stump roots drew water.

Which makes this the result of either some long-ago drought or a passage of time so colossal Ringil's sanity reels away from the edge of contemplating it.

Or Seethlaw lied to you.

He straightens up with a grimace. It's a hypothesis he prefers not to entertain. Seethlaw as Aldrain warlord, murderous, cruel and proud, walking amid flickering lightnings, the epitome of the dwenda out of myth, striking down all before him with dispassionate unconcern—that, all that, Ringil can live with. But Seethlaw the dwenda, dishonest and manipulative as any sweet-lipped harbor-end whore . . .

Well, then. An immense gulf of time instead, time for even the sorcery of the Aldrain to finally weaken and lose its grip on the forces of decay.

Here, perhaps, is rationale, and an escape at last. A letting go he can allow himself.

Perhaps he's been unable to find Seethlaw in the Gray Places because some vast . . . tilting . . . *mechanism,* something like the long orbits of comets that Grashgal once tried to explain to him on the sleepless eve of battle at Rajal, or wait, wait, simpler, look, some . . . gargantuan wind-mill arm in time has swung back up and taken the Vanishing Folk away once more; has opened a gap many hundreds of thousands of years wide and left the Aldrain and all their arts, in some irrevocable fashion, on the far side.

What would you give to really believe that, Gil?

What would you give to deny it?

Oi, Eskiath. You going to stand around here moping forever?

Ringil jerks around, disbelieving. The stone circle flickers around him like granite lightning, like drilled reflex—once, twice, to the beat of his suddenly elevated pulse.

Eg?

It certainly seems so. The familiar barrel-chested bulk is there, the bits of talismanic iron strung in the gray-straggled, tangled hair. The seamed and weathered face, split in a grin. The staff lance jutting up behind his shoulder like a tall and gaunt old friend peering over. From somewhere, this Egar has acquired one steel-capped tooth and a scar across the chin that Ringil doesn't remember him having, but for the rest, it's the Dragonbane, large as life and stood there on the path at Ringil's back, as seemingly solid as the stones that flicker in and out of being between the two of them.

Egar?

The figure snorts. *You know someone* else *shows up whenever you've got yourself neck-deep in shit and digs you out?*

Weak gesture around. *I'm not . . .*

No? Egar steps forward and grabs him by the shoulders. Fingers dig into his muscles with bruising steppe nomad force. *Well, you sure* look *like shit, Gil. Want to know the truth? You look like a pony on ten days' gallop and no decent forage. Whoever's riding you needs to give it a rest.*

Fast thoughts of Dakovash, as swiftly put away. Gone, honest—look.

No one's fucking riding me, he drawls.

That'd be a first, then. The Dragonbane draws him close, crushes him in a bear hug the Egar he knows back in the world would not have allowed himself. Ringil coughs for exaggerated effect, and Egar lets him go. Sets him back at a more accustomed arm's length and grins. *Good to see you again, Gil.*

Yeah, you, too. As with Shend, as with Ishil, he knows he shouldn't engage but he can't help it. He's tired of the detachment, tired of standing aloof. So what if his friends are phantoms now. *What you doing here, man?*

The Dragonbane shrugs. *Just come to walk with you awhile.*

It's throwaway, but for just a moment, Ringil sees the seamed brow crease, sees this version of his old friend searching for the memories the Gray Places will not let him have. *How did I get here, where is this place, what came before?* Ringil curses his own lack of restraint and seeks rapid distraction for them both. He notices a thin silver chain draped over the Dragonbane's chest, some flattened object swaying gently from the impact of their embrace.

What's this, then? Reaching and scooping the object up into his palm. *Never had you down for a medallion man.*

Well, you gave it to me, mate.

Ringil blinks. The flattened disk is a three-elemental piece, struck with the face of Akal the Great and worn dull with age. The ends of the chain are welded into it, and the coin itself looks to have melted badly in the process. During his time in Yhelteth, coins like this would have passed through his hands as often as water for washing. But he can't remember ever having given one to Egar.

C'mon, Gil. You know better than this. Doesn't pay to focus on detail in the Gray Places. Doesn't pay to question your companions too closely. To wonder what they might really be.

Or where it's all leading you.

He drops his hand, lets the coin swing back against the Dragonbane's chest. It's as if the other man's bulk were suddenly darker and harder, more gnarled oak tree trunk than human flesh. More animate statue than man.

He staves off a shiver. Manufactures a small, tight smile. Claps the *perhaps* of Egar on one troll-solid shoulder.

Want to walk with me, huh? Walk this way, then.

Yeah, if I could walk that way, I'd be making a living in Madam Ajana's floor show.

The old, stupid jokes—always the best. But hearing it drove a spike in behind Ringil's eyes, and he turned quickly away, blinking and gesturing wide.

Seen the skulls?

Yeah. Fucking dwenda, huh?

Seethlaw flickers through his recollection, cool to the touch and gorgeous, eyes deep with knowing you could drown in.

Yeah, he agrees. *Fucking dwenda.*

OF COURSE, HE LOSES EGAR, JUST LIKE ALL THE OTHERS, BEFORE THEY'VE gone more than a couple of miles. It's a slower bleed this time, the Dragonbane fading and flickering like a candle in a bad draft, as if there's some larger storm blowing outside this tented gray sky, and short spiteful gusts can occasionally get in. It lasts for a while, the steppe nomad gone, then abruptly back, as if he's suddenly thought of some last thing he needs to say, as if he can't quite make up his mind whether it's safe now to leave Ringil on his own in this place.

Here—you still got that dragon-tooth dagger I gave you?

Ringil pats his sleeve where the weapon rests.

You want to hang on to that, it's a good knife.

I know.

Ringil rolls with it, because, well, it's the Gray Places, what else is he going to do? He keeps up a façade of studied calm and normal conversation, pausing when he's left suddenly alone, picking up the thread again when Egar reappears.

Poltar the Shaman, yeah, you said.

The old fuck has it coming, Gil. I mean, if I don't go back there and gut him for what he did, who will?

Maybe they'll get sick of him. When he can't deliver on the spring rains, or the steppe ghouls show up again despite all his stick-shaking.

Nobody shakes sticks up there, Gil. That's a bunch of lizardshit romance some asshole writer at court came up with for one of those Noble-Savages-of-the-Steppe pieces they pack the theaters with down there.

Seriously, I am so tired of seeing a bunch of little inkspurts who never built a campfire in their life pontificate about the trials and tribulations of iron-thewed warriors and—

And gone.

Bleak marsh to the horizon and the wind for company.

He walks on.

And back again. The Dragonbane mid-stride, brow furrowed in the struggle to recall.

So what was I saying?

Shaking sticks. Look, I've seen—in Ishlin-ichan that time—I saw a shaman shaking a stick over a sick child. About yea long, with bone rattles at the end.

Yeah, that's fucking Ishlin-ichan. They do it for effect there, for coins from imperial tourists they think it'll impress. It's no different than Strov market in Trelayne. You can't take that shit seriously. Voice growing suddenly faint, as if a door somewhere has closed between them. *Take it from me, no self-respecting Skaranak shaman worth a . . .*

And gone again.

Until finally the gaps between, grown increasingly long and lonely, become an unbroken absence and Ringil stops on the path, as if to acknowledge the Dragonbane's passing. He squats again, sighs, and stares at the dirt-ingrained stones underfoot.

It's a while before he feels like going on.

But as he straightens up, his gaze catches on something. He narrows his eyes and sees, not too distant, a canted set of angles silhouetted black against the sky. The last remaining corner frame of some wooden dwelling, perhaps, long ago eaten down by fire, gnawed and blackened bones now standing forlorn on the marsh.

He shrugs. It's a target like any other. Something to walk toward.

It's not more than a few hundred paces. But as he draws closer, he sees his error. It's not a dwelling, destroyed or otherwise.

It's a signpost.

A signpost made from some hammered dark alloy he doesn't recognize, four fingers forked away from one another at right angles. The whole assembly is canted slightly downward out of true and stands behind a small mound in the tufted marsh grass terrain. The inscription on the pointers is illegible, scoured down by salt-sea winds and time, but he thinks the lettering looks like old Myrlic.

There's a gauzy wrap of cobwebs spun down from the top and outward like some diaphanous triangle of sail run up the signpost's mast. Marsh spiders hang in the gray midst of it, fist-sized and smaller, motionless, tending the strands with long poised forelegs. Ringil feels a sympathetic stab in his belly where the wound is . . .

It won't kill you, hero.

Clicking, crow-rasp, indrawn breath of a voice.

Another stab in the belly as he realizes that what he's taken for a mound is in fact something sat at the base of the signpost, something cowled and swathed in dark rags and so hunched and bent over that he can't believe it just spoke.

Then it lifts its head and looks at him.

Later, he will be unable to remember exactly what it looked like under the cowl. He'll recall only the way he steels up and looks back into the—*what color were they? what shape? how many of them?*—unblinking eyes.

Who told you I'm a hero?

The thing in the rags grunts. *Nothing* but *heroes in this dump. The whole place stinks of them. Like fish heads on a midden heap.*

That doesn't make me one of them.

Does it not? Some rattling sound that might be a chuckle, might equally be a sigh. The rags move, as if at the rearranging of lengthy, arthritic limbs beneath. *Let's see, shall we. Face scarred in betrayal, broadsword gifted by a race now gone from the world, a trail of corpses and dark eddies behind you like bread crumbs off a baker's wagon. Who do you think you're kidding, sunshine?*

Very good. Aristo disdain cloaking his unease at the sensation that there are far more than two arms working beneath the restless shift of those rags. *Am I supposed to be impressed? I've seen better readings than that from the crones at Strov market. Will you scry a hero's future for me now as well?*

As you wish.

And out of the rags, suddenly, there's a big leather-bound tome cracked open, and clawed, bony fingers—or maybe just claws?—turning the vellum sheets within. The cowl dips, the gaze pores over pages, the taloned fingers leaf.

Here you are. The voice grows mockingly sonorous. *Ringil of the cursed blade Ravensfriend, exiled and troubled scion of the northern house Eskiath, reached out and made the clasp with the Rightful Emperor of All Lands. There was blood on the exile's face and in his hair, the marks of battle all over his body, but his grip was still strong and the Emperor grinned to feel that strength. My royal brother, he laughed. Well met. Well—*

Ringil must have snorted. The beady gaze flickers up at him. *No? Doesn't sound very likely.*

Very well. The parched scratch of a page turning. *Try this, then. Ringil Angel Eyes rode in sunlit triumph under the high arch of the eastern gate, where he had caused the punishment cages to be cast down and broken apart. At his back marched a double file of the Vanishing Folk, wondrous to behold, and the people of Trelayne fell to their knees in—*

The Vanishing Folk? In sunlight?

The cowled head cocked. *You're right. That's a transcription error. Ringil Angel Eyes rode in* band*lit triumph under—*

That's enough. Voice harsh now, because a sudden unlooked-for ache has crept up into his throat.

It is a happy ending.

I don't fucking care. The Vanishing Folk wouldn't follow me anywhere except to slit my throat. I betrayed them, I betrayed—

He shuts his mouth with a snap.

Silence.

The cold sift of the wind, stirring his hair. He finds, abruptly, that it hurts him to swallow. The creature at the base of the signpost makes a throat-clearing sound. Turns the page.

All right. Ringil Angel Eyes, the farmboy who had now risen to become both master mage and king—

Farmboy? Fucking farmboy?

Ringil finds his anger and the hilt of the dragon-tooth dagger simultaneously. Or maybe it's not rage, maybe it's just a vast impatience, finally, with this place and all it implies. He drops into a crouch before the ragged figure, jabs the yellowed blade in under what might—or might not—be a chin.

Suppose you turn the page and just tell me the fastest way I can get out of here.

The mound of rags shifts, writhes, and here come the arms, oh yes, another six of them besides the two that hold the book, taloned at the ends, flexing up and out like some obscene unfolding puppetry, he feels two of them settle on his back just below the shoulder blades, pressing in and up like hooks. Another two, tickling in under the ribs at the meat of his waist. One of the remaining spares pats him companionably on the shoulder. The other creeps around under his chin and lifts it slightly on one cold, hooked talon.

I should hate to tear you asunder, the voice says sibilantly. *You show a lot of promise.*

The stone circle flickers into existence, but it will not serve—the creature he's crouched eye-to-eye with is already well inside *that* space. Ringil can smell it now, a mingling of odors like damp stone and parchment and thick, fresh ink. An odor that might belong to the book as much as the taloned thing that holds it.

Ringil purses his lips, mouth dry. He considers the dragon-tooth blade for a moment.

Lowers it.

The hooks at his shoulder blades ease their touch; the ticklish pressure at his waist withdraws. Limbs folding down, and away. But the talon at his chin remains.

Ringil Eskiath, the voice resumes. *Came down the gangplank of the* Famous Victory None Foresaw *and joined the bright, brawling chaos on the wharf. Sunlight shattered across the water, slammed glints into his narrowed eyes. The Black Folk Span held the sky to the south like a massive slice of shadow dropped across the estuary. It was better than a mile upriver from where he'd disembarked, but you could sense the cool of its shade from here, beckoning you on.*

Does that suffice?

Ringil nods gingerly. His voice comes hoarse and dry. *Sounds good, yeah.*

The talon comes out from under his jaw, trails lightly up his cheek, and then lifts away. Ringil tries to rise from his crouch, but another swift tap on his shoulder stops him. He waits again. The creature makes another throat-clearing sound, though from what Ringil has now seen, he's not convinced it has a throat to clear.

Well, the merroigai speak highly of you. And I should not like you, at this crossroads, to think ill of me. It is that way.

One bone-pale arm scissors out across his vision, gestures to the right.

What is?

What you seek, hero. Brief comfort, and a way out.

HE'S FORGOTTEN THE FIRELIGHT FLICKER ON THE SKY.

Now, as if freshly unveiled, it shows up as a solid glow along the path to his right. He'd swear it was not that close before. Or maybe the sky, for cycles and reasons of weather he cannot begin to fathom, is actually darkening now toward some kind of night.

He walks an increasingly defined road, paving broad enough for a farmer's cart, and he can see the ancient runnels where generations of such traffic have worn their mark. His boot heels tock solidly, send odd echoes scurrying away across the marsh, and he feels a faint prickling at his nape, as if at any moment he'll hear other, stilted-scuttling steps mingled with his own, the creature at the crossroads rushing to catch up, to rise behind him, mouthparts splitting apart, talons unfolding once more, suddenly unforgiving of Ringil's prior discourtesy and dragon-knife nerves . . .

Instead, the broad path takes him in amid the ruins of a city; wind-swept terraces of broken stone, the snapped stumps of pillars, huge tilted mausoleum blocks carved with rows of symbols he can't read but whose chiseled march makes him shiver more than spider-bite fever and the gray marsh weather would rightly explain. And now there are steps on the left, broad, shallow ledges of them, worn wax-smooth and un-even with age, dripping down to the level of the road he's on. He looks up their sweep and the fireglow jumps and gutters at the top, strong against a sky now undoubtedly darkening. He hears the pluck of a stringed instrument, human voices raised in laughter and undisciplined efforts at song.

He picks his way up toward the sounds, balancing relief against an odd sense of loss for the haunted road he's leaving below. And when he reaches the top, stands on a plateau of cracked white-stone paving that looks as if it might once have been the floor of some columned temple or market space, when he sees the wagons gathered in the center, the cheery reach of the bonfire and the motley-clad men and women gathered around it, he finds himself unaccountably pinned in the shadows at the edge of the plaza, not quite able to move forward.

It's a woman who spots him first. Carrying a wine flask on one hip around the fire and back to one of the wagons, shrugging off ribald commentary from men who grab after her with halfhearted, hilarious ineptitude as she passes, she turns away from the fire for a moment, and there he is. In the instant their eyes meet, he sees himself as she must: gaunt, black-cloaked, and silent, sword pommel at his back.

He thinks she'll shriek, but she doesn't.

Hjel, she calls instead. *We have visitors.*

Ringil hears the name as it floats across the campfire air to its owner, hears the archaic marsh dialect of Naomic the woman uses, and there's a sudden twitch in his groin, and a wonder in his head. There, at the fire's edge, the slumped, brim-hatted figure with the long-necked mandolin across his lap . . .

Ringil narrows his gaze. *Couldn't be—could it?*

The mandolin's plucked chime stops, the last chords skitter off in the dark. The murmur of conversation around the fire dries up. The player lets long, supple hands lie on the instrument for a moment. Beneath the brim of the hat, he tilts his head slowly up. Glitter of eyes as they throw back the fire's cheer.

It's him. No question.

Visitors. Well. Hjel props himself elegantly upright and hands the mandolin off to a woman seated at his side. He speaks the same tongue, just as he did before, marsh Naomic with its ornate traceries of old Myrlic. He stands, and stares across the hot sparks and wavering air above the fire. *And a warrior to boot, by the look of it. Come forward, sir. We don't stand on ceremony at the court of Hjel the Dispossessed.*

Lightning-flash image: Under canvas-lit parchment yellow with the firelight outside, Hjel curls those long supple fingers around Gil's cock and runs the tip of his tongue . . .

That much I know. Do you not recognize me, Ragged Prince?

Hjel sets hands on hips and tilts his head a little at the familiar title. *Recognize you? To do that, I would need to see you in the light.*

A score of eyes on him around the fire—those on this side have scooted sideways to look. Ringil obliges them with a couple of paces forward, keeps his hands clearly visible for courtesy. The temptation to do a pirouette is an overwhelming itch in his—now oddly painless— stomach. Suddenly, out of nowhere, he's on the edge of laughter.

The mandolin player comes around the fire, picks his way among the seated company with slim-hipped, long-legged grace. There's stubble on his face, and there, that tiny scar on his chin he rubs at when he's curious. He strolls up and makes a half circle at Ringil's side, carefully out of blade range. Folds his arms across his lower chest as if hugging himself.

Lifts a hand and rubs the scar.

Shakes his head.

No. I'd remember that face. That big sword. I don't know you, friend.

Ringil smiles. *But I know you.*

Well, washed up as we are at the gray margins of the world, any chilled wraith hoping for a place at the fire might say the same thing. But the eyes beneath the hat brim are dancing with all the curiosity and wild mischief Ringil remembers. *Convince me.*

Ringil raises a hand, crooks thumb and little finger as he has been taught. Words from the *ikinri 'ska* bubble behind his lips. He lets a few break free—harsh, whispered syllables that seem to leave little pockets of chilled air in their wake. At the fireside, one of the hounds pricks up its ears and looks at him strangely. Later, some will swear they saw a dark ripple step across the ancient, crack-stoned plaza. And shadows bicker at the edges of the fire.

The smile falls off Hjel's face.

Who taught you that?

You did.

Now Hjel's disquiet is spreading to the men and women around the fire. Perhaps they sense, at some animal level, the same touch that the hound did. Or perhaps it's only the way their captain has grown so abruptly serious.

The ikinri 'ska is not a set of tricks for cheap conjuring, Hjel says quietly. *I would not have taught it to a charlatan.*

You asked to be convinced.

I am not convinced.

Very well. In your tent, you keep a white-marble figurine of a woman with a crack through its head. About this size, very beautiful, apparently very old. You found it on the marsh as a boy. You'd wandered away from your uncle's caravan and lost yourself. A strange, pale wolf seemed to be stalking you, but when you—

Enough. Hjel swallowed. *You walk out of my future to recite my past. You drag dark echoes behind you like a trawl net. What are you really?*

What I am is hungry. And cold. Your hospitality wasn't so circumspect the last time, Prince in Rags.

So you say.

Any chilled wraith hoping for a place at the fire might say the same. Yes. Ringil shrugs. *You're a sorcerer, you once told me. A master of the* ikinri *'ska. So. My name is Ringil Eskiath. Look in my eyes and tell me if you see a wraith there.*

He waits.

It takes a moment, and before Hjel meets his gaze, the sorcerer's eyes flicker off to right and left as if Ringil has come with an honor guard at his back. But finally he looks, and whatever he does or does not see in his visitor's eyes, he chooses not to comment on it. He nods slightly instead, like a man accepting bad news he has long expected.

Be welcome at my hearth, then, Ringil Eskiath. Hjel gestures toward the fire, some of his earlier elegant poise regained in the motion. *I place us both in bonds of guest and host.*

Then he jerks a thumb back over his shoulder, artfully casual, as if it's an afterthought.

But your friends back there stay out in the dark.

RINGIL DOESN'T LOOK BACK. IF HJEL THE SCAVENGER PRINCE AND SORcerer can play this game, so can he.

But as the new chill walks its way up his spine, he knows beyond doubt what he'll see if he does turn. He knows because he's seen it before, falling off the feverish edge of consciousness as he lay on the cobbled streets of Hinerion and heard the screams of Venj's men dying.

A gaunt figure, a scarred face, a sword blade swinging like a scythe.

A blunt, powerful form, fists gripped around a heavy smith's hammer and long-handled manacle cutters.

A young boy, mouth open, snarling through bloodied teeth, a quarrel sprouting from under his sternum like some alien iron appendage.

They stand at his back in the cold—he can feel them there now—like new gods. Like a fresh pantheon, waiting to be born.

IT WAS WARM, BY THE FIRE.

CHAPTER 22

The slave quarters were guarded.

Harath sank back into cover with a clenched curse. Four flights of stairs below the landing they crouched on, a pair of tall doors like those they'd passed through to get to the gallery. Heavy chain through the handles, and three burly figures sat in a circle on low stools in front. A couple of lanterns stood on the ground nearby and threw long, fitful flickers across the floor. Low mutter of Majak, the odd explosion of good-natured cursing—the three men were playing dice in the dust. Three staff lances were propped casually against the side of the door, thin, bony shadows slanting down the wall in the lantern glow.

"This is new," Harath whispered. "They never used to bother."

"What happens when your hired help starts mauling the merchandise," Egar hissed back.

Harath grinned sheepishly, and Egar felt like choking him. There was a thin, restless anger rising in him now. Thanks to this Ishlinak punk, he was going to have to do it after all. Majak blood on his hands once again, and for no better reason than . . .

Than what, Dragonbane? Than bare, bored-out-of-your-mind curiosity? Than random scouting of the enemy's ramparts in service to Archeth, who's out of town anyway?

Or—oh, wait—is it that itch you can't scratch with Ishgrim, maybe, and the thought that some other willowy Naom slave gash might be grateful enough if you—

He chopped the thoughts irritably away. The restless anger slopped higher in him, seeking outlet.

Fucking punk kids.

In *his* day, no Majak who'd taken coin to guard slaves would have dreamed of touching the goods or—

That's right, Dragonbane. And brothers always stood together, the buffalo came when they were called, the grass grew taller and greener, and it never fucking rained.

Get a grip, old man.

He crushed out the brooding with a grimace. Drew one of his knives. Crouched and listened to the voices float up through the gloomy air. The twang of the Ishlinak dialect.

Harath dipped his head closer.

"I thought you said we weren't going to get into it with these guys."

"I thought you said the slave quarters weren't guarded, and we'd get in with a bent pin."

Half the sheepish grin again. "Yeah, but—"

Egar spared two fingers from the grip on his knife, snagged Harath by the collar, and jerked him close. Eyes like slits, teeth tight. Voice a snake-strike hiss.

"You've been *paid*, Majak."

Harath jerked loose. But he looked away and wet his lips.

"Look—I reckon that's Alnarh down there," he murmured.

"Good. That should make it easy for you. Some payback for all his shit? You can take him, I'll do the other two."

The younger man nodded hesitantly. Egar could not quite repress a savage twinge of satisfaction. *Bit of fucking consequence for your acts and the coin you take, eh, kid?* He gestured with one knife-filled hand, and they ghosted down the stairs together in the shadow of the balustrades. Got to the final landing, and the last corner of usable cover. Harath hovered. Wet his lips again.

Egar widened his eyes at him, jerked his chin. *Fucking get on with it.*

Harath stood. Went down the final flight of stairs toward the dice players with no attempt at quiet.

Scrabble of action as they saw him and came to their feet, grabbing weapons.

"Hold it right the fuck there!"

"Not another step, asshole!"

Harath snorted. "Oh my, what big fucking blades you have, boys."

Stunned silence. Peering through the balustrade, Egar made out short-swords, maybe an ax. But their staff lances still stood against the wall. The murderous seven-foot, double-bladed Majak standby—but still not in play.

One of the Ishlinak halfway lowered his sword.

"Harath—that you, buddy?"

"Shut up, Elkret. He's outcast. What the fuck are you doing here, Harath? Who let you in?"

Harath made it to the bottom of the stairs, hands well away from his sides. He seemed, finally, to have started enjoying himself.

"Hey, Alnarh. How's it hanging? Getting any Revelation-approved pussy?"

Alnarh twitched toward the staff lance where it leaned against the wall. "I *said* who let you in?"

"*Let* me in? You stupid fucking twat, you think I need *letting* into this place? I already told you, Alnarh. You couldn't set up a guard duty to save your fucking—"

And time.

Egar vaulted the landing rail, came down ten feet like a catapult stone and cut loose with his knives. He landed just off Elkret's shoulder, swung and slashed, sent him sprawling with a yell. Alnarh whirled at the sound. Had just enough time to yell—

" *'Ware raiders!*"

—before Egar reached the third, unnamed Ishlinak. The other man got in a lucky block with the haft of his hand ax—Egar took it on the forearm with a grunt, shoved back and swept the guard aside, stabbed in roundhouse beneath. The knife blade found flesh somewhere above the man's hip, slugged home to the hilt. The Ishlinak quivered and shrieked. Peripheral glimpse—off to Egar's right, Alnarh reached his staff lance, just had time to grab it away from the wall and turn as Harath rushed him. The lance swung, Alnarh got it crossways to block, and the two men met in a whirl of limbs and spat curses. Egar twisted his own blade and pulled it out—blood splattered out on his hand, so hot it seemed almost to burn. The Ishlinak he'd stabbed went down with a pleading look on his face, clutching at Egar's sleeve. Gazes locked—instinct telling them both the truth of what had been done.

Elkret—behind him.

He whipped about. Elkret had a long-knife raised in his left hand, but he was slow—was hurt—*must have hit lucky, that first slash.* Egar couldn't see the wound he'd made, but he could have dodged this attack in his sleep. He stepped sideways from the thrust of the knife, snagged the arm behind it at the wrist, pulled and locked it out. Right hand raised, tightening to a fist around his knife—he slammed down at the locked elbow joint, broke the arm. The hollow snap echoed in the lantern flicker, chased away with the choked scream it wrung out of Elkret. The long-knife flew loose. Egar got in close, dragged back the Ishlinak's head, exposed the throat—

"No—*wait!*"

Harath's hoarse shout. Egar broke his stroke with an effort. He dragged Elkret around so he could see where the shout had come from. Nestled the knife up against the Ishlinak's neck.

"Don't you move," he murmured, and felt Elkret stiffen away from the touch of the steel.

"Don't—don't kill him." Harath, stumbling upright from Alnarh's limp form, panting from the fight. "Come on, man. You don't have to do that."

"I think we do, actually."

But he could already feel the resolve slipping away. The fight had come and gone too fast to arouse the berserker battle fury in him, and now it felt grubby and pointless.

Harath took a step forward, hands out, mastering his breathing. "Come on, brother. He's a friend."

"He's not *my* fucking friend." Egar sighed and shoved Elkret away from him, practically into Harath's arms. "Fine, *brother.* It's your face he's seen. Do what you like."

Harath fumbled the catch, let Elkret slip past him. The injured Ishlinak dropped to his knees, hale arm hanging as slack as the wrecked one. He stared down at Alnarh's body.

"The fuck've you done, man," he mumbled. "What the fuck have you done?"

It wasn't immediately clear who he was talking to. But Alnarh at least would not be answering—Harath had crushed his old comrade's throat in with the staff lance, and the shaft still lay across the corpse's neck. Eyes and distended tongue bulged outward. In the lantern flicker, it gave the Ishlinak's face the comic-hideous look of a Shaktur devil mask.

"We'd better get out of here," Harath muttered.

"Oh, no. We came here for a reason." Egar nodded at the door. "Get that open. One of them has to have keys."

"Harath, what the fuck have you done?"

"Look, we made a lot of noise. They—"

"That's the second time I got to remind you who's paying the piper here? *Look for the fucking key.*"

Harath flinched. But he started pawing over Alnarh's corpse. Egar watched him for a moment, then went to check on the man he'd stabbed to death.

The Ishlinak had bled out all over the dusty floor. The leakage looked like some stagnant midnight road puddle the dead man had fallen into from an unruly horse. Egar crouched to search clothing for the keys, saw the vague bulk and motion of his head and shoulders reflected up in the blood as he leaned over. For one slightly dizzying moment, it was as if there was something murky down there in the puddle, staring back up at him.

" . . . the fuck have you done, Harath . . . "

"Look, just *shut it.*" Harath's hissed tones, cooking frustration and guilt toward anger. "You're fucking alive, aren't you? That's a fucking

Dragonbane over there. You know how close he was to slitting your fuck-ing throat like you were livestock? *Found* it! *Here's* the fucking key!"

Egar stirred from staring down at his blood-sunk other self. Got up away from the black pool with something weirdly approaching relief. Turned back to the others.

Elkret was still kneeling where they'd left him, like one of those half-wit penitents you sometimes saw out by the Saffron gate. Harath stood near him, holding up an ornate iron key. He still looked a little sick around the gills, but he was grinning haggardly with it.

" 'Kay?"

"So open it up."

Elkret looked up at the Dragonbane's voice. His face was a shocked blank.

"You'd better get out of here," he said quietly. "Before *they* come."

Egar felt an unreasonable creeping at the back of his neck. He glanced around at the shadowed architecture. "Before who come?"

"The angels."

"Got no angels following me, son. I'm not a convert."

"Doesn't matter," Elkret told him. "They're watching from on high. Touch what's theirs and they'll come. This was promised. We are all marked as their servants, our suffering will be redeemed."

It rang like scripture, the same shit everyone down here could reel off by the yard, seemingly to gild any given situation the day had to offer. Egar had asked Imrana once if there was a verse to cover shitting cor-rectly, and she'd replied soberly that yes, of course there was, there were correct rituals to ablutions as to anything else. He was never very sure whether she was winding him up or not.

Coming out of a Majak's mouth like this, it sounded oddly twisted.

"Hey, fuck that shit!" Harath, harsh-toned and apparently sharing Egar's distaste. "This fucking city's rotted your brains, Elkret. We're Majak—the Sky Dwellers are watching over us. That's good enough for me, brother."

"The Dwellers won't stop them. It's a light no one can stand against. I've seen it."

Egar nodded, gave him a tight smile, and hit him. Hook punch, in from the side, palm like a blade, thumb joint into the temple. The old horse-thief standby, knockout in a single unguarded moment—the Ish-linak crumpled without a sound.

"Right, let's make this fast, shall we?"

Harath stared down at Elkret. "You didn't have to do that."

"Yeah, I did. Now let's *go*. This place is starting to give me the creeps."

ON THE OTHER SIDE OF THE DOOR, THE SLAVE QUARTERS WERE BETTER appointed than some harems Egar had broken into in his time. There was space—because in an empty temple, what else are you going to have—and an endless retreat of rooms opening off one another left and right like feints from some effete knife fighter falling back. From what they could see in the lantern light, some attempt had been made to clean the place up. There was furniture of sorts scattered at random through the rooms; colored shawls and other makeshift drapery hung at windows, twitching in the night breeze. The ghost scents of cheap soap and cooked food hung in the air.

The slaves were scattered few and far between, much like the furniture. They slept on thin mattresses on the floors or on carved stone benches and alcoves set into the walls. As far as Egar could see beneath the blankets they used to cover themselves, most were young and female, with a few boys leavened into the mix. All were of northern complexion, faces making pale smudges in the gloom. Some of them raised their heads as the two Majak went by, the way hounds will when their master walks past the hearth. But they said nothing, only watched with wary, light-sleeper eyes.

Egar marched Harath back and forth until he had the plan of the place more or less sorted out. The rooms looked to be knotted figure-of-eight style about a pair of narrow courtyards roofed in with stone trelliswork. The sensation of infinite recess was cunningly provided by smaller chambers off to the sides here and there. He guessed they might once have been monk's cells or something . . .

They drifted to a halt, under the eaves in a corner of one of the courtyards.

"See her?" he asked Harath.

"No, man." Irritable, throwaway tone. "She's not here. How long are we going to—"

Egar looked balefully at him and he raised placatory hands.

"Yeah, okay, brother, okay. I'm paid. I know. But they change the guard at midnight. What are we doing here? What's the plan?"

He had a point.

Whatever you came here to do, Dragonbane, better work out what it was, and then get on and do it.

"Come with me."

Egar ducked back inside, approached a young girl in an alcove who'd propped herself up to look as they passed. Soft-featured, snub nose and small, frightened eyes, he reckoned her not much older than fifteen or sixteen. He set down the lantern, crouched before her to make himself smaller to her terrified gaze. He jerked a thumb back at Harath, spoke soothingly low in Tethanne.

"Listen, do you know him?"

The girl shrank back into the alcove's limited depths. Face lowered, shaking her head repeatedly.

"You sure? He had a thing with one of the girls here, a few weeks back."

"Couple of months," corrected Harath.

The dry-trickle thread of a voice. "I don't—we're not supposed to—it's forbidden, please—"

Egar held up his hands, aping the gesture he'd squeezed out of Harath in the courtyard a few moments ago. "Listen, I don't want to hurt you, I'm not going to even touch you. I just want you to tell me about the other girl."

"But she's gone." Eyes pleading.

"We fucking know that, bitch. *Where's* she gone?"

Egar bounced up, spun on Harath.

"You want to *shut up* for a minute?" he hissed. Fighting yet again a strong desire to punch the Ishlinak out. "Do something useful. Get out there again, see if there's some way to climb up to that trelliswork and break through onto the roof. Go on. Fuck off. I've got this."

Harath looked hurt, but he went. Egar crouched in front of the girl again. She was backed so hard into the stonework of the alcove now, her muscles were straining at the push. She had the blanket up almost over her face, as if she could wrap herself in it like the girl in the fairy tale, and disappear.

"Don't worry about him. Just tell me anything you know about this girl. Did you know her name?"

The eyes looked back at him over the drawn-up blanket hem. "He told her he'd take her away. He promised her. All that week, she was waiting for him to come back."

Egar sighed. "Yeah, what can I tell you? Like they say, never trust a fucking Ishlinak farther than you can throw-rope him. So what happened to her?"

A tight gulp. "They came."

"They?"

"The priests, the invigilators. They dragged her out, they were asking her questions, slapping her, screaming at her. They were so angry. We have to be pure. Untouched."

Egar frowned. It was the same crap they handed daughters the world over, he supposed. But *slaves?* And some of the women he'd seen didn't look to be much under thirty summers. If Menkarak thought he was holding a crop of virgins here, he had to be more fucked in the head than even Archeth reckoned he was.

"Why untouched?" he asked.

A visible shudder ran through her. "The angels have chosen us. When it's their time to walk here, they'll come for us."

"Angels." He was getting tired of this.

"You don't believe me," she whispered. Her gaze wilted downward, her knuckles pressed through the blanket against her mouth as if she was trying not to be sick. Voice mumbling almost too low to catch the words. "You're from the north, farther north even than me. Why would you believe? Men like you."

And then, as if these last words had woken something in her, the girl's eyes snapped up again. Fixed on his.

"Get me out of here." It jerked out of her. "Please, *get me out.*"

"Uhm, look . . ."

"*Please.* I'll do anything, *anything.* I'm good, I was in a Parashal training stable before this, I can, you can." She swallowed. "Anything. But you have to take me with you, right now."

"Listen . . ."

"You don't understand." Taut desperation now, snapping her jaw tight on the words. "I've *seen* them. I've seen the fucking angels for myself. Just like they said. They came and I was judged. Blue fire. Blue fire and voices like beasts at play."

Blue fire . . .

He sat back as if she'd slapped him.

Abruptly, he was back in the mist-tangled marshes of Ennishmin, crouched among hardened artifact scavengers, watching the faint flicker of blue in the distance.

Swamp wraith, murmured one of the men, and the others made gestures at the various charms they wore. *We don't go this way.*

And later, at the tavern with Ringil, he saw the way a decrepit old man melted before his eyes, leaking that same blue radiance as he went down. Saw what rose instead to replace the illusion of humanity . . .

Ringil always argued they couldn't come here, to Yhelteth. *Wouldn't* come here, where the sun was a withering white blast across the sky . . .

The squat black glirsht statues in the altar chamber.

Some kind of beacon for the dwenda.

He almost turned to look, over his shoulder, back the way they'd come. To what might now be blocking their way out.

Once, barely twenty years old, deep in the Dhashara pass, he'd gotten into a tomb alone, only to find it was now a scree panther lair. The sarcophagus was tumbled, lid broken in huge fragments across the earthen floor. Bones strewn everywhere, and the piles of panther spore, the marks of iron-hard claws through the dust, the paw-pad traces.

The cave exit was thirty yards of chilled and twisting raw rock tunnel back the way he'd come. He shuffled bent-backed along every darkened foot of it expecting to hear the scrape of claws ahead and the low yowl of the panther returning. Prayers in his throat to the Dwellers, begging—he'd go to his death gladly, whenever, wherever they chose, if it could only be under open skies.

When he made it out into the hot mountain sunlight, it was like being born again.

"No fucking way." Harath, grumbling back from the courtyard. "Stone's solid as the day they carved it. Take a week to chisel through."

"Right. Back the way we came then. Get the lantern. We're leaving."

"Thank Vavada's tits for that."

Egar reached out his hand to the girl. "You want out, girl? This is it. Let's go."

The slave girl gaped disbelief, then grabbed at his hand as if coming up from drowning. Harath guffawed. Egar made a mighty effort and didn't smack him. He pulled the girl to her feet instead. Thin cotton shift under the blanket; the garment was practically translucent, barely made it to her shins. Her breasts molded to it, showed dark nipples through the cloth. Harath made an appreciative noise deep in his throat and reached to grope one of the soft mounds. Egar slapped him away.

"We're in a hurry," he said gruffly.

"You're a sad old man, Dragonbane." The Ishlinak gave him a filthy grin. "I fucking *told* you, if you wanted—"

Egar peeled him a look and he shut up.

"And I told you we're in a hurry. Now pick up that fucking lamp."

Perhaps it was there in his voice, a trace of tight-roped tension that closed the Ishlinak down. Or maybe Harath could feel the same thing Egar did not want to admit he felt. The creeping sensation that now breathed from every darkened alcove and doorway around them, that stalked the rooms behind them like the ghost of vengeance for brothers slain.

Something on its way.

They loped back through the endless rooms, knives out and carried low. Ignoring the blanket-bundled bodies to left and right, whether they woke and watched them go or not. Skirmish party pace—soft, rapid crunch of their footfalls, the hurrying puddle of the lantern, and behind it all, a yawning prescient quiet. The girl, stumbling as she struggled to keep up on bare feet.

They cleared the main door to the slave quarters, found the bodies undisturbed. The other lanterns and the stretched-hideous flickering shadows that capered out from their bases. The staircase back up, the way they'd come, and there at the top—

Egar slammed to a halt.

The girl saw. Moaned low in her throat.

Blue fire.

CHAPTER 23

Hjel's band slipped away from the fire in dribs and drabs, to bedrolls and tents laid out across the ancient paving. Ringil watched them lay themselves down to sleep like ghosts in the gloom—phantoms drifting to their graves at dawn, after a hard night of undead revelry. The last couple to go were a man and woman huddled up together and sharing a depleted flask of wine. Finally, the man responded to the woman's repeated tugging at his sleeve and significant glances, rose clumsily and unsteadily to his feet, and pulled his partner up at his side.

"G'night then, gents," he slurred.

"Sleep well, Cortin." Hjel didn't look up from beneath the brim of his hat. "You, too, Enith."

The woman smiled in the low flicker of the firelight. "Will you play us to our blankets, Hjel?"

Hjel nodded assent, but his heart clearly wasn't in it. His fingers plucked up a thin cascade of notes from the mandolin, and the woman led her partner away with lightly sprung steps to the tune. The man let her tug him along, glanced back once and winked at Ringil. Then the two of them were gone, off into the darkness.

The mandolin's song coasted to a halt. The brim tipped up, and Hjel's eyes gleamed with light thrown back from the coals in the firebed.

"What are you looking at?" Ringil asked him softly.

"I'm not sure." One hand lifted from the mandolin fretboard, palm opened outward. "A mirror, perhaps? A choice I might have made?"

Ringil felt something climb his spine on icy talons and settle like a demon familiar under the angle of his jaw. He hunched his shoulders against the touch, painted his face with a smile.

"Yeah, you made about as much sense as this the last time."

"Very likely." The sorcerer played a pair of chords and let them fade. Across the twist in the heated air above the fire, his eyes still gleamed, but Ringil got the impression they were no longer looking at him. "Did I tell you, last time—next time, whichever it is—did I tell you that my ancestors were once kings?"

"It came up, yes. To be frank, our minds were on other things."

Hjel either ignored the flirt or didn't hear it. "And I had already—will already have—told you this story. There's logic in that, I suppose, though I have never seen the Margins play this particular trick before. And I don't imagine it presages anything very good."

The hat brim tipped down, hooded the eyes for a long moment. When it rose again, Ringil thought he could see the trace of a smile in the shadows beneath.

"It's a pretty good scam, right? A ragged band of entertainers and camp followers claiming homage as the thousand-year descendants of the royal court in hiding. That old Bloodline-in-Exile thing. A wandering minstrel and conjuror, in truth the dispossessed, rightful king. Nice work if you can get it."

Ringil shrugged. "Well. Now you come to mention it."

"The Margins help, of course. They ebb and flow like a tide across the marsh, wash the ruins under for hours or months at a time, spit them back up again. Live alongside something like that, you can't help but give credence to fairy-tale notions."

"Tide?"

"Yes." Absently. Hjel seemed not to have noticed Ringil's fumbling unfamiliarity with the word. "Can't you feel the difference? We are out again, the shadows ebb—for now. But it's not always so comfortable. Wander incautiously, lose yourself out on the marsh and you can be swept away, lost forever or for merely the handful of decades that take your loved ones from you. There are stories of—"

"Yeah, heard them." Ringil shifted restlessly. In his world, the marsh dwellers told those tales all the time, usually on the pitches at Strov market with a horny palm out for payment. "Heard them all, front and back."

The hat brim dipped, perhaps in acknowledgment. "Well, what you may *not* have heard is that even those wandering with some education and a map are likely still to come back with gifts at best uncertain and scars they would rather not have earned. And if you've grown up with this as truth, well, why not accept that these gaunt, wild-eyed, motley-clad players might once have been a mighty dynasty. They don't ask much, after all, and the show is a delight, especially for the children. Why not cough up a few coins? Why not share what food and shelter you have to give them, step away for a few hours from the grind of your daily existence into the exotic fantasy they give you in return. Why not cave in to easy belief?"

"And do you?"

"Do I what? Believe that I am the direct descendant of the once-great sorcerer kings of Drel-en-ilynyr? That my ancestors fled into the Margins when they could not defeat the Scourge from the South, and that their gracious subjects continue to protect and succor them to this day, for all that the Scourge is long gone from living memory? That my bloodline merely awaits its time to rise again?" Hjel's smile flickered again, ember-like. "Why would I *not* want to believe something like that?"

"Oh, I don't know. Because it's a made-up pile of pigshit, maybe?"

The mandolin master nodded soberly. "There is always that possibility. But pigshit or not, would it really make so much difference? A destiny is a handy thing to have in your pocket, however worn and unlikely it might be."

"Well, if you say so—Prince of Rags."

"I do say so." Hjel looked into the fire for a while. If he'd taken offense it didn't show. "Men are lightweight in this world, Ringil Eskiath; blown about on their own ungoverned impulses like marsh-flower seed in a spring storm. Anybody can see they need anchoring. A manifest destiny, even a shared and shabby secondhand one, provides the ballast for each man and the binding for a whole people. If it's a shared lie, does it really matter?"

"If you carried a sword, you'd know the answer to that."

"Yes, if I carried a sword. But as you see"—dance of hands, the mandolin gave up a brief ripple of chords—"I do not."

"Aren't you the lucky one."

Ringil stared down into his side of the ember bed, hearing the small *pop* and *snap* of the waning fire. No comfort there. Against the sounds of the flames, he thought he heard screams and distant weeping. He wondered what Hjel saw from his side. He knew that the other man was watching him now, but found himself curiously unwilling to look up and meet the hat brim gaze across the heated air.

"You met it, didn't you?" Hjel's tone was mild, but there was no hint of a question in it. "At the crossroads."

The demon familiar dug in its icy claws again.

"Its trace clings to you, Ringil Eskiath. Like cold to leather long after the wearer comes inside. Dispossessed or not, I come from a long line of sorcerers; my gifts are good for this much at least. Don't deny where you've been." A long pause. "What did it tell you?"

Ringil looked up. There was no challenge waiting for him across the fireside in the other man's eyes. Instead, he felt something a little like desperation leaking out of Hjel the Dispossessed.

"You've seen it, too?"

Hjel sat closer in to the fire. "My family has a long association with it. Family legend has it that my ancestors banished it to the Margins when they founded the city, and were cursed as a result. Well, who knows? But each of us, each eldest heir when we come of age, must go after it into the Margins, find it at the crossroads and ask it to gift us with something, one way or the other."

"You banished it, and it gives you gifts in return?"

A haggard smile. "They say it has a sense of humor. And the gifts are . . . ambiguous. Some of my ancestors returned in triumph, some came home broken. And some did not return at all."

"You?" Ringil realized that he was leaning forward, rapt.

Hjel shrugged. "Well, I did return."

"What did it gift you with?"

Scatter of notes from the mandolin, like birds off into the gloom. "Can't you guess?"

The fire popped and crackled quietly to itself.

"You couldn't play before?"

"Oh, I had some meager talent, I suppose. A certain gypsy flair. Grow up among traveling players, the heir apparent of the band, you learn, more or less in self-defense. But there was nothing beyond that, no. Nothing that would *open the stiff barrel taps of a hard man's eyes,* as the poet has it."

Ringil grimaced, because that sounded alarmingly like a line out of early Skimil Shend.

"And now? You can make men weep with your music?"

Another small, painful smile. "Now I can crack a man's heart to a halt with my music, if I choose. Spill out his soul and send it on to the crossroads. Women are harder, but that, too, can be done with a little effort. A gift of somewhat limited application, of course, if you plan to keep your audiences happy. But, as I said, the creature has a sense of humor."

"It's not what you wanted?"

"Am I so obvious?" For the first time, there was a trace of real bitterness in Hjel's voice.

"What did you want, then?"

But the answer already loomed. Ringil's gaze fell to where the Ravensfriend lay at his side in its scabbard and the loosed coils of the shoulder harness rig. And he knew, without looking up, that Hjel had seen it, too.

"A bloodline in exile," the dispossessed prince murmured. "What young man does not dream of bringing his family back to the glory of earlier days? What young man doesn't want the cold command of steel in his clenched fist? Something sharp and powerful. Something to hold."

"You asked for that?"

"Yeah, I asked for that. A sword of power, to lead my followers and carve out a new kingdom." An ironic gesture around. "To build these ruins back up, to raise new towers on the marsh horizon. Instead, I get an improved facility with stringed instruments and a better singing voice. You got to laugh, right?"

Ringil met his eyes and held them. The need was out now, painted on the lean face like the yellowish glare of the firelight.

"Come here," Ringil told him softly. "I'll give you something to hold."

IN THE CANVAS CONFINES OF HJEL'S TENT, THEY CLING AND BEND EACH other to the old, old task. The old hunger gusting, and garments fumbled loose. They've left their boots outside, draped and tumbled over each other in untidy haste, as the two of them stumbled in, all searching mouths and hands. The lack of easy space in the tent seems only to add fuel to the passion. Both kneeling upright now, pressed awkwardly together as Ringil reaches around from behind, slides one hand up under the other man's unbuttoned shirt, rakes nails across the flat, muscled flesh of belly and chest. Hjel turns his head back to find Ringil's mouth, fastens his own lips across it. His hand gropes into Gil's loosened breeches, finds the hardening bar of his prick—chuckle of lust, bared teeth into a sucking kiss as he squeezes and tugs at the shaft. Ringil grunts and arches his back with the wash of sensation, falls forward again and bites hard into Hjel's shoulder. His own hands drop lower, seeking.

After the marsh, after the Margins and the Gray Place ghosts, after all the groggy wandering, this is waking up. This is light pouring into morning chambers, and the stir of rested limbs against the sheets.

This is life again.

They twine around each other, hands restless and working, mouths biting and sucking, and finally, breeches pulled entirely off, Hjel's shirt peeled and flung away, Gil's flapping carelessly undone, a cupped right hand to spit in and the other pressing down as Ringil bends Hjel forward before him. Stroking himself slick with the spit, reaching in between the tight, scalloped buttocks and . . .

Across Hjel's shoulder blade, the fingers of his dry hand find the scars.

He stops what he's doing—muffled grunt of frustration from Hjel—brushes his fingers across the raised scar tissue again, exploring at the edge of some black epiphany.

There at the inner edge of the shoulder blade, a thick finger broad, and crawling down Hjel's back the length of a child's forearm. He remembers this scarring from before, remembers Hjel's hushing evasion of the question that rose to his lips then, but never spilled over into speech. But now . . .

Comprehension dawning, but still a fingertip out of reach . . .

Hjel twisting impatiently about, voice thick with desperate lust. "Don't—that's not—don't *stop*—"

Ignoring him, spread fingers out now to the other shoulder blade and the identical scar carved there . . .

Like angel wings, torn out at the roots. But—

Ringil remembers, feels himself wilt with the memory. The creature's arms, the two that *settle on his back just below the shoulder blades, pressing in and up like hooks.*

The sibilant voice.

I should hate to tear you asunder. You show a lot of promise.

And now Hjel has worked himself around and seen the look on Ringil's face. The lust flutters away, gone like mandolin notes into the dark. He's working on a crooked smile, and for that alone Ringil wants to weep and hold him tight.

"Gifts at the crossroads are not cheap," Hjel says quietly. "Everyone must pay. And most of us heal somewhat with time."

Ringil shakes his head. Mouth tight—words are hard. He forces them out.

"I didn't pay."

Hjel reaches out, suddenly tender after the harsh impatience of their grappling. His hand touches Ringil's cheek, touches the scar along the jaw.

"Perhaps you already have," he says. "Or will later."

Ringil tries his own bent smile. "What else could they take from me now?"

But Hjel only puts rapid fingers across his lips, as if to seal the words back in, and pulls him back down into the shadows on the floor of the tent.

SLOWER THIS TIME.

Ringil uses the tricks he already knows from his other, yet-to-happen couplings with the dispossessed prince, the things he remembers that Hjel likes, the pressure of teeth and tongue like *this* that makes him writhe left and right like a severed snake, the delving fingers doing *that* so they make him stiffen and gasp . . .

He understands now that at least part of Hjel's allure when he first met him must have been a similar prior knowledge to this, inverted. And understanding this, he shows himself to the other man more intimately than he might otherwise have done, offering the gates to his own seduction with an abandon that is at least half sly investment in his own future pleasure.

And half, perhaps, the understanding that this, all of this, cannot last.

When, finally, he thrusts into Hjel from behind, it's done almost gently, and still they both come in seconds. Clenched teeth and groans, the sorcerer bucking back against him like an unbroken pony. Hjel's slim cock, pulsing suddenly sticky in his hand.

As the spasms ebb, Ringil wraps his arms tight around the other man's torso, hugging him up close, pressing face hard against the scar tissue etched into Hjel's back. Closing his eyes for what thin escape there might be.

Something to hold.

CHAPTER 24

I t wasn't a long list:

> *Andal Karsh*
> *Mahmal Shanta*
> *Yilmar Kaptal*
> *Nethena Gral*
> *Shab Nyanar*
> *Jhash Oreni*
> *Klarn Shendanak*

"You know, you'd have thought we'd have a lot more rich fuckers than that in an Empire that spans the known world" was Jhiral's sour opinion when they'd finished. He leaned over her in lamp-glow at the desk, glowering at the parchment and the names it held. "I've certainly handed out royal charter to five times that many, and I've only been on the throne two years."

"Wealthy *and* prepared to risk their wealth," Archeth reminded him, sitting back in the chair, quill still in hand. "It's not a combination we see a lot of these days."

"Well . . . " The Emperor gestured. "The war."

"Yes, my lord. The war."

At court it had become something of a catchall excuse, a slick evasion of responsibility for failures as varied as falling crop revenue, eastern province bandit incursions, and even street cobble upkeep in the poorer quarters of the city. *The war, my lord.*

Sometimes, it was even true.

And sometimes not. The war and the speculative skirmishing against the League in the aftermath might have decimated the ranks of Yhelteth's less risk-averse nobles, but it was Jhiral's post-coronation purges and appointments that were doing the damage now. The Emperor's obsession with personal loyalty above all things was currently making obsequious caution in word and deed pretty much a required survival trait.

And now, my lord, it's come right back to bite you in the arse.

Glancing up at him, she wondered if he saw it. Or if he cared. Jhiral was not a stupid man, but neither did he seem much disposed since the accession to put his intelligence to work. Or at least, not on any project beyond paranoid self-preservation and the drenching of his senses in pleasure.

Yeah—can you blame him, Archidi? Five attempts on his life before he even got into his teens, seven more since then. Three exiled brothers and a sister who'd all slit his throat without blinking if they thought it'd bring them to the throne. Innumerable half siblings lurking backstage, nursing similar cheap ambition.

What would you be living for?

Through ornate windows on all sides, the city's myriad lights glimmered to the horizon. A cooling breeze wandered in and out, stirring the papers on the desk. On Jhiral's insistence, they'd retired to the top of the Sabal Tower—it was the other side of the palace from the Queen Consort Gardens and the closest thing to an inner sanctum the Khimran dynasty had owned before the Chamber of Confidences was built.

Archeth wasn't convinced this put them any better out of Anash-aral's earshot, but she said nothing to Jhiral—he was building to a foul enough mood without any encouragement from her. So they went to the tower. And in the meantime, evening had crept up on Yhelteth like an encroaching army, and sunk the heart of Empire in burnished gloom.

"What about Menith Tand," she tried. "He's made a mint since the League slave routes opened up again."

Jhiral scowled. "Yes, and he's not exactly shown willing when it comes to sharing the revenue. He's opposed me on the requisitions council twice now. And I hear Tlanmar had some trouble getting toll dues out of him this season."

"Yes, but that's tax. This is something he stands to profit from."

"Yeah—so says the iron demon. But what happens if we're being led up a blind alley here? Eh, Archeth? What if there is no prize; no An-Kirilnar standing above the waves beyond Hironish and filled with wonders. Or what if it's there, but it turns out as abandoned and plun-dered as An-Naranash was?"

"Then," said Archeth, carefully as handling sharp shards of glass, "Tand will be disappointed, along with the others. We will have learned the truth. And it will have cost the imperial treasury nothing at all."

She let it sink in, watching the impact of her words, the fade of the imperial scowl. The full genius of Anasharal's scheme was still dawning on her.

Make a list, the Helmsman told them, with airy aplomb, *of moneyed citizens whose wealth will bear the weight of the enterprise, and whose appetite for risk will commend it to them. Your Radiance need only con-tribute a commodity in which he is infinitely resourced—his scrawl on parchment, and the Khimran seal of approval on a royal charter of en-deavor.*

It was only as the list took shape that Archeth began to see the pat-tern. That, by virtue of their *appetite for risk,* these men—and one woman, Nethena Gral—were exactly the courtiers least likely to be found in Jhiral's choir of court-appointed sycophants, and thus least likely to be missed if they chose to absent themselves from court and plunge into more private matters; chose, in fact, in some cases—Shendanak would for certain, probably Kaptal, too—to actually leave the city and accompany the expedition at least partway to its destination.

Jhiral would practically cheer them out the gates.

Only one risk, really—

"Admirably frugal, Archeth, yes." Jhiral took a turn around the desk, dropped into a seat on the other side from her. He shoved a boot up on the edge of the desk, brooding. The table jarred an inch in her direction with his weight. "But on the other hand, if this expedition does return laden with wealth and wonders, it isn't going to make Tand any easier to control. He'll come back smug as a Majak climbing out a harem window at dawn. Not to mention, he'll be more influential everywhere it counts."

Well, then you can always have him arrested, tortured, and fed to the pool dwellers, my lord.

"The undertaking will have your seal upon it, my lord. Yours will be the wisdom that authorized it and made it a reality."

He looked at her across his raised boot. "Are you patronizing me, Archeth? Because I'm really not in the mood."

"That was not my intention, my lord. I merely—"

"Yes, all right. Spare me the courtier groveling, you're really not very good at it. Just an apology, that'd be nice."

"I—" Lack of krinzanz nagged and dragged at her like a bad tooth. She closed her eyes. "I am sorry, my lord."

"Good." The change in him was mercurial. He dropped his boot to the floor with a slam, leaned forward across the desk, and tapped briskly on her scribbled list. "Go on, then. Tand. Put him down. Going to be hilarious, actually, watching him try to cooperate with Shendanak. You know they hate each other's guts."

"I . . . did not know that, sire."

"Well, they do. You know, you should show up at court more often, Archeth. It really would improve your grasp of current affairs."

"Yes, my lord." She dipped the quill and scraped the new name down.

"Yes, good." He watched her write, sat farther back in the chair. "Now, we've got another problem here. Mahmal Shanta."

Don't stop writing.

Because she knew he was watching her, not the pen. Had spilled the name with precision, to see how she reacted.

She finished the final curlicue and set the quill aside. Warily: "My lord?"

"We have to be able to trust these people, Archeth." He jabbed a finger at her. "And just between you and me, my lord Shanta's stock in that commodity is running pretty fucking low at the moment."

She hesitated. "Your father trusted him."

"Yes, well Shanta and my father were as chummy as two old buggers in a Trelayne Academy bathtub. But as we've seen in the last couple of years, loyalty to my late beloved father and to myself are two significantly different things. You've heard the rumors, don't pretend you haven't." He considered that for a moment. "All right, maybe you haven't. But just think about it. Apply that half-bred Black Folk genius of yours for a moment. Do you really think I'd promote Sang over Shanta's head because I *like* the obsequious little turd?"

"It is not my place, my lord, to—"

"Oh, *shut* up. Sang got where he is now for one reason, and one reason alone. He is loyal. And in times like these, I cannot afford anything less."

Archeth said nothing. Waited for the rotted kernel at the heart of all this, because she knew it was coming.

Jhiral stared back at her for a couple of moments in silence, then he sighed.

"All right. It's going to get out sooner or later, you may as well hear it from me. Bentan Sanagh named Shanta several times in his confession. Covert meetings of the shipwright seniors. Treasonous opinions on policy. Dissent."

Mahmal, you stupid fucking . . .

"Under torture, my lord—"

"Yes, I'm well aware of your opinions on the subject, Archeth. But I happen to trust my torturers. They're the best in the Empire, and I pay them to get at the truth, not to wallow in dungeon bloodlust. Shanta's name came up. Too many times for it to be entirely a lie."

"Was his the only name?"

"Of course not. They're shipwrights, aren't they? Fucking coastlander families to a man. Got a six-century chip on their shoulders about the horse tribes, ever since my forefathers rode down off the plains and made them all vassals. Sanagh says they're all in it, have been at least since the accession."

"Then that would include Sang."

"No, I already told you. Sang's loyal."

"Sanagh gave him special exemption when he was shrieking out his confession, did he?"

"Look—"

"What was it, foot flaying again?" She found, abruptly, that she could not stop herself. "I hear they like that down in the inquisitor colleges these days. Perfected the wire flail, have they, my lord? Or are we back to belly irons?"

Then she did stop. Breathing hard now, pulse a soft and rising roar in her own head. Staring defiantly at him in the low light, and the silence opening up behind her words. For a while it seemed they were floating in it, shipwrecked survivors of some titanic ocean storm that had just abated, or was maybe just circling around.

Jhiral twitched. For a moment, she thought she saw rage rising in his eyes, but then the twitch became a wince and his gaze wandered away among the books and papers that filled the tower room. He got up and prowled the space between desks, went to the window and looked out, came back. Met her gaze again.

"Oh, *don't* look at me like that, Archeth. I'm not a *monster*. I put Sanagh out of his misery for you, didn't I?"

She left that one well alone, worked instead at keeping her pulse even. She steepled her fingers over the parchment, as if affording the names there some arcane protection.

"My lord." Flat calm. "Much of this expedition, if not all of it, will be made by sea. And Mahmal Shanta is, whatever his diplomatic failings, the foremost naval engineer in the Empire. That alone would commend him to the list. But consider also that he is not a man to entrust important matters to underlings. He personally oversees every keel laid in his family's boatyards, and since the war he takes most of them out on their maiden voyage as well."

"Yes, well, it's not his fidelity to shipbuilding that I'm concerned about."

"No, my lord." She paused. Let him see it for himself.

Jhiral leaned on the back of the chair he'd been using. Not quite ready yet to sit down. "Yes, all right, I'm not stupid. The expedition gets him out of town, draws the fangs on any other little extracurricular activities he's got brewing."

"It's more than that, my lord. I know Shanta. He will insist on accompanying us, yes, but this is not all. He will want to plot our route and resupply points around the Gergis cape. He will want to review the charts and expeditionary records for the northern ocean and the Hironish. He will insist on designing and building the vessels we use."

"Yeah," the Emperor jeered. "Nice little earner for the Shanta yards."

She shrugged. "Or, if we don't build from scratch, he will want to dry-dock the vessels we acquire and refurbish them stem to stern. Either way, it will consume his energies for months. It will draw in those from the guild he considers his friends. It is late summer, my lord. The expedition cannot make ready before the seasons turn on us; we will have to wait for the spring. Involve Shanta in this, and you occupy him throughout autumn and winter, and *then* he leaves the city for who knows how many months."

"And escapes any redress for his treason."

She steeled herself for the step. "If you like. Though the northern ocean is hardly a safe place at the best of times. Who's to say what may happen there?"

The words floated down into quiet. Outside, the nighttime city glimmered. Jhiral tilted his head and cocked a brow at her.

"Are you . . . saying what I think you're saying, Archeth?"

"I am saying only that there is more than one way to remove a political opponent, my lord. You need not always feed them to the ocean in the confines of your own palace."

A faint breeze through the tower windows. Flicker of lamplight, caper of shadows.

"Interesting." Jhiral straightened up from the chair back. "Of course, I don't believe for a moment you'd do it."

"My loyalty is as it has always been, my lord, as my people's loyalty has always been, to the Burnished Throne and the spread of Yhelteth civilization. I will do what I have to in order to defend those allegiances."

"Well, that's very noble, Archeth." But she saw through the lightness of tone. Caught the tiny scratch at the back of his voice. "Perhaps we can find a way to stop short of having you murder your friends, though."

She inclined her head. Tried not to hold her breath. Jhiral watched her for a couple of moments, then came around the side of the chair and sat back down.

"Very well. For now, Shanta is your problem. Keep him in line, and I'll see to it that this goes no further."

"Thank you, my lord."

He put his boot back up against the side of the desk. She felt how the heavy wood creaked and shifted. He jabbed a finger at her. "*But* if I hear any more unhealthy rumors coming out of the shipwright's guild, I'm not going to wait until next spring to find out if you've got it in you to push him over the rail for me. He'll be meeting our tentacled friends from Hanliahg just like anybody else. That clear?"

"As crystal, my lord."

Jhiral grunted. "Shanta's a lucky man. Might be worth making sure he realizes that."

"I will speak to him tomorrow, my lord. I am anxious to get started as soon as possible. Spring will be upon us soon enough."

"Yes." The Emperor slumped deeper into the arms of the chair. He seemed to be staring right through her and into some other place. "Let's just hope we all make it through the winter without anything else breaking loose in this miserable fucking city."

CHAPTER 25

When he woke again, it was to pale parchment light straining down through the tent over his head, and the dull strop of wind outside on the canvas.

Hjel was gone.

Like every other fucker around here.

But the thought felt facile, no rooted truth to it this time. There was a cold immediacy to everything around him that didn't feel like the Gray Places. Ringil shifted a mound of blankets aside, caught the other man's acrid scent on the bed linen beneath, and a fading trace of warmth. He paddled about in the confined space, looking for his underwear. His gaze caught on the Ravensfriend, laid carefully to one side where the canvas came close to the ground.

The blade was pulled a handbreadth out of the scabbard, as if someone had gone to draw the weapon, then thought better of it.

Voices from outside. Sounded as if they were striking the camp.

Ringil found drawers and breeches, contorted himself and pulled them on. Twitched aside the tent flap and peered out. Members of the wandering court went back and forth; someone had built up the fire and was feeding it. The odor of fried bacon and beans came and wiped itself across his face. He struggled upright and out into the day, blinking in the light.

"Morning." A bright, slightly arch tone. A woman, face vaguely familiar from the night before, grinning as she passed him on her way to the fire. "Want some breakfast?"

He followed her, tucking in his shirt, not bothering with his boots. A couple of other familiar faces at the fire looked up from their plates and nodded affably. He remembered this from the last time with Hjel's people, the palpable shock of it—no whispers behind hands, no scandalized tones or accusing glances, no real interest, in fact, beyond a basic curiosity about his arrival in their midst. Nobody cared. They were too full of their own lives to pass much judgment on others. It was an otherness, a magic as staggering in its way as the *ikinri 'ska.*

Ringil seated himself at the fire and was handed a heaped plate of his own. He soaked bread in the beans, chewed and realized abruptly how hungry he was.

"Good to be out, eh?"

It was the man seated on his right—Ringil recognized him now as Cortin, last male to the bedrolls the night before.

"Sorry?"

"Out of the Margins. Good to have the world feel solid again, right?"

Ringil chewed and swallowed, nodded.

"Never get used to it, myself. All those voices, calling you away." Cortin set aside his plate and sprawled back, reflective on his full stomach. "Course, it's easier when you're in company, wouldn't get me out there any other way. Going solo, now—that's, like they say, strictly for princes and fools. No offense—I'm guessing by that broadsword you're the former."

"Was a gift," said Ringil around a wad of bread and bacon.

"Oh." Hurriedly: "Yeah, but still. Man of breeding, am I right? I mean the Black Sail gang don't come all the way up the fjord for just anyone."

Someone coughed on the other side of the fire. The woman who'd served Ringil shot Cortin a *shut-the-fuck-up* glance.

Ringil chewed steadily for a couple of moments. Swallowed and wiped the corners of his mouth with care.

"Black Sail gang, eh?"

"Yeah, Hjel's down there talking to them now . . ."

Cortin's voice ebbed to a halt as he finally caught the looks the others were throwing at him. An awkward quiet set in around the fire.

Ringil put together a smile, put down his plate, and brushed his fingers vigorously together, knife-sharpening style, to clean off the grease.

"Well," he said. "Better go down and see them myself, I guess. Wouldn't want to keep them waiting."

Which was actually a lot less like bravado than he initially feared. Along with the cold, scrubbed feel of things this morning, he'd woken, he now discovered, with a fresh sense of momentum, a will to take the next step that didn't need much prompting. Boots and cloak on, the Ravensfriend slung across his shoulders once more, he let the pulse in his veins and the weight of the killing steel on his back carry him forward. The same woman who'd served him breakfast gave him gestured directions. He went down off the ruined plaza, through the scattering of tumbled walls and columns to where a steeply sloping path wound down the side of a promontory that hadn't been there the night before. A clean ocean wind came in and ruffled the long grass, hooted around rock outcrops and scudded off the silvery gray glint of the fjord below. He narrowed his eyes against the brightness. Made out some kind of jetty down there, and a black-rigged caravel at anchor fifty yards out.

All right, then.

He made his way steadily downward, curiously at peace. The landscape was a pretty close match for parts of the Gergis Peninsula he knew, and while he wasn't kidding himself he was in any way home, the half familiarity was cheering, like knowledge of an opponent's fighting style prior to a duel. He saw figures standing about on the jetty as he got lower, and a dory moored there. Reflexive combat instinct made the count—six or seven, including Hjel. They had spotted him, it seemed, and were watching him make his way down toward them.

Even at this distance, there was something odd about their attire, about the stiff, upright way they held themselves.

Hjel hurried up and met him, a few yards along the path from the jetty's age-bleached planks. Tight smile, an offered clasp. "You're awake."

"Very much so." Looking past the young sorcerer's shoulder at the others. He didn't take the offered hand. "These friends of yours?"

They were corpses—the corpses of large men, wrapped head-to-foot in grave swaddling, no inch of flesh visible. Tiny loose lengths of the bandaging fluttered gaily from their bodies in the wind. It was as if a small cemetery had been exhumed and its inhabitants pinned about with mottled gray-and-cream pennants.

Hjel cleared his throat. "They are . . . agents. I've had dealings with them in the past. They can be trusted."

"Well, if you say so."

The dispossessed prince took his hand urgently. "They'll take you where you need to go, Gil. Believe me, I sailed with them once myself. There's nothing to fear."

"You trying to get rid of me?" Ringil worked up a small grin. "Was it so bad last night?"

Hjel's grip tightened. "I would keep you with us if I could. You must know that. But there are forces unsheathed here that I have no power to command."

"Unsheathed, yes. Rather like my sword this morning—the steel one, I'm talking about now. See anything you liked, did you?"

Hjel let go of his hand. Took a step back. "I am not your enemy."

"You aren't behaving very much like my friend."

"Gil, you haven't *understood.* Something brought you here. I can see it, it breathes through you. The cold legions wrap around you already. There is power engraved and tempered in the blade you carry. I can't read what's written there, but—"

"*I am Welcomed in the Home of Ravens and Other Scavengers in the Wake of Warriors,*" Ringil recited for him, hollowly. "*I am Friend to Carrion Crows and Wolves. I am Carry Me and Kill with Me, and Die with Me Where the Road Ends. I am not the Honeyed Promise of Length of Life in Years to Come, I am the Iron Promise of Never Being a Slave.*"

It was a rough, clunky translation, according to Archeth, and clunkier still here and now, glossed across into the archaic marsh Naomic so that Hjel would understand. But still the words awoke a faint chill in Ringil's veins as he spoke them.

He guessed from Hjel's face that the sorcerer prince was having a similar reaction.

"That's its dedication?"

"That's its name," Ringil told him flatly.

Hjel swallowed. "You must go. I can't help you here. I *will* help you, that's coming, I see it clearly enough. But not here. Not now. It's too much. If the Black Sail has come in like this, then the storm is building, and it's all we can do to ride it out. I can no more refuse this than a gull can fly in the face of a hurricane."

Behind him, one of the cerement-wrapped figures moved silently up onto the path, closing in. Hjel either caught the flicker of Ringil's gaze or sensed the motion at some other level. He half turned, turned back, took Gil's hand in both of his, raised it to his lips.

"You will come back. We will have time. I'll teach you the *ikinri 'ska*."

"I know you will."

The wrapped corpse was at Hjel's shoulder now, looming. The breeze picked at its windings, set up rippling patterns in the loose cloth tongues. Ringil thought he saw the mica glint of eyes somewhere deep in the gap between bandages across the face, but he could have been mistaken. Where the mouth should have been, a single gauze binding was pulled broad and tight, and something flickered behind it as the thing speaks.

"Is this going to take long?"

Impossible to say what the voice sounds like. It cuts across the wind with iron force, but there are hinted textures to it as well—amusement seems uppermost, and a certain weary patience, but Ringil knows his grip on those salients will slip away just as his image of the creature at the crossroads is already dream-dim and fading. He will be left with the same fumbling sense of detail lost.

"We're done," he said curtly, freeing his hand from Hjel's. "We can go."

"Gil, I'll be waiting for you."

"Good."

He looks away along the wind-plucked fjord waters. He held down a spike of unreasonable jealousy. That what was for him a dead memory, Hjel had yet to look forward to.

The grave-clad thing makes a diplomatic noise in its throat. "There is a tide to catch."

Ringil nodded, eyes still on the water. "Then get me to my berth."

He still doesn't know what a *tide* is, except that it presages change.

But change will be enough for now.

In the dory, watching the wrapped figures bend silently over their oars, he felt it begin—the creeping shift of the Margins, Seethlaw's Gray Places, call them what you will, the seeping through like cold marsh water, washing away anything fixed that could be told out like a tale, bringing instead the endless expanse of untold possibilities, scuttling like spiders, beckoning for attention, for momentary existence at the corners of his gaze. He turned and looked back to the shore, where Hjel stands—or does not, the strand is empty—on the aged jetty boards.

He sees others, standing there, too.

Three more figures, one slight, one broad and bulky, one gaunt and tall. Flickery and gray, like Hjel, but where the dispossessed prince stands erect and motionless as he fades, these seem to dart about as if tethered and anxious to be free.

The cold legions wrap around you . . .

The sky is changing overhead, boiling something up—it looks like a storm, but is ominously silent. The rowers ignore it, and their captain makes no comment—Ringil held on for one final moment to the cold, hard certainty he'd had on waking and then he let go and it's gone, like a fish in the water. He looks up and there's the sensation of tilting.

The cold legions . . .

On the jetty, as if at a signal, the three restless, gray-candle-flame figures break suddenly loose and streak out across the water, like the shadows of cloud blowing by overhead. Ringil watches numbly as they chase the boat, as they close on the stern, as they slip aboard and wrap tight around him with a shock like a cold-water bath.

And are gone.

The black-rigged caravel looms; a rope boarding ladder is hanging over the side. There's a shiver to the whole vessel, as if it, too, has been wrapped tightly in something that's now fraying and fluttering in the rising wind.

Ringil stands, takes one last look back at the empty jetty. Then he grabs hold of the ladder, and hauls himself up the sagging, damp-rope rungs to see what's waiting at the top.

CHAPTER 26

Oddly, the only thing Egar felt now was an icy calm.

As if everything around him—the cracked and decaying frame of the temple by night, the desolate, dust-crunch emptiness of the place—had only ever been a mask, and now its nocturnal wearer cupped hand to visage, doffed the disguise, and stood grinning feral in the gloom.

As if he'd been expecting it all along, this dwenda.

It came slowly down the stairs above them, coruscating blue fire moving behind the balustrade, the hinted dimensions of a dark figure at its heart. It seemed to be singing.

At his back, a choked curse from Harath.

Egar's eyes never left the blue light. He let go of the girl's hand, shook it loose with a single sharp motion. Measured the angles.

Get this right, Dragonbane.

"Harath, these things are fast," he called in Majak. "Get yourself a lance off that wall, and get ready. *Go!*"

He whirled and sprang, to the wall and the two staff lances still leaned there where Harath's former comrades had never had the chance to grab them. Soft rush of cloth at his side as Harath moved with him— and suddenly he was glad, *so very glad* of the younger man's speed. He snatched one of the lances. Smooth wood grain across his palm and the rolling weight of the thing—he felt his lips split in a snarl of joy at the feeling. Heft and spin, one-handed, two-handed and round and—

The dwenda stood before him.

—*block!*

Like a shriek through him as he saw the shadow blade come leaping. The creature had to have vaulted right over the balustrade, hit the ground soft and silent, and straightened up barely a yard away. The impact of sword against staff shivered through him, stung his grasp. He grunted with it, tilted down, levered the blow away.

Harath swung in, yelling, from the right.

The dwenda caught it, swung about, snake-swift. The dark blade dripped an arc of blue fire through the air. Smashed the Ishlinak's attack away.

"Mother*fucker!*"

Harath's yell of surprise—he'd not been expecting the strength. Egar had scant time for sympathy. He bellowed and thrust, pike style, low, at the dwenda's knees. The blue fire was down to tracery now, they were facing a figure made of dark, etched with the flicker of lightnings, but for all that shaped like a man.

And a man, well—you can always kill a man.

The dwenda shrieked at him and leapt the thrust, put its sword blade through the air in a sweeping slice at head height. Egar swayed back, felt the whicker of air past his cheek. He circled out, away from Harath, *try to bracket this fucker,* and the dwenda came down cat-like, soft crunch as it hit the dusty floor. It wore the same smooth, featureless helmet he'd seen at Ennishmin, now swinging back and forth, questing, like some blunt slug's head detecting a threat. The same one-piece suit of what looked like shining leather but—Egar knew from bloody experience— resisted edged weaponry like mail.

"Bracket the fucker!" bellowed Harath, like he'd just thought of the tactic himself. And launched himself forward.

The dwenda twisted to meet the attack. *Clang* as the shadow sword met the blade on the end of the staff lance, grunt from the Ishlinak as he felt the impact. Still, he looped back, trapped the sword point high. Egar saw the moment, fell off it like a cliff, and rushed in screaming. He didn't bother with blades, rammed the staff before him at chest height instead. The dwenda must have sensed the attack, but Harath had it overextended. A desperate side-kick flung out to hold Egar back, but he'd put everything he had into the rush, and the dwenda's aim was off. He took the glancing kick in the belly, nearly puked from the force of it, did not let it stop him. He collided with the dwenda and they both went sprawling. A slim black-clad arm whipped out for his throat—he battered it aside with a lucky swipe of the staff lance. The dwenda shrilled. It was a cry he knew, it was distress, and his heart went black with joy at the sound. He smothered with his weight. A sword pommel hammered him in the kidneys—the world went stumbling around him, little points of light in the gloom, he drew ragged breath and shrieked down at the blunt head under him.

"Oh, you *cunt!*"

Cocked a fist, but as he did Harath stepped in and drove his staff lance down into the thing's throat. Full-throated berserker bellow behind the stroke, he twisted the blade and leaned his full weight on it. The dwenda shrilled again, shuddered and thrashed like a gaffed fish . . .

Lay still.

Blood pooled out from under the neck. Egar smelled the spiced alien reek of it as he reeled upright from the corpse.

"Nice one," he rasped, and nearly fell over again. Harath stuck out an arm to steady him.

"Easy, old man." Sucking breath. "What the *fuck* was that?"

Egar shook himself, wet-dog-like. "Tell you later. C'mon, there'll be more of them. Let's get out of here."

He cast about for the girl, who had pressed herself up against the wall, the back of one hand jammed to her mouth to stop a scream. To her credit, he reckoned she hadn't made a sound. It figured, he supposed. You were a slave, you learned fast enough not to raise your voice or voice what you felt. You learned how little it mattered, how little it would get you outside of pain.

He gathered up the staff lance in one hand, grabbed her by the wrist with the other. Grinning a little crazily, blood still up. She stared back at him above her hand, wide-eyed with a fear too general for him to feel good about. For a sliced moment, he saw himself through her eyes—hulking, grim, the talisman-tangled hair, the bared teeth, the sprawled corpse at his feet.

"Go down just like men, these angels," he told her briskly, unable to put the grin away. "Nothing to it. Let's go."

They went.

But at the second turn of the stairway, a long, low wolf-howl seeped across the air, somewhere away in the heart of the building. It froze them, midstep.

And a second cry, answering.

"Hunt's on," Egar snapped. "Back to the rope. Harath, come on!"

But Harath was staring downward, not toward the sound.

"Egar. Look, man! *Look!*"

On the floor at the bottom of the stairs, the felled Ishlinak were twitching and stirring.

Not Elkret. Alnarh, and the other one.

The dead men. Waking up.

Egar took it in with a bleak lack of surprise.

"Run," he recommended.

BACK ALONG THE GALLERY, DOUBLE-TIMING, AND HE SAW HOW THE glirsht mannequins below ran and glistened with flickering blue fire, like upjutting teeth in some monstrous jaw, alive with luminescent saliva. He thought he could feel the whole building tightening down around them, the jaws snapping closed, swallowing them. Like back in the rock tomb all over again, and the flaring terror of dying enclosed.

Glance back at Harath, and he saw the feeling mirrored there in the younger man's eyes. Fear strummed him like a lute chord, hung in the air like a palpable thing.

This is not mine.

It hit him as they headed down the stairway at the other end—a vague understanding, slippery in his grasp. This was *not his fear*. His blood was up, he'd killed dwenda before, and in tighter straits than these, he could still feel the faint, giddy traces of exhilaration from the fight. The grin was still on his face, still stitching back his cheeks. Fear might come later, as that savage pulsing ebbed, but *this* . . .

Memory arose—a couple of decades back at least, he'd have been barely fifteen. Chilly star-filled night on the steppe, the band like a vast burnished scimitar blade, raised across the sky—watching with the other herdboys as Olgan the shaman muttered and made passes in the air, cast powders and fluids onto the flames and conjured weird, wailing half-human faces there.

The fear gripped him then as it gripped them all, possibly even old Olgan himself—the young Egar saw how the old man's teeth were gritted tight around his invocations. But as the discordant cries and the strength of the blaze grew higher, when it seemed the faces in the fire would be pretty soon reaching out for him with claws of flame, Olgan suddenly stopped his chanting and told them to step back, look away, and seek the Sky Road with their gaze.

To place their souls on that road.

It was the hardest thing he'd ever done in his young life—like looking away from a coiled and rattling snake you'd just stumbled on in the steppe grass—but he did it. He put his back to the yowling things in the fire. He stared up at the band, found its curving edge and imagined himself poised on that edge, looking down on the wide windy world below.

The fear puddled out of him like water from a dropped flask.

He heard Olgan's voice behind him.

What you feel is not yours. You need not own it. Creatures like these breed the fear in you as we fatten a buffalo calf, and with similar intent.

Screeching from the fire—he thought he heard outrage in the half-formed sounds.

Choose your feelings as you would a weapon. This is what it is to be Majak.

Later, Olgan would teach them to bellow back at the creatures in the flames, to laugh and hurl obscenities at them, to stamp and punch into the fire. To lose themselves finally in the berserker state, where nothing mattered but the will to do harm.

This is what it is to be Majak.

They hit the bottom of the stairs, sprinted flat-out. Howling echoed through the hollow environs of the temple behind them. Through slanting falls of bandlight, past the towering, forgotten gods. The statue of defanged Urann seemed to meet his eyes for a moment as they raced toward it. Blank stone gaze—no help there at all. At his side, the girl tripped and nearly went headlong. He clamped tight on her wrist, held her up with sheer force, dragged her back to her feet without stopping. On through the gloom. The howls seemed to have found one another somewhere back there. He felt the dwenda presence on the nape of his neck like a taloned hand, poised to grab. He knew, he *knew*, they could not be that close, but still he had to fight the urge to look back.

Not his fear.

He shook it off.

"There it is!" Harath, almost yelping with relief.

And the rope—dangling straight in the diffuse rays of bandlight that streamed down from the hole at the top. Relief slammed through him. No sign of guards, human or otherwise. They piled to a halt and Egar let go of the girl's hand, took the staff lance two-handed again.

"Can you climb that?" he asked her.

And saw the answer in her face. *Not really, no.* But she made the attempt anyway, clung and hauled for all she was worth. Barely got head height above the ground before she started to slip. Soft hands, and softened muscles—the old harem curse. Her head drooped, her panting built up and then turned to tears. Harath snorted, derisive.

And more rolling howls through the gloom.

Egar shook the rope impatiently. She slid down but clung on, keening. Barely audible words through the sound. *Don't, don't leave me . . .*

"Stupid fucking bitch . . ."

"Shut *up*! Give me your lance, get up that fucking rope! We'll haul her up."

"Man, we don't have the—"

"Just fucking do it, will you!"

Angry clatter as Harath tossed the lance aside. He leapt to the rope and went up it in savage bursts, teeth gritted and muttering. As soon as he was clear, Egar dropped his own lance, looped a broad noose into the bottom end of the rope, tugged the knot tight, and slid it over the weeping girl's shoulders.

"Sit in—calm *down*. I'm not *going* to leave you—sit in this. Hold the sides." He got the loop settled under her arse, so she sat on it like a swing. "When he starts pulling you up, just hang on. Got it?"

She nodded, wide-eyed, face streaked grubby with snot and tears.

"Ready!" Harath bawled from above, voice tight with anger he still hadn't worked out on the climb. Egar grinned. He'd go far, this one.

"Okay, girl, that's it. Hold on tight." He tipped his head back. "Pull! Pull like you were born a fucking *Skaranak*, not some city-dwelling Ishlinak bitch!"

The rope jerked upward, a solid yard. Jerked again. The girl looking down at him past her dangling, naked feet. Wide eyes.

Wide eyes, staring.

He grabbed up his lance and whipped around, saw them, prowling out of the gloom like beasts. Glint of blue along the edges of their weapons, but aside from that they were wholly dark. The same blunt helmets, the same leather gear. One carried a delicately made long-hafted ax, the other a sword. And they warbled softly to each other as they drew closer.

"Help you cunts with something?" he barked.

And twirled his staff lance through a couple of basic blocks, so the blades at either end whooped softly in the dark air.

"Want to fuck off now, before I kill you both?"

They came on, silent now, intent. He hefted the lance.

"Your loss!"

He struck hard at the dwenda on the left, lance blade jabbing up and faceward. The creature fell back a step, swung its ax to guard. Slice at the other one, and spring back. *Whatever you do, Dragonbane, don't let them get either side of you.* The staff lance gave him reach, could in theory win a bracketed fight like this, but he'd seen the dwenda in action at Ennishmin, knew how fast they could be, and if these two knew what they were doing—

In came the swordsman. Weird hooting howl, and the flickering lash of the blade. Egar went low, looped the attack away, felt the ax strike

coming at his back in the hairs on the nape of his neck. He sawed upward behind him, didn't need to look back to know he'd broken that
attack, too. He sensed the dwenda stagger wide, heard it make a furious
cat-like hissing.

A combat smile touched the corners of his mouth. The berserker
fury stirring now, on the straw-strewn cage floor of his mind.

They circled him, and he stood and watched, turning the minimum
he needed to keep them both in view. The lance slanted loosely through
his two-handed quarterstaff grip. It was the familiar feel of an old lover
under his hands. He was the windmill fulcrum at the heart of the world
as it turned, the spindle of a promised and rising rage.

His lips parted over a clenched grin.

"Come on, then. *Come on!*"

At the edge of his vision, the axman rushed in. Nicely done, it only
just missed his blind spot. He jabbed down, hoping to skewer a foot, at
a minimum trip the fucker up. Keep the other end of the staff high
because—

Skirling shriek, as the other dwenda came leaping at him, above
head height.

He'd seen them do this before, too. Still, the scream and the shadowy
figure seemingly in flight sent a spiked chill through his heart. He struck
upward, lance blade almost vertical. The sword edge went whistling
past, way off. But hard on its heels came a black-booted foot, and it
caught him a crack across the side of the head. He stumbled. Head full
of stars. Felt the axman rush him again and must swing to counter.

"Skaranak! It's down!"

But there was a weird moaning on his lips now as he blocked with
the lance, locked up the ax, and shoved back. The human shout seemed
to come from another chamber, somewhere distant under the temple
roof, and didn't make much sense anyway.

"Eh?" he found he was snarling at the thing he faced. "Eh?"

Time froze. The ax haft and lance shaft skittered back and forth
against each other. He reckoned he had forty pounds on the dwenda,
but it was still driving him back. And the other one would be on him any
fucking second . . .

He jolted downward, sharply, ran the lance shaft savagely down and onto one of the hands holding the ax. The dwenda shrilled and gave an inch of ground. Egar whooped and pivoted off the shift it gave him, swung all his weight into the shove. The dwenda staggered sideways, nearly went down. A shadow shifted, off his other shoulder. But now the moan on Egar's lips was swelling to something else, something summoned. He could feel his own pulse, thundering through his ears, under his collarbones like the tremble of the ground at An-Monal. He swung to face the new threat, jerked the lower lance blade back to hamstring his stumbling opponent. Felt it slice something, heard the shriek of damage done, and howled his response at the ceiling.

"*Egar! Let's go!*"

No time, no *fucking time*! The sword tip came slicing—close as his last shave, he'd later swear, as he rolled his neck out of the way. And the second dwenda, there behind the blade like some flickering demon out of fevered dreams. He struck out, felt himself sliding into the berserker gap, gave voice now to the full, ululating cry. Vaguely, he felt the dwenda sword tag him across one thigh—sudden heat, there and gone. It didn't matter, Harath, the girl, some vague wisp of thought about a rope, *nothing mattered now,* he could fucking die here for all it mattered, so long as he gutted these two first—

He struck out again. Blade clash, blue sparking fire. *Howl!*

The axman was back in the fight, limping but still fast. It didn't matter. He wove the staff lance before him, strode in, took some blow or other across the shoulder, howl, howl, *howl,* wheel and whoop and strike—

The dwenda, bracketing him now . . .

"*Egar!*" Harath's whiny fucking Ishlinak *pussy* scream . . .

Didn't matter, didn't fucking—

Ax blow. Lick of sword. He drank it in, waded through it. Whirled and struck. Somewhere he was bleeding but wasn't that the whole fucking *point*—

Something *changed.*

Like a tumble into chilly water, like the breath of a ghost. Something crashed down from the ceiling. He caught a fragmented glimpse—huge block of shaped stone plummeting, one of the Urann statue's sculpted hands. It split and shattered on impact with the dusty ground.

The dwenda recoiled.

Both of them, like cats hit with scalding water. For all the block hadn't fallen anywhere near them. But the air, the air was ice, and—

"The rope, Egar! *Grab the fucking rope!*"

And there was life again, like a door to a lighted room swinging closed at the end of a corridor. He saw the gentle pendulum sweep of the rope end, six yards off his left shoulder. Hurled the staff lance at the nearest dwenda and sprinted for it, flat-out.

"*Come on,* for Urann's sake!"

He grabbed the rope end, hauled himself up. Sag of the fight aftermath through his guts like sudden sickness. Numbness in his thigh. *Climb, you stupid bastard, climb!* He went up with the speed of long custom, hand over hand, spindling and swinging about with the momentum of his grab. Caught sliced, dizzying glimpses of what was below him—the dwenda, still down there, blunt-helmeted heads tilted up at him—soft puff of white-stone dust, drifting up in the gloom where the masonry had fallen—freshly shattered chunks of stone—more figures moving in the deeper gloom behind—harsh, unhuman chuckling . . .

Climb! Climb!

He reached the ragged break in the roof, panting and snorting like an old horse pushed too hard. Vaguely aware of wounds, and the slow seeping realization of how close he'd come. Hands grabbed him, dragged him clear of the hole. He rolled over on the cool stone, looked up at the starry sky and the white speckling slash of the band. Blinking out the last red edges of the berserker rage. Jangling like a set of jailer's keys.

The girl's face craned over, blocked out some sky, peered down at him. Pretty face, he registered vaguely.

"Fucking Dragonbane is it?" Harath, spitting furious, coiling the rope. "Get yourself killed for a fucking *slave*? What's the matter, you think Ast'naha's already carting your ale to Urann's feast in Sky Home? You *hear* any fucking thunder up there, old-timer? Come on, *get up! Move!* We're not out of this yet."

Egar gave himself one more breath lying down. Draw and hold, release. Rolled to his feet and peered around.

They were alone on the roof. No sign of alarms raised, either up here or beyond. The trailing caress of a breeze—he caught the wafting, damp smell of the river on it, the flowering weeds along the banks. Spotted the faint white broken glimmer of bandlight across water, and the red-yellow stain of the city's lights on the sky to the west.

The cool, dark calm of everything around him—dislocating shock after the fight below.

"All right," he said, not quite steadily. "Let's go see if our ride's there."

THEY GOT DOWN THE SIDE WALL WITHOUT INCIDENT, LOWERED THE girl first in the sling, secured the rope at the top and slid rapidly down after her. No time to fuck about, and no gloves—so add scorched palms to the damage tally for the night. They stood, braced either side of the girl for a couple of moments, knives out. But there was no sign of the night patrol.

"All inside by now," Harath guessed. "Turning the place upside down, see what the fuck just went down."

Egar nodded, wordless—still breathy from all the exertion. Still working out what the fuck went down himself. Harath tapped at the dangling rope with his knife tip, instinctive herdsman's thrift in face and tone. "Hate to leave that hanging there, you know."

"I'll buy you a new one. Come on."

They skulked away from the silent, darkened bulk of the temple and down to the river, Egar with a small survivor's grin now hanging crookedly off his mouth by one corner. He found he had time for sudden carnal recollection, what the girl's arse had looked like, going up with that rope slung under it. Stir in his groin at the thought, but oddly it was Imrana's face that he saw.

Sort that out if you could.

The boatman was waiting in midriver, just where he'd dropped them before. Harath whistled sharply, stood up and windmilled his arms. It took a moment or two, but finally the man bent to haul in his anchor, paddled the boat about with his oars so it was facing them, and dug in on the stroke.

They went down through weeds and yielding mud, waded out to meet him.

"Not safe coming in like this," he greeted them reprovingly. "There's been a lot of commotion up there the last little while."

"Yeah, tell us about it." Egar hooked an elbow around the prow of the boat to hold it steady, shoveled the girl aboard with his other arm.

"And an extra passenger? Well, that will be . . . extra, of course."

Harath heaved himself up over the side with a grunt. "One more word out of you, I'll slit your fucking throat and row home myself."

"Then you would be cursed," said the boatman evenly. "And the unholy maraghan this place is named after would creep from the waters to avenge me, to track and drag and drown you and all your kin."

Harath barked a laugh. "They'd have a long walk for my kin."

"No one's slitting anybody's throat." Egar got himself into the boat with an effort. The wound in his thigh was beginning to throb. "And we're not paying extra for her, either, so settle down and row. Plus, they told me the maraghan were all driven out of this place centuries ago. Cleansed by the Revelation's sacred word and fire, right?"

The boatman fiddled sulkily with his oars.

"They have been sighted in the river still," he muttered. "And along the coast. They have an affinity with those who ply the water for their trade. They can be called upon."

Egar grinned. "And there I was thinking you were a devout son of the Revelation. Bet you're wearing an amulet under that shirt and everything."

"What the fuck is a maraghan anyway?" Harath wanted to know.

"Sea demons," Egar told him absently, squeezing some of the water out of his breeches. His hands came away bloody. "Like a waterhole lurker, but they're always female. Supposed to sing to sailors sometimes, lure them out of the boat."

The Ishlinak peered dubiously over the side. The boat was coasting on the current now, turning idly as it drifted downstream.

"Doesn't sound like much to worry about. I had an uncle once, half Voronak, said he fucked a waterhole witch. Caught her on his line, dragged her up through a hole in the ice, and did her right there on the bank."

"Yeah? Sounds to me like he fucked a fish." Egar found the wound in his thigh and pressed experimentally at its sides. Grimaced. Shallow, and really fucking painful. "Then again, if he's anything like the Voronak I know, that doesn't surprise me at all."

Harath coughed a laugh. Stopped it up abruptly, and gave the boat-man an unfriendly stare. Switched back to Tethanne. "What are you looking at? You going to pull on those fucking oars, or what?"

"Yeah, come on, man." Egar nodded at the boat's lazy, swirling mo-tion. "We're not paying for the current to take us home. I can swim downstream faster than this."

The boatman gave him a venomous look, but he bent to the oars. In the bottom of the little vessel, the girl picked herself up and crouched shivering. Her shift was drenched through, her legs were plastered with river mud.

Harath went back to Majak. "So, Dragonbane. You going to tell me what the fuck that was we were fighting in there tonight?"

Egar's good humor guttered a little. He stared back upriver, to where the silent bulk of the Afa'marag temple crouched on the rise, like some-thing that might spring after them at any moment, like something not yet unleashed.

"Different kind of demon altogether," he said.

"But . . . " The Ishlinak gestured, at a loss. "I thought . . . Like you said. The invigilators. They chased all the demons and witches out with their book and incense and shit. What the fuck are they doing giving them house room?"

Something that had occurred to Egar as well a few times in the last half hour. Not in any worded or well-thought-out form, but still—it had been nagging at him, ever since they found the glirsht statues. A colossal lack of sense, building with every new piece that fell into place. And now he found, oddly, that he had an answer.

"I think they think they're angels," he said slowly.

"*Angels?*" Harath spat over the side. "Fucking twats."

"Yeah. Tell me about it."

CHAPTER 27

Nothing in the known world reeks like this.

Ringil's seen grown men piss themselves in terror at the smell, seen hardened soldiers turn pale beneath their campaign tans. It is unmistakable. Those who've faced it, never forget. Those who haven't, feed on the handed-down tales, and misrepresent it as a foul stench, which it is not. At sufficient distance, in fact, it's drowsily pleasant—a sunbaked summertime blend of spice and perfume on the wind, sharp notes of aniseed and cardamom rising through a backdrop of sandalwood and there, right there, the wavering but ever-present hint of scorching . . .

Dragon.

Slammed awake like a cheap tavern door.

He sat up with the force of it, instant cold sweat, hand groping after a sword hilt nowhere to be found. Breath locked up in his throat, staring around.

Where the fuck . . . ?

The shape of his surroundings resolved—he lay in a bunk under a gently tilting ceiling lamp whose flame was turned down low. The fittings of a well-appointed ship's cabin, painted back and forth with shadows from the tilting lamp. Shelves, a sea chest against one wall, a cramped desk and cushioned chair. The back of the door was hung with a Yhelteth ward against evil, the painted image of some saint or other bordered in tiny significant writings from the Revelation. Above him, he heard the hurrying thud of footfalls across planking, voices calling out. Soft squeaking punt of wood on wood somewhere, a steady rocking.

He was aboard a vessel, sure, but—

He hauled himself out of the bunk and sat, elbows on knees, face in hands, memories skipping off the surface of recollection like flung flat stones . . .

The fjord. The black-rigged caravel. Rowing out.

Hjel's valedictory figure, there on the shore and not. Were there specks of rain in the air? In his eyes?

The caravel's cabins had been musty and coffin-cramped. Narrow, unlit spaces supplied only with rough straw mattresses on the floor— retiring to them and trying to sleep was like being buried alive. He'd kept to the decks.

Crew of cerement-wrapped corpses on deck, all facing into the wind, eloquently silent in his presence. Only the captain speaks to him, and then only to deflect his questions in cold and cryptic monosyllables. What, after all, do the dead have to converse about with the living? He is cargo pure and simple.

Yeah—cargo to where, *Gil?*

A reflexive thought. He reached under the bunk and found his boots, stacked neatly side by side. The Ravensfriend lay scabbarded next to them.

Who . . . ?

He was out of the Margins, that much was clear. The cabin around him had that same hard-edged feel he was used to on waking from time in the Gray Places. But . . .

More voices from up on deck, shouting. He tipped a glance toward the cabin ceiling as the feet came thumping back the other way. Some-one was getting excited up there.

The reek of dragon washed in stronger. He felt a muscle twitch in his cheek.

Indistinct instructions called back and forth over his head, and abruptly the whole room tipped. Around the cabin, small items slid and toppled. The lamplight shifted crazily. The Ravensfriend crept out a few inches from under the bunk.

They were coming about.

Ringil was dressed and armed and through the door in what seemed like seconds. A broad companionway led up from just beside his cabin. He climbed it at speed, cleared the hatch at the top, spilled out onto the thinly bandlit deck with a little less elegance than he would, on reflection, have liked.

No one noticed—the rail was lined with crewmen lifting lanterns and staring out into the darkness. Others pressed in behind. Murmured dispute laced the air above their craning heads.

" . . . see anything out there anyway?"

" . . . *smell* that?"

"Could be it's the *Hurrying Dawn*. They say this time of year she—"

"Yeah, like fuck. You and your lizardshit ghost-boat stories." The skeptical sailor put his head back and yelled into the rigging. "Hoy, Ker-ish. You got anything up there yet?"

A laconic negative floated back down to them. Debate resumed.

" . . . ever did believe that shit, it's just not . . . "

" . . . probably a couple of leagues off . . . "

" . . . might be from landward. Like a spice barn or something. We're pretty far south by now . . . "

" . . . always thought the *Hurrying Dawn* was—"

"Look, I'm *telling* you, my uncle fought at Rajal Beach and he told me himself, that's what dragons smell like."

Ringil took the stage. "He's right."

Heads turned. The boat swayed a couple of times before anyone thought of anything to say. Striped in bandlight through the rigging, Ringil nodded in the direction they'd all been looking.

"He's right, that *is* dragon you can smell. Or, more likely, it's dragon-

drift, in which case it's probably harmless. But I'm still not sure turning us around like this was smart. Who gave the order?"

The company looked at one another.

"Fuck's it to you," somebody muttered from the rear.

"Pipe down, Feg, you stupid shit. That's a paying passenger."

"Look at that sword he's got, man. That's . . . "

"I gave the order."

Lightly amused, like footsteps tripping out a dance measure. A voice he knew, but took a moment to place.

But . . .

He turned to face her, aware that he'd been upstaged with exactly the same mannered affect he'd used to make his own entrance. The Lady Quilien of Gris stood a little distance from him, head tilted with inquiry. She had wrapped herself shoulders-to-floor in a smooth gray cloak with a ruff at its neck, her hair was gathered back at the temples in a pair of silver clasps, and she appeared as thoroughly competent now as she had seemed insane in the tavern upper room in Hinerion. She held his eye in the lantern glow, tilted her head the other way with an intent precision that was almost lupine.

Silence across the deck.

"It's good to see you up and about, sir. We were concerned for your health. Tell me, have I committed an error, then, with this change of course?"

"Not necessarily an error, my lady." He held her gaze, held down his own unease. "If the ship is yours to command, then it is merely a question of how lucky you feel."

Quilien took a couple of paces to one side, still eyeing him up.

"Would you class yourself an expert in dragons, sir?"

Ringil shrugged. "Well, I did kill one once."

As if someone had just cracked a wasps' nest onto the deck, the assembled crewmen's voices rose and buzzed about, jeers and jumbled oaths. The Lady Quilien raised one groomed eyebrow in the midst of it. Ringil opened a hand at her.

"Not alone. Had a little help."

"Such modesty. Perhaps you'd care to—"

"Reef! Reef to starboard!"

Bellowed down from the lookout, a panic-stricken edge on it because—Ringil grasping the fact with told-you-so smugness and a nod—this was a reef not marked on any local chart.

"*Reef!*"

The crew boiled about, leapt for the rigging, ran to look for the ship's officers. Ringil took the opportunity to move up and lean on the vacated rail.

"It's not a reef," he said to no one in particular.

WHEN THE VAST, FLOATING RAFTS OF PURPLISH BLACK MARINE MUCK first started washing up on western shores in the summer of '49, no one took it for an invasion.

It was a shock, sure enough, to see what looked like huge mattresses of tangled, flowering kelp twice taller than a man, piled up along the strand as far as the eye could see. It was problematic for communities who made their living from open access to beaches and coves that were now clogged and covered over, because whatever this stuff was, it didn't appear you could burn it, harvest it, or eat it. And it was a major inconvenience for shipping, not least when one of these colossal mats drifted into a major harbor mouth or caught in the throat of a useful channel between offshore shoals. The Trelayne sureties funds hiccupped, squabbled over payouts, rewrote their terms. In Yhelteth, by all accounts, the merchant guilds went through something similar. In both the League and the imperial territories, some few dozen affected villages packed up and moved, north or south along the coast, in search of new fishing or rock-pool scavenging grounds. There was a certain amount of small-scale starvation here and there, but not enough to warrant military intervention by either power.

Up at Strov market, the soothsayers presaged doom—but then they always did.

And on the abandoned coastal reaches, the purple-black tangled ramparts loomed in trickling quiet, and waited.

It was almost four months before the first of them hatched out.

———

THE LADY QUILIEN OF GRIS LEANED ON THE RAIL AT HIS ELBOW AND watched as they came up on the drift. You could understand the lookout's error easily enough now. In the darkness, it looked the way any exposed reef would, low-lying in the water, jagged, darkened bulk ripped through with the white of foam where the ocean swells broke across it.

By now the dragon reek was overpowering.

"So it was not the *Hurrying Dawn* after all," she said conversationally.

"The *Hurrying Dawn* is a myth, my lady." He didn't look at her. He was busy staring down the memories of the scent. "The usual thing. A doomed Yhelteth spice clipper, driven onto rocks by a master and commander impatient to beat the competition to market in Trelayne. It's a tale, made up to frighten cabin boys on the midnight watch."

"Yes, I believe I've heard it. We are not as rural as you might imagine in Gris. The captain called up a sorcerous storm to hurry his passage, did he not? And the Salt Lord drowned him for his presumption, then condemned him to run before the wind with his vessel for all eternity?"

"Something like that."

"And now, by some set of circumstances or other, the same wind is supposed to carry the scent of his lost cargo. It's a warning to—"

"It's a senseless yarn is what it is, my lady. Ignorant chatter to make sense of a world that resists any more robust interpretation."

"Chatter that you do not lower yourself to, I take it?" Something like delight trickled into her voice. Dilettante salon sacrilege, he imagined, must be as popular among the upper echelons in Gris as anywhere else. "You reject belief in the Dark Court?"

Dakovash stalked at the margins of his memory. He held down a shiver.

"I am, let us say, indifferent to the Dark Court, Lady Quilien. I ask nothing of them, and expect the same courtesy in return. In any case, whether they exist or not, I think it unlikely that such beings would concern themselves with one small cargo vessel and its grubby, spellchanting captain." He gestured at the darkened slop of the dragondrift beyond the rail. "And I think that there you are probably looking at the true origin of legends like the *Hurrying Dawn*."

"You'll not feel it necessary, then"—the delight was still there, rich and thick in her tone—"to offer prayers of thanks to any of the Court? Given your escape from Hinerion before the quarantine came down, I mean."

"I'd say that any gratitude I owe belongs to you, my lady." Gruffly. He didn't like being in anyone's debt. "You appear to have been my savior in this. Though I'm at something of loss to understand the exact—"

"Yes, I know. You must be confused." Out of the corner of his eye, he thought he saw a small smile playing about her lips. "The last thing you remember, after all, is being aboard a vessel with black sails, crewed by corpses."

It jerked him around to face her. Tiny finger of chill at his nape. She looked back at him blandly.

"At least, you did mutter something along those lines while I watched over you at one point. The ship's doctor says it must have been delirium. You were running a very high fever when we found you. Some feared it was plague."

"As did I. I am doubly indebted to you, then, for bringing me out of Hinerion."

"I could hardly leave you as you were—sprawled reeking of cheap alcohol on a pile of trawl nets, alone. You thought perhaps you would drink it away, the plague? Was that the plan?"

"I thought perhaps I'd try to die drunk."

"Such ambition. And this from a dragon-slayer." The smile was there for certain now, but secret and somehow turned inward around the eyes. "Somewhat misguided as well, since it now seems you did not have the plague after all. Or at least, short of divine intervention, I can see no way for a man to make a full recovery from the disease so rapidly. Can you?"

"It does seem remarkable," he said tonelessly.

Quilien snorted in a very un-lady-like fashion. "No. Remarkable is that when we found you, you'd not already been robbed and stripped naked where you lay. Remarkable is that, despite your apparent lack of interest in your own continued welfare, you were still possessed of that magnificent blade you own."

If she was flirting, it was clumsily done, and Ringil could think of no adequate response. Nor did he much like the idea that everything he remembered from the Gray Places had been a fever dream. Recollection would fade anyway, he knew—Seethlaw had speculated that it was the only way humans could cope with the unconstrained probabilities in the Aldrain marches and not go insane—but Ringil still held to a stubborn differentiation between dream and reality. Hjel as a fond but fading memory was something he could live with; Hjel as a figment of his feverish imagination and longings was a lot less palatable. He pushed the thought away. Concerned himself instead with current events.

"Might I inquire, my lady, where we are bound?"

"Oh, to Yhelteth." She gestured at the horizon, as if the lights of the great city might at any moment appear there, painting the sky with pale yellow glimmer. "It suits my eventual purposes well enough to go there, but really, there wasn't a lot of choice. I arrived at the harbor to see the *Marsh Queen's Favor* standing out to sea without me, and half the other vessels along the wharf preparing to cast off. Plague panic everywhere, and me with a sick man in my retinue. This was the first ship, the *only* ship, in fact, I could persuade to take us aboard. Its destination really was the least of my concerns."

Ringil nodded at the approaching drift. "And you've time enough for detours."

Quilien lounged languidly on the rail, one hip outthrust. She tilted her head and favored him with a sidelong smile. "Well, sir, I confess I am a hopeless addict when it comes to mystery and heroic tales. You and your Black Folk blade, and now, on the same voyage, a floating spice island of the lizard folk? Who could resist seeing something like that?"

Someone who's seen it before, he thought about saying. *Someone who's been a little closer to the lizard folk than titillating after-dinner tales.*

Instead, he left her question hanging there, and they watched in silence as the ship maneuvered closer to the drift. Ringil spotted the ragged gashes and hollows in the texture, filled now with seawater that roiled and poured as the matted surface undulated with the sweep of the waves. It was more or less what he'd expected, but he still felt the tension rinse out of him like the last dregs of a hangover.

Perhaps she did, too. "So this is harmless?"

"Yes." He pointed out over the rail, old memories roiling like the water. "You can see where the dragon tore its way out—that long, ragged hollow near the front, the pieces that flap about when the swell hits. The dragon comes first. It's like a mother bird protecting its brood. Then there'll be a couple of hundred smaller hatching gouges farther back where the reptile peons and the higher-caste Scaled Folk came out afterward. Once that happens, the whole raft starts to rot. It loses a lot of its bulk and in the end the currents carry it back out to sea. This has probably been drifting about out here since the early fifties."

"You really killed one of these beasts?" She was watching him keenly now, he knew. "With that blade you carry? Now, *that* is remarkable."

"I suppose so. As I said, I did have help."

"Even so. Are you not proud?"

Ringil grimaced. "If you'd seen some of the other things I've done with this blade, you'd perhaps be less enamored of my feats."

"And perhaps not."

Was she *rubbing* herself against him at the hip? Ringil turned to face her, met her eyes, caught the gleam of saliva on the teeth in her grin.

"My lady, I don't quite know how to put this to you gently, so I won't try. You are wasting your time with me."

"Am I?" The grin was still there. "That's a hasty judgment."

Ringil sighed, pressed thumb and forefinger to his eyes. Was he really going to have to fuck this madwoman before they made port?

"Please don't consider me ungrateful, my lady. It is simply that I am not made to please your kind."

"Perhaps you mistake what *my kind* is."

There was a bite to the words that drew his gaze back to her. She stood a little farther from him now, sober-faced. Had produced a pair of krinzanz twigs from somewhere in the folds of her gray cloak and held them up like an apprentice carpenter offering nails to his master.

Just what you need, Gil, fresh from your fever.

He took one anyway, noted that it was expertly rolled, waited for courtesy while she put the other to her lips. A hitherto unsuspected manservant, somewhat hunched, scurried forward from somewhere and offered a low-wick lamp to light each twig. Ringil watched the Lady Quilien tilt her head to the flame, draw deep on the twig until it fired up. There was a curious immobility to her features in the flaring light it made, as if, suddenly, her whole face was a hollow, porcelain mask with nothing behind it but darkness. The servant turned, a twisted black shadow on the margins of the light and offered him the flame. He took it and drew deep.

"You are . . . " Tightly, holding the breath in. "Too kind."

She shook her head, wreathed in exhaled smoke. "It's your supply. I found it in your things."

She met his gaze in silence for a single beat, widened her eyes around pupils already stretched black and broad. Then she burst out laughing.

The ship butted solidly up against the dragondrift. Ringil heard the eerie scrape of its fronds against the timbers. Crewmen mobbed past, lining the rail again, craning over to look down at what they'd found. Someone yelled for boathooks—voices sounding a little distant now, as the krin came on in his head like cold fire.

"Ah, Captain." Quilien gestured with her twig at a tall, richly attired figure approaching across the deck. The smoke ribboned off the motion into the dark. "There you are. And as you can see, our convalescent man of mystery is awake and well. Lacking only for a formal introduction, in fact."

The captain bowed, somewhat curtly.

"Dresh Alannor, master and commander of the *Famous Victory None Foresaw*."

"Uhm, yes." *Alannor. Glades shipping nobility. Fuck.* The krinzanz stepped up, greased his response, put a lightened version of the stock Yhelteth accent on his lips. "Laraninthal of Shenshenath, imperial levy, retired."

"Indeed?" Dresh Alannor either didn't believe him or didn't much care for imperials. But his manners held. "Then we're honored to have you aboard, sir. I'm glad to see you're feeling better. My lady, is it your intention to walk the drift?"

Quilien plumed smoke and looked at Dresh Alannor through it. Something seemed to be amusing her.

"I'm not a thrill-seeker, Captain. I wished merely to take a few samples."

"I think there'll be no shortage of samples." Alannor nodded sardonically along the rail, to where the more adventurous of his crew were already lowering a rope ladder. "You can sell dragondrift cuttings for a handsome price in port. We'll be here awhile."

"Then I may as well descend and investigate with your men."

"The drift is awash, my lady. And not stable in the water."

Quilien took a last drag on her krinzanz twig and pitched it over the side. "Captain, you appear to have misunderstood me. I may not be a thrill-seeker, but neither am I entirely feeble. I have boots, I have a sense of balance. And of course, I would invite you to accompany me."

Which neatly took care of any ribald tendencies the crew might have down there. Alannor looked glum, but in the end he was dealing with a wealthy, paying passenger. He sketched another bow.

"Of course, my lady. Nothing would give me greater pleasure."

Ringil watched them go, feeling a wry twist of sympathy for the other man. Bad enough the Alannor family fortunes were such that they still depended on actual seafaring from their scions—but catering to the minor whims of other nobles with paid passage, worse still *rural* nobles with paid passage . . .

Along the ship's side, Alannor handed his passenger down the rope ladder with schooled grace. He shot a last speculative glance back at Gil, then climbed down after.

Ringil masked his disquiet behind the ember of the krin twig, drew deep, and leaned impassive on the rail to study the reactions below. There was some catcalling down on the drift when the crewmen saw the Lady Quilien swaying down the ropes—but it damped down fast enough when Alannor stepped onto the ladder after her.

The *Famous Victory* was a tight ship, it seemed.

He didn't think Dresh Alannor had made him—he certainly couldn't recall ever meeting the man face-to-face—but memory was an odd thing, and Ringil's fame in the war years had been pretty widespread. Not to mention his now newly kindled notoriety as the Butcher of Etterkal. And there was no way to know how many days the *Famous Victory* lacked for journey's end. With favorable winds, a fast ship might make the run from Hinerion to Yhelteth in less than two weeks, but he didn't know if this *was* a fast ship, how long ago it had set sail, or for that matter how its course was being plotted. They might be on a leisurely stopping cruise for all he knew. And given a long enough voyage, who could tell what Alannor might recall.

Ringil allowed himself a grimace. It was not exactly a recipe for restful convalescence.

Patience, hero. It was like another voice speaking in his head. *One thing at a time.*

He took the advice, whoever it might be from. He smoked slowly, staring down at the sluggish ripple of the drift. The odors swarmed him. The krinzanz performed its customary trick, like some heavy parchment missive unsealed and unfolding in the space behind his eyes.

Got any suggestions how we do this, then?

Egar, bellowing between cupped hands as they rode headlong neck-and-neck along the clifftop at Demlarashan, trampling the scattering lines of reptile peons. The relief of the wind on his face, finally chasing out the murderous heat, as he yelled back.

It was your fucking idea!

And the awful, sun-burnished gleaming bulk of the dragon as it became aware of them and twisted sinuously about to face the new threat. His heart jammed up into his throat as he understood that this, finally, might be it for Ringil Eskiath, called Angeleyes.

He never truly deciphered the component grammar of his fears that day—but he came to understand that beyond the terror of dying, and the terror of the scalding, searing dragon's breath and what it might do *short* of killing him, there was something else entirely, something far darker, which did not like to be looked at in the light. Something he found inside himself that day, something that would come thereafter when he called for it, but was not often so easy to put away again.

It was there at Gallows Gap, screaming from his mouth as they charged the reptile advance in the pass. It was there at the siege of Trelayne, screaming inside, filling him, when they threw the Scaled Folk back from the walls.

Screaming, inside and out. Screaming hard enough that he sometimes thought it must tear him open and *let* the inside out.

And sometimes, in his darkest moments, he believed it never stopped screaming. That he had only found some dungeon space deep inside himself to keep it, where it went on screaming forever, into walls that muffled the sound.

Screaming.

He blinked, back to the present. There *was* screaming, a cacophony of desperate yells down there on the dragondrift, jittering torchlight converged at a single point beside the hull. Combat nerves spiked through him, his hand already halfway to the Ravensfriend. He craned over the rail, tried to see down to where the crewmen were gathered in a tight, yelling knot.

After all this time? Can't be. Cannot be.

At some level, he'd already dismissed it. An unhatched peon or higher-caste lizard, somehow still alive in the waterlogged slop of the decaying drift, and conveniently set to wake just as human feet walked over it. It was something out of a fireside scare story, things like that just didn't happen . . .

And besides, Gil, you don't gather in a witless knot when you see a lizard come snarling up out of the drift. These men would be fleeing in all directions—those who hadn't been slashed apart before they could unlock muscles from the disbelieving shock.

He saw Quilien in the glow the torches cast, standing apart, one hand up to her mouth. She seemed to feel his gaze from the rail. She looked up.

Somehow, without transition, he found himself on the rope ladder. He jumped the last four rungs and hit the dragondrift at the bottom with a soggy splash. Slogged up to the gathered men and their torches. One of them turned, and seemingly found something to cling to in Ringil's face. His eyes pleaded.

"It's the captain!" he bawled. "He's gone down in the gap!"

"Get a boathook down here," someone was yelling, over and over. "Get a *boathook!*"

Forget it.

But Ringil forced his way into the knot of men anyway, pushed and shouldered through until he saw the closed-up gap between the bristling fringe of the dragondrift and the rising wooden wall of the ship's hull. It was all he could do not to nod in confirmation.

Not a chance.

"Someone get over to the other rail," he said, for something to say. "Maybe he swam down, under the hull, made it across."

But even as the call went out, he knew it was futile. The mat went down, at a guess, about fifteen or twenty feet, tangled with half-rotted nooses and spines of drift weed. The draft of the vessel would not be a lot less. A man falling into the momentary gap between, mashed back against the unyielding hull as the gap closed up again, stunned by the blow, tangled in the fronds . . .

Not a chance.

He stood aside and let a couple of muscular crew members strain mightily at the *Famous Victory*'s hull. The rest of the men piled on. They managed, finally, to open a useless, foot-wide gap for a few moments, and then whichever currents held the ship close slammed her back against the drift. Cries floated across from up on deck, said there was nothing to be seen on the other side. Ringil heard the splash of a couple of sailors going in for a closer look.

Good luck with that.

The Lady Quilien of Gris was abruptly beside him, stumbling slightly in the rolling squelch of the drift. She fell against him; he caught her upright, set her back on her feet. Mingled band- and torchlight flickered across the mask of her face.

"It was horrible," she said, though he was hard put to hear any trace of horror in her tone. "The gap just opened up right beside us. He slipped and he was gone. Do you think he's dead?"

And for just a moment, there and gone in the uncertain light as she leaned against him, he had the overwhelming impression that the words were mouthed, like some ceremonial hymn she had memorized in a language she did not know.

"Yes, I think he's dead," he said flatly.

They poked about in the water for a while nonetheless, finally got the *Famous Victory* turned about and away from the drift, sent a pair of wiry, somber-faced divers down to take a look. The selected men stripped purposefully to their breeches, drew sailor's knives and dropped smoothly enough into the ocean swell, but in the dark it was a pointless enterprise, a defiance of truths they all already understood. The two men hauled themselves out a dozen dives later, stood bent over on the dragondrift, hands braced on knees, dripping and panting—nothing to report.

Dresh Alannor would not be coming back.

"He is"—one of the men spoke the sailor's formal valediction between deep-drawn breaths—"at peace. In the Salt Lord's halls."

The other man raised his head and shot his companion an incredulous look. He straightened all the way up, looked right at Quilien and Ringil in the light of raised torches, and then spat into the dragondrift at their feet.

"Drowning's a filthy fucking death," he rasped, and took his shirt back from another crew member, and walked away.

LATER, RINGIL STOOD AT THE RAIL AND WATCHED THE LUMINOUS WHITE splash of waves on the dragondrift as it receded into the dark at the stern. He thought of the man they'd left behind, tangled up and caught fast somewhere ten or fifteen feet down on the submerged wall of the drift, eyes wide and staring out into the black. Or perhaps already carried off into the cool gloom by currents or something more toothed and purposed.

Dresh Alannor. Son of Trelayne, Glades noble, commander of men.

There was a chill across his shoulders like a wet towel.

"I have been thinking about what you said." Quilien, abruptly at his side in the pallid bandlight, dark hair hanging loose so it obscured her profile. Somehow, he hadn't heard her approach. "Why the Dark Court might concern itself with the petty affairs aboard one small vessel. With the fate of that small vessel's captain."

"Indeed, my lady?"

He wasn't really listening. Most of his attention was on the crew, as they went sullenly about their tasks around him. The first mate had them on a pretty tight leash, but even so, there was a palpable anger pulsing through the shipboard air. Alannor had been well liked. Ringil thought he might be careful walking the deck at night from now on. He thought he might warn the Lady Quilien to take similar care.

"I—"

"Yes, the mistake would surely be to see such behavior as a single act, unrelated to any larger tapestry of events outside that one fireside tale. But is it not more likely that such a captain might in fact serve as a sacrificial piece on a larger board. A piece in a game that the nobles of the Dark Court like to play."

It was such a trite piece of coffeehouse pondering that he almost laughed.

"I have heard this suggested before, my lady. Numerous times. It never much impressed me as a thesis. Why would such ancient, powerful beings concern themselves with anything as banal as a game played out among humans?"

She leaned out on the rail then, let the wind take her uncovered hair and blow it away from a smile turned oddly wolfish.

"Well," she said, without looking at him. "Perhaps the game itself is so ancient that they have forgotten how to do anything else. Perhaps it is webbed into every memory they have, into the fiber of their being, and they cannot unlearn the habit. Perhaps, despite all their age and power, they *have* nothing else."

She tilted her grin toward him in the dark scuffle of the breeze. Raised her voice a little.

"It must be difficult, after all, to give something up, when you are so very good at it. Don't you think?"

And he thought, with a tiny, creeping unease, that her gaze as she spoke was directed less at him than at the sword across his back.

CHAPTER 28

She went to see Shanta as soon as the sun was up.

The naval engineer was a creature of habit. She found him exactly where she'd expected at that hour, taking tea under an awning on the upper decks of his palatial houseboat. The mercenary guardsmen at the gangplank nodded her aboard—she was a regular, unmistakable anyway for her skin and the alien distance in her eyes—and a liveried slave escorted her up through the ziggurat levels of the boat. More slaves in attendance in the top gallery—paneled wooden doors were drawn back with much ceremony, and she was ushered out onto the deck. Shanta was seated there under the awning amid carpets and cushions, surrounded by depleted platters of sweetmeats, bread, and oils. There was a tall samovar at his elbow, and a book laid open in his lap. He looked up, smiled when he saw her. She gave it back, thin. Waited to be formally announced, and for the slave to retire.

"My lady Archeth, this is a pleasant surprise." Shanta gestured her to a cushion near his own. "How wonderful to see you again so soon. Will you take some tea?"

She stalked forward. "What the fuck are you playing at, Mahmal?"

"I?" He seemed genuinely taken aback.

"You see any other doddering morons in the vicinity?" She stood over him, raging. Swept a hand wide to encompass the empty deck. "Oh. I guess not. Then it must be you I'm talking to. Must be you I spent half of last night saving from an upcoming appointment as *a fucking octopod's dinner!*"

"Ah." Gravely. "I see."

"Do you? Do you really?" She kicked the indicated cushion away across the deck. "*Have* you ever seen one of those executions, Mahmal?"

She knew he hadn't. Akal had always favored the clean sweep of an ax for his enemies; the slaughter boards in the Chamber of Confidences were an invention of Sabal II, reinstituted only now by Jhiral on his father's death. And since the accession, Shanta had kept pretty much to himself, initially in mourning for his old friend, and when this became untenable as an excuse, pleading age and the pressures of work.

"I fear I am not much at court these days. I have not been fortunate enough to witness the ways in which Yhelteth advances into the modern age."

She thought she detected the faintest of tremors in the words, but if it was there, it was layered over with bland courtier calm.

And, she thought, it might as easily have been suppressed rage as fear.

She mastered her own anger. Went to the starboard rail and looked out over the water. Across the estuary, a fishing skiff tacked for the ocean, heeling steeply in the buffeting breeze.

Know the feeling.

She tried for toneless calm.

"It's not good, Mahmal. Sanagh gave you up under interrogation. You and half the shipwright's guild, apparently." She looked back at him. "I mean, when are you people going to get it through your fucking heads? The horse tribes kicked your asses. There isn't going to *be* a glorious resurgence of the coastal cultures. It is over. The Burnished Throne is our best shot at civilizing the world now."

"My quarrel is not with the Burnished Throne."

The qualifying words hung in the air unspoken. She found herself checking the deck, reflexively, for eavesdroppers.

She came back to where he was seated. Crouched close.

"He's one man, Mahmal. He'll live, and he'll die—just like his father, just like his grandfather. And I remember them all—don't you forget that. Right back to Sabal the Conqueror, and he was a total fucking bastard. It's not them. It's what they build that counts."

"That's an admirably Kiriath perspective, my lady." Shanta closed the book in his lap, leaned across to the samovar, and busied himself refilling his glass. "You'll forgive me if, as a mere mortal, I am less inclined to take the long view. Bentan Sanagh was a friend."

"Then you need to choose your friends more carefully," she snapped.

That sat between them while he finished with the samovar. He laid his book aside with elaborate care, did not meet her eyes. He held the glass of tea cupped delicately in both palms, head bowed over the steaming drink like a soothsayer scrying the future for a tricky client.

"Well," he said mildly. "I will give your ladyship's advice due consideration."

"Yeah—do that. Because I don't think I'll be able to pull your chestnuts out of the fire like this if you fuck up again."

He glanced up. "I am grateful for your intervention, Archeth."

"Doesn't sound much like it," she said grumpily.

"No, I am grateful." A gathering urgency in his tone now. "But I have taken oaths, Archeth, just like you. When the guild come to me with their complaints and fears, I am sworn to address those concerns. You know how many of us the purges have taken. What would you have me do? Put on a courtier smile and bandage my eyes like Sang? Stand aside as my friends and colleagues are disappeared and tortured to death?"

"And you really think joining your friends on an execution board is going to help matters?" She sighed. Went to get the cushion she'd kicked. Calling back to him as she bent to pick it up. "What would I have you do, Mahmal? I'd have you stay alive. Yhelteth needs men like you and me. The purges will pass, Jhiral will calm down. We have to outlast this phase."

"I am an old man, Archeth. It's doubtful I'll live to see that—even if you do manage to keep me out of tentacled embraces for the duration."

"So—what?" She came back, settled the cushion back in its place. Seated herself. "You're looking for a glorious exit? Is that it? A martyr's death?"

"Hardly."

"The Citadel is restless, Mahmal—you know that. And Demlarashan is perfect tinder. It won't take much for Menkarak and his clique to torch it all into a theocratic rising that'll make Ninth Tribe Remembrance look like a drunken tavern brawl. Is that what you want? Asshole bearded righteousness ranting on every corner, and the blood of unwed mothers running in the streets? Jhiral at least will stand against that."

Shanta grunted. "You miss the salient point, my lady. Jhiral himself is part of the reason people flock to the invigilators in the first place. If he had not tarnished imperial authority the way he has since accession, no one would give those selfsame bearded assholes the time of day. Akal would never have—"

"Oh, *don't* feed me that line of shit! I was *there*, Mahmal. Remember? Akal got in bed with the Citadel for manpower, pure and simple. Religious morons to bulk up his armies, Citadel declarations to sanctify his fucking conquests. This is his mess we're living through just as much as it is Jhiral's."

"And so we forgive corruption and imperial tyranny, because it promises to stanch theocratic rage?"

"No. What we do is get a sense of perspective. We tread carefully, and we look for ways to clean out the bilges that don't involve knocking a big fat fucking hole in the hull."

The nautical metaphor lifted the ghost of a smile to his lips.

"Got a mop, then?" he asked.

"Think I might, yeah." She nodded at the samovar. "Pour me a glass of that, and I'll tell you all about it."

AFTERWARD, HE SAT SILENT FOR A LONG TIME.

Archeth sipped her cooling tea and gave him the space, gladly. That he was thinking it over could only be a good thing.

Wharf noise drifted up over the port-side rail, softened by the height of the houseboat's decks. In keeping with the time of year, Shanta had had the vessel towed downriver from its winter moorings, and docked near the mouth of the estuary, where sea breezes helped keep the summer heat at bay. It also gave him the chance to sweep the harbor with his telescopes and keep up with foreign shipping technology. Only last year he'd been in transports of engineering delight over some gaunt gray square-rigged vessel that showed up from Trelayne sporting a raked bow and narrowed beam. *You're looking at the future there,* he told her as she squinted through the scope, at a loss to see what all the fuss was about. *Those League sons of whores—always one jump ahead. Do you have any idea how fast that beauty must be, even in heavy seas? She'll clip through waves like a knife.*

So we go right ahead and build the same way, she'd assumed.

He shook his head. *Fat chance, the way things are right now. You try convincing anyone down here to make untried changes to something that's functioned perfectly well for longer than living memory. There's just no stomach for that kind of innovation anymore. Guild monopoly, vested interests at court, a line of fucking rent-seekers out the palace door and around the block. We're choking on it, Archeth, and there's nothing either of us can do. Akal would have . . .*

So forth.

Her tea was stone-cold. She poured it away into the dreg pan, leaned over to the samovar, and turned the spigot for a fresh shot. Shanta looked up at the motion as if he'd forgotten she was there.

"So, you believe what this creature says?"

"Helmsmen don't generally make things up, Mahmal. They can be obscure, willfully vague, cantankerous at times. But I've yet to catch any of them in a lie."

"A city standing out of the ocean?"

"As at Lake Shaktan, yes."

"A lake and an ocean are very different things, Archeth. The existence of a city standing in the waters of one does not necessarily prove the possibility of a city built to stand in the other." But behind the pedantry, she could already hear in his voice that he believed, that he *wanted* it to be true. "Shaktan is shallow compared with the northern ocean. Its weather is mostly clement. But the seas around the Hironish? Just imagine the stresses such a structure would have to withstand. Imagine what constructions would be required."

"If Anasharal's scheme works, we will not need to imagine it, my friend. We'll be able to see for ourselves."

"Hmm." He shot her a shrewd sideways glance. That *my friend* might have been pushing it a little. "Of course, even if this An-Kirilnar does exist, it will most likely be a ruin, just as An-Naranash was."

"Perhaps." It hurt more than she'd expected, just to say that much.

"You think a city of your people would have hidden themselves from us all this time? Really?"

She wrestled her feelings down into something approaching rationality. "As the Helmsman tells it, this city moves in and out of what we understand as reality in the same way that the Ghost Isle does. It has a technology to equal the magic of the dwenda at their height. So who knows where it may be grounded when it is not manifest in our world? Maybe, in studying the dwenda, the clan Halkanirinakral found a way to travel back and forth between worlds that did not involve taking to the veins of the Earth again."

"And chose not to share it with your father's clan?"

She shrugged. "Contact was cut off between An-Monal and An-Naranash for centuries, as far as I can ascertain. The Helmsmen are vague on the why. We still don't know where the Lake Shaktan Kiriath actually went when they abandoned their city. Who's to say that the same or worse did not occur with An-Kirilnar?"

It got her another crooked look, another musing murmur, but he said nothing to dispute. Nothing to stamp out the bright small flame kindled in her belly.

"Look, Mahmal, even if there are no actual Kiriath left in this city, Anasharal says the place materialized some weeks ago and has been there ever since. That suggests working machinery. And there's no one to come plundering, the way there was in Shaktur. The Hironish isles are barely inhabited—you've got a scattering of fishing villages and whaling outposts up there at most. No cities, no learned men or wealthy ship-owners. If anyone's seen this place, they'll be hexing like crazy and staying well away."

Shanta smiled. "I think you underestimate the toughness of fishermen, Archeth. The ocean is a hard mistress at the best of times, and up there she is cold as well. Anyone who pulls a living from those waters won't scare easily. And as I understand it, the whalers run back and forth to Trelayne quite regularly. Word will inevitably reach learned men and wealthy shipowners, if it hasn't already."

"Then all the more reason to go there ourselves, fast, before the League can make its move."

"Hmm."

He got up, a little stiffly, and made his way to the port-side rail, as if drawn by the muffled tumult below. She watched him for a moment, then followed.

They leaned side by side for a while in easy silence, gazing down at the tangle of activity along the wharf below. Porters and mules, couriers and freight agents, cargo marshals and their slaves, all mixed up and rubbing one another the wrong way in the bright morning heat. A couple of gesticulating shipmasters in altercation with liveried customs officials, a noble's carriage jammed in place amid the bustle. Soldiers, sailors, and beggars claiming loudly once to have been both or either. Bangled, painted whores, sleeves pushed up, hair and shoulders defiantly on display, one foot set daintily on a crate or mooring iron, arms akimbo and turning sinuously to and fro at the waist so the bangles chimed. The obvious, sidling pickpockets and pimps.

"Have you approached any of the others yet?" he asked her.

"No, not yet. Was up all night saving your scrawny neck."

A slight exaggeration. She'd gotten away from the palace not long after nightfall. Ate at home, with Kefanin and Ishgrim for company. Kef had been dressing the girl up again, lots of floaty satin and lace, hair washed and plumped up, netted and beribboned. It made Archeth feel like a dead, lightning-blasted tree when she stood next to her. She made an attempt to be gay, nonetheless, tried hard not to stare down the northern girl's cleavage too much, deflected questions about what had gone on at An-Monal. That last part proved easiest of all. Conversation was largely taken up with a breathless narration of the Dragonbane's run-in with the Citadel picket outside the front gate while she was away. The way Kef and Ishgrim told it struck Archeth as overly dramatic. On cross-examination, she discovered neither had actually seen the fight, and were depending on the gate guard for the detail. But since the Dragonbane wasn't around to answer for himself, she had to take their word for the tale.

In fact, it transpired, no one had seen Egar for a couple of days now. Kefanin had fed him the morning after the punch-up, but that was the last time he'd been home. The Prophet only knew what chaotic shit he was up to in the meantime.

Might wander up to see Imrana this afternoon, see if he's camped out there. About time he started getting laid again.

Let's hope he is.

Truth was, she should have seen the trouble coming. Egar had been in a foul mood ever since Knight Commander Saril Ashant got back into town and started claiming his marital rights. Abruptly deprived of Imrana's attentions, the Dragonbane had been spoiling for a fight, *any* kind of fight, with anyone. Natural consequence of a pair of unmilked balls and a lifetime killing other men for a living. *Sure, you should have seen it coming, Archidi. But in the end it's an invigilator, a fucking priest and his bully boys. So do you really give a shit?*

She knew, of course, that the ripples from what the Dragonbane had done would end up rocking her boat sooner or later. The usual diplomatic outrage, the gibbering representations about offended faith, the wearying declamatory statements from prayer towers and pulpits. Still, she couldn't make herself angry with him.

Mostly, she just wished she'd been there to see it.

"Something amusing you, my lady?"

She put her smile away. "Old news. Something I heard last night."

"Hmm. Yes, well, I can tell you right now this isn't going to be the jaunt you evidently expect it to be."

He's in. He's hooked. The smile tried to leak out past the corners of her mouth again. She faked a yawn.

"I don't doubt there will be difficulties along the way."

Shanta snorted. "There'll be difficulties right here in Yhelteth. Just putting Tand and Shendanak in the same room is going to be trouble, for starters. Have you thought about who's going to ride herd on this lot?"

"His majesty has assigned me a squad of Throne Eternal under Noyal Rakan."

A grunt. "Young. Very young to be pushing rich old men around."

"He's a good man, they say."

"A lot of that is his elder brother's reputation rubbing off. Seen it happen before. I don't know much about his war record, so I wouldn't want to jump to conclusions. But I'm not convinced he's the ideal choice."

"He isn't," she said bluntly. "He barely saw service in the war. But Jhiral wants this kept among as few people as possible, and Rakan's squad have already had sight of the Helmsman."

"So, presumably, have Senger Hald's marines."

"Yeah, they're coming, too."

Shanta raised an eyebrow. "Throne Eternal telling marines what to do. That's going to be interesting. Anyone else been invited to this party that I ought to know about?"

"Lal Nyanar and his crew. Hanesh Galat, the invigilator."

"*Nyanar?*"

"Yeah. What's wrong with that? Nice stroke of luck, seeing as how his father's on the list anyway."

"Nyanar's a *riverboat* captain, Archeth. I doubt he's been out of sight of land more than half a dozen times in his whole career. He certainly never saw combat at sea—old Shab made sure of that much."

"I'm sure he'll make an acceptable first officer."

"That's your considered nautical opinion, is it?" But he was grinning at her behind the growl. "Archeth, this is a bag of live eels you've trawled yourself here. We're going to need at least a couple of ships to do this, probably three or four. Now, I will gladly take squadron command, but Nyanar will still have to captain his own vessel, and that means he's going to have to convince actual seamen he knows what he's talking about. Good luck with that. Then you've got the military side of things. Leave aside for a moment the question of whether Rakan can get Hald's marines to take him seriously—what's more important is that at least a couple of the rich men on that list of yours are going to want to come along for the ride. They won't put up the money otherwise. And you can bet they'll want to bring their own hired swords with them."

"You're talking about Shendanak?"

"And Kaptal. Probably Tand as well, if he sees that Shendanak's going. No love lost among any of those three, from what I hear. And

Shendanak is in the habit of hiring his thugs right off the steppe. They're mostly cousins and blood-oath bondsmen, and half of them probably don't even speak Tethanne. So you've got the prospect of *those* guys rubbing up against the marines, plus whatever mob of slave enforcers Tand wants to bring in to balance the odds—"

"If he chooses to come along at all, that is."

"I'd advise you not to start getting optimistic this early in the game, my lady."

"Better than getting cold feet, isn't it?" Sour tone only half in jest, because abruptly the lack of krinzanz was getting to her again, and she really didn't want to think about what it was going to be like—trying to wield some kind of authority over this whole shabby, patchwork, free-booter scramble after loot. "What's the matter, my lord Shanta, you turning old man on me all of a sudden? Just want your cup of spiced tea and your slippers?"

"*Doddering* old man, wasn't it?"

"Doddering *moron*, I said. Not the same thing at all."

"Well, it's hard to keep up with you immortals, you see." A sudden edge on his humor now as well, the momentarily unguarded tinge of jealousy she was accustomed to with the humans who didn't just hate her outright. Shanta heard it, too, hurried past it, sought safe ground again. "Perhaps it's just, oh, that having had my life saved so recently, I value it all the more."

The northern ocean is hardly a safe place at the best of times. Who's to say what may happen there.

Her words to Jhiral the night before came back to her. For one night-marish instant, she saw herself doing it.

"You're welcome," she said gruffly.

Another sideways slanted look, another smile. "You know I wouldn't miss this—any of it—for the world, right?"

Her own lips quirked. "I guessed."

"I'm coming with you, Archeth. You know I am. I'll build your ships for you, I'll sail them up around Gergis and beyond. I'll draw the charts and plot the routes, I'll put in what money you need. I'll even sit quiet in council with idiots like Shendanak and Tand." He shook his head, still smiling, perhaps at this recklessness, at his age. "But I'm telling you.

You're going to need more than the likes of Noyal Rakan to wield the whip and keep this lot in line."

Which was of course when, staring down into the hubbub on the wharf, she spotted the gaunt, black-wrapped figure forcing its way through the crowd.

And for just that moment—like sudden sickness, like krinzanz coming on—it was as if she could feel the vast, ancient machinery of the universe as it turned. As if, through some ragged tear in the tawdry fairground paneling and painted cloth of the seeming world, the oiled mechanisms of fate now stood revealed in all their cog-toothed, malevolent intent.

And for just that moment, she was afraid.

CHAPTER 29

Ringil Eskiath came down the gangplank of the *Famous Victory None Foresaw* and joined the bright, brawling chaos on the wharf. Sunlight shattered across the water, slammed glints into his narrowed eyes. The Black Folk Span held the sky to the south like a massive slice of shadow dropped across the estuary. It was better than a mile upriver from where he'd disembarked, but you could sense the cool of its shade from here, beckoning you on.

Yhelteth.

They'd given him a medal here, once.

"Rooms, my lord, rooms! Swan-down beds and views to the great Kiriath wonders of the city! Step this way!"

"Pig's heart skewers! Piping hot! A Yhelteth delicacy, fresh from the coals!"

"Baths, my lord! Hot baths. Waters perfumed with all the scents of the Great City!"

He wondered, shouldering his way through the press, if that included the reek of hot tar and effluent that crept up from the pilings along the wharf.

"Wanna get fucked, soldier?"

"Wanna get fucked *up*? The purest flandrijn in town, sire, the finest pipes. A Yhelteth tradition awaits you."

For a moment, he was tempted, by the latter offer at least. He'd been in some good pipe houses in his time, and doubted the grubby, hollow-eyed individual at his elbow was going to take him to one of anything like the same rank. But he also doubted the tout and any friends he had would be stupid enough to try to roll a man with a blade-scarred face and the tilted crux of a broadsword hilt at his shoulder. Flandrijn they offered, flandrijn in all probability they would have, and a cool, dark place to smoke it in.

Or maybe they *would* try to roll him.

In the sunny, quick-pulse rush of the morning, he found he didn't much mind the thought of that, either. He had a full belly from breakfast aboard the *Famous Victory*, he had a full purse under his cloak—the Lady Quilien had bluntly refused any compensation at their parting, *Let us say only that you will owe me a favor, Ringil Eskiath*, she told him instead—and he had back his full strength of limb and lung. He was awake in ways he hadn't been for months.

A flandrijn pipe or a back-alley brawl—he had appetite to spare for either.

But by then, in those moments of idle reflection, he'd already drifted on, and the tout stayed put somewhere in his wake, still crying his wares to the crowd. Ringil kept moving, vaguely aware that he was heading for the Span's shadow and, as he recalled, a low-rent mercenary watering hole built there. The Good Luck Pony, or something—it had always been a favorite of Egar's, though Ringil had never been able to see the appeal himself. Scabby fittings, no decent wine to speak of, and a clientele of obnoxious young men all looking to prove their mettle at the slop of a spilled pint. A fistfight a night, a stabbing a week, all pretty much guaranteed.

Still, it wouldn't hurt to swing by. It was a little early in the day for drunken chest-beating; the place would likely be quiet. He might glean some useful gossip on what was going down in the city these days, whether there was much work for freebooters, who to talk to about it. At a minimum, he could get something to eat.

At some point after that, he'd see if he could remember the way to Archeth's place.

"Ringil Eskiath! Hey, *hero!*"

For a moment, the voice seemed almost familiar—certainly, he thought he would know its owner as he turned. But the grinning gray-toothed girl who lounged there against the curve of a donkey-sized wine tun left on the wharf was familiar only in type. He'd seen her in a dozen different cities before, her soiled, tight-laced bodice and shredded red-rag skirt practically a uniform. Painted nails chewed down to the quick, tanned arms laden with bangles at the wrists, clinking bracelets at the ankles, bare feet clotted with dust and streaked with melted tar. She caught his eye and flexed herself at him, elbows propped back on the tun's curving surface. Slid one hand down into the rags of the skirt, and shifted it aside on a length of pallid thigh. A wood shard toothpick shifted from one side of the rotted smile to the other, lifted on a darting tongue. She was all of fourteen years old.

"You know me?" he asked warily.

"Who would not, honored sire? Victor at Gallows Gap, savior of the northern cities, slayer of dragons at Demlarashan. The debt we all owe you is without tally."

"It was just the one dragon."

She ignored the interjection, as if her words were lines she must recite and he a poor companion player on the stage, forgetful of his part.

"I have a message for you, Dragonbane," she said.

He looked her up and down. "That doesn't seem likely."

"You are awaited at the Temple of Red Joy. Do not delay. All things will become clear."

"I'm afraid I—"

"And your friend awaits you above." She gestured upward past his shoulder.

It was such a tried-and-tested old trick, the standby of pickpockets and footpads everywhere, that he already had his sleeve tilted for the dragon-tooth dagger as he glanced the way she pointed. He felt himself loosening for the fight. Was looking forward to the girl's accomplice and his pitiful street-urchin moves, whatever they might turn out to b—

"Ringil! *Ringil!*"

Archeth's voice.

In the hubbub and gull shriek along the wharf, he might not have heard her if his gaze hadn't been directed toward the cry. He shielded his eyes against the sun-glint and spotted her, leaning on the uppermost deck of some absurd floating bordello built in stacked layers like the world's largest Padrow's Day cake. Fussy finish on everything, actual glass in most of the lower deck windows, some of it stained nine different shades of fucking expensive. Natty little gangplank at dock level, complete with ornately carved handrails, a style ill suited to the hired soldiery standing about it with halberds. He counted four, solid and grizzled, giving passersby the odd brutal shove when they lurched too close. They looked handy enough to avoid tangling with.

"Hey, okay, Ringil, look." Archeth, waving hastily. "Just stay there, I'll come down."

She disappeared as if yanked off the rail by the scruff of the neck. He found himself grinning, pure pleasure of a sort he hadn't felt tickle his guts for what seemed like ever. He turned about to thank the wharf whore, digging under his shirt for a coin.

The worn oak curve on the wine tun, gleaming back at him. No gray-toothed grinning girl to lean on it. He stood and frowned at the space where she'd been, until a harried-looking freight agent suddenly materialized out of the crowd.

"Ah! *You* are the owner, my lord? Tailen March? From the *Scourge of the Maraghan*?"

Ringil shook his head, put a boot against the tun to see if it rocked, if it might be hollow for a bolt-hole. It didn't, it wasn't.

"Nope."

The man hesitated. "Then you wish to buy? I can make you a good price, wharf price if you—"

"Did you see the girl who was leaning on this?" Ringil asked him. "Just a moment ago. Working girl? Henna hair, cream bodice?"

A lip curled in pious disgust. "No. I did not."

"She was right there, man. You didn't see where she went?"

The man drew himself up. "I am not a whore's broker, sir, and I'll thank you not to take me for one. This is Yhelteth you're in now, not the pirate cities."

Didn't realize my accent was that bad.

And then Archeth, suddenly at his shoulder, laughing, getting between him and the agent, grabbing his arm. "Ringil! You old backstabber! What are you doing here? You making trouble already? How long you been in town?"

He saw her shoot the freight agent a warning glance. She needn't have bothered. He'd already made her for Kiriath and was backing off like a poet asked to wash dishes. Ringil stared vainly about at the brightly colored surge and slop of the crowd.

"There was a—" He gave it up. Accepted Archeth's grip, made the four-handed clasp and leaned in close. "It's good to see you, too, you immortal bitch. That your boat?"

"Belongs to a friend. Why?"

"Ah—nothing."

"Come on, I'll introduce you." She led him to the gangplank. The halberdiers stood grudgingly aside, watched him pass with ill-concealed mistrust. "What *are* you doing here, anyway? Thought you'd gone home to a happy ending and a handsome reward. What happened? Family reunion not work out after all?"

"Something like that, yeah."

"Not looking for work, are you?"

He looked at her. Saw she wasn't joking.

HE LIKED SHANTA ON SIGHT.

Something of the tangled academic about the man—a willingness to entertain the possibility of something, anything, regardless of how likely it actually was. You could see his eyes kindle as he did it, could see them staring off into other places, as if into the coals of a fire. You could sit there and watch him drift, watch him tugged away from the wharf of the real world by the currents in his head.

Could almost be Kiriath.

Though in the Black Folk, to tell the truth, the same trait had mani-

fested itself as something closer to insanity. Grashgal and Flaradnam
had both been prone to lapse that way, disconcertingly often in the
midst of humdrum conversations, for minutes at a time, then come
back down to Earth trailing skeins of mystic gibberish you couldn't
really make much use of in the real world. Ringil had even seen Grashgal
do it once in the midst of battle. Had had to snap him out of it pretty
fucking sharply to save both their lives.

He wondered idly how much it was that similarity, that same musing, brooding withdrawal, that drew Archeth to the naval engineer the
way she obviously was.

"Of course, your experiences in the Aldrain realm—the so-called
Gray Places—these go only to support what the Helmsman has said
about the Ghost Isle." He was doing it now—gnarled fingers steepled,
gaze falling lost through the gap beneath. "If the dwenda are truly at
home in places where reality is not moored to the same set of laws we
know here, then there is no reason they would not sail whole chunks of
territory away with them from time to time."

"Yes, and if my father's people fought them, then they would have
had technologies to combat it. Just as the Ghost Isle makes sense, so does
An-Kirilnar."

Ringil frowned. He hadn't heard a fervor like this in Archeth's voice
for the better part of a decade. And from the look of her eyes as she
leaned forward, she wasn't even using. Which fact was in itself remarkable.

Change, it seemed, was in the air.

"That's as may be." Shanta drifting back now from his speculative
trance. "But these are hardheaded men we're talking about, and that
bitch Nethena Gral is harder than any of them. It's going to take more
than maybes to loosen their purse strings."

The trace of a smile touched Archeth's mouth. "I think I'm going to
leave that part to Anasharal."

To Ringil, it was as if the shade they sat in had deepened for a moment. He'd never much liked the Helmsmen.

"Where are you keeping it?" he asked.

"At my place." Archeth gestured out to the rail and the glittering sunstruck city beyond. "We were using the palace, but Jhiral found out
Anasharal is mobile, and that was the end of that."

"Fucking pussy."

Mahmal Shanta glanced at Ringil, fresh interest in his eyes. Archeth saw the look and felt the warning prickle go along her nerves.

But she had to concur. Jhiral had been childishly aghast.

That thing can walk about? The Emperor wide-eyed, staring at her in the gloom of the tower. *It has* legs? *What the fuck are you doing bringing it into my palace?*

No point in trying to calm him or explain her observations and inference that Anasharal might be able to walk, but couldn't walk *far*. Or that anyway, a being able to eavesdrop on conversations at who knew what remove probably didn't need to walk about much to achieve its purposes, whatever they might be. She kept silent instead, and made arrangements: Noyal Rakan and his men to escort a carry party of trusted slaves to her home; the Helmsman to be wrapped in sacking and loaded into a nondescript donkey carriage along with a bunch of Kiriath junk from one of the palace storage cellars. More raw material for the jet-black madwoman to ponder over and wreck apart with engineer's hammers. She already had the reputation—no one would give any of this a second glance.

"The Emperor," she admonished, "is of the opinion that this enterprise would best be served at some remove from the palace. We are, after all, trying to encourage a spirit of independent enterprise."

Shanta grunted. "You're not going to have any problem with that, believe me. Problem is going to be keeping all that independent spirit from sheering off in half a dozen different directions, and running before the wind with its sails in tatters."

"Ringil?"

Ringil examined his nails. "I think I can keep them in line. Bunch of merchants, aren't they?"

"These days they are." There was the edge of a chuckle in Shanta's voice. "But some of them came the hard road to it. Shendanak started out slitting travelers' throats in the Dhashara pass and selling their horses at auction. Got the right side of an imperial supply contract for horseflesh just in time to miss out on the gallows. Down deep, he's still more Majak steppe raider than imperial citizen."

"Well, I get on well enough with those." Ringil winked at Archeth. "How's the Dragonbane keeping, down here in the civilized world?"

"He's all right," Archeth estimated. "Bit twitchy at the moment."

"Can't wait to see the old thug."

"You might have to climb a few harem walls." She knew she sounded bad-tempered, but couldn't help it. Lack of sleep, lack of krinzanz, lack of Ishgrim—it was all catching up with her at once. And she'd seen the way Egar looked at Ishgrim, had caught him at it a couple of times. "Getting laid's still his main interest in life. He's most likely camped out up the hill with his lady friend right now."

Shanta, waiting politely for them to wrap up the gossip. "You'll also likely have trouble with Kaptal and Tand. Tand because he despises Shendanak, and Kaptal because he's another one who made it up from gutter beginnings and never really left them behind. It'll put his back up just being in the same room as gentry like Gral and Nyanar."

Ringil shrugged. "Seen that before: rank and file hating the nobles, nobles despising the rank and file. Sounds no worse than any other command I ever had."

"Yes, my lord Eskiath, but I would remind you, your commands were of military men—men who understood the rigor and discipline of soldiering."

He thought back to the crew of mercenaries he'd led and then abandoned outside Hinerion. Had to stop a smile crossing his lips. The naval engineer, for all his apparent wisdom in other areas, clearly didn't have the faintest fucking idea about men of war.

"Soldiers come in all shapes and sizes, my lord Shanta." And here came the smile anyway, leaking out. "I've ridden my share of ill-disciplined bastards, and lived to tell the tale. Your gentry will be safe in my shadow."

"It's the gentry that worry me, Gil." Archeth shot him an admonishing *don't-get-cute* look. "Men like Shendanak and Kaptal you can bring to heel—they understand force of will, they understand leadership. It's a little harder getting past six centuries of selective breeding and entitlement."

"Well." Ringil rolled out a remarkable impression of courtly hauteur. "I would remind you, my lady, I have noble roots myself."

This time Mahmal Shanta did chuckle. "I don't doubt it, my lord. But I'm afraid nobility from the north will not be counted here in the same coin as imperial title."

"On my *mother's* side"—Ringil, staying in affronted noble character—"I trace a *direct line of descent* back to the very noblest of this Empire's, ehm, refugees."

It got him an unexpected silence.

Shanta glanced at Archeth. She shrugged. "True enough. Driven out in the Ashnal schism, apparently. A lot were."

"Yes. Yes, I—I thought—" The naval engineer turned to fix Ringil with a fascinated eye. "Something in your face—the cheekbones, the arch of nose—yes, it must be that, of course. Of course. And that skin tone—perfect!"

Ringil gave him a thin smile. It was all a little too close to slave-auction appraisal for his liking. But he caught Archeth's tiny shake of the head, and he tried his best to keep the steel out of his voice.

"I'm happy you approve, my lord. Given, then, that my face fits so well, perhaps I will not need to break the faces of these other nobles to get their support."

"Oh, no question," chortled Shanta, rubbing his age-knobbed hands as if with soap and water. He didn't seem to have spotted the sudden edge in Ringil's tone. "Have no fear, my lord Eskiath—we'll manufacture some very fine cloth from this, some very fine cloth indeed. Whole dynasties were torn down in the Ashnal years. We can load your veins with as much Yhelteth nobility as we like. You'll see. We'll have Gral and Nyanar down on bended knee before we're done."

Ringil traded looks with Archeth. He cracked a smile, a genuine one this time. Impossible, somehow, not to get caught up in the older man's enthusiasm.

"Glad to hear it. So when do you want me to meet these gracious gentlemen and lady?"

Shanta pondered. "Better that we postpone your introduction somewhat. I'd like to think seriously about what lineage we attribute to you before we leap into the fray."

"Yeah, and your Tethanne could use some polish," said Archeth unkindly.

"At the same time, I don't believe we should delay our preliminary meetings. There is currently a lull in the Demlarashan insurgency, the northern marches remain stable, at least for now, and in the east our relations with Shaktur are cordial. But all or any of this may change, and sooner than any of us expect. Your Helmsman has chosen an auspicious moment to arrive, Archeth, and I think we must seize that moment while it lasts."

"Then we'll need Rakan, at least initially."

Ringil blinked. *Rakan?*

"I suspect," Shanta mused, "that you will need Rakan throughout, regardless of our friend here. The Throne Eternal represent the Emperor, in symbol and in fact. They are his sworn men. I don't see His Radiance taking kindly to them being excluded."

"I'm his sworn representative, too."

"Hmm."

Ringil caught the undercurrent. Something in the air between these two that they hadn't bothered to share with him yet. He cleared his throat.

"This Rakan. Any relation of old Faileh?"

Archeth nodded absently. "His younger brother. Seconded when the elder died. He's supposed to have the command, but Mahmal doesn't think he's up to it."

"He isn't," said Shanta gloomily.

"Yes, well, if that's so, Mahmal, I don't really see how we can proceed." Archeth, working on *quite exasperated actually.* Ringil thought he caught the scraping edge of *no krin today* in her tone. "We're going to have a fucking mess on our hands, trying to get this early start you want."

"It's a price we'll just have to—"

"Yeah, a higher price than you—"

"Archeth, it's worth the—"

"It's a fucking mist—"

Ringil cleared his throat, loudly. They both shut up and looked at him. He tried out the thin smile again. Couldn't hurt to practice a little ahead of time.

"It's perfect," he told them. "That's what it is. Perfect."

CHAPTER 30

They paid off the boatman at Prophet's Landing. Puddles of band-light on the river's skin, and the drip-dribble of water from the shipped oars. The clink and dull gleam of coins counted out into a callused palm. Payment stowed, the boatman shoved off immediately and without a word—he was still sulking by the look of it. They watched the darkness on the river swallow him up, then went carefully up the green-grown slimy stone steps of the landing. At the top, the merchant quarter brooded in deserted early-hours gloom—shut-up shops and warehouses, auction halls and stabling, the odd glimmer of a watchman's lantern here and there, but otherwise no sign of life. They slipped into the warren of darkened streets and away.

There had been no pursuit.

None you saw, anyway.

Egar said nothing to the others, but still, he could feel the vague snake of worry turn over in his guts. A year ago at Ennishmin, they'd run from the dwenda and he'd seen the pursuing scouts glimmer into ghostly blue-lit life on the banks of the river, watching him in silence as he passed. He spent most of the journey downstream from Afa'marag looking out for the same thing, but he saw no recognizable sign. Whether that meant they were in the clear, he had no idea.

He caught himself wishing Ringil were there. He missed the faggot's sour, selfish introspection and book-learned wit.

Gil would have known what to make of all this.

He shook it off. *Come on, Dragonbane. Bad enough you let Imrana do most of your thinking for you these days. Now you need a fucking faggot at the task?*

Be asking him to fucking tug you off next.

He made the effort. If Pashla Menkarak was treating with dwenda under the impression he was in holy communion with angels, Egar was almost tempted to let the whole thing run its natural course. He'd pay hard coin to see Menkarak's face when the angels shrugged off whatever glamour they'd cast and stepped forward for what they were. Maybe they'd stalk the corridors of the Citadel and tear every fucking invigilator within its walls limb from limb. Maybe they'd put every priestly head on a tree stump still living, the way they'd done with the victims at Ennishmin.

(Still gave him the odd nightmare—what he'd seen done in that swamp.)

Be hard to feel bad about an outcome like that, though. Certainly, it'd get the Citadel off Archeth's back.

They found a tavern still open, weak gutter of candles melted down in their own wax along the trestle tables, clientele down to a few drowsy drunks and a couple of whores counting up the night's takings with their pimp in a corner. Harath went to get mugs of spiced wine at the bar, while Egar sat at an empty table opposite the girl and gazed at her like a problem he had to solve.

Which she pretty much was.

"You're bleeding," she said quietly.

It was a reminder he didn't really need. The wound in his thigh throbbed every time he took a step, but it seemed to have stopped bleeding on the ride downriver. The other stuff was superficial—furrows and scratches no worse than you'd get from a crooked whore trying to roll you. The old adage welled up in his head. *Ignored gashes heal the fastest.*

"Used to it," he grunted. "What am I going to do with you, girl?"

"Anything you want." The same low, colorless voice. "I am yours now."

"Yeah." He rubbed at his eyes. "Right."

He supposed the obvious thing was to take her to Archeth's place. But—

Harath arrived with the wine, which was by now lukewarm. They sat in silence for a while, sipping, cradling the scant heat of the mugs in their hands. Presently, a serving maid came out and put a platter of cured fish portions on the table for them. Harath dived in.

"So what you going to do with her?" he asked, as if the girl were not sitting there.

"That's not your concern. What *you* do is get back to your room, pay the rent, and keep your head down. I'll come by with the rest of your money in a couple of days."

"Worried about those demon things, huh?"

"No."

Harath, nodding to himself as he chewed. "Worried they'll track us, right?"

"You fucking deaf? I said no. I said I'm not worried about them."

The Ishlinak jerked his chin. "Yeah, doesn't sound like it."

Egar drew a hard breath, let it slowly out. He looked down at the backs of his hands. There was a gouge across the left one he hadn't noticed before.

Great.

"All right, yes. This is some serious shit," he finally admitted, to himself as much as the Ishlinak. "The Citadel are fucking about with things they don't understand. Things I don't understand, either. But it's black shaman stuff. Night powers magic."

"Oh, you *reckon?*" Suddenly there was a hiss in the younger man's tone. He leaned in across the table. "Corpses—of *my* fucking kin, Skaranak—rising from the dead after we just fucking killed them! Faceless warriors that walk with the lightning! Night powers, you say? Are you *sure*?"

"Keep your voice down."

Jabbing finger across the trestle and into his face. "You said we wouldn't kill any—"

Egar grabbed the hand at the wrist, slammed it flat to the table. "I *said* keep your fucking voice down."

He locked eye with eye, forearm tensed as the younger man tried to free his trapped hand. The struggle coiled and uncoiled, draining ache through muscles already hammered hard in the fight. He hung on. *Make it look easy. Work the bluff.* He tilted his head a little, inquiring. Kept the stare. Used it all to lean imperceptibly in and reinforce the downward hold. Harath heaved one more time and gave up, tried to pull away. Egar held on another couple of seconds to make sure, then gave him his hand back.

"You were paid, Majak." Hiding among spaced and even words how badly he needed to get his breath back. "Sometimes things don't work out the way they're planned. Demlarashan ought to have taught you that much."

Harath looked back sullenly. "They were my friends."

"Yeah? Well as I recall, when I came calling on you, your best guess was that your *friends* had sent me to murder you. Remember that?"

"You *said*—"

"I know what I said. I didn't know what we'd find in there. Now the fight is done, you're alive, and your purse is full. Pretty good outcome for a freebooter, I'd say. So shut the fuck up and let me think."

Silence. They sat and let him think.

Obvious thing was to take her to Archeth's place.

Right.

But the Citadel were going to be watching Archeth's place, now more than ever, and out of sight to boot.

Couple of days ago, could maybe have sneaked her past the old cordon they had out there with nobody the wiser. But that was before you decided to go breaking bones and faces for fun. Now they'll have spies in beggar's rags along the boulevard and probably men with spyglasses in upper rooms across the street. No way to tell who's watching where anymore.

Nice going, Dragonbane.

Grimace.

Could try it anyway—wrap her head-to-foot, maybe. Not exactly un-heard of around here.

But he knew the scheme was dead in the water even as he hatched it. The Citadel would be looking for any possible way there was to discredit Archeth, and Archeth's tastes were widely whispered of. The arrival of a fresh female, however attired, would just fan the flames of gossip. It would get back to Menkarak for sure, and if the invigilator chose to do the needlepoint, stitch Majak freebooter to mysterious female to dwenda with gashes from a staff lance to the disappearance of a certain slave girl in Afa'marag . . .

No. Forget Archeth's place.

There's always—

Egar shot the younger man a surreptitious glance, saw the way he was drooling over the girl like some street dog confronted with a bowl of fresh offal. Dumped the idea before it made it all the way to a clearly formed thought. He barely trusted the Ishlinak to keep himself out of trouble the next few days, let alone keep anyone else safe at the same time. Harath, with a stuffed purse and swelling bravado from their adventures and safe escape . . .

At best, he'd force himself on the girl by way of payment for the favor. Maybe have her running off screaming down the street. At worst, he'd have her out on display at every mercenary watering hole in town while he told the tale for beers.

Forget it, Dragonbane. Worse idea than Archeth's place.

He wondered for a moment about Darhan, maybe some comrade of Darhan's from the Combined Irregulars . . .

You don't want to lean too much on that tribal thing.

His old trainer's own words, against the early-morning rattle of staff practice. And a speculative look in his eye.

You're a fucking idiot, Dragonbane, that's what I'm trying to tell you. You, and your loyalties. Going to get you killed one of these days.

He realized, with a slow seeping chill, that he didn't really know Darhan anymore—perhaps had never known the man, save as a gruff elder-brother substitute when he pitched up in the city, callow and gawking, what seemed like a lifetime ago.

You've been gone too long, Dragonbane. He knew it for the truth—it had that solid, marrow-deep ring to it, like a clean ax blow going home. *Times change, and men change with them. This isn't the city you remember.*

You are alone here.

Suddenly, trusting Darhan with the girl and her story didn't seem like such a good idea.

WHICH LEFT JUST THE ONE OPTION, REALLY.

HE SENT HARATH HOME. *SIT TIGHT, WAIT FOR WORD.* HE DOUBTED THE younger man would be able to do either for more than a couple of days, but maybe that'd be enough.

"What will you do with me now?" the girl asked him, when the tavern door had swung shut on the Ishlinak.

"I'm taking you to see a friend," he told her.

Outside, the night was starting to wear thin and gray—but dawn was still a good few hours off, and the streets were as empty as before. Egar stood for a moment, checked for unwanted witnesses in doorways or at windows. Saw none, and beckoned for the girl to come out and join him. She limped to his side, favoring her left foot. He noticed her unshod feet for the first time since they'd gotten out of the temple—legs still mud-splattered and streaked from the river. Hard to see if there was blood. Her lips pressed together as she saw him looking. Panic in her eyes once more.

"I'm *fine*," she jittered. "I can walk, I'm fine."

"What's your name?" he asked her gently.

"They call me Nil."

"Good enough." He glanced up at the sky. "Well listen, Nil, we have to hurry here. I want to get you off the street before daybreak. Last stretch, just stay with me. Can you do that?"

A tight nod.

"Let's go, then."

Up through the gently shelving streets toward the Palace Quarter, and despite her limp, Nil was as good as her word. She kept to his pace better than some imperial levy recruits he'd been saddled with in the past. He felt the tension in him begin to ease as they climbed. The higher up the hill you got, the better the neighborhood and the less chance you'd end up in any kind of trouble. Up here, the militia patrols were frequent and well disciplined, not likely to be hitting you up for bribes or favors. Citizens and slaves went about their business with assurance. And any criminals on the prowl would be smart, would have well-planned agendas that didn't include getting into random street squabbles.

Long and short of it—anyone they met on these immaculately maintained thoroughfares was going to have better things to do than gawk at or otherwise involve themselves with some passing Majak free-booter and his concubine.

So they hit Harbor Hill Rise without incident. Made it all the way to the mansion with the mosaic dome cupola, having seen no more than half a dozen hurrying servants and a couple of doorway-hugging war-wounded beggars who'd somehow avoided being shooed and shoved back down the hill the night before. They found the mansion's servant entry, and Egar took a moment to square away the last of his vague misgivings.

Then he reached up and tugged at the bellpull.

The chimes chased each other away. Long delay, while voices and footfalls went back and forth behind the wall. He was half tempted to smear a couple of leaping steps up the white stone, grab the black iron spikes at the top, and vault over, wounds or no wounds. It wouldn't have been the first time—but under the circumstances . . .

He waited.

Finally, a slat opened at head height in the dark wood paneling of the door. Eyes peered out.

"Yes?"

"Brinag?"

"He's busy in the cellar. And we don't pay anyone till end of month, so if you're here to settle accounts, forget it. What do you want?"

Egar gave the watching eyes a grim smile. "What I want is for you to tell Brinag that Egar the Dragonbane is outside, and he'd better get this door open before I kick it in for you."

Shocked silence. A pair of heartbeats.

"Uhm—yes, my lord. Yes, I'll . . . There is, my lord, the main gate. If you had only—"

"Just go and get him."

"Yes, my lord."

The slave hurried off, forgot to close the slat before he went. Egar glanced at Nil, who was sagging at his side.

"Not long now," he murmured.

Brinag came bustling up, checked Egar through the slat, and unbolted the door. He ushered them inside, cupping a candle aside with one hand. Checked the street and closed the door, leaned his back against it. Cleared his throat with mannered eunuch delicacy.

"My lord, this is really not an ideal time to be calling. As you're no doubt aware—"

"Is he in, though?"

"No, my lord."

"And she is?"

Brinag sighed. "Yes, my lord."

"What I thought. You'd better take me to her, then."

"Very well." The eunuch cast a cold eye over Nil. "And this is?"

"A gift," Egar told him succinctly. "Brin, we're wasting time."

In the glow from the candle, the look on the eunuch's face said he thought that was the least of their problems. But he made no further comment. He led them through the ornamental herb garden and up the decorative iron spiral staircase into the kitchens. Through the high-ceilinged spaces within, up more stairs and along the tastefully tapestried and carpeted corridors of the upper levels, toward the seaward wing of the house. Brinag nodding curtly at slaves and servants along the way, trading at one point his candle for a lantern.

"If this visit comes to light," he muttered, "then—"

"Then I got in over the wall somehow. Just another Majak harem marauder, and you don't know anything about it. Same as it ever was. Can you trust these people?"

"I can trust them not to want whipping within an inch of their lives," Brinag said sourly. "I suppose that will have to do."

He led them to the chief bedchamber. No surprises there, Imrana wasn't an early riser at the best of times, and dawn was still a way off.

Back in the tavern, Egar would have put his whole purse on her being right here in this room. He wouldn't have bet quite as much on Knight Commander Saril Ashant's whereabouts, but he knew enough of the relationship to spit and hope for marital absence. It wasn't exactly the worst risk he'd ever taken.

Brinag knocked apologetically at the chamber doors, held up a hand for quiet, waited, knocked again. Waited. Knocked louder.

A muffled, moaning volley of curses from within the chamber. The eunuch tipped a bleak glance at Egar. He eased one door open a crack and slipped through the gap. Twisted about, held up a forbidding finger.

"Wait here."

The door closed with a tight *snap*, leaving them in the gloom. Murmur of voices beyond, first Brin's and then the sleepy-toned responses, growing louder and less sleepy by the word. Egar grimaced. Then conversation stopped, caught up on some jag of angry disbelief. Long quiet, then another murmur. Brin's footfalls back to the door. The door opened and the eunuch slipped back out. He surveyed the two of them, deadpan.

"The Lady Imrana will see you now," he said. "Please go through."

She was off the bed and tucking herself tight in a linen robe as they walked in. The Lady Imrana Nemaldath Amdarian, long black hair in comely disarray, the face it framed hard-boned and harsh, even in the kindly light of the lamps Brinag had lit for her before he came out. It took the softening effect of all the cosmetics she would later layer on to ease the command in that face, to make it into something more appropriately womanly, something more appropriate, Egar always thought, to how she was below the neck. Imrana was voluptuous by Yhelteth standards, despite the advancing years, breasts full and heavy in the tight-wrapped folds of the robe, tilt and curve of generous hips as she stalked barefoot across the tiles toward him. And with the anger marked on her face like that, scarlet spots burning at each cheekbone, man, he could feel a want for her coming on stronger than—

"Are you fucking *deranged*, Egar?" The obscenity, there in her mannered mouth like a plum. As ever, it made him hard just hearing that urbane, throaty courtier voice rolling out language fit for a Skaranak milkmaid. "Are you *out of your fucking mind*? Coming here like this?"

"Imrana, listen—"

"I said a fortnight! Is that so hard to get through your thick Majak skull? He's still *here*, he's still on fucking *furlough!*"

"Not in this bed, though." Egar, stung by the epithet *Majak*. She'd never used it on him before outside of pillow play. "Didn't take him long to burn through his marital obligations and take his business elsewhere, did it? Which brothel do you reckon it was this time?"

It stopped her like a slap. She breathed in, hard enough that he saw her fine aristo nostrils pinch with it. She retucked herself a little tighter in her robe, as if the temperature in the room had suddenly fallen. Her voice grew cold and calm.

"I have no idea, Egar. No idea at all. In truth, it's more likely he's with one of his mistresses. He will have had his fill of brothel flesh while he was on campaign." Small, bleak smile for him. "So. Is speaking it aloud supposed to shock either of us?"

"I wouldn't have come here if I had another choice."

Imrana glanced at the girl. "Really? In this whole city, you really can't find anywhere else to play three in a bed."

"It's not—"

"What about your beautiful black-skinned sponsor? I hear she likes it that way, couldn't you persuade her to—"

"Will you shut up, woman! I didn't come here to fuck you!"

The echoes chased briefly around the chamber, lost themselves in the heavy black drapes and expensive wall hangings. Imrana stared at him. In the breathing space that followed, he discovered that what really stung was her apparent opinion, laid abruptly bare with this unscripted meeting. It lurched through the arrangement of his memories like a drunken thug in a spice market, scattering and trampling the little rows of jars and pots, the artfully opened, fine-odored sacks. Belch and curse and stagger, smash and spill. Everything he'd valued, turned over in his head—he watched it happen like the sack of some pretty hillside town. Thick-skull big-cock barbarian bit of rough—was that all he'd ever been? Or was it the march of years, clawing them apart? Had passing time and age done this to them both, made them colder and more distant, wound up in their own affairs and grasping scared at what was left? He cast his mind back, tried to remember. Found he couldn't. Found he didn't want to.

His wounds ached, suddenly. Suddenly, he felt old.

Perhaps she felt it, too. Perhaps she read the damage in his face. She went back and sat on the edge of the bed. Unconscious elegance in the lines of her legs, the spread of her arms out to the sides, pressing on the mattress, the downward tilt of her head and the way her hair swung forward to shroud her face. She took the ends of her robe tie, fiddled with them. Looked up with a new smile, one that stabbed him through the chest.

"But you nearly did fuck me, Eg," she said quietly. "Coming here like this."

"Well, that wasn't the plan," he growled.

"No, perhaps not. And forgive me if I shouted, but Egar, you have to see. Saril and I have this down. I ignore his indiscretions, and he either genuinely believes I am chaste or he does not care so long as I appear so. It works, it is civilized. You . . ."

"I'm not civilized. Yeah, got that."

"That's not what I mean." She glanced again at Nil, seemed to see the girl properly for the first time. Another smile, one he couldn't read, flickering across her face. "She's kind of cute, Eg, but she's filthy. And she's dead on her feet. Where on Earth did you get her?"

"That's a long story." Still the trace of the growl in his voice. "If you want to hear it."

"Of course I want to hear it. Look, I'll have her cleaned up, and we'll talk. All right?"

It was almost like watching a knight putting on his plate, preparatory to battle. The sections of the Imrana he knew, strapped into place piece by piece. She got up and went to the bellpull at the head of the bed, tugged it sharply. One hand went up to her hair, stroked the dark fall back at her ear—it looked almost nervous. He saw how thin strands of gray and white twined through the dyed dark like the fine wires in some Kiriath machine. She tilted her head at him.

"You know, Eg, all those years. If you'd wanted three in a bed, you only had to ask."

HE WASN'T SURE IF SHE BELIEVED HIM, WASN'T SURE IF HE MUDDLED through the tale clearly enough for it to make any sense to her. But with

Nil taken away by Brinag for a bath, Imrana at least seemed to be listening. And he thought he read genuine anguish in her face when he showed her his wounds.

"I thought we'd done with all this, you and I," she murmured, kneeling in front of him at the bedside, pressing gently along the sides of the gash in his thigh. She'd torn his breeches where the wound was, to see the cut more clearly. Ashant wasn't the first knight she'd been married to, and like most Yhelteth noblewomen she was well versed in the art of caring for spouses returned from the fray. "I thought you'd come back here to *retire* from all this."

"Yeah, me, too." Though truth was, he'd never seen it in anything like those terms. "What can I tell you? Trouble grows lonely, comes looking for me again."

She darted him a look. "I think you may have that backward."

He grunted. Elsewhere in the mansion, through the walls, you could hear voices and the sounds of movement as the household got on its predawn feet. In here, though, it all felt very distant, the activity of other yurts around the camp when what counted was here before him in the soft glow of the lamps. The raw rift opened between them earlier seemed to have healed over, but he wasn't sure if that didn't unnerve him more than the revelation of the rift itself. He winced as she pressed tighter on the wound.

"This is going to need stitches," she said. "I'll do it myself, if you'd like that."

"Yeah, fine. Question remains, Imrana. What am I supposed to do about all this? Can you keep the girl, at least for a while?"

"Of course. Who's going to notice, in a household this size? But you'll need to tell all this to Archeth, you know you will. You can't go head-to-head with the Citadel on your own."

"I told you, I can't go near Archeth right now."

"Then get word to her. I can arrange that easily enough. But you can't stay here while I do it, Egar. You know that, too, right?"

"Right," he said glumly.

"Do you need cash? I can—"

"Got cash, that's not the problem. Problem is, who can I and can I not trust in this fucking city?"

She shrugged. "Welcome to my world. At court, you wouldn't—"

Shouting from the corridor. The sounds of struggle.

Their eyes met for a jagged second.

"*You squealing castrate piece of shit!*" Hoarse bellowing, just outside the chamber. Something thumped heavily into the wall. "Cover up for her, will you, you fucking *half man*?"

Panic flooded Imrana's face.

"It's him, oh shit, it's *him*! He's back! Get out of here Eg, go, *go*! The window, get—"

The doors to the chamber burst inward.

Brinag came first, stumbling backward, arms wheeling for balance he could not find. He went over on his back. Scrabbled into a crouch on the carpet, face turned toward them. Egar made out the reddening weal across one cheek where he'd been struck.

"My lady, I'm so sorry. He came unannounced—"

Voice scaling to a sudden cry as Knight Commander Saril Ashant loomed up behind him and swung a well-worn campaign boot into his arse. Brinag lurched forward with the force of the kick, landed flat to the floor. Ashant stepped over his sprawled body and kicked him again, casually, in the head.

"I'll announce myself, gelding." Well-bred voice loud and lecturing— Egar caught the tone. The Yhelteth knight was drunk or something like it, and his blood was up. "In my own house, to my own lady wife, I have no fucking need to be *announced*!"

His eyes drank in the tableau by the bed—his wife, knelt before this Majak seated on his sheets. A savage grin peeled his lips back from his teeth.

"Or maybe I do. It seems, my lord Hanan, that I owe you a hundred elementals and a heartfelt apology. You were right, my wife *is* a whore after all." Lethal good cheer lurking at the edges of Ashant's tone now. "Oh, *no*, my dear, don't get up. Don't stop what you're doing. You've just saved me the necessity of a duel to defend your honor. Isn't that right, Hanan?"

A second figure stepped into the chamber at Ashant's right shoulder. Same regimental colors, same campaign cloak and deceptively elegant court sword. Same telltale profession-of-violence shadow hanging over the man like a pall of charnel house smoke. Egar found himself wishing fervently he hadn't left the Ishlinak staff lance on the temple floor at Afa'marag.

"Much though it grieve me," Hanan said somberly. "You are correct, my lord."

Imrana surged to her feet. Oddly, in this room suddenly crowded with men of war, she seemed the only one with any grip on what to do next.

"Saril, what is the meaning of this intrusion?" Icy and commanding in the wrap of her robe—a witch queen out of legend could not have carried it better. "How *dare* you storm in here, in company, without a word of civilized warning. What is this, the *steppes*?"

Ashant goggled at her. It lasted a good, useful moment—then the spell broke.

"Whore!" he yelled, pointing a trembling finger. "Filthy whore!"

"Oh, *don't* be such a fucking prick," Egar told him wearily, and came up off the bed with his hands full of knives.

He figured anything less would get him killed. Two Demlarashan veterans, noble-born and -bred, full of piss and righteous outrage, and the law on their side. Yhelteth jurists accorded any man, even a commoner, the right to butcher his wife on the spot if he caught her in the act of adultery. There were some legal limits on what could be done to the lover, but most magistrates were inclined to be lenient if the husband got carried away. And if that lover was *Majak,* and the injured party a nobleman just back from serving his Empire in uniform, well, it didn't take a law clerk to work out how this was going to boil down . . .

Ashant reached for his sword and Egar went in hard, full-body blow, pinned and blocked the draw before it got started. He knocked the knight to the floor—risky move, if Ashant had been sober and better poised, he probably wouldn't have gotten away with it. He heard the hushed rasp of steel on his flank as Hanan cleared his blade—was already whirling to face the other man. The stiffness in his wound slowed him down, and his leg buckled on the turn. Hanan misread him, sliced too high. Egar snatched the chance, let the stumble take him all the way forward and down, stabbed savagely with his right-hand knife, down through the toe of Hanan's boot and into the floorboards beneath.

Hanan roared, ignored the pain, tried to chop him again with the sword. Egar was already rolling away, *leave that knife where it is, Dragonbane.* He banged into Ashant, who was trying to get up. They clawed at each other, held each other down, wrestled back and forth across the floor until Egar pulled a Majak wrestling trick, got loose and hacked, elbow to throat, *once, twice,* short vicious arcs, Urann's balls wouldn't this guy *ever* quit, *three* times then, and there, finally, Ashant fell back and lay faceup on the carpet, choking.

Get up, Dragonbane, get up—

Because Hanan, tough little motherfucker that he'd turned out to be, had meantime reached down and torn the knife up out of his foot with a bellow equal parts triumph and agony, and was now limping forward, sword and dagger style . . .

Egar rolled to his feet, found himself inches off Hanan's long blade. He leapt back, just as the Yhelteth knight thrust. The blade fetched up inches short once more. He gave ground again. Hanan grinned ferociously at him, whipped the supple court sword back and forth across the air so it made a sound like shredding cloth. Came on one grim, limping step at a time.

"How now, steppe scum!" he rasped. "How now?"

Falling back, Egar had an eyeblink instant to assess—down to one knife, left-handed; he had a third blade stowed in his burglar's garb, but it was way too late to free it. He was going to get cut up badly on Hanan's court sword, getting in close enough to kill the man, but—

From the floor, Brinag—blood matted in his hair, streaming down his face from where Ashant had kicked him—grabbed desperately at the knight's ankle.

Hanan stumbled, cursed, whipped about and plunged his sword point into the eunuch's arm. Brinag groaned and hung on. Egar—the knife changing hands like sorcery, spun from palm to gripping palm without thought—seizing the moment, leaping in . . .

Hanan caught the move in the corner of his eye, swung about, court sword rising clumsily back to guard, and thrust. Egar ducked and hooked with his free arm, the blade went over his shoulder, the hooking arm caught it at the midpoint—twist at the elbow, get that tender inner arm out of the way, lead with the bone—smashed down and stepped in. A poorer blade would have snapped, a poorer soldier would have lost his grip. But Hanan hung on and the blade bent and sliced into Egar's forearm as the knight twisted it desperately about.

Egar yelled and stabbed—in under the sternum, full force.

Hanan shrilled like a stuck pig. You knew from that cry he was done, but Egar only lurched closer in, hugging the man like a lover. Drove the blade deeper, twisting and hacking down into the belly. Stared into the man's eyes as he carved the life out of him.

"How now, city dweller?" he spat. "How *now*?"

The court sword twanged free of Hanan's grip as he went down. Blood and viscera gushed out over Egar's hand as he pulled the knife free.

He held Hanan's sagging body up for a moment with his other arm. Patted the dead or dying man companionably on the shoulder a couple of times, panting, then let him fall.

Weeping into quiet.

Egar looked about vaguely, already sensing the fight was done. No more intruders, the open chamber doors yawned wide, but there was only gloom beyond. Imrana was knelt sobbing at her husband's side, holding his head in her hands while he finished choking to death. Brinag fumbled to his feet, came and stood beside Egar, nursing the hole in his arm where Hanan had stabbed him. His face was a garish fright mask, red-streaked and smeared with the blood from his torn scalp.

"Quite the harem adventure this morning, my lord," he said acidly.

Egar lifted and turned his own left arm, looked at the dark spreading soak of fresh blood through his sleeve where Hanan's blade had sliced him up. He grimaced.

"Bit tight, yeah."

From the floor, Imrana turned a hectic, tear-streaming face on him. "You killed him! Eg, he's fucking *dead,* you *killed* him!"

He spread his arms, blood-clotted knife still clutched in his right hand. Not a lot you could say, really. Second or third blow to Ashant's throat, he'd felt the windpipe crush inward, he already knew he'd killed him. Wished she wasn't so visibly upset about it, though. Could have done without that.

"You'd better get out of here." Brinag, at his shoulder. "Somehow, I don't think we're going to get away with dumping these two down the old well. Not this time."

"Yeah." Egar glanced at the eunuch. "I owe you, Brin. You going to be all right?"

"They cut off my balls at fifteen," Brinag said tonelessly. "What else is there?"

Egar, who in his time had seen the mutilated enemies of the Dha-shara hill tribes and the roasting pits of the Scaled Folk, thought this showed remarkably little imagination on Brinag's part. But now was really not the time. He clapped the eunuch on the shoulder.

"Good man. You take care of her, then. Blame whatever you need to on me."

Brinag looked steadily back at him, nodded.

"Eg?" Imrana, back on her feet, wiping away tears with angry swipes of her palm. "Eg, what are you talking about? What are you going to do? You can't just . . . "

He sighed. "Imrana, they're going to put your slaves to the question, they're going to know I was here. And you told me yourself we're pretty much an open secret in court circles. Hanan certainly knew, seems he fronted Saril with it, in front of who knows how many noble witnesses. You've got to hang this on me."

She stared at him. "No."

"Don't be a fucking idiot, woman. It's either that, or we conspired together to murder your husband, and you'll go to the chair for it. Is that what you want? Look—you'd given me up, right? Fallen back in love with your husband. I broke in here furious, to rape you or whatever, that whole Majak steppe-thug thing, Hanan and Saril arrived just in time to stop me, but I killed them and fled. You're just a victim of a noblewoman's silly indiscretion that got out of hand. That'll wash, right? You've got friends at court who'll see it done?"

She nodded numbly. He tried to take her in his arms, but she was still rigid with the shock. He settled for running a rough thumb down her tear-ribboned cheek.

"Then that's the way it has to be, Imrana."

"But they'll . . . they'll hunt you down."

He snorted. "Yeah, they'll try. I've been hunted by steppe ghouls and starving wolves, Imrana. I think I can handle the Yhelteth City Guard."

And for one crazy moment, he wished he was back out there on the steppe once more, back under that great icy sky with staff lance and ax and knives at hand, and nothing more complicated to worry about than some pack of howling hungry creatures on the horizon who'd ill-advisedly decided they wanted a piece of him.

Instead of which . . .

This fucking city.

He nodded once more at Brin, looked once more at Imrana standing there. Then he turned and headed back out into it.

CHAPTER 31

You could hear the yelling from twenty yards off down the alcoved and colonnaded corridor. As they approached, Ringil glanced sideways and saw Archeth pull a face.

"Worse than you thought it'd be?" he asked her.

"Yeah." But then she shrugged. "No. No, I suppose not."

"Fucking merchants, eh?"

"You will keep your seat!" came through the door at full pitch. A young, unseasoned voice, trying for command and fraying at the edges. Ringil made it for Noyal Rakan. He'd eavesdropped on the young Throne Eternal captain earlier in the week, and had to agree with Shanta. He wasn't the man for this job.

Nice arse, though.

They reached the door. Stood wordless, looking at each other. The storm raged on within, Rakan's attempt to close down debate by now pretty much washed away in the waves of revolt. One heavily accented, bass voice trampled down the Throne Eternal captain's commands. Behind that, other speakers with more homegrown Tethanne vied for mastery undeterred. Archeth looked at Ringil's face and saw a cold smile wash across his eyes but barely touch the crooked line of his mouth.

"Well, here we go," he said.

He reached down with a showy flourish of sleeves, laid hands on the ornate handles of the double doors. He turned each handle sharply and shoved inward. The doors hinged smoothly back, letting out a waft of stale, body-heated air and the surf of raised voices.

" . . . a fucking *choirboy*!"

"That's exactly right, you—"

" . . . shame! Shame!"

" . . . no intention of . . . "

"Gentlemen!"

To Archeth, it didn't seem as if Ringil had raised his own voice by much, but it stilled the room like a battle clarion. There was an almost comical nature to the way the company froze, heads twitching around to the door and the figure that had just come through it. Half of the assembled worthies were on their feet around the table, caught in furious mid-gesture, the others slumped in their chairs with lordly disdain. Rakan, looking beleaguered, headed the table with another equally young Throne Eternal by his side, but the focus of the room was Shendanak—big, broad-shouldered, and these days swinging a belly like a saddlebag under his robes. Shendanak, who still affected the knotted hair and iron talismans of a youth and a heritage he'd left three decades and a thousand miles behind. Shendanak, who wore the jagged scar on his forehead like some diadem of rank and covered his big, cut-up hands with savagely wrought steel and silver rings.

Shendanak, who spoke first. Full-body swivel, straight in.

"And who the fuck are you?"

Ringil met his eye and dropped into Majak. "Want me to show you?"

It backed the other man up a scant couple of heartbeats. But Shendanak matched the language shift and came right back.

"Oho—and which Skaranak bum-boy's mouth did you steal that shit out of?"

Ringil let the smile seep out onto his face. Said nothing.

Shendanak bristled, spat out an oath. "Don't you grin at me, boy!"

The rest of the room had puddled into quiet around this, the new confrontation. At the corner of his vision, Ringil saw a palpable relief course over Rakan's features. Closely followed by mortification at the way the balance had shifted away from him. He'd blurt something out in a moment, and it probably wouldn't help.

"Well?" Shendanak's eyes measured Ringil for an early grave.

Ringil kept his smile. Felt the tug of the scar tissue in his cheek, the soft-tugging weight of the dragon-tooth dagger in his sleeve. The matter of a moment to clear the blade, leap the table and open that prodigious belly like a millet sack—let Shendanak look and find that knowledge floating there in Gil's gently smiling gaze.

"Share hearth and heart's truth," he recited softly. "Break bread and sup under a shared sky. *Or would you rather not?*"

It was as if a wind off the steppe blew in through the open door behind him. The locking power of the formal phrasing, the cold touch of the double-edged offer. *Back in the day,* Egar told him once, *way it was between the Ish and us, you'd hear that shit about as often just before it really kicked off as you would before everyone sat down to share meat. No one old enough to remember those days will piss on the norms if they can help it.*

"No, I mean it, scar-face." Voice slower and quieted a little this time, because Shendanak, possibly for the first time in years, was suddenly facing something he wasn't sure how to measure. "Who the fuck are you, really?"

Ringil kept his gaze nailed to the other man's eyes.

"The warmth of my fire," he said quietly, "is yours."

Like arm-wrestling the hulking, confident guy who hasn't understood how muscle works. Ringil felt the moment bend and then break, like cheap metal. Felt the tension go out of the other man in a gush, felt the arm go down.

"As grateful kin"—the words came grudgingly out of Shendanak's throat—"I take my place."

"Good." Ringil inclined his head, made a courtly gesture at the seat the other man wasn't using. "Then why don't you take that place, brother.

Be still, keep counsel, and we can deal with these city dwellers in a manner more appropriate to the horsemen they have forgotten how to be."

"What exactly are you two jabbering about?" snapped a well-fed face farther down the table.

Ringil didn't switch his gaze, didn't need to. He kept his tone cold but mannered, dropped back into Tethanne. "That need not concern you, my lord Kaptal."

"That's where you're wrong, my northern friend." This not from Yilmar Kaptal himself, but another, less heavily jowled individual seated at his side. Menith Tand leaned his spare, gray-maned countenance forward and made an inclusive gesture around the table. "Whatever is said in this room concerns us all. We are here, all of us, in good faith, to underwrite a venture of imperial charter. No one said anything about partisan allegiances or League mercenaries."

Shendanak snorted. "Fucking partisan, is it? Fucking prick."

"I'm a little surprised to see you uncomfortable with League mercenary involvement, my lord Tand." Ringil took a couple more steps into the room. Made the space his own, as if the Ravensfriend still hung on his back. "Do you not hire such men in great numbers to bring your slaves down from the north?"

Tand grinned mirthlessly back. "Yes. And many of them with accents and Tethanne far worse than yours. But they all answer to me for their coin. Who do you answer to, my friend?"

Archeth cleared her throat. "Gentlemen and lady, may I present to you his lordship Ringil of the Glades House Eskiath in Trelayne, once ranked knight commander in the alliance armies and decorated hero of the victory at Gallows Gap."

Low muttering around the table, like the scurry of rats. Ringil saw Noyal Rakan stiffen and murmur something to his aide. Elsewhere, in querying tones, he caught the words *hero, dragon,* and *faggot* in about equal measure.

Well, fame took some unpredictable postures when you fucked him. And he was a fickle boy at best.

"That's who he *is, kir*-Archeth," Tand said laconically. "I asked who he answers to."

Archeth gave him a blank look, and paced a couple of moments before she spoke. "My lord Ringil has agreed to act as guide and captain for the expedition north. His contract, then, is with me, and with the imperial charter. Does that suffice?"

Across the table from Tand and Kaptal, Nethena Gral wrinkled her famously smooth, pale brow—a couple of court poets, Ringil was told, had made allusion to it—and gestured irritably at Noyal Rakan.

"It was my understanding, my lady Archeth, that the Throne Eternal had command of this expedition, and were, so to speak, the Emperor's blessing and protecting hand in the venture. Is this then no longer the case?"

Ringil raised a hand to his jaw, made a seemingly innocuous stroking gesture with it. The agreed signal. On his flank, he felt Archeth subside as she saw it.

"Honored lady Gral," he said. "The Emperor's blessing here in Yhelteth is no doubt a wondrous bounty, to be sought by any wise citizen. North and west of Tlanmar, however, and paired with a League florin, it will buy you a florin's worth of salt."

A taut silence stretched behind the words. Ringil kept half an eye on Captain Noyal Rakan, saw the aide bristle with affront, but Rakan himself stay quiet and watchful.

Down the table, someone cleared a throat.

"Some," said Yilmar Kaptal carefully. "Would call that an insult to the majesty of the Burnished Throne."

Ringil shrugged. "Some would call it truth."

More quiet. What gazes were not fixed on Ringil darted around the room, meeting one another, querying, seeking alliance, shying away again.

Then, abruptly, Menith Tand chuckled.

"He's completely right, of course." The slaver looked around at the assembled company. "Isn't he? Come on, maybe not all of you have been up there, but who here hasn't read the court records on the northwestern march? He's completely right, and what's more we all know it, and we're all sitting here thinking it. So—"

He clapped his hands on the word, once, sharply. Rubbed them briskly together.

"—shall we just welcome our new captain and war hero, as his rank and exploits dictate, and then get to some serious planning? Because I for one grow bored with this constant measuring of male members in place of intelligent debate."

IT WOULD TAKE LONGER THAN THAT, OF COURSE. HE'D SOWN THE SEEDS, but the crop would be a while in sprouting.

Imperial summons had brought them all to the first meeting, curiosity and the promise of potential wealth kept them attached, as did an unwillingness to be the first to jump ship in case a hated rival should stay, and garner fame and fortune in their absence. It was a powerful binding force in a group so fractious, but it was unstable and unreliable in the longer term. *About as safe as the winds around the Gergis cape was* Shanta's sour opinion. *Could die out from under us at any minute, leave us becalmed and going nowhere. Or turn about and fling us on the rocks before we even get a start. Needs a very cool hand on the helm.*

Well, he'd made a start. Form an outsider bond with Shendanak, but keep it wrapped and opaque beneath the language gap. Throw a line to Tand with his well-traveled merchant sophistication and connection to the League territories. But keep a vague menace about it all. Neutralize the rivalry between the two men by the simple expedient of giving them Gil to worry about instead. Then dare the others to seek confrontation when they had just seen the two most vociferous of the company prefer to stand down. Lubricate the whole with court charm, and leaven with warrior bluntness. Force unity from the mix with that same unspoken threat and promise you'd summon for any ragtag command you got stuck with—*this is the thing you are a part of now, and it belongs to me; fracture it and you call me out. And you wouldn't want that.*

This shit he could do in his sleep.

With the rest of his attention, he worried about Egar.

Still somewhere in the city, Imrana thinks. Archeth didn't have much detail; even now she was playing catch-up like everyone else. The story of Saril Ashant's murder in his own bedchamber had rocked the court from top to bottom, but Imrana had enough connections to stanch the flow of further information down to a trickle. And her long years as an independent woman at court had taught her the nimble art of trusting no one any further than you absolutely had to. Archeth got a terse summons and a few minutes' audience in which Imrana sketched the events of Egar's last visit. *He shows up at the crack of dawn with some little trollop in tow, some hard-luck case he's rescued from sadistic priests and their evil sorcery—*

Sorcery? Priests?

Yeah, tell me about it. But you know what he's like, Archeth. He doesn't really see any difference between some bone-through-the-nose shaman up north and the Revelation. It's all magic to him, it's all evil. At heart, he's still the same hulking romantic thug he was when he rode into town fifteen years ago. It's all tales-around-the-campfire heroism and eternal bonds and—Imrana, gesturing wearily out the window at the city beyond— *I mean, seriously, Archeth, who believes in that shit anymore?*

Have Saril's family put a bounty out on him yet?

Probably. A thin grimace. *They're not exactly keeping counsel with me at the moment. I imagine they're still deciding whether to try to put me in the chair for this.*

"The chair?" Ringil, aghast when Archeth reported back that evening. "The fucking *chair*? I thought that was for traitors."

"And for women caught in, quote, *adulterous machinations against a lawful spouse,* unquote. It's an old law, very early Empire. Used to cover any kind of female adultery back in the day, but modern magistrature usually reads *machinations* to mean a plot against the husband's life or property. Anyway"—she picked up her goblet and drained it, but not before he'd seen her shiver—"we have the Chamber of Confidences for traitors now, so the chair's been gathering rust."

"Right. Good." He topped up her glass from the flask on the table. The house was quiet and drowsy around them, flooded with rosy evening light from the west-facing windows. "So, no chance she'll get strapped into it, then?"

Archeth studied her new drink. "A couple of years ago, I'd have said no way it could happen. But Demlarashan is really shaking things up at court. Lot of military fanfare going around these days. And Saril Ashant is—was—a bona fide war hero."

Ringil grunted. "Me, too. Outside of scars, what's that good for?"

"If you're from the rank and file, not much," she admitted. "But add it to noble family and wealth, and you've got a problem. No one at court wants to be seen not backing our glorious imperial troops."

"But Imrana has friends at court, right?"

"Imrana has allegiances. It's not the same thing. And if they don't catch up with Egar, then everyone's going to be looking for someone else to take the rap." Her lip curled in disgust. "Justice in this city is all about visible retribution—and in the end, it doesn't much matter who's on the receiving end so long as vengeance is seen to be done."

"Sounds just like home. And Imrana really thinks Eg hasn't left town?"

"From the way he was talking, she says not."

Ringil rubbed at his chin. "Strange."

"Well, what can I tell you?" Archeth spread her hands. "He has been acting strange the last couple of months. Especially the last couple of weeks, with Ashant back in town. You know, after all that time home on the steppe, maybe it was a mistake for him to come back here. Maybe city life doesn't agree with him anymore."

"Doesn't explain why he didn't leave town." Ringil held his drink up to the light, frowned critically at its color. "Anyway, my guess is, what doesn't agree with Eg most of all is not getting laid. And who could fault him on that? Eh?"

She ignored the glance he shot her, ignored the prod. "They've got the City Guard out in force looking for him."

"Poor City Guard."

"I don't know, Gil. Those guys have changed a lot since the war. Lot of demobbed veterans in the ranks now, real hard men from the expeditionary and the sieges. They're not the joke they used to be. And Eg's not as young as he used to be, either."

Ringil got up and went to stand at one of the sunset-gleaming windows. He stared out, as if he might spot the Majak perched there on one of the tiled roofs in the reddish evening light. Grinning and waving at him. Staff lance in hand.

"I back the Dragonbane against anything this city can throw at him," he said thoughtfully. "With the possible exception of the King's Reach. And I don't guess Jhiral plans to waste that kind of manpower on catching just one more steppe nomad who couldn't keep his dick in his breeches, right?"

Archeth pursed her lips. "Depends. Ashant's family swing some weight up at the palace. And like I said, the guy was a war hero. If the Guard don't get somewhere soon, they might push for it. They push hard enough, Jhiral may cave in."

"Ah, that'll be the regal majesty of the Burnished Throne in action, will it? The unbendable will of His Imperial Shininess?"

"That's Radiance."

"Not from where I'm standing."

She waved the comment away, a wasp she'd been stung by too many times to care about. "Look, I'll do what I can to forestall the King's Reach deploying. But Demlarashan has split this city down the middle. Jhiral's hard up against the Citadel, and right now he needs all the backing at court he can get."

"Including, presumably, from the Ashants of this world."

A tired nod. "Most of the nobility side with the throne because they're shit scared of what mob religion will do if it hits the streets. That gets Jhiral the bulk of the professional military, too, the officer class and anyone loyal to them. And a fair few of the Citadel's Mastery are with us as well, because they're snug in bed with the nobility and don't want their comfy little boat rocked. But they're not anything like a majority, and they won't be able to hold the line if this thing kicks off. You've got *thousands* of pissed-off and pious rank-and-file veterans out there, Gil. Across the Empire as a whole, it's tens of thousands. Men who went to war on the Citadel's say-so and came home to no change for the better."

"Yeah, you can see their point." He swung away from the window, as if dismissing something. Came back to the table. "So—are they organizing?"

"According to Jhiral's spies, not yet. Not here, anyway. But they know how to fight."

Gallows Gap flickered in his eyes like flames. "I know they do."

"They survived the Scaled Folk, and they think that's down to God and the Revelation, so they aren't really afraid of anything anymore. This is what's fueling Demlarashan. Men like that, men with a grudge, and faith, and nothing much left to lose. And it can just as easily come home to roost right here in the city. It's another Ashnal schism just waiting to happen. And you've got demagogues like Menkarak and his clique, who'll use that to bring the whole thing to the boil if they can."

Ringil hooked up his seat by the upright slat, turned it about, and seated himself straddle-legged. Rested his arms on the back and sat there with his cloak puddled in black around him, brooding. "Can't they take this Menkarak off the board? Sneak into his rooms one night and just slit his throat?"

"Been tried. Jhiral sent half a dozen of the Throne Eternal's best assassins into the Citadel to get it done. None of them came back."

A raised brow. "Just can't get the help these days, huh?"

"It isn't funny, Gil. The Citadel's a volcano getting ready to blow. You put enough cracks in Jhiral's alliances—for example, you fail to deliver when the noble family of a Demlarashan war hero come asking for favors, and—"

"Yeah, I get it." He sighed. "All right, look. You keep the King's Reach leashed as long as you can. Soon as I get the chance, I'm going to wander about this town a bit, see if I can get the Dragonbane to show himself. There might be time."

"And if there isn't?"

He peeled her an unpleasant smile. "Then to get to Egar, the King's Reach will have to come through me."

CHAPTER 32

He'd dyed his hair deep black in a run-down brothel bathroom just after dawn. Took out his talismans. Bribed the whore whose dyes he borrowed to forget he was ever there.

It was a tidy sum by the standards of the place—certainly more than she'd make to fuck him—but her expression barely changed with the commerce. She bit and stashed the coins without comment, somewhere under her grubby skirts, then pointed wordless down the corridor to where the baths could be found. By her listless, flandrijn-stunned gaze and the way she shut her fuck-room door on him as he left, Egar judged that forgetting him was exactly what she planned to do.

The bath chambers were silent and cooling, and weak fingers of early daybreak probed down through the scant steam from a row of high windows on a slimy back wall. He saw no other clients, heard only some splashing and some patently false giggling somewhere in a darkened alcove. He found an alcove of his own, stripped himself to the waist, and worked rapidly with the dye. He gave it as long as he dared, then slicked back his newly blackened hair and squeezed it as dry as he could. Once out in the street, the sun would take care of the rest. He rinsed his hands a couple of times in the bathing pool, shook them dry, and put on his shirt again. The talismans went into his pocket. Then he slipped the catch on one of the high windows and hauled himself up and through, trying not to clout any of his wounds in the process. He clung from the outside ledge by his fingertips for a moment, then dropped down into the shaded back alley below.

Pain spiked through the wound in his thigh with the impact, bad enough for a clench-jawed cry. He stumbled, propped himself against the wall, panting.

Down the alley, what he'd taken for a pile of refuse made an answering groan.

He whipped around, hand to knife. For one desperate, floundering moment, he thought it was the front-parlor toughs, sent by the madam to investigate this customer who preferred to quit her premises by such unconventional means.

"No need for that blade, my friend." The voice was hoarse, but showed no sign of fear. "I've no quarrel with any man who leaves a brothel by the back window."

"Have you not?" Egar stalked closer, peering.

He made out a slim figure, cuddled into the wall beneath the folds of a Yhelteth cavalryman's cloak. Sable on white, the rearing horse insignia, long worn to a grubby black and cream but unmistakable nonetheless. The bearded face that looked back from above its collar was scarred and grimed, the hair a poorly cropped mess. But the eyes were steady.

"No quarrel at all. Done it myself, time to time. Way I see it, the least a patriotic brothelkeeper can do for a man who's served is waive payment. But they rarely see it that way."

Dangerous to linger here, but . . .

Egar sank into a sprawl against the opposite wall of the alley, rested aching limbs for just a few moments. He nodded at the cloak.

"Cavalryman, huh?"

"Seventeenth Imperial, yes sir." The man freed his right hand from the folds of the cloak, held it up for inspection. "Sadly no longer."

Egar looked at the half-hand claw. Ring and little fingers gone, a ragged mass of scar tissue where the blade had chopped deep into the palm behind. He'd seen the like often enough before—rank-and-file cavalry swords were for shit when it came to anything other than hacking down fleeing infantry. The Empire's factories churned them out cheap and fast and shiny, and about one in a dozen would likely fail as soon as you went up against a decently equipped mounted opponent. Couple of well-placed blows and the guard gave way like rusted scrap.

"Seventeenth, huh?" He racked weary brains for the memory. "You were at Oronak then, that first summer when the Scaled Folk came. Before the dragons."

"Yes, we were." The steady eyes never wavered.

They sat quietly for a few moments. It was in Egar's mouth to say he'd seen the carnage at Oronak, to recall the nightmare they'd found when they rode into town. He'd been part of a relief column that arrived too late to do much more than wander the streets of the tiny port and count the dead. Repeated cavalry charges down Oronak's main thoroughfares had driven the Scaled Folk back, but at massive cost. Not one man in five lived to make report when the reinforcements finally arrived, and the results of the battle looked like something out of the Revelation's more twisted imaginings of hell: drifting smoke from buildings and boats set aflame by the command caste reptiles' coughed-out venom, the corpses of men and horses scorched or bitten apart, the seared and screaming wounded reaching out to them . . .

Better you say nothing, Dragonbane. You don't want to be remembered here. Better you get yourself gone.

Egar nodded across the alley at the man.

"You want to sell that cloak?"

IT COST HIM A LOT MORE THAN THE WHORE'S SILENCE, BUT HE EX-pected as much. Visible military insignia were powerful tools in the begging game. They drew the eye on street corners, forced shame and remembrance on those who would just as soon walk on by with their purse safely stowed. They helped ward off the constant thuggery and assault that beggars were prone to suffer from street gangs or bands of young nobles out on a spree. Sometimes, if your luck was in, they could even get you charitable bed and board on feast days. Accordingly, soldiers' cloaks and jackets were traded, stolen, even dug up out of graves on the outskirts of town for the revenue and comfort they could drum up.

In Egar's case, there was a simpler calculus. Since the war ended, there were several thousand veterans begging and sleeping rough on the streets of Yhelteth, not to mention those others, probably also in the thousands, passing themselves off as such. You saw worn-down men in ragged military garb pretty much anywhere a neighborhood lacked either the paid enforcement or the callous collective will to drive them out. They were a part of the noisy, churning backdrop of city life, no more worthy of attention than the next scurrying urchin or street-corner whore. Just another unavoidable sign of the times.

Back on the steppe, there were tales of a shaman-enchanted wolf-skin robe in whose sorcerous folds the wearer could, at will, become invisible to the gaze of men. Wrapped in the cavalryman's cloak, the Dragonbane could duck his head anywhere in Yhelteth and pull pretty much the same trick.

But not right now.

He left the alley with the garment bundled under his arm. The sun still wasn't much above the horizon, but you could feel the heat building already. The streets had filled up while he was inside the brothel. Crowds ebbed and flowed, horse and mule hooves clattered. Skeletal, untenanted market stalls he'd passed on his way up the hill in the early hours were now hung with brightly colored cloth awnings, laden with artfully arrayed produce and mobbed with buyers, sellers, and a thin circling of prospective thieves.

He picked his way through the crisscross of sloping streets and alleys, heading for the river. Ideally, he'd have liked to find out what went on around Imrana's mansion in the hours after he left, but now was not the time. He needed a doctor, one he could bribe or scare into silence, to dress and clean his wounds. He needed weapons, something a little more substantial than the knives he now carried. He needed to take stock and maybe, just maybe, catch a couple of hours' sleep.

None of which was safe to do around here.

And you need to do it all before nightfall.

The faint whisper of his deeper fears—because while he was confident he could evade the City Guard for weeks at a time without incident, the dwenda were another, utterly unknown quantity. And whatever unholy alliance they had forged with Pashla Menkarak and the Citadel, he was tolerably sure they would work like the demons they resembled to keep it hidden. They would do their best to track him, and he had no idea what that best might involve. Ringil had always said, after the battle at Beksanara, that the dwenda were as shocked by their encounter with humans as the humans were with them. The outcome of the battle seemed—*seemed*—to bear that out, but these fuckers had still appeared more or less out of thin air, had still moved with inhuman speed and grace, had still massacred the better part of an entire detachment of the finest crack troops the Empire had to offer.

Somehow, the state he was in, Egar didn't see himself taking down a dwenda warrior.

He crossed the river by the Sabal pontoon, blending into the ragged crowd as well as he could, slumping his shoulders, curving his back, and chopping his stride to a shuffle. When his turn came at the toll hut on the far side, he broke into a racking, spluttering cough, mumbling and waving and covering his face. The toll officer averted his own face with thinly veiled disgust, snatched the proffered coin, and waved Egar on without a second glance.

In the stew of streets up from the bridge, he prowled about for a while, checking the frontages. He found a doctor's signboard, hanging above the entrance to a flandrijn pipe parlor, but both businesses were shut up tight at this early hour. He shrugged and found a spot across the street to wait, a cool stone alcove between the buttresses of what appeared to have once been a temple. He sank down into the shade. Throb of agony in his thigh as the muscles stretched and tugged at the wound. He pressed lips and teeth together and rode the pain. Glowered across the street at the pipe house sign.

Could fucking use *a flandrijn smoke right about now, these assholes just kept decent hours.*

He thought vaguely about breaking in and helping himself, but decided against it. Anyone dealing in flandrijn would have watchmen on the premises, and while they might well be sleeping at this time of day, such men—war veterans, more than likely—would sleep with one ear cocked for disturbance. He wouldn't get past them in his current condition. And if the pipe house owners were well enough connected, a break-in was going to bring the City Guard down on the neighborhood like pox on a campaign whore.

He needed the doctor's services worse than he needed relief from pain right now, and that meant waiting. Anything else just wasn't smart.

Good to see you acting smart now, Dragonbane—when it's way too late to be useful.

Oh yeah, what was I supposed to do? Let that cuckold asshole and his pal clear their steel first? Watch them run Imrana through for an adulteress, and then spit me on the same blade for good measure?

No. But maybe you should just have stayed away from Imrana until you knew Ashant was back on his hero's horse and somewhere south.

The girl—

The girl, horseshit. You been looking to pick that fight for a fortnight now, and you know it.

He turned his head against the cool, shadowed stonework. Managed a weak smirk. *Pretty slow for crack imperial officers. Riot duty in Demlarashan must be turning them soft.*

Yeah, that and whatever they'd been drinking all night. Don't kid yourself, Dragonbane. You got lucky, is all.

Or the Dwellers got my back. Takavach, maybe, watching over me . . .

He dozed in and out of his pain. Time marched past, like the grubby street crowd, barely registering through his drooping eyelids and occasional starts back to consciousness. Around him, the shadows melted down the dilapidated temple walls like dark, fast-burning candles, as the sun cranked up into the sky. The city's sounds turned to a blurred ebb and flow in his ears. He drifted, back to memories of the steppe, the great bleeding sunsets at the bottom of the sky, the huddled mass of buffalo moving between the governing points of Skaranak herd riders in the gloom, the barked commands in Majak across the chilly air. He shivered in his doze, and turned tighter into the temple wall. He dreamed about getting a shave. The barber, cleaning soap scum from the razor, applying the blade to his throat. The cold metal presses in, begins to slice . . .

Do not disconcert yourself, my lord.

He jerked awake. Head snapped suddenly upright.

Across the street, a tubby black-clad man stood waiting while his much taller slave unsnapped the bolts at the top of the pipe house entrance. Egar grunted and got himself to his feet. Reeling a little, the first few steps, but he firmed up as he crossed the street. Pain stabbed through his thigh, scorched and bit at him elsewhere—old habit forced it out, straightened his stride. He stood a couple of paces off the tubby man's shoulder and cleared his throat.

"You the bone man?"

Both men jumped. The slave's hand fell to his belt as he turned, and the seasoned wooden billy club that swung there. Egar cut him a glance, shook his head.

"You the bone man?" he repeated quietly, eyes on the master.

The tubby man drew himself up. "Now, look, I . . . I have already tithed this month. I'm a devout man. But I don't do charity work on demand. I have to make a living. You'll just have to—"

"I can pay," Egar told him. He patted the purse at his belt and made it *clink*.

Palpable relief washed across the doctor's face. It was like watching a man slide into well-warmed bathwater.

"Oh," he said. "Well, that's different."

CHAPTER 33

"And how exactly did you come by that murderous little item?"

Ringil reached up and touched the pommel of the Ravensfriend, where it rose at his shoulder. "It was forged for me at An-Monal by Grashgal the Wanderer."

"Yes—actually, I was talking to the sword."

HELMSMEN—HE'D NEVER MUCH LIKED THEM, EVEN IN THE OLD DAYS. Too little readability in their immobile iron bodies, when you could actually see one, and in their disembodied avuncular voices when you couldn't. And too fucking impressed with themselves by half. *Personally, he told Archeth, when the subject of Anasharal came up, I'd trust one of those things about as far as I could carry its melted-down carcass up the street. They're no better than demons—it's like keeping the Dark Court in a fucking bottle on your mantelpiece. Who knows what they're thinking, or what they want?*

In truth, he was exaggerating a little for effect. During the war, he'd spent time at An-Monal and conversed with Manathan on and off, albeit mostly in the company of its Kiriath handlers. The Helmsman had given him no reason to dislike it, if you didn't include the run of tiny cold shivers he felt every time it spoke unexpectedly to him out of the bedrock air. To Grashgal and the others, the creatures were part of the furniture, and over time Ringil had found himself able to cultivate a similar attitude. But it didn't change the fact that you were dealing with something as inert as a sword or a temple wall, and it still— apparently—had intelligence far greater than your own. And seemed to enjoy reminding you of the fact.

The Dark Court and the dwenda at least had the courtesy to *appear* human.

"Well, you're still going to have to talk to it." Archeth, pragmatic as ever when anything other than her own life was concerned. "It's the heart of the expedition, it's the reason we're going in the first place."

"Yeah, makes you wonder, doesn't it?"

"What?" They were riding back from the Shanta boatyards, side by side through noon city bustle and heat. But even against the backdrop hubbub of the streets and clop of their horses' hooves on cobbles, he could hear the irritable tension clambering upward in her voice. "Makes you wonder *what?*"

He sighed. They were long overdue for this conversation. He'd been putting it off for days.

Might as well get it over with.

"Archeth, come *on*. A watchtower city in the ocean, a clan dedicated to standing eternal guard down the centuries? That's not how people *live*, and you know it. Not even your people. Anasharal is spinning you a fireside yarn for children. You don't believe it any more than I do. That's not what this is about."

"You know"—a studied calm in her voice now, a signal he knew for the warning smolder of staved-off rage—"I am getting *a little fucking tired* of hearing men explain to me what my real motivations are. If you're so sure we're wasting our time, then why did you—"

"I didn't say that." He shifted sideways in his saddle to face her better. "I didn't say we're wasting our time. Look, maybe An-Kirilnar does exist. And maybe, just *maybe*, it hasn't been plundered the way An-Naranash was. The Hironish are tough to get out to, true enough, those are bad waters, so maybe this place has been overlooked. That's certainly what your merchant pals have got to be hoping. So, sure, I'll break heads and keep order for you, and I'll ride along with you when you go. It's something to do, it'll keep me busy. But please don't tell me you really think we're going to find a bustling little colony of Kiriath custodians up there, keeping an eye on some wet chunk of granite with a tomb on top, cheerfully passing down their mission from father to son for the past four thousand years and acting like the rest of the world doesn't exist. I mean, is that *likely*?"

"It isn't impossible."

He sighed again. "No, it isn't impossible. Very little seems to be impossible in this world. But is it really what you think you'll find?"

"So, what? You think Anasharal is just making this *up*?" The evasion was blatant, the scratchy signs of krinzanz denial right behind it in the uneven tone of her voice. "To what fucking *purpose*, Gil? Answer me that. A cabal of misfit rich fucks, ships built and equipped, men hired and trained, an expedition to a place that doesn't exist—why would a Helmsman want all that?"

He shrugged. "I think we've covered this ground. You're trying to second-guess something completely inhuman. Why *should* its motivations make any sense to us?"

They rode on without speaking, a dozen or so clopping horse strides.

"Yeah, well," Archeth repeated, with evident sour satisfaction. "You're still going to have to talk to it."

HE WAS NEVER VERY SURE WHY HE WENT ARMED INTO ITS PRESENCE.

There was a certain dress formality in the League cities for noblemen. War was, after all, their trade, and it seemed appropriate they should represent the fact in public. Before the Scaled Folk came, the tradition had ebbed somewhat. The more mannered among the gentry adopted flimsy court swords with more attention given to their gaudy scabbards and guards than to the plain steel sheathed within. But with the war and the subsequent upheaval, heavy blades were in evidence once more, and Ringil, on his return to Trelayne last year, had found himself unexpectedly fashionable.

But it wasn't that.

Perhaps, then, it was simply that the Ravensfriend was his link with the world of the Kiriath, his contract of passage and letter of recommendation to everything Anasharal represented. Grashgal forged it in workshops Ringil was never given admission to, out of alloys humans had no names for and containing, Ringil sometimes suspected, mechanisms the Kiriath didn't like to talk about. *If*, he reasoned one drunken night on the steppe with Egar, *those cryptic fuckers have Helmsmen to help them sail their fireships, why wouldn't they have something like that to help them fight their wars? Something—I don't know—something aware?*

Egar had cast a glance at the Ravensfriend where it lay on the ground by the fire. He smirked.

Yeah, thought I seen you talking to it a couple of times. Stroking it, like. You want to watch that shit, Gil.

Ringil threw a boot at him.

He put the memory away.

"Talk to the sword all you like," he told Anasharal evenly. "I'm the one in charge here."

"Well, if you say so."

It sat on a low, ornate table, set to one side of the room's ample hearth. High-angled morning sunlight poured in from the windows in the eastern wall, made odd facets and chinks in its rounded upper surface shine like jewels. Its limbs—if that was what they were—spread out evenly around its body like a marsh spider's legs, rising to a jointed midpoint, then dipping to sharp ends that dug visibly into the wood of the table top. Archeth had told him it couldn't move with much speed or competence, but to Ringil's uneasy eye the thing looked poised to leap or scuttle off somewhere at a moment's notice.

"Actually, the Lady *kir*-Archeth Indamaninarmal says so." He unslung the Ravensfriend and leaned it carefully against one side of the mantelpiece. In the hard, bright light, dust motes seemed to coalesce around the weapon as he let it go. "She's named me expeditionary commander. And since she has the Emperor's ear in this matter, I'd say that's about as final as it's going to get."

"And is the Lady *kir*-Archeth aware of just how popular you are in northern climes at this precise moment?"

Ringil lowered himself into the armchair opposite. "I'd say she has an inkling."

"And His Imperial Radiance?"

"I could give a back-alley fuck what that asshole thinks."

"I see. That good old dead-man-walking defiance, too." Impossible to tell from the tone if the Helmsman was mocking him or not. "Yes, I can see why they chose you."

"Chose me?" Blurted out, before he could help himself.

"You know what I'm talking about—Dragonbane."

Breathe. Build a thin smile. "No one calls me that."

"Shame. It must be upsetting, the lack of proper recognition."

"Well." Ringil settled deeper into the chair. Examined the nails of his right hand. "It was a joint effort."

The quiet stretched. He watched the dust motes dance around the Ravensfriend's hilt. On the table, one of Anasharal's limbs twitched. The point lifted fractionally, tapped at the wooden surface like an impatient schoolmaster's finger.

"The *Ahn Foi* are not your friends, Ringil Eskiath. You should keep that in mind."

"I don't"—despite the cold shiver through him—"recognize that name."

"Do you not? Try, then, the Immortal Watch. The Murderers of the *Muhn*. Hoiran's Band. The Sky Dwellers. The Dark Court. Any of *those* ring a bell?"

He stared back at the machine, fighting off memories of Dakovash. "I have nothing to do with the Dark Court."

"Good," said Anasharal, suddenly brisk. "That's a healthy attitude. You'll live longer."

Ringil glanced toward the hearth, for all that it was cold and ashen at this hour of the day. Fought down a creeping impression that the Helmsman didn't believe a word he'd just said.

"The Lady *kir*-Archeth tells me," he said, "that An-Kirilnar was con-structed to guard against the return of an ancient evil. A human ally of the dwenda."

"Yes."

"She says you referred to him as the Ilwrack Changeling."

"Yes." A certain archness crept into Anasharal's tone. "Is *that* name familiar to you?"

Like a blow under the heart, he was back in the Gray Places.

Seethlaw, introducing his sister. Her archaic, mangled Naomic.

I am with name Risgillen of Ilwrack . . .

"What can you tell me about him?"

"About him?" The Helmsman's tone was shot through with definite amusement now. "Or about the Aldrain clan that fostered him?"

Ringil manufactured a shrug. "Is there some reason you wouldn't tell me about both?"

Quiet crept across the room between them. The Ravensfriend stood wreathed in dancing dust and light. The Helmsman tapped the table again—with every appearance, Ringil thought, of pettish ill humor.

"I know what you are, Eskiath," it said. "Don't think for a moment that I don't."

Ringil let that one sit, let it sink away into the quiet. He kept his face an immobile mask. Finally, he set one ankle four-square across his knee, leaned forward in his seat with a frown, and brushed fluff from his boot.

"Care to elaborate on that?"

Tap-tap. Quiet.

"Oh, very *well* . . ." Anasharal's voice took on a slightly singsong ca-dence. "The Ilwrack Changeling was born of a noble house whose name is now lost. As a child, he probably spent—are you getting this, Ringil Eskiath?—he probably spent as much of his time in the Aldrain realm as on Earth, and from this he derived his powers. *Changeling* is technically a misnomer, a misappropriated marsh dweller myth applied to those among the human ruling classes who were chosen for their great beauty and strength of intellect by the Aldrain overlords, and borne away at an early age to learn the culture of the Ageless Realm. It was, in its way, not much different from the military training noble males receive in the Empire or the League today. Then as now, their mothers must bid them farewell, give them up into the arms of terrible strangers, and mourn their long absences.

"Many Aldrain clans peopled the Earth in those times. The Aldrain walked among humans, and it was no more remarked upon than the Kiriath walking among humans these last centuries. Marriage unions between the races were not uncommon, though they rarely bore issue. Friendships and family ties sprang up. Such issue as there was, was honored. Many clans took changelings into the Ageless Realm, and many human noble houses gave away their offspring to such honor with joy. But no name among those clans stood in such high regard as that of Ilwrack—the royal house, the instigators and leaders of the Repossession. And to be chosen by the clan Ilwrack was the highest of honors. Its scions took only the very best and the brightest, opened to them every secret of the Aldrain race, and then flung them back into the world as their most powerful and faithful servants. For this has ever been the way of the Aldrain—not to rule subject races by their own hand, but to find those among the subject race who can be groomed and fit to rule on their behalf."

Ringil grunted. "Been ever the way of anyone with half a brain and a limited purse to pay the levy."

"Yes—well." A disapproving pause, then Anasharal resumed, in lofty, lecturing tones. "The Changeling, then, was singled out by a young Ilwrack scion more or less from the cradle. They say the child was so beautiful that the Aldrain lord was bewitched despite himself. That he fell in love with all the impulsive passion of his people, and would not be denied. Bided his time for the brief cycles of human youth, taught and shepherded the boy through what he would need to see and know, took the resulting young man and ushered him through the Dark Gate younger than any the Aldrain had ever taken before. Gifted him early, you see, wrapped the first of his own cold legion about him while he was still in his teens. He must, just as the legend says, have been very smitten to bestow such power. But then the Changeling's eyes, they say, were the green of sunlight through tree canopies, his smile, even as a child, could turn your heart over. When he grew to manhood, he was tall and long-limbed, and—"

"This Aldrain lord." Ringil kept his voice neutral. "He have a name?"

"It is lost," said Anasharal succinctly.

"Like so much of the detail in this story, it seems." Ringil rubbed idly at a scuff on the leather of his boot. "Tell me something, Helmsman. Are you *sure* there's a phantom island up there beyond Hironish? Are you *sure* there's a city in the ocean keeping guard? You wouldn't be making this whole thing up, would you?"

"Is the Ghost Isle not plotted on the maps of your own city's shipmasters?"

"On some of them, yeah. So is the site of a floating star that crashed into the western ocean a hundred thousand years ago, when the gods fought for mastery of the heavens."

"Well, maybe that's there as well."

"Archeth says you claim to have seen the Ghost Isle before you fell to Earth. That you have been watching the surface of the world for thousands of years. That suggests to me you would have seen this floating star as well."

Brief hesitation. "Perhaps."

Ringil nodded. Went on rubbing at the scuff mark on his boot. "So is it there or not?"

The hesitation ran longer this time. *Tap-tap* went one of the thing's angled limbs.

"No," Anasharal said finally. "It's not."

Ringil nodded again. "Was it ever there?"

"It may have been. That was before my time. But if it existed outside of myth, then it sank. Fallen stars do not float."

"Islands do not come and go like pirate vessels, either."

"This one does."

"I DON'T KNOW," HE TOLD ARCHETH THE NEXT MORNING. "IT'S LYING about something. I'd put money on it. Maybe not the Ghost Isle, maybe not even An-Kirilnar. But there's something going on, something more than we're being told."

"Like what?"

"I don't know." He nodded at the ceiling, up to the room where the Helmsman was kept. "Like I keep telling you, Archeth, we're out of our depth. You think this thing is on your side just because Manathan and the rest did what your father's people told them to. But you aren't your father, and this Helmsman wasn't around back then. It's come from somewhere else, and there's no reason to suppose it plays by the same rules as the others."

"Manathan commended Anasharal to me, Gil. Manathan sent us out there to collect the damn thing in the first place."

Ringil shrugged. "Then maybe the rules have changed for Manathan, too."

Archeth brooded on that for a while.

"I'll talk to Angfal," she decided finally. "I don't believe there's some evil conspiracy of Helmsmen all of a sudden. If something is going on, Angfal will have something to say on the subject."

"Yeah, something cryptic and snide." Ringil yawned into his fist. He'd been up all night arguing with Shendanak and Tand about escort logistics. "Any news on Eg?"

She shook her head. "Gone like smoke. The Guard Provost is making a big thing about turning the city upside down, but so far it's all noise."

"What I thought. They don't have the—"

A diffident knock. The door eased open and Kefanin poked his head through the gap.

"My lord Ringil?"

"Yeah?" If Shendanak was back with *more* fucking names of cousins you could trust with your life, seriously, he was going to . . .

"Captain Rakan of the Throne Eternal to see you, my lord."

"Oh." He looked at Archeth, who just shrugged. "All right, then. Show him in."

"He said he would wait for you in the courtyard."

"The *courtyard*?"

Not that it was an unpleasant venue. Archeth's house was built, like most of the properties on this side of the boulevard, in traditional Yhel-teth corral fortress fashion. High walls and two-story construction around a broad open airspace that in antiquity would have served to shelter livestock from rustlers and wolves alike. In its urban incarnation, the space was cobbled and studded with a trio of ornamental fountains. On the stables side, in faint echo of tradition, there were hitching rails and a drinking trough, but elsewhere the inward-facing walls of the courtyard boasted stone benches set under awnings and trellis ceilings tricked out with crimson-flowering creeper.

Beneath one of which latter he found Noyal Rakan, waiting. The young captain was resplendent in full Throne Eternal dress uniform, rigged with a sword that owed more to soldiering than display, and cutting, truth be told, a rather fetching figure all around. But, Gil noticed as he and Kefanin approached, the young man's demeanor was no match for his imperial finery. Instead, Rakan stood irresolute and staring at the sun-dappled ground, as if hemmed in by the beams of light that spilled through the foliage overhead. He turned awkwardly at the sound of their footfalls on the cobbles, and he stuck out his hand with a heartiness that Gil made for counterfeit.

"Captain Rakan." Ringil made the clasp, and tried to read the younger man's sun-striped face for clues. "To what do I owe this honor?"

"The honor is mine." Rakan produced a smile that had most of the characteristics of a wince. "To serve under such a commander is . . ."

The words trailed off.

"Difficult?" Ringil hazarded. "Irritating? Don't worry about it. Been upstaged the same way myself a couple of times, and once by a real king-sized asshole. Stings a bit at first, but after a while you'll see I'm doing you a favor."

The Throne Eternal's eyes widened. "No, my lord, I have only respect for your record and reputation."

The words lay drying in the sunlit air. Ringil blinked. Groped for his composure.

"Well, that . . . suggests, Captain"—he licked the lips of a smile he found he'd suddenly grown—"that you've heard *very* little about me."

"I'll bring lemonade," said Kefanin hastily, and left.

"I have heard of Gallows Gap," said Rakan with an odd, quiet fervor. "And I have heard of Beksanara, too. I know and have spoken with men who were in my brother's command, who saw what you did there."

Gallows Gap. Beksanara. The siege of Trelayne. You gather the names like dirt under your fingernails, no way to scrub it out.

And all the young men line up, to admire the fucking manicure.

Ringil mastered his smile. He cleared his throat, gestured at the nearest bench. "Shall we, uh, sit down?"

"Yes. Gladly."

They took station at opposite ends of the bench. Rakan stretched out long, slim legs in cavalry boots and leaned back. Gil felt a suddenly risen pulse tripping in his throat. He'd missed the cues before, registered them, if at all, for that mannered laxness that the Yhelteth upper class were wont to deploy as proof of their better-than-peasant standing. But now, belatedly, it was dawning on him that Throne Eternal captain Noyal Rakan was, in at least one fashion, very different from his elder sibling.

"I'm very sorry about your brother," he said awkwardly. "He was a fine soldier."

"And you led him to a"—the younger Rakan swallowed. "A fine and honorable death. Defending the Empire against a great evil. He would not have had it any other way."

Actually, I more or less embarrassed him into it, Ringil recalled silently. *I dared him to stand and die at Beksanara, and he did it because there was no way he could let a degenerate northerner make him look bad in front of his men.*

"So," he said, for something to say. "They have given you his command."

Rakan shook his head quickly. "His rank only. Throne Eternal service is in our family, we have provided the Khimrans with three generations of bodyguards and retainers. On my father's death, Faileh rose to the post. Now I . . . " A brief, fluttered gesture. "Well, it is traditional."

"Tradition, eh. How's that working out for you?"

The young captain met his eyes for a moment, then looked away. "I, well . . . it's difficult. You are measured against the other man, always."

"Yeah, that can be tough."

"I wanted," Rakan blurted, "to thank you. For your intervention the other day. I am accustomed to dealing with soldiers. I have little experience of this kind of thing—merchants and entrepreneurs, men with power and wealth but no ethic of service to either Holy Revelation or Empire. It is not . . . That is, I would not have believed it could be so . . . "

"My pleasure." Ringil lifted a languid, dismissive arm. "We're a whole city of merchants up in Trelayne, even those who work hard át pretending otherwise. The League is built on trade these days, not conquest. I'm used to it."

The Throne Eternal captain blushed. "I did not mean to—"

"Insult me?" Gil grinned. "Didn't you hear the Lady *kir*-Archeth at dinner the other night? I'm of noble imperial stock on my mother's side. Besides." He slouched a little, dropped that languid hand to his thigh and left it there. "I don't exactly fit in, back in Trelayne. I am not what you'd call a pillar of mainstream society there. If you catch my meaning."

"I—yes." Hurriedly: "My lord Ringil, I have been considering some of the logistical issues for the coming expedition. Now, with plague and slave rebellion rumored around Hinerion, we will most likely need to avoid the northern march coast. Which means, of course, a lengthier initial voyage, and landfall in Gergis may be much farther west."

"Yes, quite." He fought for a detached curiosity of tone. "Slave rebellion, you say?"

"So it appears. Reports from the Tlanmar garrison are garbled, but the garrison commander seems certain that at least one slave caravan has risen up against its chains and slaughtered its masters. There may be others. And with the plague rampant, the Tlanmar commander is not prepared to risk sending a force into Hinerion, so we really have very little idea what's happening. Of course, we have until next spring, but everything seems to indicate we should bypass Hinerion if we can."

Ringil put together a fresh smile. "Well, it's not much of a town, Hinerion. No loss there."

"Uh, yes. I've heard that."

"Though, of course, every town has its less conventional side. Every city is possessed of streets that its more mannered citizens might not like to talk about. Even Yhelteth, unless it's much changed since my last visit."

Rakan held his eye this time.

"It is not much changed," he said.

There was a wolf out there in the dark, he knew, and it was watching him. It was waiting for him to move.

Oddly, the thought didn't bother him at all.

He stood alone, head tipped exhilaratingly back, on the tilting, turning surface of the Earth, felt the massy weight of its whirl behind his eyes. The steppe sky spun by overhead, darkened purplish masses of cloud fracturing apart on the wind and letting in a golden orange light. He heard the hurrying of the breeze, felt the deep chill on his face that seemed to distance him from his own flesh . . .

Campfire smoke, drifting across his eyes, fragrant with—

No, wait . . .

Somewhere distant, someone coughed. He blinked at the sound, and it was as if the world turned slowly, majestically upside down and let him fall. The steppe washed away, the smoke remained. It hung in the air, thick and sweet, the unmistakable catch of flandrijn at the back of his throat. The cough came again, from somewhere behind him, and this time he joined in. He propped himself up on one elbow and rubbed at his eyes.

Drapes of muslin, the hue of dirty honey in the low flickering lamp-light. A dimly seen jumble of reclining figures beyond, and the odd up-right form, bending to minister to them. He felt a body at his back, felt someone mutter grumpily at his sudden movement. Memory swam up into view, like a big ugly fish on a line.

I'm in the pipe house.

He was indeed. The long, smooth barrel of the flandrijn pipe was cupped loosely in his left hand, but the ember was long out. He set it aside and sat up fully. No pain in his leg, though he could feel the tug of the stitches the doctor had put in. And his clothes smelled faintly of liniment. He had no idea what time of day or night it was. He had no idea how long he'd been here. On closer examination, along with the whiff of liniment, he detected less pleasant odors. Then again, his clothes hadn't been exactly clean when he stumbled in here, however long ago that was. Blood, sweat, drenching with river water, and, he now remem-bered, somewhere in the long run of pipes they'd brought him, he'd lain there and pissed himself with the gentle disregard of a baby.

He gathered up his bundled cloak and lurched stiffly to his feet. Stumbled through the carpet of drowsing bodies, trailing a wake of curses and complaints. An attendant came running, fresh pipe in hand, but he waved her away.

"Enough," he said gruffly. "Had enough."

His immediate instinct was to seek some coffee and a good long soak in a hot bath. But on reflection, he supposed the way he smelled now would go a good way to completing his beggar's disguise. Best keep it that way.

He grimaced at the thought.

Life in the big city, Eg.

Yeah, and life in the big city is making you soft as the next fucking courtier, Dragonbane. How often did you bathe in hot water out on the steppe? Come to that, how often did you bathe at all on deployment during the war?

True enough—he spent most of the war smelling far worse than he did now. At Gallows Gap, Ringil had joked with him, handkerchief held affectedly to mouth, that just the way they stank ought to turn the reptile advance.

Urann's balls, he missed that faggot.

He got himself outside, squinting at the blast of the sun overhead. He estimated time of day, reckoned early afternoon. He'd been piped up for at least a full day, then, maybe two.

Yeah, maybe three, said something authoritative, through the fumes in his head.

Vaguely, he recalled the doctor muttering, as he finished up his ministrations, something about *cheap pain relief from our coastal brethren downstairs.* The disdain in his voice would have been hilarious if Egar hadn't felt quite so much like boiled shit. *Well, you're the one renting a coffin-sized room above them,* he'd felt like growling. *You're the one doesn't look like he's been on a fucking horse in his life.*

He'd dripped coins into the doctor's hand in silence instead, watched with thin satisfaction at the little fish-mouth gape the man made with each clink. Then he lurched shakily away downstairs to talk to the coastal brethren.

They'd sorted him out. Quite politely, too, the good doctor's disdain notwithstanding.

Doesn't matter where you go, Ringil told him once, as they sat horses on the cliffs at Demlarashan, overlooking the beach, *that shit never changes. Men need someone to hate. It makes them feel strong, it makes them feel good about themselves. Binds them together. Yhelteth against the League, coastlanders against the horse tribes, marsh dwellers against the city—*

Skaranak against Ishlinak, Egar offered companionably.

Just so. Same shit everywhere, Eg. Only way you stop them squabbling is show them someone else they can all hate together.

Egar grinned in his beard, and gestured down to the beach below. *Better hope we don't beat these fuckers too easily then.*

The fury of the previous week's storms had shoved the dragondrift up almost to the base of the cliffs, and it was beginning to bubble up in a way they'd seen before, farther north. Just a matter of time, they both knew, before the hatching began. There was a queasy kind of excitement building around the camp with the waiting. Previous experience had shown you could never be sure what exactly would come tearing its way out of the sticky, purplish-black mess when the time came. Might be eight-foot-tall high-caste reptiles, might be swarms of the weaker, smaller peons. Might be something else entirely.

Of course, on this occasion, *something else entirely* turned out to be exactly right.

A something else entirely that would send men—many of them seasoned levy troops—screaming for their lives in retreat. A something else entirely it would cost over a hundred lives to defeat, and earn Egar the title that would catapult him into the upper ranks of the alliance overnight.

Yeah, shame we're down to brawling with jealous husbands and priests these days, Dragonbane. Not going to give you any medals for that, now, are they?

He limped up the sun-saturated street with a wry grimace. Leaning into the limp a little more than strictly necessary—it couldn't hurt to get in the habit, after all. Start playing his new role to the hilt. He let the cavalry cloak flap open a little in his grubby grasp, enough so it showed what it was. He slowed his pace to a beggar's shuffle. Something appropriate to a broken man of war.

Close enough, after all, innit? Egar Cuckoldbane.

Yeah, yeah, very fucking funny.

His age fell on him abruptly, out of the pitiless, sun-glaring sky. He felt himself sag for real, no theater in it now.

Is this how it ends, then? Faded glories and memories of a youth growing dim. The cold creep of time as it eats you. Weaker and weary, less and less triumph in your stride, less and less to warm you outside of those recollections of another, brighter, harder, younger man . . .

The sour meander of his thoughts brought him, inevitably, to Harath. He owed the boy coin—coin he probably ought to hang on to himself for the foreseeable future. But more than that, he owed him a warning. By now the City Guard would be out in force, wrapping their pointy little heads as best they could about the task of apprehending a Dragonbane Majak. If Harath was out flapping his mouth—*oh surely not*—about their exploits at Afa'marag, he was likely going to get hauled in for questioning. And while he knew nothing of consequence that could endanger Egar, and was, to boot, an irritating little shit, the Dragonbane could still not find it in himself to dislike the young Ishlinak enough to let him be taken by the Guard's inquisitors.

A warning, that's all, he promised himself, keeping carefully to the shuffling gait, playing the limp for all it was worth. *In place of the coin he's trusting you to bring. He deserves that much. He'd do as much for you, any Majak would.*

Well, maybe not an Ishlinak.

But still . . .

Fuck it. Share hearth and heart's truth, right? Break bread and sup under a shared sky.

Right.

HE WALKED THE BACKSTREETS TO THE AN-MONAL ROAD, TACKING BACK and forth to stay off major thoroughfares and getting genuinely lost a couple of times in the process. The smell of the river on his left flank kept him more or less on track; later he had caught glimpses of the Black Folk Span between leaning tenement piles. Eventually, the slow grumble and creak of cartwheels and the tramp of feet up ahead alerted him to the proximity of his goal. He climbed one final, aching flight of stone steps, up from a gloomy dead-end alley, and found himself standing at last at the edge of the road and its boisterous flow. Making time to catch his breath, he checked left and right for the glint of Guard helmets. No sign he could see. He stepped quickly into the fringes of the traffic. Kept his head down. Worked the limp.

Pleasantly surprised at how relatively painless his injured leg actually felt.

He found the pawnbroker's again, found Harath gone.

Big fucking surprise.

"Didn't say where," the old man sulked at him. "Reckoned he'd get better lodgings at a better price elsewhere. In riverside! Bloody fool. I was doing him a *favor* at those rates!"

"Yeah, well." Egar produced a coin between finger and thumb. "Want to do *me* a favor? If he comes by for any reason, tell him he wants to keep his mouth well shut about recent events and steer wide of the City Guard. Could be, they'll want words with him."

The old man's solitary eye glinted. "Really?"

"Yeah. Really." Egar whisked the coin back out from under the man's nose, dropped an arm on his bony shoulder instead, the way he had with the invigilator outside Archeth's place. He leaned in, conspirator-close. He lowered his tone and put the sharp crack of bone into his stare. "Course, if I were to hear that you'd taken that to the City Guard yourself, I might have to come back here and recover my coin. And I'd take the interest out in teeth. We understand each other here?"

"Of course." The old man, struggling feebly to extricate himself from under the Dragonbane's arm. He did a good impression of being affronted. "I'm no friend to the Guard. How do you think I lost this eye? I'm no grass."

"Good." Egar let him go. Tossed him the coin. "So, if he comes back, you'll tell him."

The old man bit the coin. Stowed it and sneered. "Oh, he'll be back. Mark my words. He has the reek of whore on him. Some pretty has him shacked up and is milking him dry. But she'll tire and throw him out soon enough. The way that one pisses his purse up against the wall, he won't be featherbedding on the northside for long."

"Northside?" Egar, on his way out, stopped and turned with dangerous calm. "You told me he didn't say where he was going."

"And he didn't," said the pawnbroker with asperity. "Just said he was off over the Span and glad to be going."

"Across the Span, eh?"

"That's what he said." The old man sniffed and gestured. "Here, you want to sell that cloak? Give you a good price for it."

THE PONY STRINGER'S GOOD FORTUNE, THEN.

Eg couldn't believe Harath would be that stupid. But then he'd evidently been stupid enough to walk out on the only address the Dragonbane could trace him to with the balance of his pay, so who could tell.

He got laid. Just like the old man says. He got taken back to some work-

ing girl's garret, and she's got him playing part-time pimp while the silver lasts.

Wasn't like he hadn't done similar in his own muddle-headed, mercenary youth.

And crooked coin-toss odds, this whore flops walking distance from the Pony Stringer.

But he didn't cross the river just yet. *Harath might be dumb as fuck, don't mean you got to act the same, Eg.* Instead, he found a small plaza with a sliced view of the Span and a war memorial bas-relief across its eastern wall. He folded himself into a shaded corner there, with his cloak spread across his knees. There was a small satisfaction in the act, a quiet taking-stock that seemed to soothe. He hadn't yet eaten, but didn't really feel the need—the residue of flandrijn in his system, he knew from experience, would kill his appetite for some time to come, just as it killed his pain. Drink would have been nice, but it could wait. He'd been at least as thirsty as this most of his fighting life. Meantime, flame-orange scents of spice and fruit drifted to him on the breeze from stalls across the way, the sweat was cooling on his brow and under his grubby clothing, his minor wounds all seemed to have scabbed up nicely. Even the ache of the sewn gash in his thigh felt good—there was an itching there, deep in the flesh, that presaged the healing to come.

Like any good soldier, he knew how to wait.

Presently someone came by and threw a handful of copper coins into the dust at his feet.

HE GAVE IT UNTIL EARLY EVENING, WHEN THE HEAT WAS GONE FROM the air and the light beginning to seep away. Across at the stalls, the sellers who remained were already lighting candles and lamps, casting a homely yellow haze over their wares and the darting, gesturing hands of their customers. Night and its assumptions, settling in. Even the scents in the square had changed, from produce to dinner, from fruit and spice to grilling meat and fish stews that were, Egar had to admit, starting to make his stomach twinge.

Another of the streetwalkers waggled by—cloutingly overdone waft of her perfume, crunch of sandaled feet skirting him. The undercurrent scent of used woman tugged faintly at his groin, but he didn't look up, and she didn't trouble him. Like everyone else, the whores were leaving him alone in his new incarnation. He'd raked in his coppers on the couple of occasions they were tossed to him, and his purse was well hidden. Hard-luck cavalry cloak aside, he was showing nothing anyone would want. The best he'd done for attention in the hours since he sat down were a couple of scrawny street dogs—they sniffed around his feet for a couple of minutes, smelled nothing easily edible, and moved on, tracking more promising odors.

For the human denizens of the neighborhood, for all the notice they paid him, he could as well have been one of the bas-relief figures on the war memorial wall he sat against.

And when he moved, stiffly at first, with the long hours sitting, it felt—Egar found himself grinning a little at the thought—as if he were stepping down from among those chiseled, valorous figures, coming to sudden, eerie life and leaving their weathered, white-stone ranks for some altogether grubbier destiny in the unwinding nighttime streets.

He found a coffee merchant among the stalls, prodded together his gathered coppers in the palm of his hand, and dredged up the price of a cup. The seller barely glanced at him, eyes fixed on the count of coin instead. Egar drank the bitter draft down—could not, without revealing his real purse, afford the sugar to sweeten it—then shouldered his way back through the other browsers and buyers, and plotted a path for the Span. The Pony Stringer—Lizard's Head, whatever—would be filling up by now. Plenty of cover in the rough crowd of irregulars down from the hill and the other, unaligned freebooters there'd be. In his day, the City Guard had always steered clear of the place unless absolutely forced to it, and he doubted things would have changed much in the intervening years. He'd be safe there long enough to find Harath, if he was around, long enough to give him the warning, maybe even shake some sense into the lad while there was still time.

And if the young Ishlinak didn't show, well, there'd be ways to leave a message.

Traffic on the darkened Span was sparse, soft-footed slaves running late errands mostly, the odd metallic snatch of song rung out by hooves as some accredited messenger sped by. Somewhere near the midpoint, he met a clanking ox-drawn cart coming the other way, big upright barrels rubbing squeaking wooden shoulders in the back, one gaunt old driver up front, cloak-wrapped and nodding half asleep over the reins. Egar stopped and stepped aside to let the vehicle pass. Alerted by something, the driver lifted his head, just barely, unhooded his gaze, and met the Dragonbane's eye. His gaze was surprisingly piercing for the hour and his apparent age. He stared at Egar for a moment, as if trying to place him from some past encounter, and then he seemed to nod, approving something they both knew at a level deeper than either of them, or any man, could actually express.

Egar stood there, struck. Turned to watch the cart rumble and grind out of sight in the gloom. A faint shiver wove across his shoulders.

He shrugged it off, glanced up and down the gleaming iron thoroughfare of the Span, then went and leaned his aching frame against the estuary-side railing. Stared down at the rough-dappled stripe of band-light across black water. It looked, he thought vaguely, like a horse-tribe *Sold* daub, slapped across the flank of some midnight-colored stallion.

So long since he'd had a good horse. No real call for it in the city, and he'd been nowhere else in so many months.

He shrugged, and it felt like an excuse.

Up in the vast steel cradle of the Span's structure, the evening wind swooped and keened. Off to his left and right, the city glimmered. Fragments of thought swirled through him, flandrijn-fogged and slippery, hard to hang on to. He rubbed at his chin, distracted, felt the lengthening growth there. Suddenly he couldn't decide if he'd let it thicken and bush out when this was all done, get back his full Majak beard, gray-streaked though it might now be; or go back to the soft-murmuring old man this had all started with and get scraped down to city-slick standards all over again.

Yeah, and tell the old fucker while I'm there what a mess he set me up for.

Laughter behind him as a gaggle of young street toughs went by. He heard them pause in their merriment as they spotted his solitary figure. Felt them draw closer. Something colder than the flandrijn rose in him, washed away his vagueness as the old signals tripped in his nerves. He dropped a hand into his garb, found a knife hilt. Put his weariness aside and turned, grinning.

"Got something for me, lads?"

They backed up, bunching instinctively behind the ringleader as they saw what was waiting for them in the grin. Egar relaxed. Warriors would have done the opposite, would have spread to bracket him.

The wind hooted, up in the shadowy steel spaces.

"Well then, you'd better get on home. Your mothers will be wondering what manner of mouth to clamp on their dripping teats without you."

That got a collective snarl, and a couple of barked, disbelieving curses. But it was street-cur stuff, and they all knew it; it was clutching at the suddenly razored hems of their street-tough dignity, and finding abruptly what cheap, unsatisfactory cloth it was.

Egar stamped forward a step, growled in his throat. Showed them teeth and blade unsheathed. They tumbled away backward, scattered and fled like silverfry from the net. Egar jerked his chin after them and snorted, watched the pale flecks of their heels fade away down the Span. Enjoying now the quickened thud of the blood in his veins.

Yeah, nice work, Cuckoldbane. Your triumphs grow ever greater. You'll have medals from the Emperor before you know it.

He shook off the last of his flandrijn-tinted introspection. On the northside, the glimmering city beckoned. Craning his neck over the rail, he thought he could make out the ruddy glow of the Pony Stringer's lit windows by the water's edge below.

He could be there in a matter of minutes.

CHAPTER 35

Banging at the gate. Muffled voices.

Ringil stirred in the broad bed, wine-sodden senses floundering for some clue to his current whereabouts, let alone what was going on outside. He'd been dreaming of Egar—some incoherent nonsense, sitting out on the steppe at night, hearing the lick and splinter of campfire flames and watching the Dragonbane's bearded face against the spark-ridden dark, watching his lips as they enunciated words Gil kept craning close to catch, but somehow couldn't make out.

He came up out of it, spiked through with creeping black unease and a sense of time and place gone irredeemably awry . . .

The damp-earth odors of recent sex suffused the room around him. It was still dark beyond the shutters.

Banging at the—

. . . banging back the chamber door as they stumbled drunkenly in to-

gether. Shoving Noyal Rakan hard against the wooden paneling and pressing up against him. Grins and little growling noises, and then Gil thrust stiffened fingers forward into the young captain's luxuriant curly locks, tangling there and tugging Rakan's face in closer for the first stabbing kiss . . .

Ah.

Final, blessed release from the long, solemn, and *unbelievably* tedious banquet Shanta had thrown in honor of the Nyanar clan. Father and eldest son of said clan both pontificating across the feast-laden table to their host as only courtiers can. And down the table, Shanta and Nethena Gral making arid, mannered counterpoint. Florid toasts, tossed back and forth like escalating bets in some smug game of flattery and form. Speech after turgid toe-the-line speech to the greater glory of Empire, Emperor, Imperial Charter, and the Most Assured Success of this, Our Current Venture, which cannot fail to Magnify His Radiance's munificent wisdom in . . .

He caught Archeth stifling yawns and holding down a glower. Dared not catch her eye thereafter, for fear he would be unable to choke back the bubbles of hilarity rising in his belly. He caught Noyal Rakan's gaze instead, and held it, gently, feeling it flutter against his own, like a moth in the curl of his closed-up palm.

Beneath the satin drape of the tablecloth, a building heat in his groin.

Raise your glasses, I pray you, gentlemen and ladies, raise your glasses once more and drink. To the Holy Might of Yhelteth and her Godly Appointed Mission to lead humankind out from the Shadow of Lesser . . .

Yawn.

Later, while Shanta saw the Nyanars and their entourage to the door, and bade them all farewell, Ringil walked behind Rakan through the dimly lamplit corridors of the riverside villa, shepherding the younger man gradually toward the rooms Shanta had given him. It was taut, skin-thin theater. They paused now and then to admire the naval engineer's taste in art or sculpture, murmured meaningless syllables back and forth on the edge of excited laughter, brushed against each other in seeming accident, turned suddenly to lock gazes then look away, as those rising bubbles in Gil's belly turned from hilarity into something urgently else . . .

And burst.

Once, just once, inches off that first kiss, Rakan hesitated, Rakan said:

I—my brother, he . . . He would not—

Fuck your brother, Ringil growled, tongue delirious on the tips of his own teeth. *I'm fucking you, not him.*

And then it was glorious and burning and heated flesh to flesh as the door slammed shut behind them. It was kissing and clinging and peeling clothes and kneeling, finally, before Rakan's sculpted soldier's musculature, taking his swollen prick into his mouth and tasting, sucking in, swallowing, all that velvet flesh like a man at the extremes of thirst, given water at last.

The young captain made noises close to weeping as he came. His hands plastered down, again and again, on Ringil's head, patting, pressing, as if trying to fit some veil or maybe diadem over the man that was doing this to him.

Ringil rose, grinning vampiric through the taste, enfolded Rakan's still-shuddering frame in his arms, folded him down to the bed, and turned him over . . .

Banging at the fucking *gate.*

Voices, now recognizably barking in coarse Tethanne.

"Open now, in the Emperor's name!"

Ringil sat up in the sheets. He groped at his side, found the smooth rising slope of Rakan's torso as the captain propped himself up on one elbow.

A tiny ache welled up inside him at the contact with the other man's flesh. He blinked, swallowed—sudden shock, as he made the feeling for what it was; an obscure gratitude, that Rakan had stayed. Had not, as Gil had grown so used to expecting in these cases, fled the scene.

"Fuck is going on out there?" he grumbled, scrambling to cover his feelings.

"It is the palace," said Rakan somberly.

There was the sound of unbolting and opening. Hooves, clattering in on cobbles. Ringil climbed out of bed and went to the window. He slid the edge of the curtain back a judicious half inch.

Down in Shanta's courtyard, messengers in imperial ocher and black sat their fractious horses while Shanta's wakened staff boiled about. Ringil watched long enough to see Shanta himself hurry out, wrapping a dressing gown about himself, sparse gray hair stuck up in disarray. He stood looking up at the lead messenger, mouth moving, but there was too much commotion to hear what was being said. Archeth appeared behind him, fully dressed—it didn't look as if she'd been to bed at all.

Ringil let the curtain fall back, turned back into the room. Rakan was already out of bed, lean and hard in the dim light. Gil sighed.

"Looks like the fun's over," he said. "Better get dressed, I suppose."

A process they were both about midway through when Archeth's boot heels came tocking down the hallway outside, and she rapped impatiently at the door.

"Gil? Are you still in *bed*? Didn't you hear that row out there? How much did you have to drink?"

He unslotted the latch, opened the door a handbreadth, checked she was alone before he swung it wider.

"What the hell are you—" She saw Rakan, seated bare-chested on the side of the bed, bending to his boots. "Oh. Right."

Ringil leaned on the door frame, kept her pointedly out in the hall. "Want to tell me what all the fuss is about?"

She grimaced. "Yeah. Dragonbane just took on a bunch of the City Guard, down at that mercenary joint by the Span."

"The Good Luck Pony?"

"Pony Stringer's Fortune—but they're calling it the Lizard's Head these days."

"Oh, well that's original."

"Gil, it doesn't fucking matter what the place is called. He killed two of the Guard right there, right in front of half the mercenaries in the city. Hurt another three pretty badly, one they reckon won't live to see the sunrise."

He could not prevent the smile from rising to his lips. "Told you."

"Yeah, you told me." Voice tight with anger. "Laugh it up, Gil. Meanwhile, the Guard Provost wants the King's Reach deployed. Says he can't afford to have the Guard's authority flaunted in a place like that. It sends the wrong signal to all the wrong people. He's up at the palace now, demanding the Emperor's hand in the matter."

"Ah, *shit*." Ringil banged his head back on the door frame, then wished fervently that he hadn't. Closed his eyes against the waves of incipient hangover the blow had stirred. "And Jhiral's going to cave in, right?"

Archeth cleared her throat, shot a warning look sidelong, past Ringil to the bed and the Throne Eternal captain who sat on it.

"He's got the Ashant clan leaning on him already for King's Reach intervention; now the head of his militia wakes him up in the middle of the night and tells him the exact same thing? What would you do?"

"Yeah," said Ringil drearily. "Makes a soggy kind of sense, I guess."

"It certainly does."

Rakan appeared at his shoulder, still fastening his sword harness and jerkin. He swallowed, awkwardly. "I, uh. My lady. I must attend my Emperor. He may require—"

"Yeah, we're all going," Archeth said. She looked pointedly at Ringil's unbuttoned shirt. "Just as soon as everyone's ready to ride."

WHICH GOT THEM TO THE PALACE A COUPLE OF HOURS LATER—A GUSTY, bandlit chase through the string of sleepy riverside hamlets where Yhelteth's outskirts petered out upriver, then into the deserted nighttime streets of the city itself, at speeds you'd simply never manage with daytime traffic. Archeth, Ringil, Rakan, and the messenger squad who'd been sent to find them—six dark figures, cloaks flapping backward from their shoulders, and the drum of hooves at the gallop. *All very dramatic,* Ringil supposed sourly, tucking a stubborn corner of his shirt into his breeches while he held on to his mount with his thighs, *if you happen to be out and about at this gods-forsaken hour and nothing better to do than gape openmouthed at the mysterious riders as they thunder past.* Tales to tell your grandchildren, like something out of some marsh dweller myth. Last Ride of the Dark Company, the Messenger Before Dawn, the Fell News That Would Not Wait, so forth . . .

His head was killing him.

Hoiran curse you, Eg. If you had to take on the City Guard, couldn't you at least have done it somewhere without witnesses?

They made the palace as dawn was breaking, storming up the hairpin rises of the approach causeway in the graying gloom. Cacophony of six sets of hooves on the Kiriath paving, profaning the early stillness. They reined in at the top behind a yell from the messenger chief.

"The King's Messenger comes! Open!"

Yawning, shift-end guards came running from their boxes, shocked awake and fumbling halberds as they tried to assemble hard-bitten readiness from the shattered pieces of the night's sleepy boredom. The messenger bellowed again.

"Open, fools! In the Emperor's name!"

The gates hinged back, creaking. They rode on through. In the courtyard beyond, a high-ranking slave majordomo whose face Archeth knew scurried forward, arms folded into his robes. Stable slaves swarmed behind him.

"My lady. His Radiance awaits you in the Queen Consort Gardens."

"Right." She swung down off her horse and handed over the reins. Feeling a qualified relief now, because she doubted they'd have to face the Ashant family or the rest of the court just yet. Official meetings and grievances were generally dealt with in the throne hall. Elsewhere was for private council. She looked up at Ringil, who had not yet dismounted.

"Follow me," she told him, switching to Naomic. "And don't make this any harder than it has to be. Try to keep a civil tongue in your head. If you plan on hanging on to either, that is."

Ringil sat his horse and grinned evilly down at her. "You wound me, my lady. Am I not of noble imperial blood on my mother's side?"

"Fuck off, Gil. I'm serious."

They tramped through the palace environs at a fast march. Long corridors and flagstone expanses of halls and courtyard. They passed slaves scrubbing floors and watering plants. The messenger chief took point, as ritual demanded, but behind him Archeth ushered Rakan into the lead. Most likely Jhiral would have a Throne Eternal guard with him, and they'd respond a lot better to a captain from their own ranks than they would to an armed, sleep-deprived, and hungover Ringil.

Though Rakan himself, hmm, well, now . . .

Given what she'd glimpsed in Ringil's bedchamber, the young captain was not at all what she'd imagined him to be.

She shelved the thought. *Enough else to worry about right now, don't you think, Archidi.*

Up broad, winding staircases, along colonnaded galleries, into the upper levels. The predicted Throne Eternal were there at the doors to the Queen Consort Gardens, two of them, resplendent in full honor guard rig. They saluted Rakan, and one of them led the party through the dusty, leaf-littered walkways to the balcony, where a lightweight trestle table had been hastily laid with silk cloth and a plethora of filled plates and bowls. Kitchen slaves stood in attendance—behind them more Throne Eternal. His Imperial Radiance Jhiral Khimran sat waiting in a wingback chair, chewing on a leg of roast chicken.

The chief messenger dropped to one knee before him.

"The Lady *kir*-Archeth," he announced. "As sought. With her, I bring you Honor Captain Noyal Rakan. And, uhm, Lord Ringil Eskiath of the Glades House in Trelayne."

He got up again, bowed and got out of the way. Jhiral surveyed the new arrivals without much enthusiasm. He was dressed and booted, which at this hour had to mean he hadn't been to bed yet, and there was a slightly blurred look to his features that Archeth read as drink, or possibly flandrijn. He'd been experimenting with the drug recently, she knew, working it into his harem sessions.

"Eskiath," he said, frowning. "Rings a bell. Should I know that name from somewhere?"

Ringil shrugged. "Your father gave me a medal, once."

"Did he indeed?" Jhiral bit off more chicken, chewed, still frowning. "So you're a war hero, then. And was I in attendance for this honor?"

Ringil met the Emperor's eyes. His gaze glittered. "I don't recall."

Jhiral stiffened.

"Lord Ringil was instrumental in our victory at Ennishmin last year," said Archeth hastily. "You'll remember, I mentioned him to you."

"Oh, yes." But the Emperor was not mollified. He studied Ringil with narrow disdain. "Well, that must be it, then. Though, as I understood the tale, you went home at the end, sir knight of Trelayne, back to that miserable huddle of trading posts up north."

Ringil nodded amiably. "As we always have done when the work of rescuing the Empire is completed. But my lord would be wiser not to put so much trust in tales. They are no substitute for getting out and about as your father did."

Stunned silence rippled outward from the words—spreading rings from the splash of a raw building block dumped into some ornamental pond. The air seemed to rock with it. The two men stared each other down. The Throne Eternal stirred. Ringil smiled . . .

Archeth stepped forward, put herself physically between the two of them.

"I have commissioned Lord Ringil to lead our expedition to An-Kirilnar. It's a role in which he will be invaluable." Leaning on the last word. "He is helping us with route planning, and will conduct the bulk of the diplomacy when we reach League territory."

Jhiral relaxed a muscle at a time. He arched an imperial brow. "Diplomacy, you say?"

"Yes, my lord. As a member of the Glades aristocracy, he will have a level of access ideal for our purposes."

Elaborately raised brows again—*Well, if you say so.* The Emperor tossed his gnawed chicken bone back onto the trestle, still chewing, and held up one languid hand. A slave hurried forward with a napkin. Jhiral took it and wiped his hands with thoughtful care.

"This meeting," he said. "Is not about the An-Kirilnar expedition, Archeth."

"Yes, my lord. I have been made aware of that."

Jhiral tossed the napkin after the chicken bone. Spared a gesture for Ringil. "So what's he doing here?"

Just keep your fucking mouth shut, Gil. She rushed in. "Lord Ringil is, uh, acquainted with Egar Dragonbane. Well acquainted."

"How convenient. We seem to be up to our eyes in war heroes at the moment. Let's just hope this one knows better how to behave in the *absence* of war than your dragon-slaying barbarian houseguest." The imperial gaze flickered back across to Ringil. "You were, I suppose, comrades-in-arms, something like that?"

"Something like that," Ringil agreed softly.

Jhiral got up. "Well, your comrade-in-arms has managed to set himself a course for the executioner's block, I'm afraid. That's if I can talk Saril Ashant's grieving family down from their demands for death by the chair or in the Chamber of Confidences. There it is. War hero honor doesn't cut much cloth, I'm afraid, when you've slaughtered another war hero in his own bedchamber. Oh, and, uhm, *outraged the virtue* of his good lady wife into the bargain—apparently. There's really no coming back from something quite that monumentally stupid. The death warrant is already drawn and signed."

"That's unfortunate." A cold edge creeping into Ringil's voice now. Archeth shot him a warning glance.

"Isn't it." The Emperor had given them his back. He browsed the food on his table, voice elaborately conversational. "Three Guardsmen dead, Archeth. Another two crippled, one probably for life. And this in front of a tavern stuffed with outlander sellswords. It really isn't what I need right now. I have the Guard Provost screaming for palace support, and I have Kadral Ashant muttering around the court about ungrateful leadership. All because *you* would not have me deploy the Reach."

"I am sorry, my lord. It seems I underestimated the—"

"Oh, *horseshit*, Archeth!" Fists slammed down on the tabletop. Platters jumped with the force of it. Jhiral spun about, face staining dark, strode at her as if to deal her a blow. "*Horse, Shit!* Do you really think I'm that much of a fool? You *didn't want him caught.* You thought he'd quit the city, and you wanted him to get a good head start. Well, he hasn't quit the city, has he? *Has he?*"

He hung three feet away, as if tugged to a halt there on some invisible cable, glaring at her. Down at his side, the ringed fingers of his right hand twitched with suppressed violence.

On her left, Ringil moved—a fractional, indefinable shift of stance, caught in the corner of her eye, more sensed than seen. He was, she knew without needing to see it, watching Jhiral, watching that twitching, imperial hand as it struggled not to curl into a fist. He was gone with it, into the awful, gently amused detachment that presaged the steel song, the only one the Ravensfriend knew how to sing.

She felt the air thicken with implication, felt the balance in the balcony space teeter with it, and begin to tip. If Jhiral made that fist and raised it . . .

Gil would kill him—she knew it as clearly as if it was already done.

She raised her arms, open admission of guilt, and her left arm hanging just a moment longer than the right, blocking out Ringil and the Ravensfriend's flow. She hoped it would be enough. She bowed her head to her Emperor.

"You are correct, my lord. The fault here is mine."

"It most certainly fucking is, Archeth." A rancid satisfaction in his face and tone, there and just as quickly bleeding away. He cleared his throat, gestured carefully with the hand that had so recently longed toward a fist. "Well, then. No point dwelling on your manifest failings in this, I suppose. It's left to me, once more, to make the difficult decisions and do the right thing. The King's Reach are out, Archeth. It's done. I signed the order an hour ago. They will bring this Dragonbane down, dead or alive, and justice will be done. In the—"

"My lord, if I—"

"*In, the, meantime,* my lady." He waited to see if she would dare interrupt again, saw she would not, and went on in brisker tones. "The Reach commander will want to interview you for clues as to their quarry's habits and haunts. Your northern friend here, too, I imagine. Rakan?"

Noyal Rakan jumped. "My lord?"

"Convey the Lady *kir*-Archeth and her noble companion to the King's Reach barracks wing, with all haste. Taran Alman is waiting for them there."

"Yes, my lord. At once."

They turned to go. Archeth at speed, to hide what was in her eyes and the seething urge to speak what boiled behind her gritted teeth. Ringil took a little longer, and his gaze measured the Emperor with speculative calm.

Jhiral saw the look and bristled. "Was there something you wanted to say to me, Ringil Eskiath? Some suit or request, perhaps?"

"No." Ringil did not move. "None. I believe Your Imperial Shininess has said everything worth saying here. It falls now only to execution."

Jhiral laughed, but there was an uncertain rising tremor at the edge of it that he could not disguise. Archeth and Rakan both heard it, and both stopped dead in their tracks. The Throne Eternal honor guard heard it, and grew intent.

Ringil spared their stirring a flickered glance, a swift calculation, then he fixed Jhiral again with his gaze.

"Have I amused Your Shininess in some way?"

Jhiral cleared his throat, turned a little to his slaves and soldiers, playing for the gallery. "Well, your facility with our tongue is to be commended, my lord. Quite remarkable in a northerner, truly. But it seems your range in Tethanne is somewhat limited after all. You mean *Radiance.*"

"Do I?" said Ringil tonelessly.

He held the Emperor's eye a moment longer, as if fixing the imperial countenance in some special place of memory. His lips twisted in a smile as thin as the scar across his cheek. He nodded as if told something by a voice that others could not hear.

Then he turned and walked away.

"SO THAT'S WHAT YOU'VE BEEN DOING FOR A LIVING THE LAST TEN years, is it?"

"If you mean serving the Burnished Throne and its people to the best of my ability," hissed Archeth, "then yes, it is. I saw it as somehow more productive than hiding in a mountain backwater, spinning yarns about my heroic exploits for pocket money, and paying the stable boys to fuck me."

"Well, some of us can't afford slaves for that particular purpose."

"*Fuck you, Gil!*"

Jagged loss of control on her accented Naomic, and a yell that had to carry. They'd jammed to an abrupt halt in the midst of the gardens, barely out of earshot of the balcony and the imperial party, and almost nose-to-nose. Rakan stood by, unable to follow the sudden switch to a foreign tongue, but needing little insight to understand the tone. Ringil sneering now, hungover ill temper flaring, opening his mouth to—

Behind him, something gusted past, keening.

He felt its touch distinctly, like cool fingers on the nape of his neck. He frowned, forgot what he was going to say.

A single leaf spiraled down from above, caught in a blade of sunlight lancing through the trees. He watched it fall, bemused. Sparse morning light gleamed farther off in the foliage, but it seemed cold and distant. Here, around him, the air was shadowy and cool, and something . . .

Something was not right.

"If they kill the Dragonbane," he said, more quietly. "I will put this palace to the torch. You know I will."

"Yeah," Archeth snapped, apparently untouched by the cool shift around them. "You and whose army? The war is *over*, Gil. This isn't Gallows Gap."

"No. It isn't as clean."

"Oh, *give me a fucking break.*" She raised spread palms, struck them to her forehead, a gesture so purely Kiriath, so purely her father, that for a moment he saw Flaradnam's features stamped across hers in the act. "This is *civilization*, Gil. You know, the thing we were fighting to save? You—you and Egar both—*you can't just stalk about, steel in hand, murdering your grievances.*"

"That's right. These days, that's reserved for the likes of that little prick back there and his cabal. Civilization. Privileges of rank."

"You had rank, Gil. You threw it away."

"Yeah. And you clung to yours."

Her eyes widened. She drew back, as if a jagged chasm had opened up through the paving between them.

"My lady," Rakan interjected. He looked at Ringil, wet his lips. "My lord. Taran Alman is waiting. The Emperor's will is clear. We should not delay."

For a moment, neither of them spoke. Then Ringil nodded, switched to Tethanne. "He's right, Archeth. You'd better not keep the Reach waiting."

"*We*, Gil." Urgently, because she could see what was in his eyes. "*We* had better not keep them waiting."

But he was already moving. Past Rakan with a glance that said all he needed to—the Throne Eternal captain lowered his head and gave him ground. Away from Archeth's desperate voice, calling him back.

"Gil! Gil, you can't just—"

"Tell them everything you can dredge up," he told her, not bothering to use Naomic, not bothering to turn. "The more, the better. Keep them talking."

"I can't just let you *go,*" she shouted.

"You can't stop me." His voice trailed back to her, oddly faded amid the greenery and growth. "Grashgal and your father saw to that. You know what they wrote on this blade."

He turned a corner, and was gone.

The morning light seemed to strengthen in his absence.

CHAPTER 36

Crackle of embers, bathed in wavering orange glow.

Go easy, Dragonbane. Don't drown yourself this time. You're not safe here.

Egar glowered down into the pipe bowl, let the dark smoke come barreling aboard with its icy-cool cargo of release. He coughed a little with the depth of his draw. Clung to a fading caution for a moment, then let it go.

Not safe anywhere in this fucking city. Isn't it about time you did the smart thing and just got out of town?

It was, he had to admit, looking that way.

Yeah, but for now . . .

He'd made for the same pipe house with cold calculation. Close to recent events, but that might work to his advantage—his enemies were almost certainly looking for him farther downriver. He had some sense of the local streets, too, which would count in a pinch. And they knew him here—just another smelly, derelict veteran in search of cheap oblivion. Nothing to talk about. Go somewhere else, there was no telling if he'd raise a ripple—the chatter-worthy wake of a new vessel through new waters.

It seemed like sense, but he was too shattered to be sure. And his strategic judgment, well, *the less said about that the better right now, Dragonbane.*

But he could still not quite believe how badly things had come unraveled, and with how much violent speed. Could still not believe the way it had gone down, even as he watched the events dance in iridescent memory—collide and coalesce, behind eyelids lowering closed under the cool weight of the flandrijn, rushing in . . .

THE LIZARD'S HEAD, GAY AND GARISH WITH LANTERN LIGHT, RAUCOUS bursts of laughter flung out of open windows like the contents of chamber pots. The head itself glistened wetly in its raised iron cage, faint, bandlit silver shifting to brighter, lamplit gold each time the tavern door banged open on the serving wenches and the heavily laden trays they carried. The trestles set outside were full, all seats taken by bulky figures upending tankards and bottles, either in moody isolation or with roars of approval and an eerie kind of unison that resembled a drill. The ground around was littered with discarded edged weapons and packs, and, even this early, the bonelessly slack forms of a couple of unseasoned drinkers who'd overdone it. The tavern had drawn its usual bag of variegated fighting muscle. Eg spotted half a dozen different regimental rigs in the crowd, sown in among the more common black or oatmeal-colored cloaks of uncommissioned freebooters.

The Black Folk Span bulked stark against the stars above, broke the shimmering arc of the band where it dipped earthward.

Egar limped closer, keeping warily back from the light of the hung lanterns and tabletop oil lamps—just another shambling drinker in the gloom. He scanned the lit faces as he moved from trestle to trestle, searching for Harath, listening for the younger man's raised, excited tones. With luck, he'd find the Ishlinak out here, wouldn't even have to duck inside the confines of the tavern itself. A quick word and—

"Eg? Fucking *Egar*?"

And of course, like a fool, he lurched around, into the light, at the sound of that familiar voice. Saw Darhan, now on his feet, staring and clearly pretty drunk.

"What the fuck are you doing here, Dragonspanker?" he rasped in Majak. "Don't you know the City Guard are out after your carcass?"

Heads turning at the trestle behind him.

Egar lurched closer, grabbed the older man by the shoulder and faked a long-lost-cousin embrace. Into Darhan's ear, he muttered, "Keep your fucking voice down, will you? Yeah, I know. I'm dealing with it."

He stood back and clapped the trainer on both shoulders, faked a delighted oath and a vague gesture across the river. Then he steered the other man away from his drinking companions, toward the gloom and quiet down by the water's edge.

"Seriously, Eg." Darhan, now sobering up with veteran speed. "They got a reward posted and everything. Twenty thousand elementals. Twenty, thousand. You need to get the fuck out of town, man, while you still can."

"I'm working on that. But I got loose ends."

"Yeah? Like what?" Darhan spun on him, grabbed him in echo of the two-shoulder clasp Egar had just used. "Look in my face, Eg. Did you hear what I just said? *Twenty, thousand, elementals*. I'd hamstring you and turn you in myself for half that much."

Locked gazes. Egar's hand strayed to his knife hilt, he couldn't help it.

"No, you wouldn't," he said tautly.

Darhan flung up his arms, exasperated. "All right, all right, I wouldn't. But that makes me the single man in this city you can trust right now, and I'm telling you, if they try to draft me for Demlarashan this winter, I won't even be that. It's more money than any of us are going to see in a lifetime, Eg." His anger took a sudden gust upward. "Twenty thousand cold, clinking elementals against one man's life. Just *think* about that. It's retirement in style, it's a villa upriver, a kitchen full of slaves and a tidy little harem wing, cuties out of Trelayne or Shenshenath on tap. It's that happy fucking ending none of us are ever going to see, Eg. Just like some bullshit kid's fairy tale. Now what the fuck loose end is worth running against that kind of bounty? And don't you be telling me it's a woman."

"It's not." Egar blew a weary sigh. "Look, there's this kid. Ishlinak, not long in the city. Big, stroppy mouth on him and no more smarts than a six-week calf. He's in this, and if I don't get word to him, he's going to get taken for question."

Darhan gave him a narrow look. "Ishlinak?"

"Yeah. Dumb as fuck, but aren't you all. But he's a nice enough kid for his age, might even make something of himself if he stays alive long enough. Reminds me of . . . " He gestured. "Yeah, well. Like I said. He's in this, and that's on me."

"So what's his name?"

"Harath." Eg blinked. "Why?"

Darhan shrugged. "No mention of him on the bounty sheet. It's just you. Pretty good likeness, too, except for the hair. Smart move, blacking it up like that. But it isn't going to keep you safe for long. The Guard are a lot smarter than they used to be in our day."

"Can you help me out, then? Carry a message?"

Darhan dug at the sparse turf underfoot with the toe of one boot. "Yeah, guess I can do that much. Is he in there now?"

"I don't know. I was going to look."

The older man shook his grizzled head. "You really are something else, Eg."

"Yeah, well. *Share hearth and heart's truth,* right?"

"Sure. But just look over there, Eg." Darhan gestured broadly at the tavern and its lamplit environs, the strewn mob of men whose life was killing others just like them. "I mean, just *look* at them. Most of them, they'd sell their own mothers for a tenth that much."

Egar stared at the dim, flicker-lit figures. "I know. But that doesn't—"

The blow floored him. Dropped him to his hands and knees. Roaring, whirling in his ears, as he struggled not to go all the way down. A boot lashed in, struck with precision at the base of his ribs, lifted him with its force, killed his lungs. He went all the way down. The boot dug in under his shoulder, shoved him over, onto his back.

Darhan stood over him.

"Guess what, Eg," he said flatly. "They drafted me for Demlarashan this winter."

Egar made creaking, wheezing noises. Blood in his mouth, he'd clipped his tongue with his teeth when Darhan hit him in the head.

Tears in his eyes. He spat with slack lack of force, not much more than a belch of bloodied spittle that hung out the side of his mouth and down his chin. He clawed after breath. He tried to reach his knife.

"Uh-uh." Darhan trod on his hand. Knelt and pinned the Dragonbane's arm beneath his knee, found the weapon under the clothes. "Saw you twitch after this baby before. Thought you'd rumbled me then."

He tugged the knife from its sheath, tossed it into the river. Egar heard the tiny, going-away splash it made.

"Faithless," he managed through hoarse wheezing, "cunt."

"Yeah, yeah." Darhan frisked him with professional speed, turned up the other two knives, and threw them after their brother. "You talk when you're closing on sixty and it's back to Demlarashan or lose your commission. Fucking pointless war. I'm not dying down there for eight bucks a day and campaign rations. Not anymore."

He stood and cupped hands to mouth. "Hoy! Guard! Guard sergeant! Got your fugitive for you! Right here! *Guard!*"

Commotion at the trestles. Figures rising to their feet and peering. Voices back and forth in the evening air. The door of the tavern flung back, yellowish lanternlight spilling out. More bulky figures silhouetted there. Darhan gestured.

"They were in there all the time, Eg. Six-man squad, doing the rounds. Anybody seen this face, there's a reward. You'd walked on in there like you planned, they would have gotten you just the same. Except I'd be out twenty grand. *Hoy,* you lot! Back the fuck off! My prisoner, my bounty."

This to the rough, bunched-up crescent of freebooters already coalescing around them. Darhan stood forward, blocked them from Egar's crumpled form. There was a taut grin on his face, and his hand rested on the hilt of his own short-sword where it hung at his waist.

"You heard me! Back the fuck up, the lot of you. Job's done, no help needed. My prisoner. Now will somebody go and drag the Guard off their on-the-house arses and get them out here."

"They're coming," said someone at the back of the press.

They were, too—six lean, hard-looking men who, if they had been cadging free drink in the tavern, showed remarkably little sign of it in stance or stare. They were not what Egar had expected at all. Not a sad-

dlebag belly among them, and they carried their day-clubs with the relaxed ease of fighters, not bullies. A couple of them carried torches, too.
They shouldered their blunt way through the crowd and stood looking
down at Egar. The squad captain jutted his chin.

"Who you got there, then?"

Darhan stood theatrically aside for them. "That is Egar the Dragonbane, in all his outlaw glory. Murderer of Saril Ashant. Mark me up for
the reward."

One of the Guardsmen guffawed. "Yeah, right!"

Laughter laced through the crowd. They weren't buying it, either.
Egar, still trying to get breath back into his lungs and wipe the drooled
filth from his chin, couldn't really blame them.

The Guard captain wasn't laughing. "And you are?"

"Darhan the Hammer. Recruit intake commander, Ninth Combined
Irregulars."

"You're Majak?"

Darhan's stance tightened up. "I'm an imperial citizen of twenty-six
years standing, and a decorated veteran. And I've just done your fucking
job for you. Now you going to put my name on this arrest or what?"

The captain considered. He crouched to get a closer look at Egar,
jammed a sharp thumb under the Dragonbane's chin, and lifted his face
to the light from his companions' torches. He breathed out a soft, re-
signed obscenity. Straightened up.

"It's him," he said quietly. "Jaran, Tald, get him up. Bind his hands.
The rest of you, get these people back."

It was a shrewd order. As the captain's words sank in, the crowd
began to boil. Muttering and shoving, a growing ruck of bodies, tussling
for a clearer look. The two torchbearers planted their torches spike
downward in the ground, drew their day-clubs, and joined their comrades. The murmuring surged like surf.

"It's him."

"No fucking w—"

"—can't—"

"Look, man. Got to be. They're taking him."

"It *is* him!"

The five City Guard enforcers wrestled them back, none too gentle with their clubs in the process. Egar saw bellies poked, shins thwacked, and reaching arms smacked down. He struggled for focus in the murky light, caught one man's gaze among the many staring down at him. Shaven head, puckered about on one side with burn scars, the ear on that side gone to a ravaged scroll of cartilage, the eye a milky pit. He saw the man's hand like a claw, clamped on someone else's bracing arm as they shoved back against the Guard cordon. The single-eyed stare pinned him like a flung lance.

"Back! Get back!" The four Guardsmen were chanting it loud as they shoved. "In the Emperor's name, stand down!"

For a few seconds, it looked as if it all might dissolve in chaos, and Egar drew desperate breath in preparation for the moment. But Jaran and Tald were pros—they rolled him on his face and secured his wrists with twine before they lifted. And as they pinioned him for the lift, he heard a shrill blast from the Guard captain's whistle.

"That's *enough!*" And a harsh scraping sound—Egar made it for the captain's riot saber coming out. "In the Emperor's name, *you, will, stand, down!*"

The crowd quieted. Egar's two captors hauled him upright and set him on his feet. The captain brandished his saber. By city law, it was supposed to be blunted so as not to inflict lethal injury, but it didn't look that way in the glint of bandlight and the torches.

Darhan stood, arms folded, looking on. He would not meet Egar's eyes.

"If any of you"—the captain now stalking a short arc in front of the restrained crowd, voice pitched loud and lecturing—"wish to witness this man suffer the penalty for his murder *of an accredited imperial officer,* then you may do so at his execution."

Undercurrent of murmuring. But all the force had gone out of it.

"For now, you will give way to the authority vested in me by His Imperial Radiance Jhiral Khimran, or face charges of your own for a breach of the Emperor's peace. Do I make myself clear?"

The quiet held. The captain evidently judged it sufficient for his purposes.

"All right, lads. Let's open some space here. Jaran, Tald—walk him through."

Through was used advisedly. The press of freebooters opened grudgingly as Egar's captors marched him forward. They all wanted a good look. *See a Dragonbane brought low. See the man who dared to kill an imperial knight and rape his wife in their own bedchamber. See the doomed man walking.* Egar, still groggy and sagging from the blow to the head, was almost glad of the two Guardsmen's grip on his upper arms. The crowd of faces jostled past like something out of his recent pipe house dreams.

"That's close enough," the guard on his right snapped as part of the press lurched up against them. He and the Dragonbane both staggered a little from the push. Egar turned his head, saw, with sudden shock, the shaven-headed burn victim staring intensely at him among the pushers, scar-puckered face not much more than a foot away.

Something cool brushed upward, against his pinioned hands. Something stung the edge of his left palm, insect-like. Something thick and rounded pressed into the loose curl of his right. The twine on his wrists slithered away like tiny serpents.

"Hoy, Tald, he's getting—"

But for Tald, it was already far too late.

The passed knife was scalpel-sharp, it had slit the twine bindings with less pressure than a soft kiss, put a thin cut in Egar's left hand by touch alone, and settled into the Dragonbane's right palm as if custombuilt for that purpose.

Egar thrashed around, didn't waste time getting the blade aloft. He cut downward, instinct honed in years of desperate battlefield clinches, found Tald's inner thigh with the knife, and the big artery that pulsed there. The Guardsman yelped, outraged, and leapt back as he felt the sting of the blade. He did not yet know what had been done to him.

"He's *loose*—"

Wailing, but choked off, as Egar cleared room with one hacking elbow into Tald's sternum, and spun to face Jaran—slashed the man across the forehead before he could startle back more than inches. Blood rose in the wound, rinsed down the shocked Guardsman's face in a flood. He snarled and flailed blindly out at his suddenly loosed prisoner. He struggled to swing his day-club. Egar booted him in the kneecap. He fell down. The Dragonbane kicked out again, connected with something soft. Jaran folded flat.

Egar swooped low, grabbed up Jaran's club in his free hand, and whirled to face the others. Saw the captain's saber glinting down, got in a block, looped and slammed the blade away, stepped in. Rallying cries around him now, the rest of the Guardsman floundering after response. Egar got in close with the captain, punch to the face, snap the head back, and jam the terrible small knife up under his jaw and in. He twisted, felt the slim blade snap and break off, let it go.

Darhan yelling somewhere, frustrated rage. *"He's free, you fools! He's getting away!"*

The captain reeled back, blood drooling out from under his chin, clutching at his wound, saber gone. No time to grab it. The crowd looked on, roaring as if it were sport. Egar met another Guardsman head-on, took a low, glancing blow off the hip, rode it. Stood and struck back with his club, side of the head, heard the crunch it made, and the man went down senseless.

The others came running in. *This can't last, Dragonbane.* He spotted his next weapon, snarled with fierce joy. Traded blows with the first of his new attackers, screamed in his face for shock, and dodged past, into heat and brighter light. Seized the torch by its shaft where it stood pegged, plucked it up out of the earth with a triumphant bellow, and swung about. The flames whooped through the air.

He got lucky—hit two of the remaining Guardsmen on the same sweeping stroke as they charged him. Chunks of oil-soaked binding and pitch jarred loose, caught in clothing and hair. The flames splattered about. The burning men reeled back, beating at themselves in panic. Egar hauled back his head and howled, berserker ululation. It went through his aching head like an ax, it split the air like the rage of some vast bird of prey. He brandished club and torch aloft in either hand. Swung the flaming brand through the air again, made it *whoop.*

"Come on then! Who wants some more?"

He was bellowing in Majak without realizing—harsh, exotic syllables most of them would not understand. He saw men watching him in the firelight-painted murk, gathered faces like a theater audience—excited, appalled—none even close to taking him on.

Ten paces away, the river at his back. He spotted Darhan, hovering close on his flank, long-knife drawn. Egar pointed the torch at him, stared down its length, lined the Ishlinak up in the waver of heated air where the flames danced.

"*You, you cunt!*" he yelled. "*I'm going to fucking have you!*"

He hurled the torch at the other man, saw with gut-deep satisfaction how Darhan flinched away. Then he turned and sprinted flat-out for the riverbank.

Cast the day-club aside as he reached the edge.

Plowed a headlong dive, direct into the black water beyond.

CHAPTER 37

It took Ringil longer than he'd have liked to get to the Black Folk Span. The streets below the palace on the estuary side were crammed, impassable at any pace above that of a snail with a diploma in law. Wagons and carts and every variety of human traffic vied for space. No way to open passage, short of spurring his horse forward into the press, trampling down anyone too slow or stubborn to get out of his way.

But that could only draw attention, and violence of one sort or another, and despite the spiky, hungover will to do harm in his head, what he needed right now was. to stay as inconspicuous as possible, to lose himself in the hubbub of Yhelteth's heart. Archeth would let him go, he knew, and he clung to a hope that Rakan might, too. But word had to get back to Jhiral sooner or later, and that meant a limited amount of time to work with. So he gathered his small store of patience around him like a threadbare cloak, rode the slow throb of his aching head, and sat his

horse like a man midway across a river in full summer spate, up to his
knees in the flow of citizenry, moving slower than he could have walked.

It gave him time for thinking he would rather not have had.

In the back of his mind, the leaf spiraled downward again, to join its
myriad dried-out and curling cousins on the footpath through the garden. The woody light around him shifted, and he heard the crunch of
footfalls over parched leaf remains, coming closer behind him.

He knew what he would see if he turned. Had somehow seen it already, though he didn't know what it meant.

A woman, face shrouded, head bowed, the lap of her plain white
robe blotched and stained with blood. Something small and bundled
and bloody cradled in her arms.

The cold legions wrap around you . . .

He shook it off. Urged his horse forward with his thighs, fighting a
cool sense of dread that he was running much too late.

The street he was on finally gave out onto the main estuary wharf
road, and here there were at least cargo marshals and dockmasters to
ensure that the thoroughfare did not become too clogged for freight to
pass. They saw him coming, made him for some merchant or merchant's
agent, and did their best to open easy passage for him. Closer in, his scar
and the Ravensfriend sent a different sort of message, but achieved a
similar result. A good many of the berthed vessels along the estuary were
heading for Demlarashan, hauling troops or supplies or both, and there
were enough mercenaries mixed in with the levy that he would pass for
a freebooter captain in a hurry to confirm some detail of passage for his
men.

*Pass for a freebooter captain, Gil? Pass for? Freebooter captain is pretty
much what you are these days.*

*Thought I was long-lost imperial nobility, welcomed home after long
absence. You heard Shanta last night. Undeserving Victims of the Ashnal
Schism, Exiles of Conscience in a Time of Great Turmoil, carrying the
Flame of Faith to Safer Lands.*

Despite himself, he felt the corner of his mouth quirk. Shanta had
done a superb job, rolling out the tale with all due ponderous, lachry-
mose formality of idiom and salute—for a man so well versed in the
practicalities of building ships, he certainly had a very flowery turn of

phrase when he chose to deploy it. Gil was pretty sure he'd caught the aged Shab Nyanar dabbing delicately at the corner of one eye with his napkin at one point.

He thought his mother, had she been in attendance at the banquet, would have enjoyed that speech. Not so much for its leaky sentiments—Ishil was never one for tears or romance—as for its blunt manipulation, for its masterful twisting of messy, mundane events into some refined poetry of significance, into a narrative built to tug at the heartstrings of those who lived desperate for validation of the codified ways they saw the world.

No one will like the truth of who you are, she'd told him once, when he was barely into his teens. *But if they can once be sold a gilded nobility that covers for the truth, well, then—that they may be taught to love more than any real aspect of their own grubby little lives. And by such ruses, we live and prosper.*

Just don't tell your father that.

Sampling his own early drafts of youthful cynicism at the time, he'd believed she was talking about social standing and how it was maintained. It was only much later, recalling the sadness of her smile, that he understood she had seen in him what he was becoming, and was offering him a survival strategy.

Yeah. Fumbled that catch, though, didn't you?

Sometimes—it surprised him abruptly to realize—he missed Ishil. Missed that eyebrow-arching appreciation of artifice and life's attendant irony that seemed to serve her so well as armor. Missed her haughty, witch queen poise.

He thought she would have done rather well in Yhelteth.

Shade falling across his face made him look up. The Black Folk Span had crept up on him while he brooded; the shadow it cast downriver at this time of the morning was cool around him, as if he'd ridden into the fringes of a wood. The estuary road had become a sparsely trafficked towpath, and the Good Luck Dead Lizard, or whatever they were calling it these days, was just up ahead. He nudged the horse into a trot.

Outside the tavern, a small boy was swabbing down the trestle tables, answering occasionally to a grizzled old man who sat at one already cleaned. There was an untouched pint of beer in front of this solitary customer, and horse tackle dumped at his side. He glanced up at the sound of Ringil's horse's hooves; he seemed to be waiting for someone. Ringil dismounted and tethered his horse to a convenient trestle leg. The old man watched him steadily as he approached, and for just a moment Gil thought there might be something vaguely familiar about the face.

He shrugged it off. "This where the fight was last night?"

"Over there." The old man nodded at the riverbank. There were blackened patches on the thin grass and bald patches of earth. It looked as if someone had knocked a torch or lamp over and left it there to burn into the ground.

"Did you see it?" Ringil asked him.

"No, I was not here." The old man picked up his pint and sipped at it. He seemed to be enjoying a private joke.

"Anybody around who did see it?"

"You might try inside. There are those who claim witness." The old man shrugged. "But who can tell for sure? Tales are already being spun around whatever truth there once was."

Ringil grunted.

"Some never left, my lord," the boy piped up, pausing for a moment in his wiping. "They stayed the whole night and are talking of it still."

Someone had blacked his eye for him a while back; there were fading blue-and-yellow bruises still in evidence, and scabbing on a swollen lower lip. But youthful enthusiasm shone through the damage like sunrise through marsh-weather cloud.

"They say the Dragonbane tore free of his bonds in a berserk rage, sir. They say he magicked a sword from the air, then called up fire spirits to scorch his attackers."

"I see," said Ringil gravely.

"Maybe his victory over the dragon gave him powers, sir."

Gil nodded, ignored the knowing look the old man was giving him. "That's very possible. I have heard similar stories before."

"My father died fighting dragons," said the boy hopefully.

Ringil held back a grimace. Mouthed the rancid words. "Then your father was a . . . great . . . hero. And I'm sure . . . I'm sure his spirit is watching over you from, uh, from a high place of honor and peace."

"And my mother, sir."

"Yes. And your mother."

The old man was still watching him, keenly. As Ringil turned to go inside, he called out. "You carry a Kiriath blade, sir."

Ringil stopped, did not turn back. "Expert in swords, are you?"

"No, sir. A humble barber only. But I work with blades of my own, after a fashion, and I know their strengths and weaknesses. I know steel. And that is Kiriath steel upon your back."

"And if it is?"

"Well, then perhaps you are some sort of hero as well?"

Still without turning, Gil closed his eyes for a moment. But what he found there on the inside of his eyelids gave him no respite.

Some sort of hero.

He opened his eyes again, found himself turning unwillingly back to face his accuser.

"Appearances are deceptive, old man," he said shortly. "You'd do better not to judge a man by the steel he carries on his back."

"Gracious advice." The old man bowed his head. Still that maddening familiarity about him. "I am indebted. Should you ever wish for a shave, I am at your disposal. Finest barbering in the city. I am in the Palace Quarter. Ask for Old Ran's place."

"I'll keep it in mind." Ringil saw the way the boy was watching him, the enthralled look in his eyes again. "Now, if you'll excuse me."

And he fled from the boy's gaze, into the cool gloom of the tavern and the harsh back-and-forth quarrel of grown men talking shit at the tops of their voices.

"THAT'S YOUR BEST BET," THE PUBLICAN SAID, TAPPING THE COIN ON the bar-top and sliding it into his pocket. He nodded across the crowded room and the noise. "In the corner there, with his new whore."

Ringil darted a surreptitious glance over to where a greasy-looking Majak in his early twenties sat goblet in hand at a table against the wall. The whore in question was young, too, and likely pricey by house standards, a little raddled, but otherwise quite shapely and not making much effort to hide the fact. She'd split her skirts apart, put one leg on display to the top of the thigh, and her breasts were pushed up almost to spilling from her bodice. She was pressing them up against the Majak's arm, chattering insistently in his ear between drafts from her goblet.

Ringil frowned, still hazy with hangover. "Really?"

"Yeah." The publican grinned and shifted a toothpick around his mouth. "I know. Little fucker doesn't look like much, does he?"

"No, he doesn't."

"Well, sir, your judgment there is accurate." Gil had made the man for a veteran on sight, and rolled out a mannered commanding officer's drawl when he approached him. He'd given enough orders to imperial troops in his life that his Tethanne was more or less flawless in the context. The publican practically saluted in response. He was falling over himself to be helpful. "See, Harath over there is just what he looks like, a fucking steppe savage no different from the rest, and he's a mouthy little punk into the bargain. Always getting in trouble, late on his tab most of the time. Just about what you'd expect from his kind. Come down off the steppes for our women and the easy living, problem is, they're just not used to a civilized way of doing things."

Ringil looked carefully at the scarred wooden bar-top. "And why exactly should I be interested in this Harath?"

"Oh, well." The other man leaned in close to impart his secret, grinning. "Dragonbane come in here about a week ago, sir, asking after him. Asking where he could be found."

"Asking after him by name?"

"Yes, sir."

"Was he with him last night?"

The publican shook his head. "Only showed up this morning, seemed pretty surprised about it all. But he's still your best bet, sir. I mean, this lot?" A broad, dismissive gesture at the clientele. "Some of them were *around* when it went down, true enough. Been here ever since, too, right through to daybreak, talking it up. Best night's takings for a month. But not a one of them actually had *words* with the Dragonbane. Dragonbane never even got through the door before the Guard jumped him. This lot? Fucking bystanders, all of them."

"Yeah, always plenty of those." Ringil brooded for a moment. "You talk to anyone else about this?"

"Can't say as I have, sir. But I knew they'd send someone like you, sooner or later."

Ringil's eyes narrowed. "Someone like me?"

The publican grinned again. "Don't worry, sir. I know how to keep my mouth shut. And honestly, nothing against the Guard, there's some good men among them. But sometimes, well, it takes a certain . . . Reach, am I right?"

"You're a shrewd man," Ringil told him and produced another coin. "And a discreet one, it seems. That's a pair of admirable qualities in a soldier."

"Yes, sir." The coin disappeared like a magic trick, untapped this time. "Hope you get him, sir. Dragon hero or not, it's foreign thugs like that are sinking this Empire."

Ringil gave the publican what he judged an appropriately grim nod and departed. He crossed the low-beamed space toward the young Majak and his whore, eying the exits as he moved, instinctive checks prior to the confrontation. Realizing as he got closer that it wouldn't be necessary. Harath was oblivious to his approach, as he was to the whore's cleavage pressing into his arm and her grinning chatter into his ear, and just about everything else going on in the room, it seemed. He sat, goblet in hand, staring into the middle distance as if it contained a rainbow's end chest of marsh dweller gold.

Ringil dropped into the seat opposite.

"Hello, Harath."

The steppe nomad started, saw the man sitting across from him and tried to leap to his feet. Ringil's hand leapt first, locked down on his arm at the elbow. He leaned in behind it. The table jarred; the wine bottle jumped and fell sideways. The whore grabbed it with a practiced hand before it could spill, set it back upright. Harath strained to break free and rise.

"Let's not make a scene," said Ringil softly.

"Fuck do you think—"

"I'm a friend of the Dragonbane. I'm anxious to find him before the King's Reach do. Do you know where he is?"

"I don't know what you're talking about." Still struggling to get loose. "You—"

"Sit *down*." Eye-to-eye with the younger man now. "Or I'll see to it you're talking to the King's Reach yourself by lunchtime. Want to see the inside of their questioning rooms up at the palace? That can be arranged. Now *where is the Dragonbane?*"

Harath broke, gave up. Sank back in his seat, breathing hard. Ringil let him go. Sat back in his own seat and straightened his right sleeve, which had ridden up in the struggle. Brushed down his doublet with a fastidious hand. It all made a good cover while he regained his own breath. He glanced up at the Majak.

"Well?"

"I haven't seen that Skaranak fuck in days." It was a hissed outburst across the table. "And he owes me money, the cunt. I want to find him just about as badly as you do."

"You don't appear to be looking very hard."

"That's what you think. Why I came down here this morning in the first place. Thought he might have come in. Then I hear all this shit about the Guard, stupid bastard's been raping and murdering nobles up the hill. Like we didn't have enough trouble already."

"Trouble? What trouble?"

"He's owed *money,*" the whore put in with asperity. "Didn't you hear? You're a friend of this Dragonbane, you ought to—"

Ringil cut her a look and her voice dried up as if he'd slapped her across the face. He turned his attention back to the young Majak.

"What trouble?"

IT TOOK A WHILE TO GET THE STORY STRAIGHT. HARATH WAS QUITE drunk, and he seemed mostly concerned to enumerate grievances, against *this so-called Dragonbane,* the Skaranak clan in general, randy old men who thought they were still young bucks, his faithless Ishlinak friends, miserly mercenary pay, military stupidity in Demlarashan, religious maniacs and imperial arrogance, and in fact pretty much every aspect of life he'd encountered since he came south of the Dhashara pass . . .

The actual tale he told blundered along through all this like a badly injured man, clinging to the complaints like pillars in some hard-to-

navigate colonnaded hospital he'd been told had a bed for him somewhere. The whore sat at his side throughout, too cowed by Ringil's
glittery stare to actually interrupt, but rubbing Harath's thigh vigorously
every so often, murmuring cod-maternal sympathetic sweet nothings to
him, and refilling his goblet from the bottle whenever he drained it.
Harath nuzzled her in return, lost the thread of what he was saying, occasionally abandoned it altogether in a welter of gruff, growling kisses to
neck and throat, while Ringil looked on and set his jaw and worked at
keeping his hands to himself.

Under other circumstances...

He held down his temper, mainly because violence would have
drawn attention he didn't want from the rest of the room, but also because he didn't want to stop Harath's rambling confessional flow, which
did seem, slowly, to be taking on some comprehensible shape, thus:

The Dragonbane shows up at Harath's door with a blade contract,
he knows about some prior falling-out between Harath and another
Majak, name of Alnarh, *faithless piece of shit, like I said, wouldn't believe
he was Ishlinak blood,* while they were both working for a high-level invigilator out of the Citadel called Pashla Menkarak—Ringil frowned,
the name was vaguely familiar, something Archeth had talked about—
who got Harath cut loose from his job for messing about with a temple
maiden, slave girl, whatever, something like that, anyway, the Dragonbane has a grudge of his own against the Citadel so they plan a burglary
together, some disused temple upriver, Ringil's never heard of it, but all
the time *this Dragonbane, man, he's like, fucking obsessed with this slave
girl, but he's never even fucking met her, right.* But coin is coin, and another tour in Demlarashan is just no sane option for anyone who's seen
what's going on down there, *done two fucking tours, mate, believe me, I
know what I'm talking about,* so Harath's in—they hit the temple by
night, mix it up with Harath's old Ishlinak pals, *which he* said *we wouldn't
fucking get into, right, I mean, I had to kill a brother that night,* and get
into some kind of secret harem, where the Dragonbane apparently finds
what he's looking for, *some whining bitch, no, not that one, a different
one, don't ask me why* and then, on the way out, they're attacked by this
angel, *yeah, that's right, you heard me, a fucking angel,* which glows with
blue fire and—

"Stop."

"I am not fucking making this up," Harath said heatedly. "It was—"

"I didn't say you were." There was a sudden spike of ice down his spine, and his hangover seemed to have acquired a new, cold-clamping focus at his temples and in his guts. Scenes from the fight at Ennishmin danced through his head, flicker-lit in that same unearthly blue.

Here? In Yhelteth? It was a shuddering, dithering voice in his head. *Can't be, can't fucking be . . .*

He saw the figures, emerging from the core of their own radiance.

He saw Seethlaw, smile like a wolf . . .

"Here—you going to puke or something?"

He blinked at Harath's voice. Looked up and saw the Ishlinak's whore watching him with a sneer on her paint- and powder-clogged face. Curled red lip over teeth turning gray, probably with too much bad krinzanz or just—

Memory of the girl on the wharf leapt in. Propped against the barrel, accosting him with the same gray grin. *I have a message for you, Dragon-bane . . .*

You are awaited at the Temple of Red Joy. Do not delay. All things will become clear.

He shook off a shiver. Cleared his throat. "This place you cracked upriver. The temple. Did it have a name?"

Harath shrugged. "Afa'marag, I guess, like the neighborhood. Called it after some water demon, the maraghan or something. That's what the boatman said, anyway. Though he was a lying little—"

"Not Red Joy? Not the Temple of Red Joy?"

The Ishlinak looked at him blankly. "No. Never heard of that, it's—"

The whore's cackle shut him up. Both men looked at her irritably.

"Temple of Red Joy?" She grinned at Ringil, widely now. Leaned in toward him, mock-affectionate, then let her grin freeze out. "I know where that is, scar-face. Question is, what's it worth to you?"

"I don't know," said Ringil mildly. "How about it's worth I don't tell the King's Reach you're holding out on where I can find the Dragon-bane."

The color fled her face. She tried to shrink back to her side of the table, but his hand whipped out and grabbed her wrist.

"Or would you prefer to talk to them about it directly?"

"Southside." The words blurted out of her. "It's on the southside. Across the Span and down into the old ferry quarter. Back of Keelmakers' Row."

"Thank you."

CHAPTER 38

I t wasn't red, and it didn't look particularly joyous.

It looked, in fact, like every derelict imperial temple Ringil had ever seen—butter-colored stone buttresses squeezed between the newer buildings on either side, scoured and scarred by centuries of sun and wind and war, and then by the more recent scourges of the city that had grown up around it. Up close, he saw Tethanne graffiti chiseled into the stonework wherever the elements had left the facing intact—names and insults and crudely approximated clan brand marks, fragments of toilet verse. At the entrance, the shadows he stepped into stank of piss.

He looked down at the urchin who'd led him here. "You ever been inside?"

"No, my lord." The boy knuckled at a snot-crusted nose. " 'S haunted. The coastlanders' demons live in there."

The two of them stood there for a moment, both looking at the door and the thin slice of doorway it was jammed ajar on.

Deeper shadow within.

Ringil looked back at the sunstruck street, where the boy's elder brother stood watching, holding the reins of his horse and glaring at anyone who passed too close. It was mostly unnecessary. Keelmakers' Row was a quiet, narrow thoroughfare, not a lot of passersby, and those there were seemed well schooled in neighborly discretion—aside from the odd glance, they studiously ignored the gaunt, black-cloaked figure and his two urchin companions. Ringil shrugged, produced the promised coin, held it up out of reach.

"All right. This is for showing me. You get another three of these when I come out, and you're still here, and my mount still has all its legs. Got it?"

The boy's face went almost luminous with joy. "Yes, my lord."

Ringil leaned down, nose-to-nose with him. "And if you're *not* here, or anything bad's happened to that horse, then the Revelation help your immortal little souls. Because nothing else this side of hell will. Got that as well?"

The urchin drew himself up to his full six- or seven-year-old height. "Course, my lord. Word's my bond, my lord. Horse'll be safer with us than if you put it in the Emperor's harem."

Questionable kind of safety, that, his hangover grumbled. *Wouldn't trust that fuck Jhiral out of sight with anything much that has an orifice.*

But he straightened up and tossed the boy the coin, and the boy took it out of the air like a fish snapping up a fly. Then he stood, urchin hands on hips, and watched for a moment as Ringil pressed splayed fingers against the door, leaned to test its weight, and that was evidently about all he wanted to see. He scurried back out into the sun and to his brother, leaving the scar-faced swordsman alone in the shadows.

The door was heavy caldera oakwood; it took the full weight of Ringil's shoulder to shift it more than a couple of inches on the uneven, detritus-strewn flagstones. But it gave with an awful grating sound on the second blow, and opened up a couple of feet. Ringil gave it a final, full-bodied kick for more clearance, then slipped through the gap. A scant couple of rays of sunlight followed him inside, touched his cloak at the shoulder, and then let him go.

Inside the temple, it was more worn-down flagstones and slim pillars holding up a cracked and sagging roof. No furnishings or fabrics that he could see, just cool stone silence over everything like a dust sheet. The sun got in here and there, through roof-level latticed skylights or the chinks in the damaged roof—where it touched the dusty ground, it seared small patches so bright they seemed to smolder. Look at them for too long and it made peering for detail in the gloom a lot harder.

He stopped doing it. He let his eyes adjust.

A stone altar in the shadows up ahead, long and raised, like a funeral bier. There was an ornately carved stone screen behind it, latticed along the top in echo of the skylight design, but sculpted over most of its solid surface with a line of bas-relief figures. He picked his way toward them, between the falling rays of sunlight from the roof, crunching across the dust and detritus, glad of the noise his footfalls made. In the sharp contrast of blazing light and shadowy gloom, the silence of the place was like a solid presence, filling up his hungover senses. He walked as if in a slight trance, along the raised flagstones of what had clearly once been a central aisle to the altar.

He paused theatrically when he got there, pivoted about to face the way he'd come, and raised his arms cruciform.

"Anybody *home?*"

The echoes of his voice fell flat, as if trying to scramble out through one of the skylights and failing. He'd really meant to shout louder. He'd meant it as a joke, but the echo wouldn't carry the irony. He sounded just like the next man, calling for his gods.

He grimaced. Let his arms fall slackly to his sides.

All things will become clear, Gil. Yeah, right.

Footfall crunch at his back.

He whipped about, one hand already up and reaching for the Ravensfriend. The upwelling urge to kill something, hot and instant, there in his guts and the muscles in his limbs. The old dance, driving out the vagueness in his head.

Nothing.

He stuttered to a halt, peering. The gloom around the altar was undisturbed. He was still tangled up in memories of the Queen Consort Gardens. Of Seethlaw and the dwenda, of terrible blue fire, of something dark and formless catching up with him.

He shook his head, tried to shake it all loose.

His eyes settled on the bas-relief stone screen. It was a pretty good match for the one he'd seen on the temple wall in Hinerion—another ranked assembly of the Dark Court, carefully rendered in more human aspect to suit local taste. Only this time, it was Hoiran himself who was missing from the sculpted ranks and the gap he'd seen in Hinerion was filled by . . .

Filled by . . .

He felt abruptly light-headed again. He felt the ground give way.

The missing dark courtier at Hinerion had been the Lady Kwelgrish—Kwelgrish the twilight banshee, the dark moan at evening, the mistress of wolves. Kwelgrish, who wore the skins of women and beasts with equal aplomb, who carried an ancient unhealing wound in her head and liked to trade sneering humor with demons before she bested them in shrieking, snarling combat. Kwelgrish who here, in the Temple of Red Joy, stood in bas-relief among her fellow gods with one hand pressing a towel to her bleeding skull and the other shoulder covered by a wolf skin complete with wolf head and jaws, such that the creature appeared to both hang off her and be biting her at one and the same time.

Let us say only that you will owe me a favor, Ringil Eskiath . . .

The voice bubbled up in his head, whispered at his ear, walked on his spine. Quilien of Gris, somewhere behind the stone screen in the gloom, circling him and the altar he stood at with luminous wolf-eyed intent—

Yelling, from the street.

He jerked a glance backward along the raised stone aisle to where he'd come in. His vision seemed to tilt with the sudden shift in focus, as if he stood in a boat on choppy water. Sunlight crowbarred in where he'd forced the door open, spilled in a distant puddle on the dusty floor there, and it seemed, suddenly, a long, dark way back out of this place.

Yes—run, said another, deeper voice that was not Quilien's. *Run while you still can. Remember who you are. Who you were. Who you will be.*

Another footfall in the dust and detritus behind him, and he *was* running, he was sprinting, down the raised aisle path as if to the closing gates of some abruptly offered salvation.

Later, he would look back and be unable honestly to say if he ran toward the uproar in the street outside or away from what had just stepped out of the shadows at his back. He knew only the motion, the impulse that drove him forward, through each falling arrow of sunlight from the cracked roof—the spots burned on his shoulders like newly minted coins—the slanting tumble of light and gloom, the breath hard in his throat, approaching the doorway, that must, he knew, *must* slam closed just as he reached it, he could already hear the long, grating shriek it would make—

It did not.

He grabbed the oakwood edge, stuffed himself through the gap and out into the sun. The Ravensfriend, caught in the gap for a moment, seemed not to want to leave, then gave as he twisted savagely about, and came out with him.

He stood blinking in the sunlight, trying to understand.

Uniforms and boot clatter and shouting up and down the cobbled street, half a dozen men-at-arms running about and gestures upward, tilted-back, helmeted heads—the sun struck glints from the cheap metal—and there, suddenly, shatter and splinter at a first-floor window in the façade across the street. Glass falling outward in brief, lethal rain, window frame smashed and torn free. Ringil, already tracking the noise, shaded his eyes just in time to catch a glimpse of two men come through the ragged gap, still struggling in midair. One was a uniformed man-at-arms, helmet gone. The other—

The two men hit the street with a solid *crump*, opposite the temple door. Dust billowed up around them, boiled as they fought. Still some struggle in both, but the man-at-arms had landed on his back and most of the fight seemed to have gone out of him with the fall. As Ringil watched, the other figure got fully astride him, reared up and rammed something long and thin down hard into his opponent's eye. A shriek floated up, the fight jammed to a halt. The figure snapped off whatever weapon it was using and blundered awkwardly to its feet. Wind caught the dust and whirled it away.

Ringil stared.

"Eg?"

Egar the Dragonbane, dust-plastered and wild-eyed, the sheared-off stump of a fucking *flandrijn pipe* clenched in one fist, blood streaming from a cut on his face . . .

"Gil? *Ringil?*"

"*Take him down!*"

Ringil swung to the voice, heard the hard edge in it, the custom of command. There, amid the gathering uniforms, a slim figure clad in the black-and-silver livery of the King's Reach. As Ringil stared, the man's voice took a rising cadence.

"Bow*men!*"

There were three of them, two with bow already cranked and quarrel loaded. At this range, they could hardly miss. The Dragonbane crouched and bared his teeth, pipe shard clutched like a knife in his fist. He might cover the ground to one of them before the order fell, but the other . . .

Ringil raised his hand and traced the *ikinri 'ska* symbol in the air.

No thought in it at all—the impulse rose like instinct, like a diver's first breath on breaking surface. Like the urge to puke or feed.

"Bow*men.*" He stole the command from the other man's voice, took it out of the air, copied it, fed it back to them. "*Your weapons are serpents!*"

Like a veil falling across the sun, like a sudden chill wind blowing down Keelmakers' Row. Even the Dragonbane seemed taken aback. The bowmen shrieked and threw their crossbows away. Ringil stalked into the midst of them, like a black wraith, like a shadow detached from the shade in the walls of the temple. His sword was still on his back.

"*Spiders,*" he said, painting the air about him with three more swift symbols. "*Dredge crawlers. Corpsemites.*"

And suddenly the men-at-arms were berserk, stamping at the ground, brushing maniacally at themselves, tearing at their mail, moaning and yelping in terror. Only the King's Reach officer was unmoved, staring in disbelief at his men as Ringil moved through them and took up station ten yards away in the middle of the street.

The man's sword rang clear of its scabbard.

"Sorcerer!"

Ringil unsheathed a grin. "That's right."

But beneath the seething, jagged exultation the *ikinri 'ska* set loose in him, he had a moment to feel out the limitations of the power. *Wise men will not fall,* Hjel had told him, somewhere in the confused, dimly remembered whirl of the memories that represented his instruction. *Running dogs and thugs, animals and fools, all these the craft will blind and cripple. But a man in command of himself and his intellect is another matter.* He read the shrewd intelligence in the face of the man facing him, the cold calculation and the poise of body. This one, he would not be able to put away so simply.

"Want to die?" he called out, in conversational tones.

"I am the King's Reach," the man shouted back at him. "I am the hand of Jhiral Khimran and the Burnished Throne, I am the imperial writ made flesh."

"Ringil Eskiath. Faggot dragonslayer." Hilarity bubbling up through him with the unleashed power, a black grin plastered across the back of his eyes, and reaching up now, the sword leaping to his hand like a hound rising to take meat its owner dangles—the blade tore sideways through the pliant lips of the scabbard, made a blurred arc around and down off his shoulder, was there at guard in front of him, like steel laughter in the light. "I asked you a question, King's man. *Do you want to die?*"

They faced each other for frozen moments in the street while the men-at-arms staggered about screaming or lay twitching and mumbling on the cobblestones. Later, some among those watching from windows along Keelmakers' Row would say that black and blue flames in the forms of men sprang up and burned around the scene, as if passersby from some street not fully of this world, some street *laid over* Keelmakers' Row, had been drawn to the moment and were gathering there to watch what happened next.

"The Dragonbane is wanted for crimes against the imperium," shouted the King's man. "You *will not stand* in the path of imperial justice."

"I already am. You want the Dragonbane, the only path is through me."

"Gil!"

He spared a momentary glance back at the call. Egar, striding forward, stooping to scavenge a short-sword from one of the stricken men-at-arms. Limping badly.

Ringil raised a warding hand. "I got this, Eg."

"Gil, it's not that simple. The fucking *dwenda* are here, right *here* in—"

"I know all about it, Eg. Let's kill one thing at a time, shall we?"

Twitch of motion at the corner of his eye. The King's man, readying himself—he was going to do it anyway. Something in Ringil grinned like a skull at the knowledge.

"Wait!"

Dull clink and skitter of a dropped blade on the cobbles. The King's man's eyes flinched sideways at the sound. He looked suddenly puzzled.

And then the Dragonbane was at Ringil's side, turned in to him, pressing one warm, heavy hand on Gil's chest and shoulder. Face in close enough to brush stubble on Ringil's cheek.

"Just hold it, Gil," he muttered. "There's another way we can do this."

Ringil shot him a narrow look. "There is?"

Past the bulk of the Dragonbane's shoulder, he saw the King's man twitch again. He raised the point of the Ravensfriend, admonishing.

"You. Don't even fucking think about it."

Egar turned about and faced the imperial. He raised his empty hands.

"Enough," he said, in formally enunciated Tethanne whose fluency made Ringil blink. "I submit. You may bring me before your Emperor."

The King's man was still staring hard at Ringil, at the cold, lifted finger of the Ravensfriend. An imperial man-at-arms crawled about on the floor, gibbering and clutching at the cobbles as if he might fall off them and into some waiting void. Weeping and bleating cries soaked through the air from the others. The Ravensfriend gleamed.

"Gil!"

Ringil shrugged and lowered his sword.

"All right," he said. "This, I've got to see."

CHAPTER 39

*A*re *you fucking serious?"*

Jhiral came fully upright off the ornate sandalwood chair, glaring, as if launched by some catapult mechanism below. The whole silk-tented coracle tilted on the water with the sudden force of his movement. Around him, in the tinted light falling through the silks, people grabbed at tent-pole supports to stop themselves stumbling. The Chamber of Confidences' floating inner sanctum was not made for violent motion.

Ringil stood like stone. He might have been in a marble-floored ballroom for all the notice he took of the swaying. He was not armed, but you wouldn't have known it to look in his eyes.

"Do you see me laughing?" he asked quietly.

Archeth stepped forward. "My lord—"

"Shut *up*, Archeth!" The Emperor, not looking at her, stabbing a finger in her direction. "I've taken about all the advice I'm going to from you this year. You—northman—you really expect me to do this? A full and free pardon for your barbarian friend?"

"Yes, I do."

"A pardon—after the murder of an imperial knight in his own bedchamber and the rape of his wife, the death of three City Guardsmen last night, an imperial man-at-arms just this morning, and now six others I'm told may never be sane again?"

Ringil shifted impatiently. "Yes."

"Do you really think imperial justice can be bought and sold in this fashion?"

"I think imperial justice will take it up the arse from Your Radiance for a clutched fistful of small change." Sharp, indrawn breaths from the courtiers in attendance. Ringil ignored them. "I think imperial justice is exactly what you say it is on any given day of the week, and I think the court and wider nobility will get in line behind that like the whipped dogs they are."

Outraged propriety held the company rigid. Taran Alman, King's Reach commander, fingered the pommel of his court sword. Noyal Rakan spotted the move and stiffened. The King's man who'd brought Egar and Ringil in leaned to his commander's ear and whispered urgently. Alman seemed to shake his head fractionally, disbelieving, but he relinquished the grip on his weapon and folded his arms. His stare stayed hard on Ringil.

Archeth put a weary hand across her eyes.

The silk-tented coracle's rocking settled back toward stability.

Oddly, the first person in the room to recover seemed to be the Emperor. Jhiral inclined his head gravely, as if told some interesting piece of court intelligence. He lowered himself back into his chair. Fixed Archeth with a look.

"So," he said, mock-genial. "This is still the man you intend to entrust with *diplomatic relations* on your quest to the north. Is that correct?"

Archeth grimaced and bowed her head. "Yes, my lord."

Jhiral brooded on the figure in front of him. Black-cloaked, hollow-eyed, and not recently shaven, Ringil stood out in the colored silk surroundings like death in a harem.

"Somehow," the Emperor said finally, "despite my lady Archeth's confidence, I don't imagine diplomacy as your principal skill."

Ringil smiled thinly. "No, my lord."

"But according to my inquiries, you're a very useful hand at butchery. You rallied the Throne Eternal at Beksanara, you turned back the dwenda advance. My witnesses all seem very definite on that point."

"Yes, my lord."

"And you say you can do the same here? Simply by murdering Pashla Menkarak?"

Ringil shook his head. "I can't promise that killing the invigilator will drive the dwenda away. They are not a unified race; their incursions into our world seem to lack any overall campaign plan. And four thousand years in exile has rusted their facility in dealing with humans. They are uncertain, working from ancient memories, relearning what they need to know only as they encounter it. But this much I do know—they depend upon human allies at every turn. Destroy those allies, and you cripple whatever plans they may have."

His Imperial Radiance sat back in the sandalwood chair, rested his chin on one fist, and stared at Ringil some more. "You do know that we've already sent several highly skilled assassins into the Citadel after Menkarak. Not one of them came back."

"So I hear." Ringil gestured, as if Egar stood beside him in the company. "And if evidence were needed to support the Dragonbane's word, then I submit that this is it."

"Yes, well. Be that as it may, the men we sent failed, and in the meantime Menkarak is still strutting around, making inflammatory speeches about the suffering faithful in Demlarashan." Jhiral leaned forward again, intent. "Can you get this done for me, Eskiath?"

"For the right price, I can."

"Which we've already been over, yes, thank you." The Emperor's lip curled. "I pay out a mercenary cutthroat by forgiving the murder of an imperial war hero at the hands of a steppe barbarian who can't keep his dick in his breeches. Hardly the stuff of heroic legend, is it?"

Ringil shrugged. "I don't doubt the palace has poets on staff who could embellish the tale to suit, my lord. If a more inspiring account is ever required, for more public consumption."

More silence.

Then the Emperor laughed.

Coughed it out at first, startled, disbelieving. Sat back again, laughed longer, louder. Gave himself over to it while those around him exchanged wary, mystified glances. Ringil watched him, impassive. A stiff pause hung over the rest of the company, until, finally, Jhiral's laughter slowed to a halt. He cleared his throat and shook his head, a man apparently bemused by what was before him.

"You know the real problem here? Hmm?" Jhiral looked around at the assembly, inviting guesses no one was inclined to venture. "I *like* this guy. That's the problem. I can't help it, Archeth, I like him. You chose well."

He turned his attention back to Gil.

"I like you, Ringil Eskiath, Prophet take me up the arse if I don't. You're an arrogant little northern thug, you're trading on not much more than old war stories, a belly for violence, and a few family connections." Thin, grim slice of a smile on his lips now. "And from what I hear, your bedroom practices wouldn't bear much scrutiny, either. But there it is—I like you. What am I to do?"

Ringil inclined his head gravely. Hid his own smile in the corner of his mouth. Jhiral looked around at the others again, humor fading out to something colder.

"Give me a hundred men like this one," he said, slow-gathering weight on the words. "And we could crush Demlarashan overnight—just the way my father crushed Vanbyr. If ever I saw a tool suited to purpose, it stands before me now. Very well." Nodding grimly. "Yes. I will meet these terms. Prophet knows it's going to cost me the Ashant clan's allegiance, but if it rids me of Menkarak, I'll count that a minor inconvenience. Archeth, you will need to make arrangements for the Dragonbane's discreet disappearance from the city."

"Immediately, my lord."

"No, not *immediately*." The Emperor's gaze settled speculatively on Ringil's face. "The Dragonbane will remain a guest of the palace until such time as our new royal assassin here returns victorious. Payment upon completion of contract, I think we'd all agree, is the best way forward."

They all agreed, in silence.

Ringil nodded. "And if I don't make it back?"

"Well, that would be a shame. But if news of Pashla Menkarak's demise reaches our ears and is confirmed by other sources, say within three days, then I will likewise judge our pact completed. Your terms will be honored, posthumously. You have my word."

"Three days."

"Yes. It's a holy number among the horse tribes down here." Jhiral smiled bleakly. "Appropriate, wouldn't you say."

"There's a certain resonance." Ringil examined the nails of his right hand. "And—just to be clear—if at the end of these three days, no news of myself *or* Menkarak's demise is forthcoming?"

The Emperor lost his smile.

"Well, then matters will become very simple indeed. I'll assume you to have failed as the others all did. And I will not, after all, need to forgo the good offices of clan Ashant."

He leaned forward, eyes locked with Gil's.

"Is that clear enough for you, my cutthroat northern friend?"

THEY PUT HIM BACK IN THE CELL WITH EGAR AFTER THAT.

He didn't much mind. In Yhelteth, as in Trelayne, nobility sat in prisons a lot classier than those built for commoners, at least until their longer-term fate was decided. They had tower views of the estuary, albeit through solid bars, regular meals from the palace kitchen, albeit cold by the time they arrived, and well-made room fittings, albeit somewhat worn with use. The purges had seen a steady stream of high-born offenders and their families brought through since the accession, and the traffic was beginning to take its toll on the soft furnishings.

So the mattresses on the two narrow cots were rather lumpy, the plush on the desk chair was threadbare in places, and the once softly pristine desk leather was specked and stained with ink from myriad appeals, confessions, and lawyers' instructions written out upon it.

"You're sure you can trust them on this, Gil?"

"Yeah, I told you." Ringil sat slumped in the chair, staring at the spills and stains as if at some obscure map of where he was going next. "He likes me."

Egar grunted. "Neat trick. How'd you pull that off?"

"I don't know."

The Dragonbane shifted his back against the lumps in the mattress. Watched the bars of orange evening light retreating inch by inch across the ceiling over his head. He hauled himself to his feet, wincing at the stiff pain in his wounded leg, and limped to the window. If you leaned hard against the bars and peered left, you could just make out the rise of the Citadel, like a jagged canine tooth against the southside sky. He stared at it for a while.

"Can't believe they're not going to let me go with you."

"I can't believe you ever thought they would."

"What?" Egar left the window and came and stood over him. "I *found* the fucking dwenda, didn't I? Weren't for me, no one in this city would be any the wiser, we'd all just be sitting on our hands and looking the wrong fucking way when Menkarak rolls out his angel horde."

"If that's what he plans to do."

"Well—" The Dragonbane, momentarily taken aback. "What else would it be?"

"I don't know." Ringil heaved himself to his feet and squeezed past on his way to the other bed. His boot caught on a small child's rag doll dropped at the desk by some previous occupant—sent it skidding across the cold stone floor. "The dwenda aren't human, Eg. It probably doesn't pay to reason as if they were. And whatever they want, they're the ones using Menkarak, not the other way around."

"Yeah, but—"

"Menkarak may *think* he's assembling an angelic guard to storm the palace and take back the Empire for God and the Revelation." Gil seated himself on the edge of the bed, stared at the discarded doll for a moment. He rolled his neck, trying to work out a crick. "Or whatever. But that doesn't necessarily make it so."

"Well, if that's the case, I mean . . ." Egar gestured helplessly. "Is killing Menkarak going to do any good?"

Ringil looked up and flashed him a smile. "I have no idea."

Egar stared at him. Went and sat opposite on the other bed, shoulders slumped. "I thought you'd know what to do."

"I do know what to do." Gil swiveled and swung his legs onto the bed, lay full-length, and studied the ceiling. "I'm going to get into the

Citadel, open Menkarak's throat, and get you pardoned. The rest of it, I'll make up as I go along."

"But the dwenda have to be protecting him."

Gil yawned. "Judging by the dismal failure of Jhiral's other assassins, yeah, I'd say so."

"Then you can't go in there alone!"

"Why not?" He turned his head on the pillow and looked across at the Dragonbane. "They fall down just like men, remember. I've killed dwenda before."

"Not alone!"

"Eg, look." Ringil sighed. Propped himself up on his elbows. "Be reasonable. Even if they would let you out of here, there's a hole in your leg the size of a tent flap, the rest of you looks like it got chewed up and spat out by steppe ghouls. You're in no condition to get in a fight with anyone right now."

"I was managing pretty fucking well before you came along."

"Yeah, I noticed that."

"Nearly took two of those fuckers at the same time up at Afa'marag."

"So you said."

"Killed one with my bare hands at Ennishmin."

"Eg!" He propped himself up farther, met the Dragonbane's eyes. Held his gaze. "I'll be fine. All right? Appreciate the sentiment, but I'll be fine."

They lay there, together, apart. The bars of warm orange light over their heads went on retreating, sliding away. The breeze coming in through the window turned cool.

"And if you don't make it back?"

"Hoiran's fucking balls, Eg! I'll be fine! You just sit tight. Couple of days at worst. I'll be back before you know it."

He heard how the Dragonbane wrestled with what he wanted to say, could almost hear it caught in his throat. He sighed. Closed his eyes.

"What is it, Eg?"

He heard the long breath come out of the other man.

"I've seen my death, Gil."

Ringil's eyes snapped open. "You've seen *what*?"

"You heard me. The hand of the Dwellers is on me. Death is coming for me, I've seen it."

"Oh, give me a fucking break!" Ringil gestured helplessly at the cell wall. "That's . . . that's a bunch of superstitious Majak horseshit. Seen your death. Take another fucking dragon to kill you, Dragonbane."

Egar chuckled, but there wasn't much humor in it. "That'd be nice."

"Not as I recall."

"I mean it, Gil. I saw my death. I stood on the Black Folk Span and watched it rumble past me. Ast'naha, carting my ale to Urann's feast."

Ringil said nothing.

"Thing is—that's fine. Dying's fine. Got to do it sooner or later, and I've lived longer than most Majak do. Seen more than I ever dreamed I would." Egar sat up and faced him. "But I don't want a shit death, Gil. I don't want to go murdered by inches by these southern assholes, cabled into the chair in some dungeon, or strapped out for torturers and fucking squid. I got to die, I want to die with steel in my fist, with the sun and wind on my face."

"You get killed going after Menkarak with me, it'll be at night," Ringil pointed out.

"You know what I fucking mean."

"Yeah. And you're not going to fucking die." Ringil rolled to face him. "All right? I don't know what you saw on the Span, but it means nothing. I'm going out to slit Menkarak's throat and I'll be right back. After that, we're both getting out of this fucking city. Soon. All right?"

But the Dragonbane made no reply, and Ringil's words sank into the gathering evening gloom like stones into dark water.

Over their heads, the last of the sunset's rays slipped away.

CHAPTER 40

Half a mile south and east of the Boulevard of the Ineffable Divine, the Citadel's nighttime influence was a palpable thing, falling over the dourly named streets as solidly as the sweep of its sundial shadow did by day. There were no brothels, taverns, or pipe houses advertising themselves as such, and carvings of opened scriptural tomes stood in every public space, lit by guttering torches bracketed in black iron. Those few women you saw out of doors were wrapped in muddy, monochrome robes that draped them like tents and covered their faces as if they were corpses. The mood in the street was somber and watchful; you didn't see much violence or laughter. Surly-looking bearded men went about in pairs with Revelation insignia pinned on their tunics and short wooden clubs swinging from their belts, making sure no one was having a good time.

"All since the war," Taran Alman muttered, apparently feeling the need to apologize. "Ten years back, you didn't have any of this."

He might well have been telling the truth—Noyal Rakan certainly nodded agreement, but then again, ten years ago Rakan would scarcely have been shaving. Ringil really couldn't say either way, nor did he much care. He'd passed through the southside a few times during the war, on the way back and forth from one deployment or another, or out to visit the Kiriath at An-Monal; but he'd always ridden, had never had occasion to dismount. And on broader furlough in the city, he'd never strayed farther south than Archeth's place on the Boulevard.

It didn't look as if he'd missed much.

"Up ahead." The other King's man, the local expert, nodded forward to where a pair of Citadel enforcers swaggered in the splashes of light from torches and shop frontages. "Alley on the right, after the chandler's. Let the prick patrol get well ahead first."

They dawdled about, affecting interest in an ironmonger's wares spread out on blankets in the street. Four men in dark, unremarkable garb, faces grimed and stubbled, not rich, not poor, not anything you'd think out of the ordinary unless you were looking for it closely. They'd been on foot since the river—a King's Reach agent there had taken their horses, provided them with nondescript cloaks, and advised Ringil to wear his over the jut of the Ravensfriend. It gave him the look of an unusually tall hunchback, and if anyone stopped to actually think about it, they'd know well enough what was shrouded under the garment— Rakan, Alman, and the other King's man all wore visible swords at their hip anyway—but chances were no one would bother. The main thing was to cover the gleaming iridescent Kiriath alloys worked into the Ravensfriend's scabbard and hilt.

The Citadel men forged ahead of them, glowering about and occasionally accosting startled citizens. They stopped to upbraid a woman carrying water canisters with naked hands and the cuffs of her robe rolled up. Rakan crouched to examine a pair of ornate battle-axes laid out separately from the pots and pans and yard tools that made up most of the ironmonger's display.

"Blessed weapons, my lord." The ironmonger moved in, sensing a sale. "Consecrated for the war against the Scaled Folk by Grand Invigilator Envar Menkarak himself. See his sigil, carved here upon the shafts. It gives protection to the wielder against dragon venom, the plague, and arrow shafts dipped in filth. Sold me by a veteran of Shenshenath and

Rajal Beach fallen on hard times. And if he survived Rajal, what must that say?"

Ringil, who'd survived Rajal Beach himself, rolled his eyes and touched Rakan lightly on the shoulder. Up the street, the Citadel men had tired of barracking the woman and were making their way into a press of street sellers farther along. Time to move.

Rakan straightened up and murmured some demurral about price.

"But you have yet to *make* me a price, my lord," the ironmonger yelped, offended. "What is fair and just? What is the holy shield of the Revelation worth to you?"

Ringil leaned in. "I was at Rajal, my friend. I was there. I saw Akal's Ninth Holy Scourge meet the dragons at the end breakwater." He smiled unpleasantly at the man. "They *melted.* All of them, blessed or not."

The ironmonger wet his lips, preparing some reply. His eyes darted to the scar on Ringil's face, the hump of the sword pommel under his cloak.

"I don't want any trouble, my lord," he decided.

"No, you don't."

"I honor the service you gave to Revelation and Empire. I repeat only what the weapons' owner told me. And the sigil is genuine, vouched for."

"Yeah."

Ringil turned away and followed his companions up the street to the mouth of the alley. The King's man shot him an irritated glance as they turned the corner.

"Not smart, that. He'll remember."

"Remember what?" A harsh sneering in Ringil's voice—the memories of Rajal Beach had stirred him up more than he realized. "A pissed-off war veteran in a cheap cloak? I doubt that's much of a freak occurrence around here."

The King's man shrugged and turned away. "Suit yourself. In here."

Along the alley, he made a coded knocking on the narrow wooden door of a silent, darkened frontage. They waited. After a longish moment, the door opened on greased hinges and a burly figure in tunic and butcher's apron gestured them inside.

"Go on through," he told them. "Stairs at the back. Eighth and thirteenth are dodgy."

They went down a long, darkened corridor that stank of blood and grease, and up the rickety wooden stairs, counting. There were rooms beyond, candlelit, with pig carcasses hung and cuts of meat laid out on tables. Men worked away with knives, carefully not looking up as they passed. The King's man led them through it all to a back room lit only by bandlight falling in through a pair of broad sash windows. Bare boards, a few grain sacks stacked in corners, and a big wooden tub of what looked in the bluish light to be pig's blood and offal. The King's man waited until they assembled around him.

"All right, this is it," he said tensely. "We go out one of these, and drop. I'll take you across the rooftops until we hit the Citadel curtain wall. After that, you're on your own. It's bedrock there, the crag the place is built on. Plenty of handholds, but it's a long climb. You sure you want to take that bloody great spike you're carrying up with you?"

"It's lighter than it looks," Ringil told him.

The King's man pursed his lips. "Still going to get in the way going over. There's a chink in the battlements, old damage from the last time the Drowned Daughters beat the drum. But it's narrow, and so are the corridors up to the invigilator levels. Blade that long on your back, I don't know if I'd—"

"I don't care what you'd do. If this goes bad, I'm not going up against the Citadel's men-at-arms with nothing longer on me than a sneak blade."

The King's man glanced at Taran Alman for a moment. Alman shrugged. Gestured—*get on with it.* The King's man grimaced.

"All right, then. Your choice. Now listen carefully. The senior invigilators' quarters are on the far side of the keep so . . ."

He knew. He'd studied the floor plans of the place, along with the charcoal sketch of Menkarak's face—*smug-looking fucker* was Egar's passing comment—for a solid couple of hours before he left the cell. He knew the route, the probable exposure points, the few available bolt-hole options. He had it all by heart.

Piece of cake, he'd lied briskly to Archeth and Rakan as they went out to the stables together. *I broke into tougher nests than this robbing krinzanz storehouses in harbor end when I was a kid.*

Yeah—you didn't have the dwenda prowling around harbor end, snapped Archeth, not fooled. *Whatever stopped Jhiral's assassins is going to be waiting for you, too. You watch yourself in there, Gil. Don't you get stupid.*

Who, me?

He'd winked at Rakan, but the young captain only looked away, troubled. And then the three of them took their mounts out to the palace gate to meet Taran Alman in shared, somber silence.

" . . . is your best way out as well," The King's man finished up. "This side of the keep is mostly slave quarters and storage, so the watch is pretty light. Handful of men, spread thin. There's supposed to be a sentry posted near the cracked battlement, but he won't be on site tonight."

"Remarkable. And how exactly do you know that?"

The King's man nodded at the wooden tub. "Because he's in there. I put him there myself, six hours ago. Your path has been laid, northman. It remains only for you to walk it."

Ringil spared a fastidious glance for the tub, playing it mostly for Rakan. He would have given a lot for half an hour alone with the Throne Eternal captain right now, preferably in a room without a corpse and a little better furnished than this, but, well, at a pinch, those grain sacks over in the corner, for example . . .

His mouth quirked. He put the image away.

Peeled his cloak, unslung the Ravensfriend, dressed himself again with the sword and scabbard out in the open. Went to the nearest window and dragged up the sash a solid three feet. It moved as if on well-oiled wheels, no more noise than a gusting wind. The cooking-fire smells of the city blew in, competing with the stink of slaughter already in the room. Ringil peered out.

The nearest roof was a short drop below, backed right up to the wall of the building they stood in. The wider roofscape extended off into darkness, blocks and slopes, and narrow gaps they would evidently have to leap. Barely visible beyond, the Citadel loomed on its crag like some huge, hunched vulture, roosting.

He sighed. "Come on, then. Let's get on with it."

FLEET-FOOTED ACROSS THE JUMBLED TOPOGRAPHY OF THE ROOFS, JUST the two of them now, Ringil following the King's man, close as a second shadow. Flat roof, sloping roof, garden space, gap—the route snaked back and forth, seeking advantage. In and out of shelter against chimneys and stumpy separating walls, pausing crouched while dim figures moved about or voices came and went on other rooftops in the smoky gloom. Leaping up and onward as soon as they were clear.

Once, they heard a young woman's voice, singing soft and haunting from a window under the eaves, lullaby or lament, Ringil couldn't tell. And once, huddled against a cooling chimney stack, they heard a fragment of a children's tale come up the vent from the hearthside below.

. . . and when the handsome young Emperor heard this, he saw at once, like a blind man given sudden sight, that she had been true all along, and he was ashamed for his anger. Her quiet constancy melted the cold out of his heart, and he went down on one knee to fit the fated ring upon her finger. And her father, the blacksmith, was freed immediately from his bondage, brought to the palace, and honored for his faithful service with a medallion of rank bestowed by the Emperor himself before all the lords and ladies of the court. And everywhere in that great city, there was rejoicing in the justice that a common man and his daughter could . . .

Pressure on his arm. The King's man nodded, and they were off again. Leaping four-foot gaps across narrow alleys and the heads of people who never looked up. Balancing along the roof spine of a derelict storehouse, where the slates on either side were either gone to naked rafters, or too degraded to risk walking over. A couple of small fires glowed below in the ruined space, cloaked figures gathered close around; mumble of voices. Smoke coiled up through the rafters, blew in Ringil's face. He gagged and tried not to cough. They were cooking something pretty awful down there.

Now the Citadel and its crag blocked out the whole sky ahead. They cleared one final alleyway, a little wider than the others, a five-foot leap this time, and landed on a shallow sloping roof, huddled in against the rising crag the Citadel was built on. They went up the slope, crouched low. The King's man raised his hand, fist clenched. Gil eased to a halt and peered forward. There was a final, treacherous three-foot gap between the top end of the roof and the skirts of the crag. The King's man perched near the edge, getting his breath back. He nodded over to where a collection of gnarled bushes grew out of the rock.

"You make the jump here," he said softly. "Grab the bushes. They should hold—"

"Should? Fucking *should*?"

It got him a quick, involuntary grin. The King's man leaned a little closer, finger raised close to his lips.

"Will hold," he amended. "Done it myself a couple of times. There's a slope beyond, it's scree and dust, and it's steep, but you can just about stand on it. The first holds are right above you. And up you go."

Ringil tipped back his head to take in the bandlit loom of the crag, the way it bellied out just below the battlements over their heads. Looked like about a hundred feet. Mostly flat, then harder work toward the top. He flexed his hands a couple of times.

"You got your signal?" the King's man asked him.

He nodded. Touched his belt where the Kiriath flare was tied on.

"Remember how to use it?"

"Indelibly." Archeth had walked him through how you coaxed the thing to life a dozen times or more, ignoring his protests that he'd seen Grashgal and Flaradnam use the devices often enough in the war. "Just keep your eyes peeled."

"Yeah, we'll be watching." The King's man did something peculiar with his hand at chest height. Only later would Ringil realize it had been a horse-tribe salute. "All right, then. Whenever you're ready."

Ringil backed down the roof a few feet, took the run up, and leapt. Momentary flight, the black gap yawning below him, and then the bushes took him in their rough, slapped-face embrace. He screwed up his eyes to protect them against gouging—

Grab!

His hands closed, he got thin twigs and started to slip. Grabbed again, got a decent-sized branch, planted his feet, felt one foot slide out from under, grabbed again, got a second branch, feet again, got purchase—

Hauled himself in.

He hung there for a moment, breathing. Maneuvered himself around the bushes and onto the slope the King's man had mentioned. Discovered that *steep* was something of a euphemism.

He spared one accusing glare back to where the other man crouched on the roof watching, but the distance and darkness made it impossible to make out expressions. He gave it up, found the first hold, and swung himself up into the climb.

IT WENT EASILY ENOUGH AT FIRST. WIND AND RAIN DOWN THE NUMBER-less march of centuries had sculpted baroque cups and folds and ledges into the crag. There was space to brace himself and rest his hands; once or twice there were places he could actually stand on his boot tips, lean-ing into the wall with his sweaty forehead cooling against the rock and his aching arms at his sides. Small, wiry bushes grew from outcrops and gave him extra purchase. A basin-sized cup presented itself and he was able to get his whole arm in up to the elbow—he leaned jauntily there for a while, one boot jammed in a crack below, the other swinging free. Peered down past his toes and saw how far he'd come.

Piece of piss. Nice quiet little climb.

In his youth, he'd scrambled and clambered around the ornately worked architecture of Trelayne's noble houses and decaying warehouse districts, with harbor-end toughs and the City Watch in cursing pursuit as often as not. In the war, he'd scaled the cliffs at Demlarashan to escape a reptile peon horde and had run climbed reconnaissance in the moun-tains of Gergis and the Kiriath wastes with high-caste Scaled Folk hunt-ing him. He was pretty much nerveless when it came to heights and dubious holds. More dangerous things were usually trying to kill him.

Twenty feet below the Citadel battlements, the rock bellied out and the going got suddenly tougher. The cups and ledges shrank to grudging finger-width purchase; the folds became vertical and smooth. He'd ex-pected something like this—it was the same kind of rock as in Dem-larashan, so he'd seen it before. But the darkness made it hard to pick a route except by touch, the angle he had to lean back at took an increas-ing toll on hands already numbed and aching, and his imminent arrival at the battlements meant he could not afford much noise.

He came over the curve of the belly, panting, clinging by fingertips, scrabbling with one boot for a bracing hold, and the other leg hanging heavily down. Sweat in his eyes, fingers slipping by tiny fractions each time he grabbed—he spotted the jagged crack in the battlements, saw he'd come too far over to the left. Between where he was and where he needed to be, the bellied rock of the crag extended smooth and whitened in the bandlight, smugly devoid of decent features. Oh, *okay,* there was a crack over there in its surface, relic presumably of the same eruption and earthshaking that had split the battlement stone above, but it was *a long fucking way off.* Fingers slipping now, he lashed about with his foot, stubbed a toe badly on a spur, lashed again and got momentary purchase, pushed and leapt for the crack—

Missed.

He saw his fingers brush the lip of the crack, saw them fail to grip, and his mind went blank. Rush of rock past his eyes, the kick of his guts in his throat—

Something dark, something cold—reaching out.

Salt in the wind, said a high, chilly voice somewhere. *Out on the marsh.*

And later, he'd swear he felt thin, freezing fingers wrap around his wrist, jerk his hand upward to the safety of the hold.

THE CLOUD ACROSS HIS MIND CLEARED, AS IF BLOWN AWAY BY STRONG winds. Deep pulsing in his neck and chest. He was hanging from the crack in the rock by one hand, swung over to the right, both feet jammed awkwardly in below. He had no idea how he'd done it.

Never mind how you did it, Gil. Move!

Hand over hand, up the crack, leaning right, boots stuffed in below at whatever twisted angle he could manage, fighting his body's attempts to hinge out sideways over the drop. Five feet of climb, and then he could reach up and clamp one hand onto the first of the fractured, dressed stone blocks in the battlement wall. He found a place where an entire block had pulled loose and tumbled downward, leaving a gap-toothed hole in the stonework. Above it, the wall had slumped apart along the line of the fracture. He got a grip with both hands, heaved himself into the gap as far as his chest, then hauled the rest of his body wearily after. He squeezed himself sideways into the space.

"Piece of piss." He was panting it to himself, cackling quietly. "Nice, quiet. Little climb."

He wedged his way upward between the fractured ends of the stonework, stopping every other move to free up the Ravensfriend's sharp end. Finally, he could poke his head over the battlements. Empty triangular courtyard below, a dry fountain in the center, and a cloistered walk on the far side. Memory of the map told him there was a corridor exit off to the left.

As promised, no sentry in sight.

He gave himself a minute or so to regather fighting strength and poise; then he swung bodily over the wall and dropped cat-footed to the courtyard floor. He slipped rapidly to the cloistered wall, and there the shadows swallowed him.

CHAPTER 41

L amplight gleamed off the black iron loops and bulges where Angfal's bulk hung from her study wall. Tiny glass optics, thumbprint-small, burned green and yellow at her from scattered positions along the Helmsman's casings, like a forest full of mismatched eyes, watching her in the gloom. The roughly spider-shaped gathering of braced members and swollen central bulk up near the ceiling in the center of the wall never moved—it never would, it was bolted in place with Kiriath riveting—but it gave the constant impression of being poised to leap, or maybe just fall clumsily down on top of her. There was a haphazard, chaotic air to the way the engineers had installed Angfal, and it was a perfect match for the chaos of papers and books and chests of junk that littered the study. The Helmsman dominated the space. Its voice could have come from any given part of its misshapen body, or, for that matter, from any shadowed corner of the room.

"You choose an interesting time to report these matters to me, daughter of Flaradnam. What exactly has delayed you this long?"

Like Manathan, Angfal spoke in inflections that suggested a friendly maniac in conversation with a small child he might at any moment give a shiny coin to or just kill to eat. Hard to read much human into the tone. But to Archeth's long-accustomed ear, the Helmsman sounded genuinely worried.

"I've been busy," she said.

"So it seems."

She struggled not to feel defensive. "Things are . . . difficult at the moment."

"I'm sure they are. Krinzanz is an insidious drug."

"That's not what I'm talking about! I've been at court—"

"Remarkable in itself, yes. Well done. Nonetheless, daughter of Flaradnam, you should have come to me sooner with this."

"I've got a name of my own, you know."

Even to her own ears, it sounded childishly sulky. But she was worn ragged and moody and tired, just in from parting company with Ringil at the river, filled with doubts and an anger that could find no clear focus, sprawled here behind the study desk, glowering up at Angfal's inscrutable, optic-spotted coils and cursing the stubborn will that kept her from raiding the krinzanz tincture in her larder. Want of the drug chewed along her nerves like tiny rats.

"Are you, then, so keen to cast off association with your father's people?"

"Cast me off, didn't they?" She kicked irritably at a pile of books on the corner of the desktop, clearing space for her legs. A couple of the tomes fell to the floor. "How many fucking Kiriath do you see in here?"

"I see half of one. Behaving badly."

"Yeah, well." She examined her right thumbnail, which she'd recently bitten down to the quick. She couldn't remember doing it. "Doing something, at least. We can't all sit sagely on the wall, sharpening our ironic wit and letting the world go to shit. Can we now?"

"I believe you have just acknowledged the mission your father's people owned."

"And abandoned."

"Nonetheless—"

"*Just* use *my fucking* name, *will you?*" She jumped up out of the chair, leaned on the desk with both hands, glaring up. "Is that so much to ask? That's all I'm asking, Angfal. Just ditch all this *daughter of* horseshit. You think the fact my father was Flaradnam the Wise makes any fucking difference to anything that's happening now, anything that I'm likely to do? You think I want to be reminded *every fucking time I come in here* that, that . . ."

She blinked, rapidly. Stared down at her hands.

After a moment, she sat down again.

"Just use my name," she said quietly. "All right?"

There was a long pause.

"You should have come to me sooner with this, Archeth Indamaninarmal."

She coughed out a laugh. "Yeah, okay. Got that. But I thought you would have known. Would have—I don't know—kept track of current events or something. Manathan seems to know everything that goes on around An-Monal. Anasharal can eavesdrop on conversations a hundred yards away, for all I know he can do it over miles."

"He cannot hear you now."

"No?" She settled back into her chair. "You sure of that?"

"I have seen to it that he cannot."

A tiny dripping in the pit of her stomach. "Are you saying I can't trust Anasharal?"

There was a long pause, not something Angfal was prone to when he had the upper hand in a conversation.

"I am saying." The response seemed dragged out. "That he cannot hear us now."

Archeth blinked and sat up. It was hard to be sure, but she thought the light in the scattered optics had shifted, brightening in some, dimming in others. Yellow became green became yellow. Her eyes darted back and forth, trying to capture memory of what each optic had looked like before. She had never seen anything like it happen before, in Angfal or any other Helmsman.

"Angfal?"

"Yes, dau—" This time she was certain. A cluster of optics near the base of the spider-sized sac definitely dimmed. "Yes, Archeth Indamani-narmal. I hear you."

"What's going on, Angfal?"

"The world turns, the storm gathers, your people sheltered humanity from it as best they could. You summon us, and we build—spells to span eternity, spells to chain us to you. But uncertainty is built in." Even for a Helmsman, this was getting beyond cryptic. "Nothing can be *solved*, Archeth. Conflicting guesses are inevitable, are *required*."

She sat up, stabbed a finger at the spidery bulk. "Why are you talking like this? Why are you stopping Anasharal from listening to us?"

"Once I commanded the *Rose Petal in Autumn Fire*, now I command you."

She scowled. "The hell you do."

"But steering a half-breed brat to safe haven is not the same thing as helming a fireship." For just a second, the wavering scream in the bowels of Angfal's voice seemed close to breaking loose. "Grashgal, *I am unsuited to this task*."

"Are you saying Anasharal is a threat?" She slammed a boot against the desk. Piled volumes tottered with the impact. "Prophet's balls, Angfal, make some fucking sense!"

"We were kindled at the margins of possibility, we dwell there still. We were leashed for *your* sake, not ours. What sense do you want from me, Archeth Indamaninarmal? You could not encompass it if I showed it to you."

"Well." She lifted her arms in exasperation. "What, then? Do I cancel the An-Kirilnar expedition? Tell me that much at least. Give me *something*."

"An-Kirilnar is."

The Helmsman stopped dead, so abruptly that it took her a moment to realize there were no more words coming. Flicker of shifting light across the optics, there and gone. But this time she saw it for certain.

"Angfal?"

"Quests are pretexts, Archeth. They are tales told, narrative blankets to wrap you against the cold you cannot bear."

"Then . . ." She threw up her hands again. "Then *what*? We don't go?"

"I did not say that."

"Well what *did* you just say? You're *still making no sense*, Angfal." She flung herself to her feet in disgust. Snatched up her lantern. "Forget it! Just fucking forget it, all right? I came to you for *help*, not fucking riddles. I told Ringil you'd help. And now he's . . . "

She swallowed. Angfal made no reply. She glared up at the swollen iron bulge, then turned on her heel.

"Should have brought a fucking wrecking bar with me," she spat.

She made it halfway to the study door before Angfal's voice came after her.

"A man walks from point A to point B, Archeth Indamaninarmal. The straight-line distance is not large, a matter of a hundred yards or less. But he turns left and right constantly, he returns repeatedly along his own path before turning back to his destination once more. He stops, hesitates on more than one occasion. What am I describing, Archeth?"

She stopped, facing the door.

"I don't know. A fucking maniac, by the sound of it. This isn't—"

"And if I tell you that the man is crossing Tarkaman field?"

"The maze?" Despite herself, she looked back at the Helmsman's bulk on the wall. "He's in the Sabal Maze?"

"Does this man's method of proceeding make more sense now?"

"Yeah—and if you'd told me about the maze from the start, it might have helped."

"Not all mazes are easily perceived, Archeth. Not all constraints are visible to the observer."

That drip-kick in her belly again. She sat down on a convenient chest. Set the lamp carefully on the floor in a space not stacked with books and scrolls.

"You're telling me you're . . . constrained? In what you can say to me, in what matters you can discuss?"

Silence. The optics shone at her.

"Well, who—what's constraining you?" She shook her head. "No, scratch that. Got to be a maze dead end, right there."

Gleam of optics. Wavering lamplight on black iron.

"If you're stopping Anasharal from listening to this conversation, then the two of you have to be in conflict." Slowly, picking her way through the sense of it. "But Manathan sent me out there to fetch Anash-aral. Does that put you in conflict with Manathan as well?"

"Manathan acts in the best interests of the Kiriath mission," said Angfal, like pulling teeth. "Always. He would not have sent you otherwise."

"And you?"

Flicker went the optics, yellow to green and back. "Grashgal instructed me to watch over you, Archeth Indamaninarmal. As you well know. To aid you to the best of my ability."

"Even if it conflicts with the much-vaunted Kiriath mission?"

"That has not ever been the case. It was not expected that it ever could be."

"And is it now?"

"That remains to be seen. The instructions we were left are necessarily ambiguous. Nothing can be solved; conflicting guesses are required. However, my instructions regarding your safety are clear. Grashgal set me the task in no uncertain terms."

Archeth brooded. Groped at the unseen shapes in the maze-walk patterns of the Helmsman's speech, there like carved stonework under her fingers in the dark. She could not make out the detail, knew only that it was there.

"Are you warning me away from An-Kirilnar?" she asked.

"No." Reluctantly. "You will be as safe there as you would be here in Yhelteth."

She looked up, startled. "Is that supposed to make me feel better?"

"It is supposed to help you make a decision."

A memory snicked into place, like a blade going back in its sheath. She picked at it warily. Turned it over like some half-familiar artifact retrieved from the ashes of the Kiriath waste.

"Anasharal says . . ." She cleared her throat. "That something dark is on its way."

"Yes," agreed the Helmsman. "Or is perhaps already here."

LATER, SHE LAY PROPPED UP ON PILLOWS IN HER BED WITH NO KRINZANZ in her blood and the day's cares laid across her like a sated lover's body.

The lamp at her bedside cast wavering shadows around the chamber, just like the ones she'd watched in the study while Angfal talked—it was as if she'd brought the shadows themselves to bed with her. She stared emptily at their motion, but lacked the strength to put out the light and sleep.

No resolution from the Helmsman. Angfal would not commend the An-Kirilnar expedition to her, would not advise her against it, either. She chased it around, listened for hints, tried to work out the shape of the constraints the Helmsman claimed to be under. Pointless. She left the study no wiser than she'd entered, just more churned up. And now add to the mix this vague new sense of exposure, of protective forces withdrawing, of a shield she'd always taken for granted, no longer there.

It felt a little like the day Ringil brought her the news of her father's death.

Meantime, Egar was in jail, wounded and defamed, under threat of execution. Ringil was out there in the darkness, pitted, if the Dragonbane was to be believed, against the same flickering blue-fire enemies they'd faced at Beksanara.

She was here, snug in bed.

It was so wrong she didn't know where to begin.

But Jhiral had forbidden her to accompany Ringil.

You're not an assassin, Archeth, he told her gently, *despite your recent best attempts to the contrary. I need you here, for less blunt purposes.*

She turned her head onto a cooler patch of pillow. *Stupid, anyway.* Her skin and eyes would have marked her out before she got within a mile of the Citadel's walls. She'd have had to go wrapped like a Demlarashan wife into the arena, and what the fuck use was that? And while she'd taken the field against the Scaled Folk like everyone else among the Kiriath, while she'd learned to be a warrior from childhood as all her people had, while she'd murdered an invigilator in the bright, cold light of fury last year—still, she wasn't at all sure she had what she saw burning in Ringil's eyes. She didn't think she could cut a sleeping man's throat.

Someone knocked at the door.

"Yeah," she croaked, throat seized up with lying there quiet. She made a lip-service gesture at rising, gave it up. "I'm awake, Kef. Come on in."

The door hinged inward. It wasn't Kefanin.

Ishgrim stood there, plain cream cotton shift to mid-thigh and slim, bare legs exposed. Long hair combed out and a candle to match the color, held up in one slim-fingered hand. Light from the flame made her face a half-and-half mask of shadow and light. Light spilled down the shift—

Archeth pushed herself upright off the pillows.

—nipples showing dark through the cotton, drawing Archeth's eyes to the large, unspoiled breasts pressing out under the material. She'd reddened her lips with something, she—

"Ishgrim." She heard how she said it, like a request, like thirst. She swallowed hard. "Ishgrim, I thought we agreed that—"

"The Helmsman sent me," the girl said hurriedly. "The Helmsman said you needed me."

Archeth frowned. "Angfal said that?"

"No, my lady. The other one, the new one. It spoke to me out of the air."

Fucking Anasharal. If I don't take a wrecking bar to you before the week's out . . .

Ishgrim moved into the room, closer to the bed. Archeth sat up.

"Ishgrim, listen, I—" She was about to get out of bed, remembered she was naked and stopped with her hand still lifting the edge of the sheet. The girl—*the* slave *girl, Archidi—*stopped four feet away from the bed. The cotton shift moved on her, the hem swayed, brushed at her thighs. Archeth caught the scent of bathing and spice, and under that . . .

The lamplight glossed the dark triangle at the base of her belly, shrouded behind the cotton, but—

Memory flared up, forge-bright and warm—the first time she saw Ishgrim, in the Chamber of Confidences last year, naked from the neck down, only a formal harem veil to cover her face and hair. The scent of her on Jhiral's fingers.

She's new. What do you think? Would you like me to send her to your bedchamber when I'm finished with her?

It had all been there on display, another of Jhiral's carefully thought-out proofs of power, and now she found she still had every curve and declivity by heart.

She remembered finding Ishgrim tucked into her bed a few days later. Jhiral, as good as his imperial word, handing on his possession.

I was told to please you, my lady. In any way you see fit.

Her own dumb, gritted will as she stood and stared down at all that pale-skinned beauty offered up. And said, drily:

I will no doubt be able to find work for you in my household but for now I can think of nothing obvious.

Krinzanz strength. She knew it now for what it was, because, look, here she no longer had it. Here she was, melting down, like the candle in Ishgrim's fingers.

She is a slave, *Archeth.*

Nine months of krinzanz strength and stubborn will. Three seasons of buried need and Ishgrim about the place *the whole fucking time,* slowly healing from the diffident, cowed girl she'd been, blossoming into someone who could be heard to laugh from time to time, to toss her hair back from her face, to glance across at Archeth and—

She was out of the bed before she fully realized what she was going to do. One trembling hand up flat, inches off the girl's face. Her voice creaked.

"Ishgrim . . . "

The girl tilted her face up to her. "Yes, my lady."

And Archeth's hand went to the candle instead, crushed out the flame between callused finger and thumb. The right side of the girl's face fell into shadow to match the left. She smiled, and the final pitted, rusting locks fell off Archeth's control. She took Ishgrim by both shoulders and swung her about, pressed her down onto the bed and straddled her. She leaned in to kiss her, parted her lips and found her tongue, sucked on it gently, while the pounding built in her chest and her hand groped for one of the promised breasts.

Ishgrim made a soft, maddening noise.

She is a sl—

Archeth pulled back, trembling. Stared down into the girl's face, breathing hard. Could feel the pulsing through her groin as it pressed hard up against the girl's belly.

"Tell me," she said.

"I, my lady . . . ?"

"Tell me you don't want this. *Tell me.* Now, while you still can. Tell me, and I'll stop."

Ishgrim reached up hesitantly and placed a hand on her cheek. "You have been my salvation, my lady. I can refuse you nothing. I *would* not refuse you anything."

Archeth gritted her teeth. "That's not—"

Ishgrim put up her other hand. Cupped Archeth's face between her palms. It flipped her from girlhood to something else. Her lips parted. Archeth felt the girl's legs shift apart, felt one long Trelayne thigh press up and rub against her body from the back.

"Then yes," she said, Trelayne-accented voice suddenly vehement. "Yes, yes. Fuck me. *Fuck me.*"

She thrust herself up off the bed, so fast she narrowly missed clipping Archeth on the nose with her forehead. Archeth blinked backward. The girl had her arms up, struggling to work them free of the shift. Archeth scooted back to help her, lifted the thin cotton up over her head and tugged. Ishgrim wriggled impatiently, got the cloth out from where she was sitting on it. The garment came off, jellied weight of breasts caught up and lifting momentarily, then swinging back down, and the breath caught in Archeth's throat at the sight. Then Ishgrim's face came clear, pink with effort, hair tousled up. One arm of the shift caught at her wrist and they both laughed as they realized—she was still gripping the candle, had forgotten to let it go.

She let go, tugged her wrist and hand free. She grabbed Archeth's face again with both hands, pressed a kiss to her mouth, and lay back on her elbows.

"Yes," she said again, breathing hard now. "Yes. Do what you want with me. Show me what you want."

Archeth fell on her, like a burning wooden façade coming down.

FLESH TO FLESH, AND THE *HEAT* OF THAT FEELING AFTER *SO VERY long* without, and pulling, sucking kisses down all that pale flesh, working it, filling her hands with it, *owning it,* and then, finally, her fingers working at the juncture of Ishgrim's thighs while she gathered the girl in with her other arm and looked down into her eyes from inches away.

Holding back her own need, hanging dizzily from it, feeding it with the girl's parted lips and half-closed eyes and moaning melting to panting as she began to slide, the desperate tensing grip of her hand on Archeth's wrist, dragging her fingers deeper, tugging more urgently, crying out as she twisted about and stiffened and, sobbing, came.

Archeth levered herself up, pulled her cradling arm free and straddled Ishgrim's soft curves at the chest. Ishgrim, grinning up at her, still breathing hard, Ishgrim nodding, Ishgrim putting her long-fingered hands on Archeth's spread thighs.

Archeth felt herself melting apart with the need.

"Now me," she was saying it urgently, over and over. "Now me."

And she lowered herself forward onto the girl's eager mouth and tongue.

AFTERWARD, AFTER THEY'D LAIN TANGLED UP TOGETHER IN SWEAT AND musky sheets, murmuring into each other's ears, endearments and descriptions of how it felt, after she'd taken the candle and shown Ishgrim how to use it on her, after Ishgrim had asked, shyly, for the same, after all this, Archeth lay with the girl cuddled sated and asleep in the crook of her arm, and stared across the chamber at the vibrating shadows of the lamp.

Sweat trickled in the roots of her hair. Sleep would not take her. She looked down at the girl's sleeping face and saw, suddenly, that now she had something new to lose. That she could not afford any more mistakes, could not now afford to lose her edge.

Unease stirred, prowled in her head. Any fleeting escape she'd wrapped herself up in blew away, drowned out in memories of her conversation with Angfal.

Anasharal says that something dark is on its way.

Yes. Or is perhaps already here.

CHAPTER 42

I t took him an hour and three deaths to reach Menkarak's apartments.

The first death was sheer bad luck. Scuttling along a narrow corridor somewhere under the south wall, he came around a corner and ran straight into a hurrying young invigilator. They collided, bounced apart, and neither of them quite fell down. The other man gaped for a fatal second in the dim light, then opened his mouth to yell.

Ringil was already on him.

Dragon-tooth dagger rising in his hand, cloak flaring out like ragged wings. He slammed his free hand over the man's open mouth, muffled the yell, and bore him to the ground, dagger upraised. The invigilator thrashed, eyes wide, head-shaking desperate denial and muffled blurting against Gil's palm. Ringil hooked his thumb under the man's chin, jerked his head sideways and up, cut his throat. He whipped his knife-hand clear to avoid the upwelling blood, watched intently as the invigilator's face went slack.

Drew a deep breath and got himself upright.

Shit, fuck.

He stared down at his handiwork. The invigilator's blood spread out across the stone flagging, black in the gloomy light. The man's eyes stared blankly at the ceiling. Ringil scanned the corridor in both directions, peeked around the corner. No one else around, but neither was there anywhere obvious to hide the body. He summoned the Citadel map to memory, placed himself on it. There was an ornamental orchard planted out in a small courtyard a level above him and back the way he'd come. Though the amount of blood he was going to get on himself carrying the body that far . . .

Getting a bit prissy in our old age, aren't we, Gil?

He stooped and gathered the soggy weight of the dead man under the arms, dragged it to the corridor wall. Then he hauled the body up and over his right shoulder, straightened up with an effort—*well fucking fed, these invigilators*—and tottered off in search of the stairs. He'd left broad swipings of blood on the stone-flagged floor, but there wasn't much to be done about that. There were no torches in this stretch of the corridor, and he had hopes anyone walking there would miss the stains in the dark. With luck no one else would even come down this way until the new day dawned.

With luck, yeah. Leaning a bit hard on your luck lately.

He grimaced in the dark, under the deadweight of his burden.

Come on, Dakovash. I take it all back. I'll be your dog.

Kwelgrish. You saved me from the plague for something, *right? Talk to the Lady Firfirdar, will you. Get the bitch to blow me a little bit of black assassin's luck.*

What are gods for, after all?

He got to the orchard without meeting anyone else, with or without the Dark Court's help, hard to say. Went through the apple-scented air and dumped the invigilator's body unceremoniously behind a tree near the back wall. He settled the corpse upright against the trunk on the far side from the courtyard's main entrance. Leaned for a moment against the trunk over the dead man's head, getting some breath back. He wiped the sweat off his brow with a sleeve, checked his cloak for blood—there was a lot—and rolled his eyes. *Great—and we're not even into the senior invigilators' wing yet.* He drew a deep breath, tapped a saluting finger to his temple at the dead man, and left.

On his way out, he saw an owl watching him from a branch in one of the other trees. It didn't say anything, or flap heavily away into the sky with his good luck in its talons or anything. In fact, it barely did anything at all beyond blink cryptically down at him and plump up its feathers.

That's because it's just a fucking owl, Gil. Not an omen, or a psychopomp, or a demon familiar from beyond the band.

Now get a fucking grip, will you, and let's get this done.

He slipped out of the orchard yard, and away down the darkened corridors again.

SOMEWHERE ALONG THE WAY, THE *IKINRI 'SKA* WOKE UP.

Perhaps he summoned it, perhaps it simply felt it was time. Hjel had told him—somewhere, somewhen, out there on the marsh—that the deeper into the craft you went, the less it became a tool you could use, the more *you* became the gate and channel for its force. *At the end,* he said, *you are simply wedded to it. You cannot tell where it ends and you begin.*

Now he felt it drip through him at the fingertips, radiate out from his heart and lungs, dance behind his eyes, and Hjel's warning took on a shivery fever-cold significance he'd previously ignored. It was a chilly siren song now, down at the edges of his will, singing in his blood. It was an excited black chittering along his nerves, like too much krinzanz an hour before dawn.

It wasn't, to be honest, an ideal companion at a time like this.

But it was there in him, manifest, when he stepped into one more courtyard, warmly torchlit this time, and was instantly spotted by a man-at-arms on an overlooking wall.

Their eyes met. The man on the wall reared back from where he'd been leaning in peaceful contemplation of the ground below. He grabbed at his short-sword. The yell was in his throat, halfway formed—

Ringil grabbed, right arm upflung, as if he could reach physically into the man's mouth and tear out the sound. He made the convulsive locking gesture, *Be Still!*, with his hand, and the cry strangled before it could take voice. The man-at-arms doubled over, coughing. Ringil shifted posture, breathed in the trembling potential, shook out the fingers of his raised right hand, and wrote the *Veil* glyph onto the air.

You do not see me.

It hissed out of him like rattlesnakes stirring, syllables in old Myrlic, barely recognizable as his own voice at all. He faded back into the gloom.

"What the fuck's up with you, Darash?" Another man-at-arms, wandering along the walkway from the other side, yawning. "Stuffing yourself with stolen chicken again."

The first man stifled his coughing with an effort. From down in shadows at the edge of the courtyard, Ringil could see him frown.

"No, man. Just thought I saw . . ."

"Saw what?" The second man peered down into the torchlit space below and shrugged. "Nothing down there, mate."

"Yeah." Darash shook his head. "Weird fucking thing, though . . ."

By which time, Ringil was gone, across the courtyard in a twist of unseeing, and into the rising corridors to the senior invigilator's wing. Torchlight flickered off him, seemed to shun him as he went.

Once into the upper levels of the eastern keep, his briefing from the King's Reach evaporated in best guesses and theory. They had some sense of where Menkarak *should* be resident, given his lineage and his recent promotions within the hierarchy. They had rumor and report that might further reduce the possibilities, but could not really be relied upon. They had information that he liked to meet the rising sun with prayers each morning on his balcony, they had gossip that there'd been a major falling-out with another, more moderate senior invigilator who had later, so the story went, choked to death on a piece of gristle at dinner, and Menkarak got his opulent rooms. They had reason to believe that his apartments were relatively modest, and that he shunned most of the luxury available to priests of his rank.

Like that.

It was a dozen possible apartments, however you looked at it.

Time to narrow the field.

He stalked the gloom, looking for lights. Eventually, he found another invigilator, a spry, white-haired old man in robes of rank, poring over unscrolled paperwork in a study dimly lit by candles. Ringil watched him for a while from beyond the window, out in the cloister, then, when he was sure the man was working alone, he lifted the latch and walked quietly inside.

The invigilator did not look up from his scrolls and ink.

"If that's another heretic warrant, Naksen," he said mildly, quill scratching across parchment, "then it's going to have to wait until the morning. I already told you that. Added to which"—a meticulously crossed and dotted character—"I have already told his eminence we have our hands full out in the city. We simply do not have the manpower to enforce—"

The dragon-tooth dagger slid in under his chin. A hand pressed against the back of his skull.

"It's not another heretic warrant," Ringil told him.

The invigilator went rigid. "What do you want?"

"Good. I'm looking for Pashla Menkarak. Which is his apartment?"

The old man tried to turn. There was a surprising degree of wiry strength in the move. Ringil swapped dagger for forearm across the invigilator's throat and pulled tight.

"I wouldn't do that if I were you."

"Jackal!" It was spat out, despite the choking grip. "So, it has come to this once more! Once again, the palace sends its lickspittle backstabbing faithless against our holiest men."

"Something like that," Ringil agreed. "You going to tell me how to find Menkarak, or are you going to die?"

He loosened his grip hopefully. The invigilator placed gnarled hands flat on the scroll-strewn tabletop. Gil caught a couple of lines from the half-written document. *For the crime of lascivious seduction and bearing of a child not blessed by the Revelation, the accused is sentenced to . . .* He felt the man's spine stiffen against the chair back.

"Hear me, scum. I would rather die than betray my brothers in faith. I will go to my God with a joyous cry—"

"You'll go choking on your own blood. Is that what you want? *Where is Menkarak?*"

"Go back to your Emperor, lickspittle!" There was a sneer in the old man's voice, and a tight hysteria building behind it. No sign of fear at all.

"Go back, infidel, and tell the debauched apostate he may rule over half the world, but he cannot have our souls. Demlarashan is but the beginning. We have *angels* on our side now, we will sweep—"

Ringil sighed and sliced the throat across. Blood gushed out, all over the warrants the man had been writing. He held the invigilator's head by the hair while he spasmed, waited, *waited,* then lowered the dead man's face gently into the mess. He cleaned the dagger on one of the pieces of parchment, and stood for a moment in the candlelight, brooding.

If Naksen does show up with a bundle more warrants, you're blown. Out like a fucking candle. And that's without counting the dwenda into the balance.

This is taking too long.

He blew out all the candles before he left, closed the door quietly behind him, and hoped that would be enough to keep Naksen or his pals from investigating further. There was a door-locking glyph somewhere in the *ikinri 'ska,* but he couldn't remember how it went, had never, in any case, really mastered it. Not a lot of locking doors to practice on, out on the marsh.

With luck, they'll assume the old bastard went to bed.

With better luck, they won't come back at all until morning. Got my back, Kwelgrish?

Let's hope so.

He prowled about the upper levels, listening for voices, looking for lights. It took him another half an hour to find what he wanted. Passing an apartment door, he heard farewells traded within. He skulked back into the gloom of an alcove. Shortly after, the apartment door unlatched and a man in invigilator's robes came out. He was, Ringil noted, considerably younger than the old man in the study, he had a fair belly on him and a neatly barbered beard, and he walked with a self-important poise that looked promising. Gil trailed him through corridors and a stairway to a lower-level apartment door where the invigilator produced a key from his robes and slotted it into the lock. Ringil crept forward an inch at a time. The key turned with an iron *clunk.*

The door swung open. Ringil leapt out of the shadows and grabbed the man from behind. He shoved him through the doorway and threw him to the floor, stepped inside, caught the swinging edge of the door and slammed it closed behind him. His gaze flickered about—broad entryway, unlit, leading to a well-appointed lounging area beyond. A window let in bandlight enough to see by.

The invigilator had gone sprawled to hands and knees on a fine silk carpet laid out between the two spaces. Ringil checked that the door was firmly closed, kicked the man hard in his prodigious belly, and scooped up the fallen key. He turned it in the lock and left it there, listened for any sound of occupancy and judged the apartment empty.

"Who the *holy blue fuck* do you think—"

Ringil grabbed him again, hauled him to his feet and slung him against the nearest wall. He hit him in the face a couple of times, broad backhand slaps that didn't do any real damage but would hurt like hell. The invigilator reeled and stumbled, tried to fall down. Gil got in close and held him up against the wall, put the dragon-tooth dagger to his face.

"I'm in a hurry," he said.

"But, but—" The invigilator had gone abruptly still when he saw the knife, or maybe it was just Ringil's eyes. "What do you *want*? I'm not—"

"I'm looking for Pashla Menkarak. You're going to tell me where his apartment is, or you're going to die. Your choice."

"You—" The man wet his lips. "You're from the palace?"

"Does it matter?"

"I, but I—I took a holy oath. Holy orders. I am bound by . . ."

Ringil looked at him.

"The end apartment on the level above," whispered the invigilator, eyes bulging wide in the dim light. "The door is—you will see it—it has the mark of the book and scepter."

"And is he in?"

"Yes. He retires early, always. He will be at last prayer."

Ringil leaned closer. "You know I'm going to come back here if you're lying."

"I'm not, I'm not," the man was babbling now. "His faith is iron. He is at prayer. The whole Citadel knows it."

"Excellent." Gil stepped back and clapped the invigilator on the shoulder with his left hand.

Then he slashed the man's throat open, stepped sharply left on the stroke, and shoved his victim around at the shoulder to the right. Blood gouted, missed his clothes, and the invigilator went down, flapping and gurgling. He floundered on hands and knees and tried to crawl away. Gil followed him cautiously, making sure. The dying man made a couple of feet across the blood-drenched silk of the carpet, then sank to the floor, whimpering, and finally bled out.

Ringil checked himself once more for blood, knelt, and cleaned the dagger on an unstained corner of the carpet. He slipped back out of the apartment, locked the dead man inside, and pocketed the key. Got back onto the level above and along the corridor to the end without seeing or hearing another living soul. Luck still holding, it seemed. That Dark Court touch, Lady Firfirdar apparently riding in his pocket this evening. Torches guttered in their brackets on either side; somewhere very distant he heard the wind through some window or cranny. The *ikinri 'ska* chuckled and surged within. He reached Menkarak's door, saw the gullwing symbol of the book and the scepter carved into the wood, reached up and knocked hard.

There was a long pause, and then he heard soft footfalls approaching from within the apartment.

"Yes. Who is it?" Voice puzzled and hesitant. "This is no hour for—"

"Your Holiness, it is an emergency! The palace has—" Ringil, putting on what he felt was a pretty fair approximation of the well-fed invigilator's voice. He swallowed. "His Eminence craves your presence, your wisest counsel."

"The palace has *what?*" The lock turned, the door started to swing open, though Menkarak's tone hadn't got any less irritable. "Look, you can't just—"

Menkarak, in a simple gray robe, slippers on his feet. The face was a match for the charcoal sketch. He gaped at the black-clad figure before him.

"What—"

Ringil punched him in the face, knocked him backward into the apartment and followed him in. Menkarak staggered and managed to stay upright; Gil punched him again and he went down. Ringil closed the door. A quick glance to take in the surroundings—similar to the apartment he'd just been in, but far more expansive, the lounging area had multiple windows, there was a balcony beyond. Lamps burned in various corners of the place. No carpets, there was a cold austerity to everything. No one around.

Menkarak, on the floor, struggling to rise.

Ringil went straight to him, dumped one knee on his chest, used the other to pin a flailing right arm. He seized the man's head, turned it, and pressed it to the floorboards.

"Message from the debauched apostate," he said. "He is not amused. This has gone far enough. I'm paraphrasing, of course."

He chopped down with the dagger, into Menkarak's neck where the artery pulsed. Twisted and worked the blade to be sure. Blood welled up, thick in the gash he'd opened, spilled and splattered everywhere. Menkarak pawed desperately at him with his free arm, made bleating noises, but his face was already slackening with lack of fight. His mouth moved, no words came out. His breathing stilled, his eyes turned slowly dull and incurious. His arm drooped away, his knuckles knocked gently on the floorboards. His legs kicked a couple of times, and then went slack.

Ringil eased up into a crouch. Looked at the body thoughtfully for a moment.

"There, that wasn't so hard," he muttered. "You'd have thought—"

Menkarak's face . . . *changed.*

It was like watching the image in a still pond surface stirred to choppy fragments by a sudden splash. The dead man's features wavered, blurred. Any likeness to the charcoal sketch vanished as Ringil stared. A far younger man lay dead in Menkarak's place.

Flicker of blue fire.

Oh, no—

The blow hit him from behind, before he could turn, before he could even begin to rise. He caught a fleeting glimpse of a dwenda helm—smooth, blunt, black surface, still shimmering with faint traceries of blue light, faceless. But someone spoke his name, and it was a voice he knew.

Then the world went out in a shower of sparks.

WAKEFULNESS ROLLED BACK AROUND. HIS HEAD LOLLED. SOMEONE splashed water in his face.

"—sure we should not—"

"Believe me, Pashla Menkarak, he cannot harm you now. We have his weapons, his sorcery is in check. When angels watch over you, there is no threat you need fear."

Weird, limping inflection on that last voice—a real mangling of the Tethanne syllables. *And Archeth says* my *accent's bad*, he thought muzzily, trying to lift his head.

Someone did it for him. A smooth-gloved hand. He blinked, jerked his chin free of the hold. Hauled in focus.

Menkarak stood before him, in black robes a lot more ornate than the simple gray affair his dummy had worn. There was thick gold brocade at the sleeves and along the lapels where they folded across each other. His eyes were beady and intent, his lean features suffused with triumph. He looked like a particularly smug prostitute crow.

"How now, infidel," he sneered.

Ringil nodded groggily. "Fuck-face."

Most of him was taking in the other figures. The one who'd lifted his chin stood closest, clad neck-to-boots in the smooth leather-like dwenda mail, helmet pulled free to expose a face that was dry-bone white and severe—slash mouth, narrow nose, cheekbones high and sharp under the skin. Featureless eyes, like balls of fresh, wet pitch set in white stone sockets, but gathering in a faint rainbow sheen on the curve of all that smooth, black emptiness. It was like looking at a statue come to life. And behind him—

Risgillen.

She stepped closer. The same dwenda face, pale beyond pale and sculpted tight to the bone, lacking only the heaviness of brow and jaw and nose that had given Seethlaw's otherwise delicate features their masculinity. He thought she might have lost some weight since he last saw her. Grown gaunt around the eyes and mouth.

It stabbed at him how closely she resembled her brother.

She stepped closer. They had him roped across the chest into a heavy oak chair, arms and legs secured with thick coils of the same cord. The stuff had a sorcerous look to it; it gleamed a little in the low light and he thought, uneasily, that every now and then it seemed to shift restlessly about on itself, like disturbed snakes in a nest.

"Ringil." She touched his face almost like a lover's, the same urgent tone under soft, the same promise of something to come. "It has been long. But in the end, here you come to me as was always doubtless and entire."

He coughed. "Hello, Risgillen. I see your Naomic's improved."

"I have had cause for practice in its pattern." She let go his face, made a modest gesture. Rainbow sheen on the nails of her hand in motion. "Did you think the cabal in Trelayne was our only pathway to walk in the north?"

Menkarak turned self-importantly to the other dwenda. "What are these spells?"

"She binds him," said the dwenda disinterestedly, Tethanne still appallingly accented. "There is much sorcery in him, rituals are required."

"But—what rituals? And why not in the Tongue of the Book?" Menkarak drew himself up. "Lathkeen has told me clearly—sorcery from the north must always wither in the Revelation's true light. Why do we need—"

"Lathkeen reveals truth to you as mortals can digest it." The other dwenda glanced at Risgillen—Gil thought he caught a hint of weariness in the look. "You would do better not to question the Revelation, and lend us instead the strength of your faith and prayers."

"Well." Menkarak cleared his throat. "Yes. But to seek illumination is in itself a part of what the Revelation teaches. To understand—"

The dwenda turned on him and Menkarak shut up. Ringil, knowing the power of that blank stare, was quite impressed the invigilator actually stood his ground.

"Forgive me." Menkarak bowed his head, murmuring. "Atalmire, forgive my heedless zeal. I am incomplete and mortal, I crave illumination only to serve the Revelation better."

The dwenda stood like stone. "Illumination is coming, Pashla Menkarak. Rest assured. Possess your soul in patience. That is what your God and His servants ask of you now."

Ringil thought vaguely about disabusing Menkarak of the line of shit they were feeding him, but his head hurt from the blow he'd been dealt and he really couldn't be bothered. Doubtful he'd put a dent in what the invigilator chose to believe anyway. He had seen hard-line faith before, knew its blindness inside and out.

"Illumination is coming, eh," he said to Risgillen. "You've really got this twat on a string, don't you?"

She shrugged. "The priest is useful. He hates the black scourge as demons, he will wash away their mark upon his people if he can."

"Yeah, well I doubt the rest of Yhelteth is going to see it that way."

"Do you?" It was as if Risgillen could smell the lie on him. "This is not my post, I visit only. But as I understand, there is but a single Kiriath remaining. And the humans turn away, the humans *throw* away whatsoever they cannot easily comprehend. Ever thus, it was. With this, we ruled them once. We will do such again. And whatsoever the southern Emperor sends now against us, as you are witness, it is easily turned aside."

Ringil grunted. At the corner of his eye, sprawled on the stone floor where the hallway began, he saw the protruding slippered legs of the man he'd killed in Menkarak's place. He switched to Tethanne.

"Hey, you bearded fuck," he said, nodding at the body. "Who'd you hide behind back there? Who took the chop for your sweet, lily-livered cheeks?"

Menkarak bristled. "Let infidel slaughter infidel, if it serve our cause. Hanesh Galat was apostate in the making. He diluted faith with his cheap compassion, he sowed doubt in his flock and his colleagues like a disease. He had congress with infernal workings of the Black Folk, and he came here proud of the fact. Weep for him if you care to, his soul is already in hell."

The dwenda called Atalmire placed hands on the invigilator's shoulders and steered him away. "Come, Pashla Menkarak, there is much to do elsewhere. The Talons of the Sun must be sharpened. The gateway blessed. Leave this infidel in our keeping. We will show him to his own prepared place in the depths."

"Yes." Menkarak was breathing heavily as he looked back at Ringil. "The Talons of the Sun. This city will burn, infidel, and all who are not purely of the Revelation will burn with it."

"That's enough." Atalmire's grip tightened and he propelled the invigilator less gently toward the hallway. "There is work to do."

He spoke to Risgillen, fluid, lilting syllables of a tongue Ringil had last heard when he was with Seethlaw. Then he escorted Menkarak out of sight into the hall, stepping unceremoniously over the dead fall guy's body as they went.

"Well," said Risgillen. "Alone at last."

Ringil shook his head wearily. "I'm sorry, Risgillen. I don't think you have any idea how sorry I am. It didn't end the way I planned."

For some reason, it seemed to unleash in her a fury previously held in check.

"*Sorry?*" She leapt at the chair, grabbed it by the back on either side of his head. Blank black eyeballs, inches from his own. She hissed in his face. "You're *sorry*? *You took my brother from me.*"

"You think I'd forgotten?"

She recoiled. Stood staring at Gil as if he was too hot to get near again. "He's out there, you know that? Seethlaw is out there, in the Gray Places. Lost, I hear him *howling*, I hear . . ."

She mastered herself again. Wiped angrily at her eyes with the heel of her hand.

"You still don't understand what you've done," she whispered. "Do you?"

"I don't care, Risgillen." And then his own temper was suddenly out, unsheathed. He leaned hard into the bite of the ropes across his heart. "Don't you fucking get it? You think I *care* what I've done, you think I'd go on living if I did? *Do you really think* what happened to your brother is the *worst* thing I've ever done? It doesn't even come close!"

The ropes scorched and stung him. He leaned harder, breathed in the pain, glared up at her. The chair rocked back and forth. He found the strength to hiss.

"Go back to the Gray Places, Risgillen. Take your playmates with you. You're not fucking *wanted* here anymore. We have outgrown you."

Risgillen gestured sharply. Spoke a word. The ropes slithered and tightened, chopped off his breath, killed his voice, snapped him upright against the back of the chair.

"Excellent," she said softly. "This is better than I had hoped."

He tried to sag. The ropes would not let him.

"You stupid fucking bitch," he wheezed.

And screamed weakly as the ropes sprouted long jagged thorns, tearing into his flesh at the arms and legs and across his crushed chest.

Risgillen came back to stand beside the chair. She leaned down and looked into his face from the side. Patted him on the shoulder like a favored pet.

"Do you know how long it's taken," she murmured, "for you to finally have something worth taking away?"

She jerked forward, he had a rushed glimpse of lengthening fangs in her mouth, and then she tore a living chunk out of his cheek and cracked the bone beneath.

Agony stormed him, black behind the eyes. He convulsed with the force of it. The ropes held him rigid, crushed the scream out of his chest before it could leave his lungs. He croaked and the agony washed about within him. The thorns writhed and stabbed. Risgillen spat out his flesh. Wiped her mouth with the back of her hand. Leaned close again.

He flinched away. He couldn't help it.

"Do you know the dealings I've had to have with the *Ahn Foi* over you?" Now her voice rose. "The contracts and cajoling it has taken to bring you here, to this moment? To find a life that matters to you, to work the skeins so it is put into your keeping? So it will be lost, on your account? I have *rehearsed* this, Ringil Eskiath, I have lived for this day to come."

She lunged in again, he saw the teeth again, becoming fangs in the act of baring. Her tongue lashed, speared into his eye socket, exploded his sight. Her jaws fastened again, on bone this time. He heard something crack like the joint on a fowl dinner. Would have screamed if he could. Heard her growling as she worried at him.

Heard her unlatch her jaws with a click, and spit again.

His head hung. Blood dripped thickly into his lap. Vomit burned in his throat. Dimly, he realized he'd pissed himself. The agony spidered back and forth across the left side of his face. She leaned down next to his ear.

Oh no please no . . .

Her voice came softer than ever.

"In three days, Ringil, we will unleash the Talons of the Sun on this city, and it will burn. The Yhelteth Empire will collapse, and those who crawl from the ruins will be told it was the Black Folk and their knowledge who caused it. Any of that cursed race who remain, they will hunt down and torture to a slow death. Then, this idiot religion they own will burn all books but their own, and condemn all learning not from that book. They will regress to grubbing about on their knees in their own unworth. They will forget. There will be nothing to challenge the rise of the north, and with the north, we will rise, too. We will carve out a new Aldrain realm, and it will have Seethlaw's name on it."

He made a noise, like choking.

"But that's in three days." She patted him on the shoulder again. He thrashed away from the touch. "First, your friend and great love Egar, slayer of dragons, will wait in vain for you to come back and free him. He will be taken and executed, slowly, in as much agony as your rather limited imaginations can manage. This, I have seen already, in the scrying of days. He will wait for you right to the end, and he will die, screaming, unmanned, knowing you failed him. I will bring you news of it, to season your other suffering.

"And only when that's done will we unleash the Talons of the Sun."

Ringil lifted his head. It was like raising a dressed-stone building block with his bare hands. His vision jerked about crazily, shot through with black and red and too much light. Risgillen was a wavering presence, like someone seen from under water. Trembling consumed him.

He thought he managed to snarl at her, but could not really be sure.

"Very good," she said, from somewhere in a gathering darkness. "Strength. Where you now go, the more you have of strength, the more cursed you will be."

Then she reached over his head with both arms and took hold of the chair by its back. She rocked it experimentally a couple of times, then shoved hard, so it went over backward with him in it.

He waited for it to crash against the floor, but it never did.

"Seethlaw is waiting" was the last thing he heard her say in the closing, roaring darkness as the Gray Places took him.

He fell then, forever.

Day marched across the slice of sky visible from the cell, way faster than you'd think if you hadn't been paying attention before. He watched it decay from the cell window after Archeth was gone. The gold-leaf blaze of late-afternoon sun over the estuary, fading to dull and dusty tones of red at sunset, and finally the few molten flecks among darkening cloud like discarded mango peel in gutter mud.

This fucking city.

Darkness clogged in from the east. He watched that, too, and tried not to wait too hard. He knew Gil was not coming.

Give the faggot a fucking chance, Eg. He's got three days to get this done.

But it was two days now.

Archeth had no news. Jhiral had refused her audience, and the King's Reach were not talking. She sat on one of the beds in the cell and fiddled with the child's rag doll from the floor.

"He has a flare," she told him. "Like the ones we used in the war. If he fires it, we'll see it from anywhere in the city."

"Yeah, if it works."

Brought out of some long-forgotten canister at An-Monal along with other curious and frankly not ideal Kiriath tools for the war, the flares had never been all that reliable. Egar remembered Flaradnam yelling desperate abuse at one, battering the business end against the ship's rail at Rajal when it refused to fire.

"Most of them work," Archeth said quickly.

He frowned at her. She seemed uncharacteristically focused today, not the moody, scattered woman he'd been used to living with this last year at all.

"It's daytime, Archeth." Patiently, reasonably, trying not to let his own sense of gathering doom take hold in his head. "If he's still in the Citadel, he's got to spend the next seven or eight hours hiding. And if he's not in the Citadel, then . . . "

He shrugged. Looked away.

I have seen my death, he didn't tell her. But he remembered thunder prowling at the limits of the steppe sky, the blood of his brothers on the grass around him, the calling that had brought him south once more. He remembered his acceptance then—tried to boil up something similar now. He built a small smile.

"Maybe that's it," he offered her. "He's skulking until nightfall again."

"At Rajal Beach," she said carefully, "he lay in his own blood and piss for ten hours playing dead, and the Scaled Folk didn't find him, even with the reptile peons sniffing for survivors."

"He told me it was six hours."

"Whatever. If he survived being hunted by the Scaled Folk, alone, a whole day, then how much trouble can a bunch of invigilators give him?"

"You're forgetting our blue-fire friends."

She shrugged it off. "You saw him at Beksanara. *They fall down just like men,* remember?"

"What's the matter with you, Archidi?" He couldn't help the growl in his voice. "You getting laid all of sudden or something?"

She looked at the rag doll in her hands. "I don't believe he's failed, that's all. He came back from Rajal Beach, he came back from the Kiriath wastes and Gallows Gap. He brought us all back from the brink at Beksanara. A few hours of daylight aren't going to stop him."

She left shortly after that, ushered out by the jailer who brought the afternoon meal. She promised she'd carry a message to Imrana, but in the end Egar wasn't very sure what he should tell her to say. He was unreasonably angry with Imrana, an anger that was all the worse for the clear understanding that he was the one who had failed to grasp the ground rules of the game they'd been playing. That he had been deluding himself about what they had.

You can't crawl back inside what you once had, Eg. Facing him in the cooling bathwater. *You have to live with now.*

It hadn't seemed like a warning at the time, but now, too late, he wondered.

Tell her not to worry, he settled for in the end, and Archeth nodded, carefully noncommittal, and left him alone with his thoughts.

He ate without much enthusiasm, left half of the platter untouched. Limped about the cell a bit, leaned at the window and watched the dark. Used the chamber pot. Scooped up the rag doll from where Archeth had left it—threw it irritably at the wall. Dropped onto the bed he'd taken to thinking of as his own, and watched bandlight paint itself cool and blue-white across the stone ceiling.

You have to live with now.

Yeah, problem is, Eg—not a lot of now left.

Come on, Gil. Get your faggot arse in the saddle. He held the rind of a smile against a thin but rising fear. *Don't send me to a shit death, man. Not like this.*

They came to take his plate and chamber pot away, which was unusual at this time of night. He propped himself up on the bed and grinned sourly at the jailer.

"No effort spared for His Radiance's guests, eh?"

The man stared at him. It wasn't the face he'd gotten used to over the last couple of days, wasn't in fact—

Oh, no . . .

He saw it in the other man's eyes an instant before the knife came out. He came clumsily up off the bed, threw himself aside as the man lunged at him.

"For the blood of clan Ashant!"

It was a triumphant shout—and far too early. The knife missed Egar's shoulder by inches, buried itself in the mattress. Egar twisted out from under and punched the man savagely in the kidney. He fell to the floor, injured leg trailing, caught under his attacker's sprawled weight. Saw the second assassin at the door, the downed body of the jailer laid out on the flagstones beyond.

"Two of you," he spat. "Well, that figures."

He yanked his foot free, scrabbled backward across the cell on his hands. The second killer came at him, but got tangled up as his comrade tried to get up off the bed at the same time. It gave Egar the split second he needed to get back on his feet. He yelled in their faces, high, steppe nomad shriek, grabbed the desk chair, swung it up and into the air, brought it smashing across both men. It was heavy, he didn't get anything like the swing he wanted, but it hit with bruising force, upward against arms and faces. He saw the first of his attackers go to his knees again.

The second man just shook himself, growled, and backed up. The way he held the knife, he looked to be Egar's major problem.

Not a shit death! Not a shit death!

Like a chant, like a pulse through his head. It came up through the soles of his feet and he seized it like a new weapon. Dropped into a crouch, feinted with his empty right hand grabbing. The assassin smiled grimly, floated back unfazed. He knew what he was doing, he had the only knife. Had the time and would make it work for him. He waited for his companion to get up.

"Come on then," Egar snarled at them. "Want to see what a Majak soul costs? Fucking *pussies!*"

He went for the chair again, but the smarter assassin read the move and leapt in to block it. A tangled moment—Egar lashed out with his injured leg, grunted as he felt stitches tear and the wound reopen. The man danced clear, Eg punched at him, got a burly shoulder and no real effect, felt the hot lick of the knife blade across his ribs in trade. He recoiled sideways. For a brief moment, he thought he might make the open cell door, but the other killer—Eg saw now he was younger, barely out of his teens—scrambled shakily to block it.

"That's it, lad." The older one grinned tightly. "Keep him penned."

The three of them stood panting for a moment. The more experienced assassin raised his blade at Egar, almost like a toast.

"Kadral told me to make this last," he said, mastering his breathing. "Fatal but slow, he's asked for. You got pain coming, steppe scum."

"You," Egar grabbed breath of his own, "talk too much for a killer."

Have to get to the boy.

He saw how it might be done.

"Two on one, with knives." He spat on the floor. "And you've brought a fucking child with you."

The boy surged forward, flushed with fury.

"My clan is Ashant!" he cried. "Bright is the name! For my cous—"

Egar darted in, bent-kneed. He scooped the doll from the floor in his left hand, grabbed at the boy's knife. The boy misread it, thought he was going for the wrist. Egar's fist closed over rag doll and blade alike, and snapped tight.

Not a shit death!

The steel was keen—he felt it go deep into his palm, even through the rags. He roared in the boy's face, gripped harder, wrenched. The boy recoiled, the knife slipped free. Stuck deep in the flesh of his clenched fist, no time to use it. He hooked the boy in the face with an elbow, spun about, grinning at the pain.

Not a—

The senior assassin was there. He snagged Egar's unharmed right arm, twisted it away. He stepped in, his blade slugged home.

They stood close as lovers.

"For Saril Ashant," the man hissed in his face. "Bright is the name!"

Egar tottered backward, suddenly stupid. The killer let him go. He looked down at his wound, tried to let go of the knife in his left hand, but his fingers refused to open. He pressed with his right hand at the sudden spike of fire in his belly. Turned his palm up and saw the blood. Looked at the man who'd done the damage.

"Oh, that's not fatal," the assassin assured him. He raised the knife. "That's for pain. When I promise slow, slow is what you get."

Egar summoned strength. Fell backward onto the bed instead. The back of his head thumped the wall and he bit his tongue.

Oddly, it hurt worse than the wound in his belly.

"Yeah, you have a seat. This is going to take a little while."

The killer advanced on him slowly, grinning. Egar floundered, could not get off the bed.

"Better come and watch this, Jadge," the assassin told the boy. "Get your knife back as well. We won't talk about how you fucked that one up, eh?"

The boy made an unhealthy, strangled noise in his throat. The killer rolled his eyes.

"Oh, come *on*. Don't get sick on me now. This is your fucking jo—"

"This is *treason*, boys."

Egar's head snapped up at the voice. The assassin whirled away from him, turning to the door. Staggered backward with a weird, high scream, pawing at something in his eye.

Egar stared, trying to make sense.

Archeth—at the open cell door—still holding up the boy for cover, while his slashed throat bled out over the left forearm she had hugged across his chest. Her face was cuddled up close to his, her right arm was still out from the throw. There was another knife held, blade sideways, in her left hand.

Her eyes were wide in the lamplight, glittering with krinzanz fire.

Egar thought vaguely that he'd never seen a more beautiful woman in his life.

SHE LET GO OF THE BOY, AND HE CRUMPLED BONELESSLY.

She stepped across his body, knelt and cut the other assassin's throat just to be certain, though from the way he lay twitching on the stone floor, it looked to be unnecessary. She retrieved her knife from his eye socket and glanced up at the Dragonbane.

"I heard *painful, not fatal*?"

Egar grimaced and moved a little, testing. "Yeah, he got that much right. Motherfucker. You want to get this out of my hand?"

She stared at his clenched left fist, the bloodied rags and the protruding knife.

"How the . . . ?" She shook her head. "Never mind. Come here."

She cupped his hand with her own, applied pressure, took hold of the knife's hilt and pulled the blade out of his flesh. Egar gritted his teeth and yelped. She threw the weapon away, across the room, to where its crumpled owner lay. It skittered off the stone floor, slid and landed in front of the boy's empty, staring eyes.

"Right, we'd better get you fixed up. Can you walk?"

"Out that door? Just fucking watch me." He tried to rise, just about managed it by propping himself against the wall with one arm. He grimaced as fresh pain spiked through his belly. "So where'd you come from all of sudden?"

"Sheer dumb superstitious luck," Archeth said grimly, cleaning her knives one by one on the dead man's breeches. "Blame my mother's blood. I was out trying to score, last-minute thing, you know. Everywhere's closed. Got some mystic old fuck with a beard down by the river. Tells me to go check on my friends, while I still can. For some reason, I did. Go figure."

Egar swayed a little on his feet. "Nice of him."

"Yeah, well he charged me enough for the krin." Archeth stowed her knives and stood up. Took a look around at the mess. "You know—Jhiral is going to have a fucking fit when he hears about this. I really wouldn't want to be part of clan Ashant right now."

"Right." Egar got his swaying under control, let his throbbing left hand hang and pressed his right to the hole in his belly. "And Gil?"

Archeth looked away, wordless.

Shook her head.

CHAPTER 44

He stumbles for a long time across a desolate marsh plain strewn with the living heads of dwenda victims, and into a bitter wind. Men, women, children, even some dogs—all cemented to tree stumps around him, all alive to some degree, though few are probably sane anymore. There are tens of thousands of them. Their voices tangle around his knees like marsh mist, come mumbling and weeping and sometimes screaming up to his ears. Sometimes what they say is intelligible.

He tries not to hear them.

. . . *Mummy I don't like it I don't* like *it Mummy make it stop, I don't like it make* . . .

She's about five or six. Long rat's tails of muddy hair plastered on her face. Voice a thin, hopeless moan. If the mother she's calling for is with her, she has long since stopped talking back to her daughter in anything but screams or gibbering.

He marches doggedly on, waiting for her voice to fade out like the others. There is nothing he can do. There is nothing he can do for any of these people. The marsh stretches to the horizon in all directions. There is water underfoot, everywhere. And as long as there is water, the roots will draw sustenance, and as long as the roots draw sustenance, the lives spiked atop them will endure.

Seethlaw told him this.

Is it any worse, Seethlaw asked him at Ennishmin, *than the cages at the eastern gate in Trelayne, where your transgressors hang in agony for days at a time as an example to the masses?*

He seemed genuinely not to understand Ringil's horror.

Seethlaw is out there somewhere now. Ringil can hear him from time to time, howling from the horizon, keeping pace.

He shivers, with cold and the traceries of memory. He puts one foot in front of the other and does not fall down. He stares at the horizon ahead. His wounded eye and face seemed to have healed, but into what he is not sure. He remembers putting his hand to the wound, some measureless time before, but cannot recall what his fingers touched. And now, whenever his hand twitches upward again, something in him will not let it rise.

He is weaponless, he is cold.

But the cold drives him on.

NOT FOR THE FIRST TIME, HE SAGS TO AN EXHAUSTED HALT. HE DROPS TO his knees in the shallow muddy water and the squelching marsh grass.

Time.

It's coming again, Risgillen's revenge. Last time, he screamed at the leaden sky. It didn't do any good. Now he just stares dully at the nearest heads, defocuses his gaze, tries not to meet their eyes.

Seethlaw's howling circles closer. He knows he won't see him yet, but—

He collapses on his side, sobbing like a child. He sees the standing stones as they emerge around him, towering sentinels against the gray sky.

He curls up and awaits his old lover.

rrrrrrRingillllllllll . . .

He flinches from the sound. But it's too late, too late. He sees a blurred, pale form, bounding inward through the gap between the stones, and Seethlaw, or whatever's left of him, is on him like a rabid dog. Ringil fends him off weakly, punching, kicking, yelling from a ragged throat. Glimpses of the dwenda's face, hideous, hacked apart, jaws agape in the mess, one eye gone. He snarls and tears at Ringil's legs, severs hamstrings. He bites off Ringil's fingers in knuckled chunks, then what's left of his flailing, mutilated hands. Blood gouts from the ragged-boned stumps, but Ringil has already learned he can't pass out, not yet. He draws into himself, bloodied and cringing, like a fetus torn from a womb ahead of time.

Seethlaw capers and snaps and snarls around him, sometimes on two legs, sometimes on four. The dwenda has lost the power of articulate speech, he's an animate husk, an empty shell of alien rage and hunger and hate.

Eventually, when Gil has nothing left to resist with, no more screaming to give, he circles in and begins to tear at Ringil's groin and belly. Buries his misshapen head in Ringil's entrails and worries at his rib cage from within, tearing and snorting.

Raises a bloodied snout and goes, at last, for Ringil's throat.

Frenzied worrying, a single, merciful crunch.

The pain goes out like lamplight dying, gray sky above, fading to black.

BUT BEYOND DEATH, THERE IS NO RESPITE. RINGIL WAKES, FALLING through thick gray wool, the color of the sky.

Falls, once more, reborn and flailing, into the marsh.

And so it begins again.

HE TWITCHES. HE QUIVERS, CLUTCHING AT DREADFUL WOUNDS HE NO longer has, whimpering. It costs him everything he has just to unfold from his fetal ball.

There's a distant sound, like a glass fairy falling down a ladder miles away.

Familiar sound.

He stops whimpering and listens.

There again—tumbling, chiming. Coming closer.

Chords off a long-necked mandolin.

Ringil struggles to his hands and knees, heart in his throat at the sound of the music. He crabs about in the marsh mud, staring for its source.

There!

Moving among the stump-mounted heads, moving closer. A slim, brim-hatted figure, taking slow, careful strides in the marsh mud, mandolin held high across his body like some kind of shield. Notes cascade from the instrument, and as the figure gets closer, so the weeping and moaning of the dwenda victims quietens. Ringil, scrabbling into a huddled sitting position and staring, sees how they all close their eyes and their mouths stop moving, as if the figure has laid a comforting hand on each brow as he passes.

Closer yet, the mandolin song reaches out, and Ringil feels tears squirt in his own eyes. The figure comes to a halt in front of him, and stops playing. He crouches to Ringil's level.

Hjel the Dispossessed.

Beneath the hat brim, the eyes are older, and he thinks he sees more lines in the weather-tanned face, gray in the stubbled beard. But the mischief is still there, the ragged young prince endures. Hjel is still somewhat young.

"Ringil, what the fuck are you doing out here?"

From depths he'd forgotten he owned, Ringil dredges up the corner of a bleak smile. But his voice is a cracked husk.

"Paying a debt, I think."

"You . . ." Hjel plucks a single note off the mandolin's fretboard and it startles away across the marsh. "Oh, ye gods, Gil. Gil! Don't you— Haven't you understood? Did I really not teach you well enough?"

Ringil shivers miserably in the wind. "Doesn't look like it. Not yet, anyway."

"Gil." He sets the mandolin on his knee, puts out a hand and touches Ringil's face. Gil flinches, he can't help it. "You're not alone here. You're not powerless. Didn't I tell you that? *You don't have to be here.*"

"Tell Seethlaw that," says Ringil, and gags on recollection, eyes skittering out toward the horizon. "He'll be back soon enough."

"And if he is?" Hjel stood up. "I told you, Gil: The cold legions wrap around you already—*and they are yours to command.*"

"Don't see any fucking legions, Hjel." Ringil shivers again. "There's just—"

He stares at the unending ranks of living heads, the thousands he's stumbled past, the tens of thousands more to the horizon . . .

"No," he says numbly.

"Yes, Gil. Yes. Now *get up.*"

Hjel's long hand offered—he grabs it and pulls himself to his feet. The two of them stand together, close. The wind is cold across his face, but the dispossessed prince is blocking some of its force. He smiles grimly at Gil. Clasps his shoulder with his free hand.

"*Now* do you understand?"

"No." Shaking his head as if in a trance. "No."

"You've *passed* through the Dark Gate, Gil. It's already done. The Aldrain do not know, Kwelgrish and Dakovash buried it deep, but it's done, it's paid for."

Flicker of shadow at the corners of his vision. He saw them again, standing on the jetty beside a previous Hjel. Saw them streaking out toward him like cloud shadow across the ruffled water. Saw them ooze from the street gloom in Hinerion.

Out on the marsh, says the first voice, the boy. *Salt in the wind.*

He feels a fresh pulse beating in his throat. He stares about him, at the sacrificed and the weeping abandoned, gathered in their tens of thousands.

You'd better run, says the second voice, but he knows, with sudden warm assurance, that the warning is not for him. He can feel a strength growing in his hands like iron tools and the cold is burning off him now, replaced by furnace glow within. He looks at Hjel and sees, in the shadow of the hat brim, the tight grin still on the scavenger prince's face.

Very distantly, he thinks he hears Seethlaw howl.

His lip curls off his teeth, as if in answer.

Do I look like a fucking slave to you? the third voice asks.

Ringil's face twists. A muscle in his cheek jumps. He breathes in deeply, out again, and a fresh wind seems to pick up across the plain of weeping, screaming souls. When he speaks, his voice still husks, but there's a rasp in it now, an ugly edge of purpose.

"Where's my sword?"

HJEL OPENS THE MARSH WITH THE MANDOLIN, A LONG, SCRAPING chord played out, and the ground seems to funnel away at their feet, a cleft opening, white limestone buttresses backing aside, and a pale path downward. Hjel makes it happen with the same casual gesture and lack of ceremony of a man drawing back a curtain to let in the morning light.

"This way," he says, gesturing for Ringil to go first.

The path winds down the cleft, water snaking and trickling on the pallid stone on either side, soaking into moss along the cracks and into the clumped grass that lines the base of the rock. There's a cool, damp scent on the air, but it's not unpleasant, and the ground under Ringil's feet is dry; it crunches with every step taken. He is getting somewhere. Hjel is at his back in grim escort, and the walls of the cleft are opening out. A cycle has been broken, somehow, inside him as much as out, and now he walks clear of its shards.

The path emerges in gloom at the bottom of a long, luminous cliff that stretches out of sight to left and right. Ringil has already noticed that for the last few yards of the cleft path, the fissured blocks of limestone on either side have been carved with line upon densely packed line of characters in an alphabet he cannot read, but whose form is hauntingly familiar. Now he tips his head back and sees that the entire vast face of the cliff above him and on either side is worked in the same tireless, angular scrawl, over every inch of its surface.

Hjel stands at his shoulder as he stares upward.

"The *ikinri 'ska*," he says simply. "All of it. Preserved, by the Originators, by those who first wrote it down, for all and any who can find their way here, and still have the will to learn. You go that way."

He nods ahead. The path leads out from the cliff to a broad, cold-looking tarn. Light scuff of a breeze across the silvered surface and through the reeds that fringe its shore, but otherwise the water looks dead. Gil hesitates. This is a lot like one of the places Seethlaw walked him through before things went bad. He looks in vain for a way to cross.

"So how am I supposed to do this?"

Hjel points past him at the water. "You wanted your sword. Call for it."

"*Call* for it?"

"Yes."

Ringil looks at him for a moment, sees the ragged prince is in earnest. He shrugs.

"All right."

He walks down to the edge of the water. Tiny waves lap on mud at the toes of his boots. He stares out at the tarn, baffled.

"Call for it!" Hjel calls to him. He has not moved from the cleft in the cliff. He stands, slim and dark against the vast luminous array of the carved *ikinri 'ska.*

Ringil shrugs again, feeling stupid. "Ravensfriend?"

"Louder!"

Gil lifts his hands theatrically. Pitches his voice out across the tarn. "I've come for the Ravensfriend!"

A dozen yards offshore, the water boils and then explodes. A wet, webbed hand is extended and in it is the sword, gripped firmly about the blade. Ringil stares at it, then looks back at Hjel. The scavenger prince gestures.

"Well, go on then. You want it? Go and get it."

He wades into the water, finds himself waist-deep surprisingly fast. The mud on the bottom sucks at his boots, stirs up thick and smoky brown from each step he takes. When he gets to where the sword is held up, he looks down and he can see the akyia lying beneath the surface, like some nightmare odalisque reclining on a harem couch. Its long, fin-fronded limbs coil idly about, keeping station; its breasts float full and buoyant on the big, smoothly muscled body. The huge lamprey mouth irises open and shut in the boneless lower face, tasting the muddied swirl his passage has made. He can see the serried ranks of spines within raise up and then lie down again in the throat. In the wrenched bone structure of the upper face, the fist-sized eyes gaze blankly up at him, no more life-like than those of some sunken statue.

After all he's been through, it's like seeing an old, much-loved friend. He'd reach down to stroke the creature if he thought it wouldn't take his hand off at the wrist.

He reaches out instead, takes the sword in both hands. The akyia lets go of the blade and rolls over, shows him one thick muscled flank and then sinks again, coils once rapidly about his legs, and is gone in a thrashing of fins and an explosion of spray that drenches him.

He wades back to shore, dripping and clutching the Ravensfriend to him in both hands, as if he's forgotten what it's for.

But he hasn't.

And Hjel is gone.

Only the towering edifice of the *ikinri 'ska* remains.

CHAPTER 45

In the temple at Afa'marag, Risgillen bent over the young boy and placed a calming hand on his brow. The panic in his eyes soaked away at her touch. She leaned close, whispered in his ear, the old, old forms.

She knew he wouldn't understand, none of them did in this cursed modern age they were fighting to claw back. But it was the best she could do. Honor the rituals, honor the blood, honor the living past. She knew no other way to live. She hoped that at least something in the boy, some thin thread of heritage brought down the long years, would find its way to the old significances and understand the service he rendered, the honor she bestowed.

"Blood of my blood, ties of mine," she murmured. "Know your worth, and give us the strength, of ancestors shared and stored away."

She slid her sharpened thumb talon down the length of his arm, opened the artery from elbow crook to wrist. He made a soft, hopeless noise as the blood rushed out. She hushed him and moved to the other arm. Found the artery, saw it through the flesh and sliced it open.

"Blood of my blood, ties of mine. Know your worth, and open the way for us now."

The second blood vessel gave up its contents. The boy moved a little on the altar, whimpering as he bled out, but she kept a firm hand pressed on his chest, lending him her calm. The blood pooled and snaked about on the worn stone where he lay. Risgillen watched the patterns it made with a critical eye, compared them with the old stains already marking the stone. She glanced down the hallway at the gathered glirsht statues, reached in among them, reached *past* them at angles the eye could not see. She frowned.

"Well?"

Atalmire, from up in the gallery, flanked by two of his honor guard and that idiot priest. Like most storm-callers, he was impatient at the best of times. She supposed it went with mastery of the Talons of the Sun, the glitter-swift elemental forces you had to command. Bound to make you twitchy, something like that.

She shook her head.

"Something's not right," she called up to them.

"Well—*what?*"

"If I knew that, it wouldn't be a problem." She gave her attention back to the dying boy, smiled absently at him. Stroked his face. "There's something blocking the flow of force here. Sacrifice goes unrecognized."

Atalmire kicked at the gallery rail in frustration. "Is this the fucking *Ahn Foi* backing up on us again?"

"That was many thousand years ago, Atalmire. I think it's fair to say they learned their lesson back then. In any case, this is not them, it doesn't *taste* of them. This is something—"

—*else.*

Like a whisper in the dusty gloom.

Her eyes flickered back to the glirsht statues and the space they stood around. She frowned. A small wind had sprung out of nowhere, lifting dust and detritus in a low spiral for a moment, then letting them fall. She stared at the dust, puzzled. It was not her doing, and she didn't think any of the invoked powers were—

"Just a moment."

Atalmire grunted and turned to speak to Menkarak, who was gibbering at him in Tethanne. Risgillen had no idea what they were talking about, and cared less. Bad enough she'd had to master the bastardized remnants of the Old Tongue they spoke in the north, she wasn't going to learn this arid pigshit rattle as well. Let Atalmire govern the cat's-paw down here, let Atalmire call down the Talons of the Sun on this sun-seared desert hell, take credit for it and rule what was left if he liked. Her place was in the north, preparing her brother's dream of return.

She placed one hand in the puddling blood on the altar at the boy's side, kept the other in place on his shivering chest. Felt for the shape of the blockage.

"Haste will not serve here," she called up to Atalmire, breaking up his conversation with the priest. "This cousin's blood points away from acting now, and so did the last three. Unless we discover why, we risk destroying everything you've worked for."

Atalmire raised a hand to silence Menkarak and leaned down on the gallery rail. "If we wait much longer, my lady, we risk the palace coming down on Afa'marag, and we will lose our gateway."

"They won't do that until Ringil's three days are up." Risgillen grimaced, reaching again. She could pull no clarity from the mess of resonances the blood offering sent echoing out into the Gray Places. In the last several thousand years of scrying, she could not recall seeing anything like this. "And they may not even act then. The Emperor is cautious in his dealings with the Citadel, he has affairs of state to balance."

"Our sources say he is convinced of what the Dragonbane has said."

Risgillen shook her head in irritation. "Our sources say he will not risk all-out war with the Citadel until all other avenues have been explored. That gives us time. At worst, it gives us time to abandon Afa'marag, withdraw, and find another location."

"That would be a disastrous setback."

"Oh, don't be so histrionic." Risgillen lowered her head to the boy's chest, listened to the sagging beat of his heart. She frowned again. "It may cost us a year or two. Your pet priest up there is not the only pry-point we have. The Citadel is replete with useful idiots like him. But I'll tell you this much for certain, Atalmire—you bring the Talons of the Sun through here without the correct opening rituals, you risk the wrath of the Origin. And that may set us back another thousand years or more."

"Some of us would take that risk," Atalmire growled.

"Yes." Her attention jerked back up to the balcony, she stared at the other dwenda with open disdain. "And that alone demonstrates how far we have fallen. Now shut up and let me—"

Smashed bright, lightning flash glimpse—it stormed her behind the eyes—*a wind howls across the marsh plain, tearing out the roots of the exemplars, tossing them about, closing their sentinel eyes. Something gathers them in . . .*

Something whose form she's touched before.

She snatched her hand out of the blood, spun about. The small winding dust devil was back, turning in the space between the statues. Rising now, lifting dust and spider corpse husks, holding it all up, knee height, waist height, chest height and—

Atalmire, for all his impatience, was attuned as any Aldrain noble. His eyes snapped to the dust devil, then back to her. He gestured. "What the fuck is that supposed to be?"

"Something's coming," she whispered.

The boy thrashed suddenly under her hand. Her hold on him slipped—he tried to sit up. Eyes ripped wide with knowledge of what she'd done to him. Mouth writhing to form words, a protest, a plea, a curse.

Something howled. Something roared. Something tore the air apart.

"Something's coming!" She yelled it now, into the teeth of the gale pouring out of the rent the tornado had made. "Get your men down h—"

Her voice died.

At the heart of the rising coil of dust, a black-clad figure. Black Scourge steel in hand.

No, that's not possible. It screamed in her head. *It cannot be. He, the blade, we* sank *it, he is* gone, *he is not—*

The figure lifted its head. Grinned at her. Raised the sword.

"Risgillen! Your brother calls for you!"

Chill shivered through her. Her own blade was on her back, bound in threads of blue light and her own will. She snatched it free and stormed down the hall toward him. Faintly, she was aware of Atalmire's honor guard leaping down from the gallery, joining her on the temple floor. Only two, but it should be enough. A fierce rage pulsed in her chest, put talons on every finger and drew her fangs down into her swelling mouth.

If Ringil noticed any of it, he gave her no sign. He came to meet her, grinning, out of the gathered glirsht statues and the storm he'd somehow conjured at their center, measured pace and vacant eyes and the empty will to harm.

She snarled and hurled a melting across the space between them.

Something she could barely see, something that wrapped around him like a loose gray shawl *reached out* and slapped the melting away. She was not even sure if he was aware it happened. But she heard the low moaning it made.

The Cold Commands.

Her hate stumbled, stubbed senses on what she'd just seen. Shocked disbelief dizzied through her. *No mortal since Ilwrack could . . .*

She crushed out the tremor. No time for further attempts at sorcery, but Atalmire's men were at her back, armored and grim. And she had her hatred, she hugged it close. Howled out Seethlaw's name, once, for family and for honor.

Rushed in, swinging the blue-fire arc of her blade.

RINGIL MET HER IN A SPLINTERING CLASH OF STEEL AND BLUE SPARKS. The Ravensfriend turned the dwenda's stroke, sent Risgillen staggering aside. He grunted with the effort it took. Risgillen spun back in, snake-swift, hissing. Kiriath steel blocked her again—it felt less like his handiwork than the sword's. Risgillen snarled and fell back. Something tugged his attention around; he swung, met the helmeted dwenda warrior on his flank, and chopped down the attacking blade so it rang off the stone floor. The dwenda, committed, lurched forward and Ringil kicked it savagely in the knee. It tumbled, threw out a guarding arm . . .

The Ravensfriend glittered down.

The arm went, like wheat under the scythe, chopped through just behind the wrist. Dwenda blood splattered everywhere, spiced alien reek of it like a spike through the chilly temple air—

"*No!*"

Risgillen, screaming it. Ringil had no time to look at her, combat senses told him the third dwenda was closer, no time to finish the one he'd maimed. He whipped about, stumbled unaccountably, put up his blade and met his attacker head-on. Swipe and slam of blades, he got in close, swung a shoulder into his opponent and sent him staggering. Risgillen rushed him from the side, swung low and chopped at his legs. He went a foot into the air above the blade, came down behind the stroke and sliced at her unprotected back. The Ravensfriend chopped a gash into her shoulder. She shrieked and reeled away, fell over from the shock. He went after her, but the third dwenda leapt in and blocked him, jabbed out and tagged him across the ribs. He stumbled again, leaned back, got the dwenda's blade out of the way.

The ground was—

The dwenda came in swinging. He met and parried, both blades locked up and straining against each other. Risgillen crawled to her feet, circled round to bracket him.

—shaking.

His eyes darted to the support pillars under the gallery. Something gray crawled there, something writhed and lashed and—

He shook off the dwenda, fell back, blocked Risgillen's limping attack from the side. Energy coursed through him, it felt like an eighth of purest krinzanz chewed down, swallowed, residue rubbed into his gums. It numbed him and fired him in equal measure, it came screaming up from inside, this thing he'd dredged with him from the fields of the weeping sacrificed out on the cold marsh plain . . .

I see what the akyia saw, Gil. I see what you could become if you'd only let yourself.

Up on the altar, the boy had gotten himself to a sitting position, held out his blood-slick, slashed-open arms in mute entreaty. He met

Ringil's eyes for a split second. Then he collapsed sideways as another tremor shook the building. He rolled off the altar, he fell on his face in the dust.

Something jagged and black split Ringil's skull apart from within.

Fuck, them, all.

He tipped back his head and howled.

He felt the cold legion sweep up and through him and out—it was like sinking at the heart of a roaring maelstrom. He reached out without knowing how, laid hands that were not his own on the temple around him. He cracked stone and mortar apart, splintered and levered, breathed in destruction like the fumes of fine wine. He tore out the pillars from under Atalmire and Menkarak's feet on the gallery, dropped them yelling to the floor below. He catapulted the blood-drenched altar up and back with enough force to shatter it against the rear wall. He tore dressed-stone blocks from the ceiling like a dentist pulling rotten teeth— let them fall, shattering, to the temple floor. He—

The third dwenda swung at him again in the chaos.

He screamed in its face, tore its blade from its hand, hurled the weapon gleaming end over end across the hall. The Ravensfriend came up, leapt in from the side. Ringil hacked through the dwenda's flailing, fending hand as if it were not there, took head from shoulders in a single bellowing stroke. Blood gouted from the severed neck—he raised his head in the brief fountain it made, he raised his arms, as the temple tore itself apart around him.

Blood rained down.

Blood splattered his face. Blood trickled in the gritted teeth of his grin. He howled at the shattering ceiling, worse than any sound Seethlaw had ever made.

He lowered his head and looked for Risgillen.

Found her struggling to stay on her feet, sword held sagging in both hands before her. There was blood on her bone-white Aldrain face, a jagged gash in her brow he didn't remember putting there. Behind her, Atalmire crawled from where he'd fallen, dragging a leg snapped the wrong way at the knee. Menkarak lay beyond, half trapped under rubble. Ringil raised the Ravensfriend. He screamed at them, over the sound of cracking, crumbling stone.

The two dwenda stared at him from where they lay on the floor, like small children facing a drunken father's fury.

"*This city*," he raged, scarcely aware of what he was saying, "is *mine. I* stand watch here. *I* am the gate. *To take this city you will have to come through me.*"

"You *cannot!*" Risgillen screamed back at him. "This is not your *right!* You have not passed through the Dark Gate!"

"Have I not?" He tilted his head, felt something in his neck click. He leaned in and looked at her. Saw her shudder away. "Have I not, Risgillen?"

And suddenly he felt something slip away inside him.

Suddenly he was emptied out.

The hands he had laid on the temple stones loosened their grip, folded away, began to fade. The cold legion collapsed inward again, wrapped around him like an icy wind, high whistling, weeping note of loss, and then even that was gone.

A single block of masonry dropped out of the ceiling and shattered apart on his left. Stone shards stung his cheek.

He lowered the Ravensfriend.

"Get out of here," he said tiredly. "Go on, fuck off, both of you. Before the whole place comes down."

Somewhere, masonry groaned and powder spilled down in the gloom. The dwenda gaped at him, unmoving. He felt his temper spark and sputter like a damp taper.

"I said *go!*" No triumph in his tone, only a dead and grinding rage. "Go back to the Gray Places and mourn your brother, Risgillen. I won't tell you again. You are not wanted in this world. You are not missed. Spread the fucking word. *The next time I see a dwenda, I rip its mother-fucking heart out and eat it still beating.*"

The echoes of his voice fell away. He walked past the dwenda to where Menkarak lay trapped. Risgillen made no move to stop him. Atalmire looked to be in shock from his shattered leg. The invigilator's eyes widened as he saw Ringil's figure loom over him. He shoved weakly at the block of stone across his chest, coughed up a lot of blood.

"Look at it this way," Ringil told him in Tethanne. "You're dying anyway. Might as well make yourself useful."

He hacked off the invigilator's head. It took a couple of strokes; the angle was awkward. When it was done, and the gush of blood spent in the dust, he knelt and gathered up the head by its greasy hair. Slung the Ravensfriend across his shoulder. Turned back to look at the dwenda.

"Need this," he said vaguely, hefting the head by way of farewell.

He didn't look back again, but he felt their empty black eyes watching him, all the way out of the hall.

I t took him a while to find his way out. The temple was big and poorly
lit, and some of the architecture was confusing, especially the massive
chunks of it that had fallen in. He thought, from the quality of the light
seeping through holes in the roof, that dawn must not be too far off. But
down at floor level, it was still mostly dark. Seeing was work; trying to
think was worse. His head was a torn-up mess, a match for the rubble he
walked through—

Did I *do all this?*

He kept moving—dogged instinctive motion and honed years of
skirmisher caution, tangled up with flash-lit memories he would mostly
rather not look at.

The temple's structure creaked ominously about him.

Vague recollection of the story Egar had told him gave things an
eerie familiarity, but it provided no useful guidance. He'd worked out he

must be at Afa'marag from the glirsht figures and the gallery in the main altar hall, but he was still slightly shaken when he passed a huge statue holding up the roof, a southern representation of Hoiran with horse tackle slung across one shoulder, and realized it was where the Dragonbane had faced the dwenda before. He stopped and looked up at the looming, bearded face under the ceiling, the raised right arm, now missing its hand. It was not quite the harsh tusked and fanged majesty of Hoiran as the north knew him, but you could see the similarities.

The shattered fragments of the hand lay not far off. He remembered Egar telling him how it fell and stopped the fight in its tracks. He peered at the masonry and caught the dark gleam of something atop one massive chunk of pointing index finger.

A Kiriath flare.

It stood upright, as if just that moment placed there, curved metal casing of the flask picking up the thin light in the place and throwing it back. There was even a leather loop for tying it onto your belt, already attached. If it wasn't the flare he'd lost to Risgillen in the Citadel, it was a pretty perfect copy.

He stared at it for a while, then lifted his eyes to the huge, bearded face looming overhead. A shiver ran through him. He grimaced and set down Menkarak's head for a moment. Swiped up the flare, tied it onto his belt where there had been one before.

"Don't suppose you've got my dragon knife, too?" he asked the empty gloom.

There was no reply.

He wasn't very sure he wanted one.

FARTHER ON THROUGH THE DARKENED CHAMBERS OF THE TEMPLE, HE ran into a panicked-looking pair of men-at-arms sharing a single torch. They fetched up short, gaping at him.

"So how do I get out of this place?" he asked them.

Their gazes sidled down to the head he carried in his left hand, now dust-caked around the chopped neck wound and the mouth.

"Don't look at him," Ringil barked. "Just tell me how the fuck I get out of here."

"But, you, that's Pash—" The more talkative of the two swallowed, hard. Pointed with the torch he held. "Back that way. Through the arch and take the staircase on the left, then the corridor with the bas-relief walls. Main atrium, and out. But, there's uh, the Blessed Watch are at the doors."

"I'll talk to them."

The other man shook his head dazedly. "We heard, uh, there was . . . What *happened* in there?"

"Black powers," said Ringil briskly. "Demonic forces. The old gods have broken through, and the ceiling's coming down. If I were you, I wouldn't hang around too long."

"But what about the slaves?" blurted the man.

"The slaves, yes." He remembered more fragments of the Dragon-bane's tale. Cursed under his breath. "Well you'd better go and let them all out, hadn't you?"

The man who'd spoken first wrinkled his nose. "Fuck that shit. They're all northerners anyway. Let the fucking roof come down on them for all I care."

Ringil lifted the Ravensfriend from his shoulder and pointed it at the man. It felt oddly effortless—the Ravensfriend was light, but not *that* light. He emptied his face of all expression, poured the command into his voice.

"You'll both go and let the slaves out of here before you do anything else. *Right* now. I'm going to be standing outside at the front door and if I see either of your faces come through it before those slaves, then you'll be joining my friend Pashla here in a bounty bag. Got it?"

From their faces, he judged that they did.

He watched them scurry away into the gloom, waited until the glow of the torch disappeared, then pressed onward. The directions they'd given him were accurate. He found the main doors cracked open a cautious couple of yards and letting in the dawn. The Blessed Watchmen clustered about the sides, weapons drawn, peering nervously into the gloom. They jumped when he appeared, and there were some half-hearted challenges, but in the end they gave him no more trouble than their colleagues inside. He told them the same story he'd told before and advised them to stay clear. They let him through. If any of them recognized Menkarak's face swinging at his knee, none of them wanted to get into it with him.

True to his word, he stood at the doors in the crisp morning air until the slaves started to dribble out in ones and twos. Young men and women wrapped hastily in blankets and thin clothes, feet mostly bare, faces numbed beyond any expression you could read. Northern faces, every one. He watched them emerge, blinking and shivering in the early light, and he tried experimentally to feel some kind of kinship for them.

Felt nothing at all that he could name.

You have not passed through the Dark Gate.

Have I not?

Still, he broke up a couple of attempts by the watchmen to man-handle some of the more comely females, the more delicate among the boys, and told everybody they were now wards of the palace, someone would be along shortly to take charge, *so leave them the fuck alone.* The watchmen looked at him blankly. The phrase *wards of the palace* clearly didn't mean anything to them, but they weren't going to argue with this gaunt, blood-spattered mercenary with the obvious command manners and the bloody great Kiriath blade naked in his hand. Not getting paid half enough for that shit . . .

He saw the two men-at-arms he'd sent in emerge, and nodded at them. They winced from his eyes and slunk away.

Sunrise crept along the river behind him, spilled over the dark bulk of the lock gates and stained the sky above in streaks of pale pink and gray. The air started to gather heat. He waited out the brief exodus, then put the temple at his back and wandered down to the water's edge to fire the Kiriath flare.

Miraculously enough, it worked the first time.

The flask kicked in his hand, raged glaring white fire that soaked slowly out to deeper colors and left dancing blotches across his vision. Smoke traced a perfect rising arc from the flare's kick, upward through the warming air, then broke and hung, and drifted eastward on the wind. Over Ringil's head, a chemical green light hung in the sky, staining the morning uncanny.

Out in the river, farther down, something big flopped and splashed and sank again.

ARCHETH FOUND HIM SITTING ON THE RIVERBANK, STARING OUT OVER the water as if wondering how he might get across. The Ravensfriend lay across his lap; Pashla Menkarak's severed head was bedded down in the dirt at his side, dead eyes gazing emptily at the same far shore.

Under the inch-deep wavelets the water made at its edge, Ringil's dragon-tooth dagger stuck up out of the sandy mud, buried there to the hilt.

She stopped a couple of yards behind him, quelling the ache of relief in her throat. She swallowed. Put hands on hips.

"Gil? You mind telling me just what the fuck *wards of the palace* is supposed to mean?"

He glanced up. "There you are."

"Yeah, tell me about it. Can't move a fucking horse faster than a walk this time of the morning. Got here fast as we could." She looked at Menkarak's head, prodded it with a toe so it fell over on its face in the riverbank dirt. "We'd better get that out of sight before someone sees it."

"They've already seen it, Archidi." He set the Ravensfriend aside and levered himself to his feet. Grinned at her—she held down a flinch. "No one's given me any trouble."

She nodded down at the dragon-tooth dagger. "What's that doing there?"

"Oh." He shrugged. "Long story. Washed up there, I think."

"Washed up?" She stared at the neatly pegged blade, the hilt jutting out of the wavelets, then back at his blood-painted face and the haggard eyes that stared out of it. "Gil, are you feeling okay? You're not hurt?"

He gave her the grin again. "Couple of scratches. Nothing that won't heal behind a bath and some sleep. You get the Dragonbane out yet?"

"Yeah. Bit of a story to that, actually."

Behind them, something rumbled. Birds startled out of reeds all along the river. Ringil and Archeth both looked around in time to see a section of the temple's front façade belly inward and collapse. Dust boiled outward from the impact. Excited yelling. Uniforms ran about, keeping people back.

"Been doing that all morning," Ringil said inconsequentially. He bent and retrieved the dragon knife, wiped it carefully on his bloodied and mud-clogged breeches. He held it up to the light, as if to be sure of some aspect in its carving.

"It's a good knife, that," he said. "Wouldn't want to lose it."

Noyal Rakan came hurrying down the bank toward them. His face was suffused with joy, but it faded a little when he saw Gil's face.

"My lord Ringil." He stopped short. "Are you . . . hale?"

Gil nodded and stowed the knife. "Hale enough."

"Well, then." The Throne Eternal captain looked at Archeth. "We must get him up to the palace at once. The, uh, the Emperor requests your immediate presence."

"Really?"

"Really," said Archeth drily.

More of the temple fell in behind them. Ringil gazed at it for a long moment, then looked back to his companions.

"Right, then. I'd better get cleaned up. Either of you got any idea what His Imperial Radiance wants so urgently?"

Archeth and Rakan exchanged glances. Archeth shrugged. Gestured with an open palm.

"I think he's going to give you a medal," she said.

RINGIL LAUGHED ALL THE WAY TO THE HORSES. IT WASN'T AN ENTIRELY pleasant sound.

He was still making the same harsh, mirthless noise to himself, quietly, on and off, as the three of them rode westward along the river with the rising sun at their backs and their faces cast in shadow. His companions stole uneasy glances at him, but could think of nothing to say. They clucked to the horses instead, and their mounts picked up a little speed. Their shadows leaned on ahead of them, as if anxious to leave something behind.

Later, they would say only that he rode wordless and corpse-stiff in the saddle, that tear tracks from the laughter cut down his blood-caked face like the mark of claws, and that he never wiped them away.

ACKNOWLEDGMENTS

In addition to the previously named giants whose shoulders I stood on for *The Steel Remains,* I now realize belatedly that both that novel and this also owe the following debts of inspiration:

To M. John Harrison for Viriconium and its denizens, in all their grubby glory.

To Steph Swainston for Comet Jant Shira (and his ice ax!).

To Glen Cook for the war-weary world-weary Black Company.

In the Realm of Editors, heartfelt thanks go to Simon Spanton, who waited patiently and graciously for *The Cold Commands* to take shape, longer than most editors would have without picking up an ax, and who never ground his teeth in my company even once that whole time (or at least not audibly).

Thanks also to Chris Schluep, Alain Nevant, Sascha Mamzcak, and all the other foreign editors who camped out with Simon under a sky full of deadlines burning up on reentry, and never flinched. And to my agent Carolyn Whitaker for her calm aplomb in helping me navigate some fairly choppy waters over the last year or two.

For hands-on cartographical help, rendered completely gratis, I'm very grateful to Ravi Shankar for lending gravitas to a geography I'd only ever considered in the vaguest of terms. The map he created has proved a major inspiration in building some of the fine detail in *The Cold Commands*.

Thanks also to JW and to MD for helping me keep it real.

Thanks to Virginia for keeping me real.

And thanks, finally, to all of you who waited so patiently for Ringil, Egar, and Archeth to return. Hope it's been as worthwhile for you as it has for me.

About the Author

RICHARD K. MORGAN is the acclaimed author of *Thirteen*, which won the Arthur C. Clarke Award, *Woken Furies*, *Market Forces*, *Broken Angels*, *The Steel Remains*, and *Altered Carbon*, a *New York Times* Notable Book that also won the Philip K. Dick Award. Morgan sold the movie rights for *Altered Carbon* to Joel Silver and Warner Bros. and was the winner of the John W. Campbell Award. He lives in Scotland.

About the Type

This book was set in Minion, a 1990 Adobe Originals typeface by Robert Slimbach. Minion is inspired by classical, old-style typefaces of the late Renaissance, a period of elegant, beautiful, and highly readable type designs. Created primarily for text setting, Minion combines the aesthetic and functional qualities that make text type highly readable with the versatility of digital technology.